THE TRIALS OF THE FAVORED

Also By Logan Young

The Power of Princirum Series:

The Vanquisher of Water

Coming Fall 2022
The Power of Princirum,
Book 3

The Power of Princirum, Book 2

THE TRIALS OF THE FAVORED

LOGAN YOUNG

To Dale, Ed, and Jessica—

~

For always pushing me beyond what

I thought I was capable of,

and showing me the power of

dedication and hard work

~

CONTENTS

The 8 Elements

INFERON
IGMONTIS
SOLARIS
ALFONBURG
THE CITY OF LUXMONT
THE CITY OF SILVAURA
LUXMONT
SILVAURA
CRYSTAL PALACE
TERMUBRA
TERADON
CONTELLUS
THE CITY OF CONTELLUS
THE CITY OF TERMUBRA
UNDARUNE
THE GREAT FORTRESS
WADITA

THE TRIALS OF THE FAVORED

C H A P T E R O N E

T H E U N K N O W N
S I C K N E S S

KYM GAZED OUT THE WINDOW, WATCHING THE COUNTRYSIDE ZOOM by as the carriage sped down the road. Outside, all she could see was a mass of grey. It hadn't stopped snowing for days, and the thick clouds hadn't let any real sunshine through for even longer. A shudder ran through Kym's body, and little bumps rose all over her skin. Uneasy, she pulled the thick cape she hadn't wanted to bring more tightly around her.

Kym knew she should be grateful. Hadn't she wanted to get out of the palace? Being confined there for over two months, she dreamed of her old life, but she never thought she'd actually return. Kym took a breath, unable to stop her hands from shaking. Would her parents recognize her after all this time? Kym doubted it. She hardly recognized herself when she looked in the mirror these days.

The grey gloom worsened as the carriage raced inside the city walls. A mixture of greying mud and snow splattered the windows, kicked off the ground by the carriage wheels. Kym peered through the muck-covered window, eager to catch a glimpse of the world she once knew—a packed street, weekend shoppers. But there was no one there. She settled back in her seat. They wouldn't reach her parents' house for a while. She had time to prepare.

The carriage jerked to a stop much sooner than Kym expected. She squinted out the grime-coated window, but all she saw was the mass of muck. What was going on? They couldn't have made it to her parents' house yet. Why did they stop?

The carriage door opened, filling the inside with faint, pale light. A small, round man stood outside, his hand outstretched, ready to

1

take Kym's. He beamed at her, who smiled back as she took his gloved hand, which matched the rest of his faint blue clothes.

"We've arrived, Miss," he said in a high, singsong voice.

Kym stepped onto the paved ground, excitement coursing through her like electricity. Finally, after months of wanting nothing else, she was home. There was just one problem. Kym's home was nowhere in sight. They weren't even in her neighborhood.

Kym didn't understand. Massive buildings towered on either side of them, stretching high into the air. Kym's parents' house was near the city walls, where none of the buildings reached such a height. Why were they in the middle of the city? She was supposed to be visiting her parents. Where was her home?

"Blessed One." A woman dressed in dark, form-fitting robes stood a few feet away from Kym's carriage. She bowed, her back parallel with the ground, her arms held wide in greeting. "You honor this city with your presence."

Kym stared at the woman and the six others, all dressed in identical robes, on either side of her. The sight of them turned Kym's muscles ridged as stone. Anger boiled up inside her like fire, and she squeezed her hands so tightly her knuckles turned white. Priests.

"What are you doing here?"

The priests were the reason Kym spent most of her childhood alone. They killed her aunt and uncle for speaking out against the gods. After that no one wanted anything to do with Kym or her parents. And now they were bowing to her.

"We are here at Lady Nila's request," the woman said, lifting her head slightly. "I am Pro Ormana."

If Ormana thought invoking Nila's name would calm Kym, she thought wrong. Her hands shook as Nila's name washed over her, and Kym did nothing to calm herself. Why should she? Nila had made her life miserable since the Festival of Creation. Kym turned back to her driver, unable to look at the gang of priests for one more second.

"This isn't right. My parents don't live here."

"They do, Miss," Pro Ormana said before the driver could

speak. "They're inside." She gestured to the closest building while two of her fellow priests pulled open the doors. "I'll show you the way."

The last thing Kym wanted to do with her first day of freedom was to spend it with a group of priests. But if Nila sent them, how could she get rid of them? She followed Ormana inside, unsure which of them looked more bizarre—the black-robed priest or the young girl wearing a flowing blue gown. Kym certainly felt out of place. All of the lights, blinking screens, and floating images looked so foreign to her. How could these objects that filled her old life seem so odd?

They exited the elevator on the seventh floor. Ormana led Kym down the dark corridor, stopping at a door about halfway down the hall. She opened the door without knocking, stepped to the side, and inclined her head to Kym. Tentatively, she stepped over the threshold. What were her parents doing here?

Kym shut the door behind her, plunging the already-gloomy room deeper into darkness. A lone man stood amongst the mismatched chairs, table, and couch, a pained smile on his face. He was short, with a kind face and a slight bald patch on the top of his head. All of Kym's fears melted away as she took in the blue eyes that so resembled her own.

"Hello, sweetheart."

"Dad," Kym breathed.

Kym walked toward her father, barely containing her excitement. It was odd; being back in the city felt so strange, but now she felt entirely like herself. She'd been devastated when Nila took her away, and for a while, all she'd wanted was to get back home. But this wasn't her home. This wasn't the place of her happiest memories.

"What's wrong?" Kym's dad asked. After all their months apart, he could still tell when Kym was upset. "You don't seem like yourself."

At the Festival of Creation, Kym and her friends had stopped Melana, the Ruler of Darkness, from stealing Princirum's source of magic. After that, Kym thought she'd found her place among the Favored. But, instead of praising her for her efforts, Nila, the Ruler of Water, feared the bond Kym and her new friends had formed. She ordered Kym to stay away from them, and as a result, she'd hardly spoken to anyone in months. But that wasn't what troubled her now.

"What is this place?" Kym asked, looking around the room. The old couch from the living room was there; so was the worn kitchen table. "Why aren't you at home?"

"Kym," her dad said slowly, "this is our home now. Our neighborhood was reclaimed by the city's Expand Upward Initiative. I think they're gonna build living complexes there."

"Oh." Kym felt empty. How could the home she'd dreamed of so often, with its tiny rooms, worn furniture, and creaking gate, no longer exist?

"We moved here a few months ago," her dad continued, looking around the little living room. "It's not too bad. We're closer to everything now."

"Where's Mom?" Kym asked. She looked around her dad, sure her mother was standing just out of sight. But there was no one else there.

Her dad's smile vanished from his face. His skin turned pale, and his breathing became shaky and shallow. He seemed to be deflating.

"Come and see," he said hoarsely.

He turned and led the way through the hall. Kym followed, her hands shaking slightly at her sides. What was going on? Why hadn't her mother been there to greet her? Why was her father acting like something terrible had happened?

He stopped at the first narrow door they reached, his hand resting on the worn knob. Kym's stomach felt like a giant knot. He didn't want to go into the room. But why? What did it have to do with her mother? Taking a breath to steady herself, Kym grasped her dad's hand and together, they opened the door with trembling fingers.

The room was full of medical equipment. Doctors surrounded

the bed, their hands busy with scanners, while a nurse took notes by the single, small window. A woman lay on the bed, her eyes unblinking and colorless. Her skin was snow-white, and her hair, once the same faint, golden color of Kym's, curtained her face.

Kym's body froze. The motionless woman couldn't be dead. She wouldn't believe it. She stared at the woman, and watched her slight chest rise and fall the tiniest amount. Kym's body relaxed, a glimmer of hope sparking inside her. There was life in Kym's mother, but only just.

Kym crossed to her mother's bedside in three quick strides. She dropped to her knees and took her mother's limp hand, which lay above the blankets. It was cold as ice. She shoved her mother's arm beneath the covers. Why weren't the doctors trying to warm her? Under the blankets, her mother's body felt like ice. Did she know that the daughter she hadn't seen for months was there?

"Any news?" Kym's dad asked a doctor, his eyes locked on a hologram floating above his screen.

"I'm sorry, Marek," the doctor stated. "At this point, we've—"

"What's wrong with her?" Kym cut across the doctor, not taking her eyes off her mother.

"Oh, Miss," the doctor stammered, "We…we're not sure. I've never seen anything like this. She's unresponsive to any stimuli we provide. She's stopped retaining heat, and our treatments aren't having any effect."

Kym stood up, the chill of her mother's body lingering on her skin. She faced the doctors, who shuffled back—one stumbling into the wall behind her. Kym stared at them, unsure what to say. Why were they retreating from her? It was like she scared them.

"Let's take this to the kitchen," Kym's dad said slowly. "Give Elena some rest."

Kym waited to follow her dad and the doctors out of the room. Nobody moved. Everyone just stood there; heads bowed in silence. What was going on? Why were they acting like Kym, a sixteen-year-old girl, was in control? Then it hit her. She was a Favored. No one would leave or do anything without her permission. Here, she was in charge. Kym gave her dad a quick nod, and he led the way out of the small bedroom.

The doctors gathered around the old wooden table in the kitchen. Kym's dad hurried over to the sink, pulled clean glasses from the rack, and started filling them. Kym walked over to help, but her dad shook his head.

"Go sit down," he said, jerking his head toward the table. "They're waiting for you."

Sure enough, the doctors hadn't sat down. Apparently, they also needed Kym's permission to sit. Kym's stomach lurched uncomfortably. Why did she need to tell them what to do? Sure, she lived in a palace with the Ruler of Water, but that didn't make her special. If Nila hadn't found her all those months ago, she'd be normal, just like them. But Kym was anything but normal.

"There has to be something you can do," Kym pleaded. "You have to keep trying."

"Forgive me, Miss, but like I said, we've done everything we can," the doctor said, his voice shaking slightly. "Please, tell her we did everything we could think of."

"What?" How was Kym supposed to tell her mom anything? The doctors said she couldn't see or hear. Was there a chance she could wake up?

"We did everything she asked," the doctor continued, his voice trembling even more. "Your mother has been our sole focus for weeks. We've barely seen our families since coming to care for her. But we've run out of tests. There's nothing else we can think of. Please, tell her."

Kym couldn't think of a single thing to say. What was the doctor talking about? Clearly, he wasn't talking about her mom. Who'd he think she'd talk to? And why was he so frightened? Kym had to be missing something.

"I'm sorry," Kym said, trying to keep her voice gentle. "But—"

"Please!" There was a real note of panic in the doctor's voice. "Tell Lady Nila we did everything she asked."

All the air vanished from Kym's lungs as the doctor's words

sank in. When Nila stopped Kym after her training session the previous day, she'd said she wanted Kym to visit her parents. She hadn't mentioned any of this. But Nila had known about Kym's mom, apparently for weeks, and never said one word about it. Anger raged inside her like a wild beast. Kym tried to keep herself calm, but her body shook violently.

"Miss," the doctor said, his eyes wide.

"Get out."

"We did everyth—"

"Get out!"

Kym slammed her hands on the table. Bright blue spirals appeared on the backs of her hands, wrapping around her forearm up to her elbow. The water in the glasses flashed blue, then exploded outward. Shards of glass flew in every direction, water spraying the walls and table. The doctors sprang from their seats and ran from the little room, bumping into each other as they scurried away. A moment later, she heard the front door slam.

Panting, Kym stood still, her Marks fading like dying embers. She hadn't meant to make the glasses explode. She hadn't meant to use magic at all. She'd just been so angry. She hadn't lost control like that since her first sparring match.

Kym's dad, who'd run after the doctors, walked silently back into the room. He stared at her, his eyes narrow and his forehead covered in lines. He opened his mouth, but no sound came out. He walked to the counter, grabbed a worn dish towel, and started mopping up Kym's mess.

"Dad, you don't—"

"Quiet, Kym," he sighed, not looking up from the floor.

"Really, you don't need to do that."

Kym raised her hand, invoking her blue Marks again. The water floated up from all the surfaces, collecting in the middle of the room. She waved her hand, and the ball of water drifted to the sink. She flicked her wrist, and the water rained peacefully down the drain.

"Kym." Her dad was standing, and his voice was stern. "That's enough."

"What?"

Why did he look so upset? All right, she knew he probably wasn't happy she yelled at the doctors, but it wasn't like she'd meant to blow up the glasses. She got upset. He had to know that.

"What's going on with you?" he asked, sweeping the glass shards covering the table into the trash. "I could tell the moment you walked through the door. You don't seem like yourself."

"I'm fine," Kym lied.

She couldn't tell him the truth. How could she? She didn't even know where to start. When Kym found out she was one of the Favored—a select group of people in Princirum who magically controlled light, darkness, fire, water, air, or earth—she'd promised her parents she'd make them proud. How could she tell her father the magical world she'd spent most of her life distrusting was worse than she imagined? Sure, she stopped Melana from declaring war on the gods, but at what cost? She'd lost everything she cared about that night. And in the end, the gods, who Kym always doubted, let Melana go with only a warning.

"You're not fine," Kym's dad repeated. "You look miserable."

"I...This whole Favored thing isn't what I expected."

Kym's dad shook his head. He finished cleaning up the kitchen while Kym stood off to the side, unsure what to do. When he finally pulled the last pieces of glass from the curtains, he walked past her and into the living room, where he sat on the couch. Kym hung in the doorway, still feeling uncomfortable.

"So, how's life as a Favored?" Marek asked. "What's the Palace of Water like?"

"Um..." Kym didn't know what to say. She couldn't tell him how she really felt, not with her mom in her current condition. He had enough to worry about.

"It's been an adjustment," Kym said truthfully.

"We thought it would be," Kym's dad smiled. "You were never the biggest fan of the Favored growing up. And you showed the signs of magic so late."

"Yeah, the magic was tough to learn at first, but I'm getting the hang of it now."

"And look at you." He looked Kym up and down, and she saw pride replace the pain in his eyes. "Look at how far you've come. You will serve Princirum and the gods well by battling death."

"Right," Kym said evasively.

Her dad seemed genuinely proud of her, which just made the whole thing even worse. He thought his daughter was off fighting death demons, protecting the people and the gods. How could she tell him this was the first day she'd been out of the palace since the Festival of Creation? Of course, that wasn't her choice.

"How long do you get to stay?" Kym's dad asked.

"Not long, I think," Kym said, happy for the change of subject. "Nila wants me back at Wadita in the morning. I'm supposed to collect some guards and take them back to the palace."

"Well," Kym's dad said, standing up abruptly. "I wouldn't want to keep a Water Favored from her duties."

"Dad…"

Did he think she'd rather be running Nila's errands than visiting him? After becoming a Favored, Kym thought about returning home for weeks. She'd missed her old life so badly some nights she cried herself to sleep. But she stayed. Her magic was a gift from the gods, after all, and there was no way for her to leave. The gods created the Rulers to rule Princirum in their absence, and they weren't fond of disobedience. So, Kym did what they asked.

Marek walked over to his daughter, grabbed one of her hands, and pulled her into his arms. Kym sighed, feeling all of the built-up tension inside her melt like ice. She remembered standing in a very similar embrace on her parents' porch months before, wishing the moment would never end. And now, standing in this strange apartment, Kym found herself wanting the same thing.

"Is Mom gonna be all right?"

"I don't know," he whispered, stroking her hair. "I pray to the gods every day. It is not her time to wander Nothingness."

Kym's body tensed. Why would her dad say something like

that? Nothingness was the place where the dead wandered, trying to find peace. Her mom wasn't that sick, was she?

"If her return is in their plan, all I have to do is wait. Reta's waters will cleanse her. I know it."

"Reta?" Kym asked, pulling away to look into her dad's eyes. "Dad, Pheil is the goddess of health. Why would you pray to Reta?"

"Kym," her dad smiled. "You're a Water Favored. Your power is Reta's divine gift. Your mother and I have prayed to her ever since Lady Nila took you away."

Kym couldn't stop the smile from growing on her lips. Marek Collins, always the believer. Of course, he'd put his faith in the gods over the doctors. He had hope. And if he thought Kym's mom had a chance, Kym could hold onto hope too.

"You should see her again. Before you go."

"No," Kym said slowly, letting go of her dad. "I don't want to see her like that."

"But, Kym—"

"I'll see her again." Kym grabbed her cape from where she'd thrown it on the couch. "When she's better."

"All right. And Kym," he added, opening the front door. "Keep making us proud."

"I will." Kym only hoped she could keep her word.

Pro Ormana stood waiting in the hall. She followed Kym silently into the elevator, through the lobby, and out onto the worn pavement. Kym's carriage sat on the other side of the street, the horses fidgeting in their harnesses. The other priests who'd greeted Kym closed in around her as she crossed the road, their arms held in front of them while they stared at their shoes.

A man darted out from around the carriage. His clothes and hair were ragged like he hadn't been inside for days. His eyes were sunken and dark, not unlike Kym's mother's. He squinted at Kym, panting loudly as he swayed from side to side.

"You don't deserve that," he snarled, gesturing at Kym's jewel-covered cape. "Why should you have that when we have nothin'?"

Kym opened her mouth to speak, but Pro Ormana stepped

between her and the man before she uttered a sound. She maintained her demure composure as the man stared her down, his eyes darting from side to side.

"Leave," she ordered, although her voice remained gentle. "No good can come from this."

"No good comes from her," he spat, pointing at Kym.

"Very well."

Ormana stepped back in line with the others. She nodded slowly to the priests around her before looking back at the man.

"*Agni!*" Ormana shouted, her voice harsh.

Two priests rushed forward faster than Kym expected. They reached inside their robes and withdrew slender, metallic rods. The man tried to run, but he was too slow. The first priest slid across the ground, kicking the man's feet out from under him. The rod in the second priest's hand grew taller than she was. She swung it down on the man's middle, forcing him to the ground.

"No!"

Kym rushed forward. Why were priests attacking a helpless man? He'd done nothing wrong. More staffs appeared in the hands of the remaining priests. They held their weapons around Kym, caging her back from the fight happening feet in front of her.

"Please," Kym said, looking at Ormana, "Stop this."

"As you command, Blessed One," Ormana said, inclining her head. "Protectorate, *d'naity!*"

The priests in the street stopped their assault at once. Staffs shrank around Kym as the priests stowed their weapons. Ormana turned to Kym, her face as serene as ever. Kym stayed rooted to the spot, her mouth hanging open. The man was clearly starving and upset. Why did they attack him for it?

"We must hurry, Blessed One," Ormana smiled. She and her fellows all stepped forward, shepherding Kym toward her carriage. "We can't keep Lady Nila waiting."

"We?" Kym's mind raced at the word.

"Oh, yes. Lady Nila requested the Protectorate provide her additional security. We're accompanying you back to Wadita."

CHAPTER TWO

THE
QUAKE

ORMANA HALF LED, HALF PUSHED KYM INTO HER CARRIAGE. KYM stared out of the window, her heart pounding in her ears. The other priests dragged the semi-conscious man out of the street, while another group arrived with new horses. Ormana and her fellows mounted them, and Kym's carriage rushed through the city streets. Half of the Protectorate rode out in front, while the others stayed in the rear.

Kym couldn't think straight. She kept seeing that man, curled up on the ground while long strips of metal beat against his skin. What had she just seen? Priests led people through rituals and prayers; they didn't attack people. But Ormana hadn't called them priests. She called them Protectorate.

This, of course, didn't help Kym. She'd never heard of any priests being called Protectorate—if they were priests at all. This group seemed like something else altogether. They fought like they'd trained to do so their whole lives. She'd always thought regular priests had captured and killed her aunt and uncle. But after watching the Protectorate, she wasn't so sure anymore. And what had Ormana said to make the priests attack? Kym had never heard words like that before.

Exhausted, Kym leaned back in her seat. The constant whirl of color flying past the newly cleaned window calmed her nerves. She wanted to wipe the whole thing from her mind. She reached up and dimmed the lamp. Maybe the darkness would help ease her raging mind? The grey sky outside grew steadily blacker, and Kym's eyes began to droop.

Kym swam out to sea. She didn't look back, always pushing herself forward. Surely it was better than the world she'd left behind. The water around her grew darker. She was too deep for even the light to find her. After a while, the dark ground split open, revealing a vast, deep trench.

Kym stopped, squinting at the blemish in the smooth ground. What could exist in such a place, unseen by all? She dove down to investigate, reaching the dark edge in seconds. A school of bright yellow fish burst out of the trench, surrounding Kym. She raised her glowing arms, ready to blast them out of her way. One of the fish glided up to her, its mouth open.

"Kym," it boomed in an echoing voice.

A sharp, jabbing pain bloomed in Kym's left side. She winced, looking around for the source of the pain. But there was nothing near her.

"Kym," the fish said again, louder and more clearly than the first time.

"What do you want?" Kym winced, another sharp pain erupting in her side.

"You need to get up."

Kym's eyes snapped open, bright light obscuring her vision. Kym tried to force her surroundings into focus, tears streaming down her cheeks. She was still in the carriage, now full of early morning light. But she wasn't the only person there. A girl with dark, shoulder-length hair stood over her. She poked Kym hard in her side, her lips right next to her ear.

"Kym, wake up. You're home."

Kym groaned. Maybe, if she closed her eyes, Kenna would get bored and go away? But Kenna hadn't left Kym alone for months, so why would she stop now?

"Knock it off," Kym said flatly, shoving Kenna away with her foot. "What time is it?"

"Around ten. They said you'd been here a while."

Kym climbed out of the carriage, her joints stiff. The sight of Kenna's smiling face was enough to make Kym's blood boil. After Nila had forbidden her from seeing her friends from the other palaces, Kenna became one of her jailers. She followed Kym wherever she went, always claiming to be there as a friend, and would only leave when another Water Favored would take over her watch.

Kym stood on Wadita's sandy front drive. With its high towers and shimmering blue walls made of solidified water, the palace looked just as magical as it had when Kym first saw it. However, the sight of her home no longer filled her with awe and wonder. She'd been confined there for so long her short trip to the city felt like a vacation.

"So," Kenna said, following Kym up the front steps. "How was your trip? Is Elena okay?"

Kym stopped dead in her tracks. Even after all of the time they'd spent together, she'd never told Kenna her mother's name. How did Kenna know her mom was sick, or where she'd been?

"Lady Nila told me where you went," Kenna said, not allowing Kym time to answer. "I hope your mom's doing better."

"Just stop!" Kym couldn't take any more of this. Of course Nila had talked to Kenna about Kym. "I know you don't care. Just drop it. Okay?"

But Kenna wasn't the type to give up easily. She followed Kym up the palace steps. Protectorate stood in lines on either side of the massive front door, their hands held in front of them with their heads bowed. Kym would've thought they looked weak if she didn't know what they were capable of.

But as she was about to walk past them, Kym stopped. There were more Protectorate guarding the door than those who'd come with Kym from the city. Many more. Had Nila called more Protectorate from the other cities? It wasn't like she didn't have enough guards.

After the Festival of Creation, Nila's paranoia reached new heights. She used her magic, which was more powerful than any of the Favored, to create her guard. Molding water into the shape of soldiers, she gave them consciousness, allowing them to act on their own. Now, she never went anywhere without them.

Nila only made seven guards to begin with. But as time went on, she seemed to think she was in even more danger. More construct guards appeared inside the palace, but they always stayed inside the walls. That must be why the Protectorate were there; to guard the outside while Nila's constructs stayed inside.

Kym made a beeline for the stairs once she was inside the massive, round entrance hall. She wanted to get out of her dress and into something comfortable. Kenna's hand closed around her wrist before she could move.

"Where are you going?"

"To change," Kym spat, yanking her hand free. "Is that okay with you?"

"Don't you think you should tell Lady Nila you're—?"

"I thought telling Nila everything I did was your job," Kym cut across her. "I wouldn't want to deny you the honor."

"That's ridiculous," Kenna said, a little too loudly.

"Whatever. Now, if you don't mind, I'd like to go train."

Training was all Kym had left. Unable to sneak out to see her friends, since the other Water Favored watched her every move, she focused all of her energy on honing her magic. It was the reason she was there, after all, and she'd promised her parents she'd make them proud. It was also a great way to burn off aggression, which Kym admittedly had a lot of these days.

"Fine," Kenna said, her voice clipped. "I'll train with you. Meet you back here in five minutes."

Kym didn't bother to stifle her groan. All she wanted was to train alone. Was that too much to ask? But now Kenna would be there the whole time. So much for some time alone to clear her head.

Kym stomped up the spiral staircase to her bedchamber. She

opened the door and was relieved to find it was empty. The last thing she needed was to manage her lady's maids, Isabel and Veronica. She threw her gown into the open space in the middle of her room and hastily pulled on a plain blue shirt and pants.

Kym was back in the entrance hall three minutes later, happy to see Kenna wasn't there. She'd gladly train without her, but there was a problem. All of the training rooms at Wadita were underground. Usually, the Water Favored gathered in the entrance hall at sunrise for Nila to open the stairs concealed in the floor.

Thanks to Nila's growing paranoia, she only opened the stairs at sunrise and when training finished in the evening. Kym missed sunrise by several hours. And despite all her training, she still wasn't able to unseal the training room stairs. Sure, she'd managed to shift the floor in her room a few inches, but even that was enough to exhaust her. So, her temper rising, she waited for Kenna, one of the few Favored who could unseal the floor.

She didn't have to wait long. Kenna emerged from one of the many doors ringing the entrance hall walls. Kym stared at the door as it swung silently shut. Nila never let Favored into those rooms, but Kym always suspected they led to her private chambers. So why was Kenna allowed in there?

"Ready to go?"

"What were you doing in there?" Kym asked. "Nila never lets Favored in her rooms."

"Lady Nila needed to ask me something," Kenna said importantly.

"Whatever." Kym would have bet all the jewels on her dress that Kenna went running to Nila the second Kym left. "Just open it."

Kenna stepped into the middle of the hall and raised her arms. Her blue Marks appeared, glowing just like Kym's, although hers coiled around her forearm a few more times. Kenna slammed her hands down on the floor, which trembled at her touch. The ground split open, revealing the stairs that led to the training rooms.

Kym walked down the steps, Kenna hurrying behind her. They

passed several doors as they moved deeper below Wadita, but they never stopped. Finally, after walking for nearly five minutes, they reached the bottom of the stairs. The landing was dark, small, and lit by several torches. There was only one door, with small basins of water on either side of it.

Kym placed her hand on the door, and water rose from the basins. She staggered back, staring at the glowing blue water as it took the shape of people. The shining water constructs stood in front of the door, blocking Kym and Kenna's way.

"State your purpose," one of the water constructs ordered, its deep voice issuing from the center of its body instead of its mouth.

"Seriously?" Kym turned to Kenna. "Why the Thed did she add constructs down here?"

"I am Miss Kenna, Favored of Water," Kenna said superiorly to the construct, ignoring Kym, "and this is Miss Kym, Favored of Water. Let us pass."

The constructs bowed, their glows fading like dying embers, and sank silently back into their basins. Kenna stepped forward and pushed open the door. The vast, domed room was where Water Favored practiced advanced magic. Kym and several other Favored spent most of their time training in the water dome. Kym followed Kenna inside the vast room, which was empty except for them.

"Where's everyone?"

"Not sure," Kenna shrugged, clearly uninterested as she stopped in the middle of the room. "You ready?"

Kym nodded, eager to get started. Kenna invoked her Marks, raised her arms, and panels rose along the base of the curved walls. Water poured into the dome, reaching above Kym's head in seconds. Luckily, this didn't bother her in the slightest. Of the many things she'd learned at Wadita, underwater existence was by far the coolest. Kym relaxed, opened her eyes, and saw her Marks glowing. She sighed, breathing in the icy water like it was air.

She swam around the base of the room, barely needing to move her arms or legs as the water continued to rise. Kym's energy coursed through her like warm drink. She imagined her energy around herself, pushing her through the water like a missile. She shot forward with increased speed, trying to burn off the anger bubbling inside her.

Kym circled the room several times before Kenna joined her. Kym shot forward, trying to get away from her, but Kenna kept pace with her. She looped around Kym, taking the lead as they shot through the clear water. Kenna wasn't one to break from tradition, no matter how many times Kym asked. They'd done this so many times Kym could do it with her eyes closed.

As one of Kym's instructors, Kenna always structured her lessons the same way. They started swimming around the dome before moving on to perfecting the skills they'd practiced the previous day. So, Kym swam up to the middle of the dome while Kenna situated herself near the floor. Kenna jetted upward so quickly Kym barely had time to dart out of her way. This was a good thing since Kym wasn't supposed to move too much when evading attacks.

"Okay," Kenna called after they'd worked on evasion for nearly ten minutes. "Let's switch to reaction drills."

Kenna and Kym drifted to opposite sides of the dome. Kym took a deep breath of icy water, trying to clear her head. Her energy flowed through her arms, following the path her Marks led to her hands. She imagined a sphere of water floating above her palm and let her energy flow into it. A glowing orb of water appeared above her hand, emitting the same blue light as her Marks. It pulsed gently against her palm, feeling like a tiny heart above her fingers.

Kym threw her water bolt as hard as she could. She pushed it through the water with her energy, willing it toward Kenna on the other side of the room. Kenna's circular shield formed right as Kym's bolt reached her. The bolt exploded in a flash of blue light, shattering Kenna's shield. But Kenna's shield blocked the worst of her attack, and she merely floated backward a few inches before settling.

"Nice shot," Kenna said, her voice clipped and her brows knit.

Kym braced herself. Kenna wouldn't waste any time returning

fire. Kenna's water bolt soared through the water, but Kym was ready for it. She'd trained with Kenna for so long she could read her like a book. Kym's shield was fully formed before Kenna's attack left her hand. The bolt bounced off Kym's shield, causing only a slight push against her palms as the bolt ricocheted into the curved wall.

Kym waited for Kenna to attack again, but no bolts or blasts came her way. Instead, Kenna directed her hands at the blue ground, and several tall pillars rose out of the floor. Kym let herself drift down. Clearly, they were moving on. These targets, like the rest of Wadita, were made of energy-infused water. Kym wouldn't be able to break these targets, no matter how powerful her attacks were.

But that didn't stop her from trying. Kym threw attacks at the pillars, while Kenna floated off to the side, her arms crossed. She'd call out different targets for Kym to hit at the last minute, no doubt trying to trip her up. Kym didn't miss a single one. And with every attack, a little anger vanished from Kym's raging mind.

"Blast! Bottom right!"

Instead of throwing her bolt with one hand, she pushed it forward with two, like she was trying to knock someone over. A long jet of glowing blue water shot from Kym's hands, hitting the bottom of the right-side pillar. Kym's arms shook as she forced her energy into the blast, keeping it going longer than usual. Her arms felt like boulders after a few seconds, and when they fell, the attack faded away.

"Sloppy," Kenna smiled, drifting in front of Kym. "You can do better than that."

Anger burned away Kym's newfound sense of calm. Why did Kenna take such pleasure telling her she'd done something wrong? She'd held the attack as long as she could, which wasn't much shorter than Kenna's record. Why did she care?

"Let's do a little one-on-one," Kenna said, still smiling. "Don't worry. I'll go easy on you."

Normally, Kym would spar with the other members of her training group. But, since Jax, Jean, and Ryland were off doing who knew what with Aidan, Kenna was Kym's only choice. And that wasn't her only problem. Kenna had at least three more years' experience than Kym. But, after Kenna's comment, Kym didn't mind letting off a little steam.

Kym and Kenna swam to opposite sides of the room. They faced each other, their dominant hand pointing toward their opponent. Kym locked eyes with Kenna, and she knew she was in trouble. Kenna's blast flew through the water, filling it with bright blue light. Kym arched her body upward over the attack, her shirt blowing around her from the force of the blast.

Kym quickly formed two bolts and threw them, one right after the other, at Kenna. But Kenna's shield was strong; both of Kym's attacks bounced right off the shield without damaging it. Kenna spread her arms, ripping her shield apart before swinging her arm out in front of her. The shining blue arch caught Kym in the legs, spinning her through the water.

Kym slammed into the wall with a thud. Lights popped in her eyes as she shook her head, trying to clear the ringing from her ears. She hurtled through the water at her top speed, right at Kenna. Kenna waved her hands through the water, and four water bolts appeared in front of her. Kym stopped dead in her tracks. What was she doing? Kenna flicked her wrist, and the bolts launched through the water.

Kym swam in the opposite direction, her heart pounding, as the bolts raced behind her. She changed direction as fast as she could, hoping to shake them off, but Kenna's attacks followed her erratic path. What was going on? Bolts couldn't change direction midflight. The first bolt exploded a little ways behind her, while the other three drew closer to her feet. Kym focused her energy, trying to steady herself, and the last three bolts overtook her.

Kym flailed through the water, her ears ringing from the combined assault. She didn't know which way was up or down. Her body slammed into the wall with such force she bounced off of it. She focused all of her energy, and her surroundings stopped spinning around her. But that didn't stop her body from shaking with suppressed anger. Kym knew Kenna had just started using tracking bolts. How was Kym supposed to compete with magic like that?

Kym spun around, energizing enough water to fill a small pool. If Kenna was going to play rough, so was Kym. She brought her hands together as fast as she could. The glowing blue water soared to her, forming a sphere no larger than an apple above her hand. The inside of the bolt felt like a million tiny hands were pressing against it, fighting to escape.

Kym threw the compact bolt, her eyes locked on Kenna, her head pounding. The explosion sent both Kym and Kenna flying through the water. Kenna slammed into the wall, her shattered shield useless against Kym's attack. Kym focused her energy and stopped herself before she slammed into the wall again.

"What the Nothingness, Kym?" Kenna shouted through the rippling water. "There's no need to get that aggressive.

"I thought we were going for it," Kym said, pretending to be confused. "Isn't that why you used tracking bolts?"

"I—we weren't—I think we're done for the day," Kenna spluttered, her face red.

"Sounds good to me."

Kenna raised her arms, and a deep rumbling filled the room. The water level fell as the targets all around the floor sank back into the ground. Kym stayed where she was, her body completely dry as the water level dropped. Her first breath of air felt oddly warm and light in her throat. When the last droplets of water trickled out of the room, it looked exactly like it had when they'd arrived.

Kym yanked open the door and left before Kenna was even near her. If she could just get to her room, maybe she'd finally get a little peace. About halfway up the dark passage, Kym heard a cough behind her. She tensed, her skin growing hot as her heart pounded in her chest. She took a deep breath, trying her best to stay calm, and turned around. Kenna was a few steps below her, her face shining with sweat.

"What now?" Kym asked.

"Okay," Kenna huffed, wringing her hands. Why did she seem

nervous? "So, when I talked to Lady Nila earlier, she asked me to find something out for her."

"Oh yeah?" Kym said, her temper rising. She had a feeling she already knew what this was about.

"Yeah. She asked me to find out why you're so unhappy."

"Seriously?" Kym couldn't stop her voice from shaking. "She can't figure that out?"

"We're all worried about you," Kenna pressed on, and even through her anger, Kym could hear the sincerity in her voice. "You haven't been yourself for a while."

Kym couldn't believe this. If they were all so worried about her, they wouldn't have kept Kym locked up in the palace for months. They would've let her see her friends and not spy on her for Nila. How could they not know what was bothering her?

"If Nila's so worried about me," Kym said through clenched teeth, "she should've told me my mom was sick instead of telling everyone else."

"Hey," Kenna said defensively. "Don't bite my head off. I'm just doing what Lady Nila asked me to do."

"And that's the problem."

Kym turned on her heel and ran up the stairs before Kenna could say another word, her eyes hot with fury. She didn't stop when she reached the entrance hall and kept running until she reached her bedchamber. She threw open the door with such force it bounced off the wall with a crash. High-pitched screams joined the echoing boom, but Kym barely registered Veronica and Isabel in the corner. She stormed across the glittering blue room and pushed open the glass double doors.

Out on the balcony, Kym closed her eyes, trying her best not to scream. Nila knew why Kym was upset. There was no way she couldn't. Kym's hatred for Nila, and Wadita, and the whole situation, all blended together in a blaze of fury.

She'd only been back at the palace for a few hours, and she was already itching for an escape. If Nila would only allow her to leave the palace to fight death demons. At least she'd get a break from her giant blue prison. Of course, that hadn't happened since the festival, because the friends she wasn't allowed to see would also be there fighting the demons.

Kym clutched the railing, breathing in the crisp sea air. Slowly, her heartbeat no longer throbbing in her throat, she opened her eyes. The waves rolled gently onto the sandy shore, filling the air with their soft, rushing chorus. The sun already hung low over the horizon, filling the grey sky with flashes of yellow, orange, red, and pink.

Kym sighed, remembering her time spent exploring Princirum with her friends. Kat and Amber driving each other nuts. Ashlyn's warm smile and Tomark's gentle nature. She even missed Pupil, even after he attacked them at the Festival of Creation. She'd give anything to see them again. If the gods always had a plan, why couldn't that be it?

Everything around Kym shuddered violently. She heard Veronica and Isabel scream as the air filled with the sound of breaking things. The palm trees along the beach shook and swayed, and flocks of colorful birds screeched in alarm. Kym lost her footing, slipped, and landed hard on her back as the world rattled around her.

The trembling stopped, and the world fell instantly still. After the crashes and bangs, the silence was eerie. Kym clutched the railing, gingerly pulling herself up. Her body shook uncontrollably, but for the first time in months, it wasn't from anger.

When she was little, she'd learned about the gods' fury. Her father stressed it would never happen as long as Princirum stayed faithful to the gods. Kym didn't want to believe it, but what other explanation could there be for what just happened? She'd just experienced an earthquake, the first one since the creation of Princirum.

O U T   O F   T H E
F I S S U R E

"Is everyone okay?"

Kym's bedchamber was a disaster. Many of the delicate statues covering the tables and shelves lay in pieces on the ground. Several of the large urns around the room had fallen over, and water crept across the blue floor. Veronica and Isabel sat huddled in the corner, their arms wrapped tightly around each other, their bodies trembling.

"We're fine, dear," Veronica said, pushing herself to her feet. "The god of earth must be angry."

"But Thray hasn't shown anger since Rai's Great Compromise. How are you?" Isabel added, looking Kym up and down as she grabbed her shoulders. "Are you hurt?"

"I'm fine," Kym said, wriggling out of Isabel's grip. "Let me help you clear this up."

"Oh, no!"

"That wouldn't be right, Miss," Veronica said.

"At least let me handle the water," Kym insisted, pointing to the soaked floor. "It'll take me no time at all. After that, I promise I won't do anything ever again!"

They agreed. Kym directed her hands at the water-soaked floor, closed her eyes, and took a deep breath. Her Marks glowed as the water rose silently into the air. Kym sent the water soaring out the balcony doors, unable to put it back in the smashed urns. It drifted silently past the beach and out over the ocean. Kym dropped her hands, and the water fell like rain into the sea.

Kym sat quietly on one of the couches, even though every fiber of her body told her to get up and help her maids. They'd just been through an earthquake. Couldn't they loosen their grip after something like that? Of course, Kym knew she shouldn't complain. With all the Water Favored at Wadita watching her every move, her maids were the only people she actually liked to have around. Even if she still hadn't gotten used to the way they waited on her hand and foot.

She watched her maids scoop up the shattered pieces of pottery. What could the gods be so angry about that it would result in an earthquake? It couldn't be what happened at the festival. The earthquake would've happened months ago if the gods were going to punish the Rulers for their behavior. But if the gods weren't angry at the Rulers for trying to overthrow them, what was the earthquake about?

The bedchamber door burst open. A tall, dark woman dressed in a simple black and blue robe stepped inside. Kym had never seen her before, but the uniform was the same as all the other Protectorate guarding the outside.

"Are you all right, Blessed One?" the Protectorate asked.

"Why are you here?" Kym snapped, unable to keep her voice calm.

Kym wanted to throw the woman from her room. This was the only place she had left. Her bedchamber, which she hated so much when she'd arrived at Wadita, was the only place she could be herself anymore. She wasn't going to have a Protectorate in there if she could help it. Not after what they had done to her aunt and uncle.

"We're checking all the rooms, Blessed One," she said, bowing low. "Are you hurt?"

"We're fine, Pro Veilix," Isabel said before Kym could speak. "If that is all, I'm sure you have other rooms to check."

"Miss Kymbralyn," Pro Veilix plowed on as if Isabel wasn't even there. "Stay in your room. We'll inform you if any new developments arise."

Pro Veilix bowed and backed out of the room, leaving Kym

where she was. Why had she been so rude to Isabel? Sure, they got on her nerves, but Kym never spoke to her maids like that, and she wasn't going to let some new Protectorate do it. Why did she need to stay in her room? And what 'new developments' could there be?

"I'm gonna go see what's going on," Kym said, turning to face her maids. "I know she said to stay here, but—"

"Go," Veronica said curtly, smiling at Kym.

"Really?" Kym couldn't keep the shock from her voice. She'd expected Veronica would make her stay.

"Really," Isabel said, opening the door and sticking her head into the hall. "She's gone. We'll cover for you if she returns."

Kym ran into the hall, not wanting to give her maids a chance to change their minds. Apparently, she wasn't the only person at Wadita who didn't like the Protectorate. But why? Veronica and Isabel were very devoted to the gods—they considered caring for Kym their god-given duty. Why would they go against the orders of a Protectorate? The Protectorate were priests, after all.

The halls and stairways were full of running servants. Kym walked as calmly as she could, trying not to draw attention to herself. Luckily, no servants stopped her, and she saw no other Favored roaming the halls. When she reached the bottom of the stairs, she pushed open the door as quietly as she could. The entrance hall was full of people, and not just servants. The Favored were all there, standing together in the center of the room. Servants ringed the edge of the hall, nervously watching the gathered Favored. Kym stuck to the edge of the group, trying to stay as small as possible.

This didn't make sense. Why was everyone gathered in the hall? They all couldn't have snuck out. Just like Kenna, the rest of the Water Favored did whatever Nila asked them. Then it dawned on her. They'd been asked to be there. They weren't told to stay in their rooms. Only Kym was.

They waited nearly half an hour before something happened. Finally, the doors to Nila's chambers opened, and silence fell over the crowd. Nila glided into the hall, flanked on either side by four

Protectorate. An incredibly tall woman dressed in a bright blue, jewel-covered dress, Nila didn't look at anyone as she drifted through the crowd. She held her head so high Kym expected her towering crown to fall off.

"Thank you," she said when she reached the other side of the hall, "for gathering with such haste." So, Kym was right about Nila having everyone meet in the entrance hall. "You must have questions, but severe matters required my attention."

"What happened?" asked Jean, a girl from Kym's training group with spiky brown hair. "Was that really an earthquake?"

"Unfortunately, the great Thray, creator of earth and bringer of the harvest, shook Princirum with his might today. His displeasure is apparent. The earthquake was centered at Crystal Palace."

Kym's mouth fell open. Crystal Palace was the home of Lady Zara, the Ruler of Life and leader of the Rulers. But why would the gods strike Zara? She hadn't tried to overthrow the gods a few months before. It would have made more sense if the earthquake had been at Melana's palace. Zara always respected the gods. This couldn't be part of the gods' plan to help Princirum. So what was it?

Kym's mind struggled to find an answer. After the festival, Zara let slip that the gods already knew about the Rulers' plot to overthrow them, and that they had a plan of their own. Could this earthquake, this show of natural force, be a part of it? It was possible, but Kym couldn't think what good it would do. What would attacking Zara's home prove?

"The Rulers must gather at Crystal Palace with Lady Zara to assess the damage. Wadita will be under Kenna's charge in my absence. She will oversee all training since it is unclear when I shall return. Aidan," she indicated a tall boy with dark hair standing at the front of the crowd, "and…"

Nila's eyes locked on Kym, still standing at the very back of the hall. Kym stared back at her, and even from across the sea of people, she saw Nila's stony expression falter. Her eyes narrowed as her cheeks flushed. The sight brought the tiniest smile to Kym's lips.

"Jean," Nila continued, her voice as cool as ever, "will accompany me to Crystal Palace."

The crowd dispersed. Most of the Favored headed for either the bedchambers or dining hall, but Kym stayed put. Why was Nila taking Jean with her? Jean had never been to Crystal Palace in her life. If anyone should go with Nila, it was Kym. She walked straight toward Nila while everyone else filed out of the hall. Kenna, Aidan, and Jean stood around Nila, deep in whispered conversation. But Kym didn't care. This was her chance to leave Wadita and figure out what was going on.

"Why are you taking Jean?" Kym demanded, cutting Kenna off mid-sentence.

"Kymbralyn," Nila said coolly, staring down her nose at Kym. "Why are you out of your room?"

"You've never taken Jean to Crystal Palace," Kym said, choosing to ignore Nila's question. "She doesn't know the rules. I do."

"No," Jean said frantically, stepping forward. "Kym is needed here. I'm ready, Lady Nila."

Kym suppressed a snort. Of course, Jean wanted to go to Crystal Palace instead of Kym. Before Kym got on Nila's bad side, she'd take Kym to the Rulers' Summit each month. She even made Kym the first Vanquisher of Water and let her leave the Wadita to fight death demons all the time. Kym wasn't eager to spend another two and a half months trapped in her blue prison before being allowed to leave again. She knew what she had to do, even if every part of her body screamed in protest.

"Lady Nila," Kym said, her voice calm and quiet, "if you let me go, I'll...I'll do whatever you say."

Nila stared at Kym, her face blank. She glided forward, her hands clasped in front of her, until she was inches away from Kym. Slowly, the corners of her mouth curled upward.

"Pro Hayden!"

One of the Protectorate, a man no older than thirty, ran forward. He kept his head bowed as he approached Nila, who never took her eyes off Kym. Her whole body tensed. Did Nila seriously think this Protectorate could stop her? Sure, he had his staff, but Kym had her magic. She could knock him back before he even drew his weapon. As subtly as she could, she shifted her feet, ready to attack.

"Escort Miss Kymbralyn to her bedchamber," Nila said. "If she is to join me at Crystal Palace, she must be dressed properly. Have her ready to leave in ten minutes."

Kym couldn't stop her mouth from falling open. After everything Nila had done, Kym hadn't expected her to let Kym go. She sighed, and it felt like a giant weight vanished from her chest. She'd done it. She was leaving Wadita again.

Pro Hayden bowed to Nila and started walking toward the bedchamber stairs. Kym hurried after him, ignoring Jean's look of outrage as she stammered at Nila, who didn't say a word. Pro Hayden led her through the many stairwells and halls, reaching her bedchamber in record time. This struck Kym as odd. The Favored held higher rank than Wadita's nonmagical residence. Why was he leading the way? Shouldn't it be the other way around? And how did he know where her bedchamber was?

Kym expected him to step aside, but he walked right into her room. He didn't even let her in first like her maids usually did. Veronica and Isabel stood in the middle of the room, their arms full of Kym's clothes. They looked even more shocked to see Pro Hayden then Kym was by his odd behavior.

"Miss Kymbralyn is leaving for Crystal Palace," he barked at Veronica and Isabel. "Have her ready to leave in five minutes."

"Nila said ten," Kym corrected him.

"Very well," Veronica said, her usually soft voice much darker.

"Come here, dear," Isabel gestured Kym over to her.

Kym joined her in the closet, but Veronica stayed where she was, staring at Pro Hayden. He hadn't moved, standing in the middle of the room like a statue. Isabel grabbed Kym's arm and pulled her back.

"You will wait outside," Veronica said to Pro Hayden. Isabel swept around him and pulled open the door. "We'll send Miss Kym out when she's ready."

"Lady Nila instructed me to escort this Favored. I will not leave her side," Pro Hayden said, slipping his hand between the gap in his robes. "Step back. Now."

Veronica did not step back. She took several steps forward, stopping right at Pro Hayden's feet. Kym watched his eyes narrow, and she could see his arm tense as his fingers tightened around something. Pro Hayden stepped back, his staff expanding as he pulled it from inside his robes.

"No!" Kym reached forward, but she was too far away to offer any assistance.

Pro Hayden lunged at Veronica, who stepped to the side with incredible speed, avoiding the staff. Stepping back toward the staff, she trapped it underneath her arm while grabbing it with her free hand. Veronica lunged back, wresting the staff from Hayden's grip. She twirled the staff nimbly in her hands, turning the weapon on its owner.

She stepped forward, prodding Pro Hayden in the chest with his own weapon. He staggered back, Kym's shock echoing all over his face. What were her maids doing? Veronica tossed the staff to Isabel, who caught it and swung it around her in one motion. She guided Pro Hayden out the door, holding the staff sideways in the doorframe, blocking his path.

"You will wait here," Veronica said calmly, "Until Miss Kym is ready."

"Your weapon." Isabel tossed the staff into the air and closed the door before the weapon reached him.

Kym stood frozen, her hand still outstretched, her mouth gaping. What just happened? How had Veronica and Isabel done that? In all the time she'd known them, never once did they show they could move like that. And the way they worked together without even speaking. They had to have done that before. But when, and where?

"Well," Isabel bustled into the closet, her voice once again light and singsong. "We need to work quickly."

"Crystal Palace means the other Rulers," Veronica called to Isabel. "She'll need her best clothes."

"Her sapphire gown is still in the laundry."

"What just happened?" Why were they acting so normal?

"Miss Kym, please. Your clothes."

"I—I'm not gonna change until you explain what's going on," Kym stammered at Veronica.

"My dear, I promise we'll answer your questions. But we need to get you ready."

Kym nodded, and Veronica led her to the dressing platform. Isabel hurried out of the closet, a sea-blue dress draped in her arms. She slid it over Kym's head while Veronica removed Kym's training clothes.

"Miss Kym," Isabel smiled, helping Kym fit her arms through the long, sheer sleeves, "you said you had questions for us."

"How'd you do that?"

"What?" Veronica asked.

"Get Hayden out of here. I saw the Protectorate fight in the city. They're crazy. But it was like you knew what he was going to do before he did it."

"Of course we did," Isabel said plainly.

"What? How?"

"My dear," Veronica said, a slight edge to her voice. "Did you think we'd done nothing with our lives before coming to serve you at the age of fifty?"

"Um…"

Honestly, Kym had never thought about it. Of course, she'd questioned her maids' strange desire to serve someone for the rest of their lives. To her, the idea of serving someone because they were a Favored was absurd. But after taking care of Kym for months, she'd never asked either of them about their lives before Wadita. Kym seemed to deflate at the thought.

"Before choosing to serve those touched by the gods," Isabel said, gently lifting Kym's chin with her finger, "we were Pro Isabel and Pro Veronica."

"You were priests?"

"It's not as simple as that," Veronica said, helping Kym into a pair of high-heeled shoes. "Priests are the members of the Temples who perform the rituals and lead the people of Princirum through the gods' plan. The Protectorate protect the faith and those faithful to the gods."

"So how'd you end up here?"

"My dear," Isabel laughed, "we couldn't stay in fighting shape forever. When our time to leave the Protectorate came, we decided our time serving the gods wasn't done. We joined the Servitude, a branch of the faith devoted to serving those who do the work of the gods."

"Which, of course, led us here," Veronica smiled, fastening the jeweled buttons of Kym's cape.

Kym stared at her maids like she'd never seen them before. No wonder Veronica and Isabel were so devoted to her. To them, this wasn't a job. It was their religious duty, their life's work.

"Well, Miss," Isabel said, running a brush quickly through Kym's blond hair, "you're all set."

"You'd better hurry," Veronica advised, leading Kym back to the door. "Better not keep Lady Nila waiting."

Hayden stood silently in the hall, his face turned deliberately toward the floor. This time, he did not lead Kym back to the entrance hall but followed a few paces behind her. She couldn't stop herself from smiling. It must have hurt, getting beat by two women old enough to be his mother. And he deserved it. There was no need for him to be so rude to Veronica and Isabel.

Nila and Aidan, along with Nila's new Protectorate guard, were waiting in the entrance hall. If she was going to follow the rules, she might as well start now. She took her place behind Nila, standing next to Aidan. She looked down at her shoes, her hands held behind her back. She didn't make a sound and waited for Nila to make the first move.

Nila glided out of the hall, and her entourage hurried to keep up with her lengthy strides. Nila's carriage, much larger than the one

Kym used earlier, sat ready on the graveled drive. But something was wrong. There was no driver, and if that weren't bad enough, there were no horses either.

"Um, Lady Nila," Aidan said, seeming to follow Kym's thoughts. "Forgive me. Where are the horses?"

"Those beasts couldn't possibly get us to Crystal Palace in time," Nila said flatly. "I will provide the horses for this journey myself."

Nila turned from the carriage and faced the sea. She raised her hands and her blue Marks glowed brightly in the faint afternoon light. Streams of water flew through the air, forming four large orbs as they stopped where the horses should've been. Nila moved her hands through the air, tracing small circles with her fingertips. Thin streams of water branched out from the balls, bending and reshaping themselves until four watery horses stood before the carriage.

Nila flicked her wrists. The horses glowed brightly, like when Kym put her energy into water, and pawed at the ground. Two stable hands hurried forward and hitched the water constructs into place as the driver sat at the front of the carriage.

"Very impressive," Aidan said quickly, like he wanted to be the one to say it first.

"It is not the time for flattery, Aidan," Nila said smugly. "We must leave with haste."

Nila climbed into the carriage, Aidan right behind her. Kym stepped forward, and she could feel Nila's Protectorate guard closing in behind her. Curious, she risked a glance over her shoulder. Four of the Protectorate stood right behind her, while two others climbed onto the carriage's rear.

"Nila—Lady Nila," Kym corrected herself, sitting next to Aidan. "Is bringing all the Protectorate really necessary?"

"Do not be foolish," Nila snapped. "Only two of them will join us. Any more would slow us down. Besides, I have no idea what awaits us at Crystal Palace. As a Ruler, I must be protected at all costs."

Kym wanted to say the only thing Nila needed protection from was the other Rulers. Besides, Nila's magic was one of the most powerful things in Princirum. Why did she need guards when she had her magic? But she bit her tongue. She needed to stay on Nila's good side. She'd spent too long in Nila's bad books to get put back in after five minutes. So, Kym nodded, her mouth firmly closed.

Nila raised her hand, and Kym saw her Marks glowing beneath her sleeves. She flicked her wrist, and the carriage shot forward with the force of a cannon. Kym reached to the side, grabbing onto the windowsill, her body sliding down the seat several inches. Aidan wasn't as quick. He fell right off the bench and onto the carriage floor. Kym barely suppressed a snort.

"That was unexpected," Aidan grunted, pushing himself up.

"Yes, they are fast," Nila smiled. "Much faster than those stinking beasts we usually use. The constructs will not tire or slow down. We should reach Crystal Palace in about six hours."

Kym looked out the window, but all she could see was a multi-colored blur as they raced down the road. The carriage stayed oddly still, and she knew Nila must have done something to it. Nila wouldn't sit in a constantly bumping carriage for six hours.

The trip to Crystal Palace took no time at all. The sparse palm trees of Undarunic, Nila's realm, were quickly replaced by hills that grew into mountains. The great, black mountain bloomed on the horizon, and even with its snow-capped peak, Kym could still see the glittering palace twinkling there.

The carriage jerked to a stop when they reached the mountain's base. Nila pushed open the door and was outside before Kym could stand. Five other carriages stood closely together. Light, darkness, fire, earth, and air constructs all stood still as statues before the various carriages. Apparently, the other Rulers shared Nila's desire for a hasty arrival.

Kym and Aidan followed Nila out into the cold, grey gloom. The Rulers stood together in a tight huddle, surrounded by their own Favored and Protectorate guards. Did the Rulers really need this much protection to investigate an earthquake? It made no sense. A shiver ran through Kym's body, and her insides turned to ice.

Kym pulled her glittering cape more tightly around her. There must be something else going on here that Nila wasn't telling them.

"We should seal it straight away," Evanna, the Ruler of Light, was saying as they joined the group.

"Yes, Evanna," James, the Ruler of Fire, sneered. "What a cunning idea. Seal it before we know what caused it. I expected nothing less from the daughter of the goddess of Light and Wisdom."

"Lord Kai." Everyone fell silent as Zara stepped forward, her long, white dress floating around her. "Now that Nila has arrived, ensure the mountain is safe before we proceed."

Kai, the Ruler of Earth, stepped toward the mountain. Kym turned to watch him and gasped. A giant fissure, at least two hundred feet tall, ran up the side of the black mountain. How could she have missed the massive scar across the mountain's face when they'd arrived? It wasn't exactly small. Had the earthquake been powerful enough to split the mountain in two?

Kai raised his hands, and green Marks appeared on his arms. Nothing happened. Then, the ground beneath their feet began to tremble. The bare bushes around them quivered as a flock of birds took flight from a nearby tree. Kai lowered his hands, and the earth fell silent and still.

"The mountain is safe," Kai informed the others.

"Good," Zara nodded, and Kym could hear the relief in her voice. "Before we seal the fissure, we need to look inside."

"What?" So many Rulers spoke at once, Kym had trouble telling one voice from the other.

"Whatever is down there does not concern me or my Favored."

"A hunk of stone is not our concern!"

"Send in the Protectorate. They can report anything worthwhile."

Kym bit her tongue to stop herself from crying out. Her hands clenched into fists, and her entire body shook. The Rulers, the all-powerful children of the gods, were afraid to look inside a cave. They wouldn't risk themselves or their Favored, but they'd gladly send their non-magical guards in their place. Even though Kym wasn't a fan of the Protectorate, they didn't deserve that.

"Enough!" Zara's enraged voice brought an end to the protests. "We need to know what is down there. You can feel it. That icy power we vowed would never enter our paradise."

Zara's words echoed around Kym's head, growing clearer every second. The icy discomfort inside her had nothing to do with the gloomy weather. It was the feeling she felt whenever she fought a death demon. Her magic was warning her; the enemy was near. The power of death was seeping out of the mountain.

"There is no need to investigate, Zara," Melana said, her voice silky and cold. "Look."

She pointed at the fissure. Two figures emerged from the gash, one much taller than the other, walking toward the Rulers. Kym invoked her Marks, rushed forward as her months of training over-rode her confusion. Metallic clicks filled the air, and Kym knew the Protectorate had drawn their staffs.

She stared at the newcomers, who were completely unfazed by the Rulers' show of force. They were both male, with the shorter of the two walking slightly behind the taller. Both had the same pale complexion and slim frame. How long had it been since they'd seen sunlight? The two men stopped a few feet in front of the lined Favored, where the taller of the two spoke, his voice low and powerful.

"Greetings. I am Phillip, Ruler of Death."

T H E   P O W E R
O F   D E A T H

KYM COULDN'T BELIEVE THE MAN'S WORDS. THERE WAS NO SUCH thing as a Ruler of Death. When the other gods defeated Thed, they banished him to Nothingness to rule over the souls of the dead. Thed wasn't there when the gods created Princirum thousands of years ago. He never made a Ruler in his image. That was why the Favored battled the death demons when they appeared—to keep Thed's power out of Princirum.

"What do you mean, sir, by calling yourself the 'Ruler of Death'?" Zara's icy voice cracked through the air. "The power of death belongs to Nothingness, not Princirum. You were not created in the image of the gods, and therefore hold no claim to the title of Ruler. Your words are unfounded and treasonous."

Kym expected Phillip to recoil at Zara's words. She'd only heard Zara speak that way once before; after Melana betrayed the rest of the Rulers to Thed. She, and the other Rulers, were at least a foot taller than Phillip, who looked like a good breeze would knock him over. But Phillip didn't look frightened. In fact, his slight smile grew under everyone's gaze.

"My patron god, Thed, said you would not believe."

Phillip stepped closer to the Rulers, and the sound of expanding metal erupted behind Kym. As subtly as she could, she glanced back. Long, sharp spear tips protruded from the ends of the Protectorate staffs. A few of them caged in the Rulers like they did to Kym back in the city. The remaining Protectorate directed their spear tips right at Phillip.

"Thed's presence and power, though weaker than the other

gods', has grown since you let him into Princirum," Phillip continued, coming to a stop a few feet from the Favored. "He demands I represent his will and virtues to maintain balance."

"Demands?" Kym heard the fury in James's voice. "You dare make demands of us, as though we are equal? How could we be? We are blessed with magic you cannot possess."

"Forgive me, James," Phillip said, and Kym could picture James seething with anger at not being addressed with his proper title. "My magic is just as potent as yours."

"Impossible!" Evanna shouted. "Death magic does not exist!"

"Evanna," Melana said silkily. "There is no need for rudeness. My good sir, if what you say is true, you would not object to a demonstration of your prowess."

"Indeed, I would not," Phillip beamed, bowing his head slightly to Melana.

Philip walked to a fallen tree near the edge of the road. Its bark had blackened, and snow covered most of the outside. Kym could tell, even from far away, that the tree had been dead for months. It looked like it would fall apart at the slightest touch.

"First," Phillip smiled, "I would ask Zara to confirm that no life remains within this tree."

Zara didn't move. She stared at Phillip, who simply smiled back at her. Slowly, Zara raised her hand. Her white Marks shone brightly against her skin as she directed her fingertips toward the tree. Kym watched the tree, expecting its life energy to appear at Zara's command. But nothing happened.

"The tree is lifeless," Zara confirmed.

"Excellent," Phillip said. "For in the absence of life, there is only death."

Phillip raised his arms, shaking back his billowing black sleeves to reveal thin, skeletal arms. He took a deep breath, and a look of intense concentration fell over his face. Marks, jet black and shining like the night, appeared on his pale skin. Black mist oozed from the tree, forming dark tendrils in the cold air. Phillip pulled his hands quickly into his chest. The mist soared toward him, condensing into a small black cloud.

Kym couldn't stop her mouth from falling open. The whole display looked all too familiar. She'd seen Zara do almost the exact same thing when demonstrating life magic at the Festival of Creation. She'd removed the life from several plants, reducing them to dust in the process. Kym tore her eyes away from the energy in Phillip's hands and instead looked to the dead tree.

But the tree was no longer dead. It still lay on its side, but brown, healthy bark replaced the rotten black stuff from moments before. Bright green leaves covered the once-bare branches, which looked very out of place against the snowy ground. If Kym didn't know any better, she'd have thought it had just fallen over.

"I trust you are convinced."

Phillip pushed his hands forward, and the death energy drifted back around the tree. Kym watched him bring his hands together, and the black cloud forced itself inside the healthy bark. The color drained from the surface as the leaves withered and fell to the ground in a blackened heap.

"I suppose we have no choice," Zara said coldly.

"Zara, what are you saying?" Nila demanded.

"This man is no Ruler," Kai said, his voice shaking.

"Protectorate," Stailin boomed. "Take him!"

The sound of a cannon blast boomed around them before the Protectorate could move an inch. Kym jumped, looking this way and that. What had made that noise? It didn't take her long to find it. Zara's white Marks glowed once again, and she held her hand above her head.

"Enough!" Zara called. "I said we have no choice but to believe he possesses the power of Thed. This does not make him a Ruler. We must decide how to proceed from here. I am calling an emergency Summit of the Rulers."

"What is the meaning of this?" Phillip demanded, and for the first time, he sounded angry. "Thed made me a Ruler to help repair the imbalance your carelessness caused."

"You have proven your power," Zara said firmly. "Being a Ruler of Princirum is not something you can simply lay claim to. This is a decision for the gods and the gods alone.

"We will proceed to Crystal Palace to conduct the Summit at once. None of the Favored are permitted in the throne room, as this is a matter for the gods. Phillip, you may accompany us and wait in the palace while the gods pass judgment on you. The boy must stay behind. Only those blessed with magic may enter that part of my palace."

Kym hadn't given the boy a second glance since he arrived. She'd been too focused watching Phillip's magic. He stood a little behind Phillip, staring at the snow-covered ground with his arms crossed. He was older than Kym—maybe eighteen—with choppy black hair that fell over his pale, thin face.

"Splendid," Phillip said, recalling Kym to the conversation. "Then, there will be no issue with him joining us."

"I beg your pardon?" Zara asked sternly.

"Once plagued by sickness, Jazin has spent the past month learning to harness what once caused only destruction. He is a Favored—a Death Favored."

Kym watched the Rulers, waiting for the bomb to go off. Evanna looked like she wanted to throw a light bolt right at Phillip's head. Stailin balled his hands into fists at his side. Red blotches shone on Nila's cheeks, and she trembled with suppressed rage.

"Very well," Zara said, barely maintaining her composure. "The boy may come. But he will wait in the hall with the rest of you."

The Rulers hurried to their carriages, their anger emitting through the silent air like heat from a flame. Kym, Aidan, and Nila's Protectorate hurried after Nila, already climbing back into her blue carriage. Kym barely stepped inside when the construct horses leaped forward, surging the carriage up the winding mountain path.

Slowly, Kym's mind ground into action. The shock of Phillip and the boy's sudden arrival faded, and concern began to bloom in its place. Of course, she knew what the Rulers were worried about. They didn't want to share power with anyone, especially someone they didn't know. They barely worked well with each other as it was. But that wasn't what worried Kym.

Phillip's death magic was more concerning. She'd spent nearly all of her time as a Favored battling the power of death. Fighting death demons and protecting Princirum was the whole reason the Rulers were supposed to train the Favored in the first place. But would that change if Phillip was a Ruler? Would his involvement make the death demons go away, or cause more of them to appear?

The carriage jerked to a stop, and this time Kym was ready for it, not even sliding down her seat. She and Aidan followed silently behind Nila, who practically ran up the steep, glittering front steps. With its twinkling white stone walls and vast towers and wings, Crystal Palace looked just like Kym remembered it. She hadn't been back since the Festival of Creation, when Nila stripped her of all responsibility and confined her to Wadita.

The massive front doors opened of their own accord as they approached. The Rulers, along with their Favored and Protectorate, walked across the empty entrance hall to two curved staircases, which led to the balcony above. No one spoke as they mounted the steps and began working their way through the vast, empty halls.

Kym stayed a few feet behind Nila, her hands held behind her back and her head down. She could hear the other Rulers hurrying to catch up with them. If she just lifted her head slightly, she could see who else was there. Kym turned her head and saw someone in a bright red dress walking a few feet to her right. Aidan stomped hard on Kym's foot, and she looked back down at the floor. This was going to be harder than she thought.

The vast, wooden doors to the throne room were already open. The Rulers filed inside, leaving their Favored to wait in the middle of the rounded hall. Zara, along with Phillip and Jazin, were the last to arrive.

"You will wait here," she ordered, "as we call on the gods to aid us in our decision." Zara walked into the throne room, and the doors closed silently behind her.

Kym followed Aidan out of the middle of the hall, while the

Pros backed out into the joining corridor. Kym and Aidan stopped at one of the many pillars supporting the glittering ceiling. For the first time since entering the palace, she looked around. All of the other Favored stood at the edge of the hall, leaving Phillip and the boy alone in the center. No one spoke.

Kym hadn't looked to see which Favored came with the other Rulers. There'd been too much happening out at the fissure to notice. She scanned the hall, taking in the others in their yellow, green, red, purple, and silver outfits. With every new color she saw, she had to fight the urge to run forward.

Kat, her short brown hair the same color as her eyes, leaned against one of the white columns, ignoring the Earth Favored trying to talk to her. Amber, her head held high, stood perfectly still as her narrow, golden eyes swept around the room. Pupil towered over the other two Darkness Pupils, though Kym thought he looked nervous.

Ashlyn stood a little behind the other Light Favored, smiling her usual warm smile. Tomark stood beside the other Air Favored. His brown, wavy hair fell to his shoulder, and his kind green eyes looked right at Kym.

Her heart swelled at the sight of them. There they were. The friends she hadn't seen for months. The people Nila thought would influence her loyalties. How could they all be there? She stepped forward without thinking. She needed to see them, and hug them, and speak to them. Aidan's hand closed tightly around her upper arm, stopping her from moving any farther.

"Don't even think about it," Aidan hissed, pulling Kym back to his side.

"Let me go," Kym jerked her arm out of his grip.

"This is exactly why Lady Nila didn't want to bring you," Aidan whispered in her ear. "She knew she couldn't trust you."

A flash of multicolored light shone through the gap between the throne room doors and the floor. Aidan turned his head so quickly Kym was surprised she didn't hear it crack. And he wasn't the only one. All around the hall Favored, along with Phillip and Jazin, stared at the door. Then almost all at once, they ran over to the door.

Kym didn't follow Aidan as he hurried to listen to the Rulers' conversation. With the lure of secret information occupying his mind, this could be Kym's only chance. Slowly, trying not to draw attention to herself, she walked to the opposite side of the hall. Joy spread through her like warm fire as she watched the others, all of her friends, do the same.

Kat got there first, Tomark right behind her. She punched him affectionately on the arm before Tomark pulled her into a one-armed hug. Amber got there next, her face impassive, but Kym could see the smile she tried to keep from her lips as she nodded to Kat and Tomark. Ashlyn wrapped her arms around each person's neck, warmth radiating from her smile. Pupil shook Tomark's hand, who smiled as he gave each of the girls a quick hug.

Kym couldn't believe what was happening. She ran the last few feet to rejoin her friends. She flung her arms around Kat, who half-heartedly tried to shake her off as they both laughed. Amber, Ashlyn, and Pupil each wrapped their arms around her, and with each new pair of arms, Kym's body grew lighter. And as Tomark placed his arms around Kym's neck, an odd shiver ran down her spine. She didn't want to let go.

"It's great to see all of you," Tomark beamed, turning away from Kym.

"I've missed you so much," Ashlyn said, her green eyes shining as she flipped her long, fiery hair from her face.

"Really?" Pupil said, his eyebrows raised. "Even me?"

"Yes, even you," Kat barked. "Even after you tried to get rid of us at the festival, I still missed your face."

"I agree with the short one," Amber drawled, making Kat's nostrils flare. "We did decide to let it go, after all."

"I don't care about the past," Kym smiled. "I'm just glad we're finally together again."

"It only took a life-altering event for us to pull it off," Kat smiled.

Kym laughed for the first time in what felt like months. She couldn't help it. It was like a weight lifting from her chest. Here, with her friends, all of her worries seemed so unimportant. She glanced over her shoulder. Aidan's eyes were trained on her, but he still had his ear pressed against the throne room door. Hopefully, whatever he was listening to was more interesting than Kym's reunion with her friends.

"This is nuts," Ashlyn said. "I can't believe this happened."

"Really?" Amber said superiorly. "I don't find it strange at all."

"Of course you don't," Tomark said. "Why would you be shocked by a Ruler of Death appearing literally out of nowhere?"

"Zara said Melana let death into Princirum after the festival," Pupil said, his large body deflating slightly. "Something was bound to happen."

Why hadn't she thought of that? She racked her brain, trying to remember Zara's words that night in the throne room. She'd said something was coming, and death was like a parasite. But she'd been talking about the actual power of death, and Thed himself. She hadn't mentioned a new Ruler showing up. What was going on?

"I'm just glad I finally got an excuse to leave Terradon," Kat groaned. "Kai hasn't let me leave since the festival. He even had my maids move into my room to 'better serve my needs.' He's really just making sure I have no way of getting out."

"Same," Tomark said. "Stailin's had the Air Favored watch my every move."

"You're lucky," Amber said. "Lord James hasn't let me leave his side. I spend every waking minute with him."

"So they've all kept us locked away," Ashlyn shook her head. "You'd think they'd be grateful after everything we did. But instead, they make our lives miserable."

"Melana's been worse."

"She couldn't get worse than she was," Kat said.

"She found a way," Pupil sighed. "The tasks she gives me to stay at the Great Fortress as one of her three Pupils have been crazy. She orders me not to leave but then tells me to get a rock from outside. I never know what to do."

"What did you do?" Ashlyn asked.

"I used shadows to pull the rock inside."

"Nila let me go home," Kym whispered.

Silence followed Kym's words. The others stared at her, and Ashlyn's mouth hung open. Kym shifted uncomfortably. Did they all need to stare? It reminded her oddly of the other Water Favored. Sure, Nila let Kym leave Wadita when they were all confined to the palaces. It didn't warrant them gawking at her. But there was something else in their eyes that made Kym pause. They didn't look mad, or even upset.

"Why'd Lady Nila let you leave?" Amber said. "Lord James wouldn't let me visit my father, and his estate isn't far from Inferon."

"My mom's sick. She's been sick for a while, and Nila knew the whole time. I found out after I got there."

"That's terrible." Ashlyn wrapped her arms around Kym. "Is she gonna be all right?"

"The doctors don't even know what's wrong with her. They say they're doing their best."

"They'll figure it out," Kat said, her voice uncharacteristically soft.

"Are you okay?" Tomark placed his hand on Kym's shoulder.

"I'm fine," Kym sighed, trying to hide the mixture of pain and affection in her voice.

She'd received more compassion in the past few minutes than she'd gotten in the past several months. They didn't care what she did or if it was what Nila wanted. Their only concern was Kym and how she was doing. Kym sighed, her eyes brimming with tears. Why wouldn't Nila want Kym to have support like this?

"So, this is the first time any of you have gotten out since the festival?" Kym asked, eager to change the subject.

"Yup," Kat said. "Kai's even had other Favored going to fight death demons in my place."

"Same," Pupil said. "I don't think the Rulers wanted to risk us getting out."

"Why?" The frustration in Tomark's voice was evident. "What would happen if they let us leave?"

"This," Amber said plainly. "Us reuniting."

"You're not serious," Kat said, rolling her eyes. "They literally have a million more important things to worry about."

"At least now with the new Ruler," Ashlyn said, "us speaking is the last thing on their minds."

"You believe him?"

"Tomark, how can't you?" Ashlyn sighed.

"You saw his magic," Pupil said. "We have more experience with death magic than any other Favored. It was the real thing to me."

"And what about that boy?" Amber's usual superior tone wavered. There was a little too much interest in her voice.

"What about me?"

Kym hadn't notice the thin boy dressed in black standing a few feet away from their tight little circle. He stepped closer to them, the ghost of a smile on his lips. Kym's first impulse was to step back as he drew nearer. His skin was so pale it seemed to shine white in the light from the torches. If Kym hadn't seen him walking around, she would've assumed he'd been bedridden for months.

"Hello," Amber said in a breathy voice. Kym had never heard such a sound pass Amber's lips before. "I'm Amber."

"Jazin."

Kym's eyes darted between Amber and Jazin. She'd never seen Amber soften so quickly. As the legendary Fire Princess—the first Favored to ever present magic at birth—Amber always acted like she was better than anyone. She barely gave Kym the time of day when they first met. So why was she staring at Jazin, and why was he smiling faintly back? Amber's face looked so soft it was unsettling.

Next to Kym, Kat started coughing uncontrollably. Kym smiled. Kat wasn't the subtlest person. Luckily, Amber got the hint.

"Oh, yes," she said, shaking her head slightly, as though dazed. "These are my friends."

Kat opened her mouth to speak, but Kym was a step ahead of her. She stamped hard on Kat's foot, causing her to close her mouth and glare up at Kym. Kym merely raised her eyebrows in response. The last thing they needed was Kat saying something to make Amber roast her alive.

"So," Ashlyn said, clearly trying to cover up the awkward moment. "You were sick?"

"For a long time," Jazin smiled.

The doors to the throne room opened before anyone could press Jazin further. All the Favored gathered around the door scattered. Kym and the others hurried to join the Favored from their palaces, meeting them around the edge of the hall. Kym stood beside Aidan, who didn't say anything as they waited. His brows were furrowed, and his hands were balled into fists. He obviously wasn't happy with Kym, and she knew she had no defense. She'd broke Nila's rules after all. Maybe, once Phillip was officially not a Ruler, Nila would be so happy she'd forgive Kym for breaking the rules.

"Enter." Zara's voice rang out from the throne room.

Everyone hurried past the large wooden doors. The vast, domed room had seven thrones; six around the perimeter and one in the center. The floor between the outer thrones and the center one was sunken several inches, and the center throne sat on a raised plat-form, looking down on the others.

Kym and Aidan stood slightly behind Nila's throne, which was closest to the door. To her left, Kat and the other Earth Favored stood behind Kai's throne, while the three Darkness Pupils stood behind Melana's throne to Kym's right. Phillip and Jazin stood on the sunken portion of the floor. They gazed at the center throne, where Zara stared down at them.

"The gods graced this hall with their presence and made their will known," Zara said, her raised throne rotating slowly. Her voice was oddly clipped, like she didn't want to say the words passing her lips.

"From now until the end of time, this man shall be known as Lord Phillip, Ruler of Death."

Kym couldn't believe what she was hearing. How could the Rulers let this happen? There couldn't be a Ruler of Death. There just couldn't. How could this be part of the gods' plan?

"This will not be disputed," Zara continued. "Priests will place notices in the four cities, which will receive the Rulers as we tour Princirum to present the Ruler of Death to the people. This Summit has concluded."

Kym barely had time to think before Nila was on her feet, leaving the throne room before the other Rulers stood. Kym and Aidan ran after her, Aidan glancing at her every few seconds. Kym's heart pounded in her throat. Was he going to tell Nila she broke the rules? If he did, Kym had a feeling she was going to be in for a very uncomfortable carriage ride. They finally caught Nila as she descended the curved stairs to the entrance hall, where her Protectorate gathered around her.

"My Lady," Aidan panted, clutching at his side. Panic jolted through Kym's body like an electric shock. He was going to rat her out. "What happened in the Summit?" Kym's body relaxed. She should have known. When it was a choice between getting Kym in trouble or knowing secret information, Aidan would choose the information every time.

"Exactly what Lady Zara said," Nila spat. "The gods said Phillip, once a lowly mortician with no magic of his own, is now the Ruler of Death. He is not even made in the gods' image," she added bitterly.

"Will he have a palace?" Kym asked, feigning interest. It was better to keep Nila talking about Phillip. At least then her own indiscretions wouldn't be up for debate.

"He already does," Nila said. "Inside this very mountain. Its appearance caused the earthquake and the mountain to split open. The gods have named the Palace of Death Obsidian."

Kym had to stop her mouth from falling open. In the span of a few hours, she'd witnessed a new type of magic, met the Ruler of Death and the very first Death Favored, and been told a palace appearing out of nowhere caused an earthquake that shook all of

Princirum. Lord Phillip and his death magic must be there to stay. A shiver ran down Kym's body, and little bumps rose all over her skin.

They reached the front drive. Nila waved her hand, and the water-construct horses pulled their carriage up to the front step. The carriage door swung open and Nila climbed swiftly inside. Kym and Aidan clambered in behind her, both huffing from trying to keep up with Nila's lengthy strides. Kym barely sat down before the carriage jerked forward, racing down the black mountain and back to Wadita.

CHAPTER FIVE

JUST A
GIRL

KYM TURNED THIS WAY AND THAT, BUT NO MATTER WHERE SHE looked, there was only blackness. Her body trembled uncontrollably, and her insides felt like she'd swallowed a bucket of ice water. The sensation felt oddly familiar, but she couldn't remember from where.

Off in the distance, a faint light bloomed in the blackness. Kym ran toward it, her heart pounding in her ears. What could it be? The cold inside her intensified as she drew nearer. Something stood in the middle of the light, growing larger the closer Kym got. What was it? She pushed on, her curiosity outweighing her growing discomfort.

A woman stood in the glow, staring blankly into the darkness. Kym stepped around her, trying to see her face. It was her mother. What was she doing there? Tall, thin men dressed in black appeared around her, shimmering strips of black silk in their hands. Slowly, they wrapped the fabric around Kym's mom. They started with her hands and feet, covering her until she was just a darkened silhouette.

Kym reached out. She needed to grab her, to save her. But the cold inside her was so intense she couldn't move. Her panic rising, Kym tried with all her might to summon her energy, but no matter how hard she tried, her blue Marks never shone in the blackness. Something tight wrapped around her feet. Looking down, Kym saw more people dressed in black, now wrapping their silk strands around her.

"No!"

Kym sat bolt upright, her body covered in sweat. She rolled around, unable to see where she was. The world fell out from under her, and she landed on the floor in a heap. She ripped the sheets off her, expecting to see her feet wrapped in black. But aside from being twisted in the light blue fabric, they looked perfectly normal. Kym took several deep breaths. Her heart pounded in her head like she'd been running for her life. She'd never had a dream like that.

Still shaking, Kym clambered to her feet. Glowing embers were all that remained of the fire Kym's maids had made. The room smelled warm and musty, and the walls slowly closed in around her. She needed to get out. She needed air. She walked over to the balcony doors and flung them open.

Kym's body felt oddly dull and stiff as she stepped out into the frosty morning air. But why? The only time she'd ever felt that was when a death demon was near, and she hadn't seen one for months. There couldn't be a death demon near Wadita, could there? No. They weren't stupid enough to wander too close to the Rulers. So why did she feel so strange?

Images from her dream flashed clearly through her mind. Her mother standing there motionless. The men wrapping the black silk around her. The all-consuming cold of death as her body faded from sight.

"No," Kym breathed, shaking her head. "It can't be."

Kym's hands wrapped around her stomach, and she could almost feel the icy cold blooming inside her. Her mother's body had been so cold when she touched it. It was the same cold she'd felt in her dream; the icy dullness of death she'd experienced every time a death demon was near. She'd felt it oozing from the fissure at Crystal Palace, but only now realized what it meant. The doctors would never be able to help her mom, even with their technology. It wasn't a sickness that was affecting her mom—it was magic. Death magic.

For the first time in months, Kym wanted to speak to Nila. If she was right, and she hoped she wasn't, the Rulers needed to know. Of course, the increased presence of death would find its way into the cities. And if it was indeed death magic making her mother ill, then one of the Rulers should be able to fix her. They had to, after everything Kym had done for them.

There was just one problem—Nila hadn't been at Wadita for weeks, and Kym had no idea when she'd return. She'd left the day after the emergency Summit to tour the cities and introduce Phillip to the people. Aidan and Kenna were in charge of Wadita in Nila's absence, but Kym didn't want to tell them of her suspicions. They were still mad at her for breaking the rules at the emergency Summit, which Aidan wasted no time telling Kenna about. She couldn't risk them not passing the message on to Nila. They'd already given her extra-long training sessions, pushing her until she was on the verge of passing out.

The sound of galloping horses filled the pre-morning air, along with the unmistakable sound of a massive carriage hurtling down the drive. That could only mean one thing—Nila was back.

Kym ran inside, not bothering to close the balcony doors, and hurtled into her massive closet. She threw off her shimmering nightdress, pulled on her training clothes from the day before, and jammed her feet blindly into her shoes. She was out the door in seconds, bouncing off walls as she ran down empty stairwells and hallways. She needed to get to Nila before she went into her private chambers—before Aidan or anyone else could stop her.

Kym burst into the entrance hall, her insides searing with pain. Panting, she looked wildly around. Nila had her hand on the door to her private chambers, her Protectorate guard walking back outside. She looked even more exhausted than Kym.

"Nila—Lady Nila!" Kym panted, running over to her.

"Kymbralyn!" Nila said coolly, her eyes flashing. She was clearly not in a good mood. "Why are you out of your room?"

"I'm sorry. But I…this couldn't wait. I think I know what's making my mom sick. It's death. I think there's so much death in Princirum it's starting to affect the non-magical people."

Kym expected Nila to react in some way to her theory. Instead, she stared down at Kym, a narrow crease forming between her eyebrows.

"We are aware."

"Wh-what?" Kym hadn't expected Nila to agree with her. How could the Rulers already know?

"While touring the cities to present Lord Phillip, we felt Thed's presence around us. The priests showed us one of the recently deceased, and Lady Zara and Lord Phillip confirmed the presence of Thed's power in the body."

The bottom fell out of Kym's stomach. Someone had died. But who? Could it be Kym's mother? No. If it had been Kym's mom, Nila would've told her, wouldn't she? And why weren't the gods doing anything to stop Thed's power from growing? He was their enemy, after all. They should be protecting Princirum from death, not letting it consume people. How was letting people die part of their plan?

"Can you stop it?" Kym asked, her voice barely more than a whisper.

"Thed's support in the cities has grown since Phillip's arrival," Nila said angrily. "More sickness will come as others flock to him. However, Lady Zara believes she can—"

Nila's entire body tensed, and her eyes widened with terror. She clutched at her stomach, taking shallow, rasping breaths. It was like Kym wasn't even there. Nila turned her back on Kym, facing the door to her private chambers.

"Nila," Kym said, her voice shaking. She'd never seen Nila act like this before. What could she be feeling that filled her with such dread?

"Nila," Kym repeated, trying to keep her voice calm. "What's wrong? What's going on?"

"I..." Nila panted. "Something is in Luxmont. Near Solaris."

"What? It's not a death demon, is it?" Death demons wouldn't appear so close to the Palace of Light.

"This is unlike anything I have felt before," Nila breathed. "So much power."

"Let me go," Kym said a little too quickly. This was her chance to get away from Kenna and Aidan.

"No," Nila said firmly, frowning at Kym. "I will send Aidan or Ryland."

"No," Kym said, her voice breaking slightly. "There's no time. If this thing is as powerful as you think, shouldn't an experienced Vanquisher handle it? If you send me, I promise I'll come right back."

Kym didn't dare to move. If Nila didn't let her go, then the only chance she'd get to escape the palace would slip hopelessly through her fingers.

"Very well," Nila said slowly, her voice regaining its usual clipped tone. "You will return as soon as the demon is vanquished."

Kym bowed her head to Nila, unable to stop the smile spreading on her lips. She sprinted from the entrance hall and out onto the front steps before Nila could change her mind. She'd done it. She was out.

Kym trembled from head to foot. Her clothes, while offering excellent mobility for training, weren't designed for cold weather. She needed to get underwater. She'd never felt cold underwater, even after training for eight straight hours one day. She'd be fine once she was in her element.

Kym ran as fast as she could, her feet sliding slightly on the greying snow. She rounded the palace wall, sand and muck spraying around her as she sprinted across the damp beach. She sprang into the air, invoked her Marks, and dove into the gently rolling waves.

Kym let her energy flow around her and sped through the water like a rocket. The current provided little resistance as she followed her familiar route up the coast. She'd been to Luxmont, Evanna's realm, many times to fight death demons. All she needed to do was follow Contellus's jagged coast until it turned smooth. Then she'd enter the first river she'd find and make her way inland.

Kym found the river mouth with ease. She turned into the river, and started making her way inland. She pushed herself upriver, fighting against the current. Kym refocused her energy on herself, and it felt like pushing a boulder up an icy hill with her mind. She directed herself down, and her stomach scraped against something hard. She looked around. The water level was significantly lower than it had been months before. Even keeping her body as flat as possible, there was only a few inches between herself and the rocky riverbed.

She'd swam for nearly an hour before she felt it. The cold numbness bloomed inside her as her insides turned to ice. Kym stopped, trying not to let the river push her back as her body shook uncontrollably. The last time she'd felt death this intensely was when a death demon was right beside her. She rose to the surface, sticking her head above the water. She moved closer to the bank, and the cold inside her intensified. The demon must be close—very close.

Kym climbed onto dry land, but she couldn't see the demon anywhere. Her heart pounded in her ears, and every little sound sent a jolt through her shaking body. She needed to find it, and fast. She stepped to the right, and the cold inside her lessened slightly. Her heart pounding, Kym sprinted off to the left, scanning the horizon for some sign of the demon.

After running for only a few minutes, something caught Kym's eye. Off in the distance, flashes of red light filled the grey sky. But those weren't the usual first rays of morning light. Kym knew fire magic when she saw it. That had to be where the demon was. Kym quickened her pace, ignoring the growing cold both in and outside her.

Kym could tell the battle had been going on for quite a while. Sections of grass were charred and burned, while large boulders littered the ground. The Fire Favored, who was closest to Kym, pointed their hands at a section of flaming ground. The fire shot into the air, arching toward the demon, which was at least a hundred feet away.

"Amber!" Even without seeing her face, Kym knew who the

Fire Favored must be. Who else did she know who sent flaming comets at death demons?

"What kept you?" Amber yelled, sending another comet at the demon.

"Don't worry about it." Kym looked frantically around for some water. There was only snow and grass. "I need water!"

Without taking her eyes off the demon, Amber flicked her wrist. A tongue of flame shot from her fingertips. It soared into a pile of snow beside Kym, reducing it to a giant puddle. Kym smiled and made two steaming water bolts.

Kym threw her first bolt at the demon. Without even waiting to see if it made contact, she used the second bolt to shoot a blast at it. Each of Kym's attacks hit the demon, exploding in flashes of bright blue, but nothing happened. The demon just kept moving slowly forward.

"Nothing's working!" someone shouted to Kym's left. "It's not even attacking, and we're losing!"

Kat stood twenty feet away, her eyes locked on the demon. She directed both of her hands at it. A wall of earth rose right in front of the demon. Kym threw a pair of bolts, trying to direct the demon into Kat's wall. But it kept walking forward, and Kat's wall began to blacken. Cracks spread through the earth as Kym's bolts exploded on the dark figure, and the wall crumbled into a pile of blackened sand.

Kym squinted at the demon, which was so far away she couldn't see what it was. How did it destroy Kat's wall without even touching it? Death demons killed anything they touched, but that was it; they had to touch it. Kat's wall fell before the demon even made contact. It was unlike any demon she'd ever encountered, and she had no idea how they were going to stop it.

Flashes of yellow and purple exploded around the demon as Light and Darkness Favored tried and failed to stop the demon's slow progress. High in the air, an Air Favored sent down a series of air bolts, but that too did nothing. How were they supposed to stop something that didn't even seem to know they were there?

"Has anything stopped this thing?" Kym shouted. She threw a water swipe at the demon's feet, hoping to trip it up. It didn't work.

"No!" Kat shouted. She jerked her hands around multiple times, and massive stalagmites rose around the demon. They lasted no longer than the wall.

"Compact bolts?" Kym asked frantically, shooting a water blast at the demon. It exploded against the black creature in a flash of blue.

"I tried when I got here!" Amber shouted as a wall of flame burst to life in front of the still-moving demon. "It didn't even faze it."

"Did you try together?" Kym threw two swipes at the demon's feet, which exploded as dust filled the air. Neither Kat nor Amber answered. "It's worth a shot."

"Tomark!" Kat shouted at the flying Air Favored. A smile grew across Kym's lips as Tomark descended toward them. "We're all gonna try compact bolts. Tell the others."

Tomark flew high over the demon to tell the other Favored. The earth beneath Kym's feet trembled. Kym looked around. Streams of earth rose from the ground, swirling around Kat as she forced it into the bolt in her hands. Next to Kym, Amber set the remaining grass ablaze.

Kym acted quickly. Before Amber's fire vaporized all the water, Kym pulled it toward her. She focused her energy, letting it flow into the water as she forced it into the smallest space she could. Her compact bolt quivered in her palm—a million tiny hands pressing from inside it. From the other side of the demon, Kym heard Ashlyn's light voice ring through the air.

"Everyone ready? One! Two! Three!"

Kym threw her bolt, willing it to hit the demon at the same time as everyone else's. The bolts collided in an explosion of multicolored energy. The force of the attack lifted Kym off her feet, and she flew back through the air. She slammed to the ground, pain radiating from her shoulder. Gingerly, she pushed herself to her feet. That had to have done it. There was no way a death demon could survive being hit by six simultaneous compact bolts.

Tentatively, she took a step and sighed. She couldn't feel the cold of death radiating inside her. Kym ran forward. They must've beaten it. But what demon was so strong that it emitted death like that? Kym reached the demon, and her mouth fell open. It wasn't a creature, like nearly every demon she'd faced. It was a girl. A little girl, no older than ten. Her skin was snow-white, and her eyes glittered like black gemstones.

"What the Thed…" Kym hadn't seen Kat walk up.

"Oh, Pheil," Pupil breathed, approaching slowly from the other side. "It's a kid."

The girl stirred. She took sharp, shallow breaths as she slowly sat up. Then, the girl opened her mouth and screamed. There wasn't a trace of anger in the girl's voice. There was only pain.

"Look out!" Tomark shouted.

A wave of death energy blasted out of the girl. They scurried back, narrowly avoiding the blast, which blackened and killed everything in a ten-foot radius around her.

"What are we gonna do?" Amber asked, throwing a bolt at the girl. "Our most powerful attacks didn't do a thing."

"Amber!" Ashlyn yelled, deflecting Amber's bolt with one of her own. "I don't think there's anything we can do."

"How are we supposed to destroy it then?" Amber snapped.

"We aren't destroying it!" Kym said, dumbfounded. "She's a little girl."

"A little girl who nearly killed us," Kat said, backing away from the girl. "I doubt we'll be able to reason with her."

The girl reached up, and Kat fired an earth blast at her. Kym threw out her arm, and a water shield appeared in front of the girl, blocking Kat's attack.

"You're taking Amber's side?" Kym couldn't believe Kat would attack a little girl.

"Ash," Tomark turned to look at Ashlyn, and Kym could hear

the panic in his voice. "This is out of our league. Get Evanna. Maybe she could—"

"I can't," Ashlyn said, her face falling. "Evanna told me I wasn't allowed to go back until we destroy the demon."

"Seriously? And it's not a demon! It's a little girl!" Kym shouted.

Another wave of death energy burst from the girl. They all ran back, barely avoiding it for a second time. If they didn't find a solution soon, they might run out of time.

"If Evanna won't help, what are we supposed to do?" Kat burst out.

"I can help."

Kym turned around, as did the others. Jazin stood behind them, dressed for a fight, an amused expression on his face. A smile spread across his lips as his shoulder shook slightly. White-hot fire replaced the dull cold inside Kym. Did he think this was funny?

"What are you doing here?" Tomark asked.

"Lord Phillip sent me after he felt a disturbance. He said other Favored would be here, but that they might need my help."

"Well, what could you do?" Ashlyn asked skeptically. "Everything we've thrown at it hasn't done a thing."

"I'll give it a try," Jazin said.

Jazin stepped up to the waves of death pouring from the girl. He extended his hands, and Kym saw his black Marks glittering on his arms. The black mist flew from around the girl into Jazin's outstretched hands. She screamed, and Kym's insides shuddered at the sound. But Jazin didn't stop until all of the black energy floated before him.

Kym expected Jazin to stop there. Instead, he stepped forward and wrapped his hands around the girl's wrists. More black energy oozed from the girl. She cried out, her body trembling, and slumped to the ground as the blackness vanished from her eyes. Jazin shoved his hands over his head, the death energy from the girl floating between them. The energy soared into the air, where it disappeared.

"That was incredible," Amber beamed, stepping forward. "How'd you do that?"

"I'm a Death Favored," Jazin said quietly. "Controlling death is what I do."

Kym couldn't stop herself from rolling her eyes. Did he have to be so cocky? And why was Amber acting like he was the coolest person she'd ever seen?

"Well, thank Pheil," Pupil said, almost as excitedly as Amber. "We'd have been screwed if you hadn't shown up."

"Thanks, Xander," Jazin smiled.

Kym stared at Jazin. Who was he talking to? There was no one named Xander in this field. And why did Pupil look like Jazin just kicked him in the gut?

"Who's Xander?" Ashlyn asked, clearly just as confused as Kym.

"I am," Pupil sighed, looking at his shoes. "Xander's my real name."

"Woah, back up. How does random death kid know your name?" Kat asked, jabbing her thumb at Jazin. "We don't even know it!"

"I know all of your names," Jazin said flatly. "Lord Phillip told me everyone who was here before I left. I didn't know Xander went by another name. I'll call you something else if you want?"

"No," Xander said slowly. "Call me Xander. All of you," he added, looking at the others. "I don't care if Melana gets mad. You should know my real name."

Kym must have misheard him. Xander did whatever Melana wanted, without question. But now he was okay with them knowing his name, and all because this new guy let it slip by accident? He'd turned on his friends and attacked them at the festival because she told him to. Why was he suddenly okay with disobeying Melana now?

"Well, I'd hate to ruin such a meaningful moment," Kat said, bringing Kym back to her surroundings. "But we still need to do something with her."

Kym looked down at the little girl, still lying on the snow-covered ground. Her body twitched every couple of seconds, and her breathing sounded shallow and weak. Kym knelt beside her and brushed the girl's light brown hair from her face. What happened to her, to make her like this? Did she fall so deeply into death that it started pouring uncontrollably out of her? If Kym was right about her mother, could the same thing happen to her? A shiver ran through Kym's body at the thought.

"I don't know," Ashlyn said. "But I can go to Solaris now and ask. Since the fight is over, Evanna might actually speak to me. I'll be back in a minute."

Ashlyn invoked her yellow Marks. There was a flash of pure, yellow light, and Ashlyn was gone.

"Where'd she go?" Jazin asked, looking around.

"She went back to Solaris, just like she said," Kat huffed, crossing her arms.

"Light Favored," Amber said gently to Jazin, throwing Kat a dirty look, "can travel at the speed of light. She'll be back in a sec."

"Oh," Jazin said, "I didn't know."

"Clearly," Kym said, a little more forcefully than was probably necessary.

Maybe it was the way he spoke—always smiling like he was better than them—but there was something about Jazin that rubbed Kym the wrong way. How could he not know the Darkness Favored were called Pupil? Phillip had told him everything, after all. Did he reveal Xander's name on purpose? Why?

Another flash of yellow filled the air, and a breathless Ashlyn stood before them.

"So," Xander said, "what did Evanna say?"

"Well," Ashlyn panted, "she didn't believe it was a little girl. I had to tell her about five different ways, and she only believed me after hearing how Jazin removed the death energy from her. She said Thed's power is in Princirum now, so this girl might be the first of many."

"That's great, Ash," Tomark said gently, "but what are we supposed to do with her?"

"Oh yeah," Ashlyn said, hurrying on. "She said to take her to Tenbatter."

Both Xander and Kat tensed. They exchanged a look with each other, their expressions grim. They'd heard of Tenbatter before. Kym, on the other hand, had never even heard the word. It had to be a place if they were taking the girl there. But what was it? Where was it?

"I don't know where that is or how to get there," Ashlyn finished, apparently on the same page as Kym.

"I do," Xander said darkly. He looked almost uncomfortable. "I can take us there. Jazin, can you carry her?"

Jazin nodded and hoisted the girl over one of his shoulders.

"Okay," Xander said, "Form a circle and put one hand in the center."

They did as Xander instructed. Kym put her hand in the middle of the circle, standing between Ashlyn and Kat.

"What's Tenbatter?" Kym whispered.

"I'll tell you when we get there," Kat said quietly. She looked just as uncomfortable as Xander.

Trying to ignore her confusion, Kym looked across the circle to Xander. His purple Marks shone bright, and he had a look of intense concentration on his face. He stared so intently at their grouped hands, veins appeared on his forehead. Kym looked down at their hands and gasped, but stopped herself.

Their group of hands was a mass of varying black shades, all wrapped around each other. Darkness crept slowly up their arms, and Kym felt like hers had been plunged into a bucket of ice water. Xander was turning them into shadow.

When her body was icy cold, Kym felt Xander's hand twist amongst the others. Her body lurched forward, pulled into the place where their hands met. Their bodies collided into one massive collection of darkness. The world blurred around her as they spun into one another, then everything was dark.

T E N B A T T E R

Darkness pressed in on Kym, compressing her body into the smallest of spaces. She gasped, but no air entered her lungs. Only her arm, still stuck out in front of her, felt normal, her fingers still intertwined with the others'. She felt them pressed all around her, beside her, inside her. She closed her eyes, but it made absolutely no difference. Hopefully, whatever Xander was doing would be over soon.

Kym's feet slammed into solid ground and her body exploded outward. Her eyes snapped open. The world seemed overly bright, and her body felt oddly light and cold. She blinked several times, but her eyes didn't seem to be working. Disgruntled murmurs flew around her as she tugged her hand from the wriggling mass of fingers. Clearly, she wasn't the only one who didn't enjoy traveling through shadow.

"Xander." Kym heard Ashlyn next to her. "A little warning would've been nice."

"Seriously," said Tomark's shaking voice. "Is it always that uncomfortable?"

"Warping is a difficult skill," Amber said superiorly. "Few can manage it at all, and that's before taking others along. It took me over a year to master it completely. Of course, I was eleven—"

"Amber," Kat groaned. "Do us all a favor, and shut the Thed up."

Amber had once fire-warped Kym, Tomark, and herself to their secret hangout spot in the middle of the night. Kym remembered traveling through the flames. It had been so pleasant and warm. And while she'd felt oddly pulled apart, never once did it feel uncomfortable. Maybe Xander did need more practice.

"It doesn't matter," Xander snapped. "I got us here in one piece."

Kym looked around, her vision slowly growing clearer. Something very tall and dark loomed overhead, blanketing them in shadow. Kym rubbed her fists into her eyes, trying to help them adjust. Slowly, the massive thing came into focus.

They were standing in front of a giant, stone tower at least two hundred feet high. A massive, wooden door was the only blemish on the worn, grey surface. Kym craned her neck, hoping to see the top of the weathered facade. A chill ran down her spine. There was no hope here. Not even a spark. Why would they bring a little girl here?

"What is this place?" Kym wasn't surprised to hear her voice was no more than a whisper.

"This," Xander said darkly, "is Tenbatter."

"We know what it's called," Amber snapped, also looking up at the massive tower. "What *is* it?"

"Can't you tell?" Kat's normally lighthearted tone was oddly cold. "It's a prison."

"A prison?" Tomark asked, although Kym thought she knew the answer. "For what?"

"The Rulers' enemies."

Kym shook her head. So, instead of trying to make Princirum a better place, the Rulers decided the best way to spend their time was to build a prison? How was this supposed to save Princirum from the power of death?

"The Rulers don't have a prison," Ashlyn said. "The only prisons in Princirum are in the cities."

"That was before the Festival of Creation," Xander said. "After everything that happened, the Rulers felt they needed to build it to protect themselves. Those who the Rulers view as a threat are now brought here."

So, not only did the Rulers feel they needed extra protection at their palaces, but they also needed somewhere to put their so-called enemies? Kym didn't want to hear this. Who could even threaten the Rulers? They were the children of the gods, after all.

"How do you two know this?" Amber asked, bringing Kym back to the conversation. "Weren't Lord Kai and Lady Melana keeping the two of you out of the loop like the rest of us?"

"Kai tried." Kat snorted. "I was stuck at Terradon for weeks by myself while Kai sent the other Earth Favored to build it. Finally, I got one of them to spill his guts."

"And since they built it in Lady Melana's realm," Xander said, "she sent her Pupils to oversee it. That was one of her tests. She told me I couldn't leave the Fortress, then filled me in about Tenbatter. She said the Darkness Pupils needed to supervise the construction."

"Did you stay at the Great Fortress?" Tomark asked.

"If I hadn't, I wouldn't be one of Melana's Pupils. For all I know, Melana would've called me an enemy and thrown me in there."

"Wait," Kym said. She stared at the little girl, still draped over Jazin's shoulder. "Evanna thinks this little girl is a threat? That's crazy. How could this girl be a danger to the Rulers?"

"Kym, you saw what she did," Ashlyn said. "She's dangerous."

"I don't know," Tomark said, "Did she even know what she was doing? I don't think she was in control."

"That makes her even more dangerous, Tomark," Amber said briskly. "She needs to be separated from others."

"Guys," Jazin said quickly, a note of panic in his voice. "I think she's waking up."

The girl fidgeted and wriggled in Jazin's thin arms. Kym stepped forward. She wanted to do something to calm her down. She reached out her hand, and the cold dullness of death bloomed from her fingers down to her stomach. The girl's eyes snapped open, once again black as night. Kym couldn't touch her. She backed away, Jazin trying to retain his grip on the little girl.

"Follow me," Xander said, looking warily at the girl.

Kym and the others followed Xander to the massive wooden

door at the base of the tower. Two Protectorate stood on either side of the entrance, their faces set with emotionless stares. They didn't move as Kym and the others drew nearer. Xander reached out his arm to push open the door, and spears appeared almost from nowhere, blocking the entrance.

"State your purpose," the guard on the right said in a deep, slow voice.

"Um…to deliver an enemy of the Rulers," Jazin said tentatively. He turned so the guards could see the girl draped over his shoulder.

"Excuse me?" the other guard snapped, glaring at the group of teenagers in front of her.

Kym's eyes darted between the two Protectorate, her insides growing hot. Why didn't they believe them? Why would they be there if the Rulers hadn't sent them?

"This girl," Amber said in full Fire Princess form, staring down at the two guards, "poses a severe threat to the Rulers' power. We defeated her, and now she must pay for her crimes. Let us pass. Now."

The guards shrunk at Amber's words. They looked defeated, and Kym couldn't stop herself from smiling. She knew Amber hated being the Fire Princess, but at least it came with a few perks. And scaring the pants off of a few Protectorate was a nice bonus.

"O-o-of course, Miss," stammered the guard to the left of the door.

The guards hurriedly stowed their spears and opened the door, almost melting into the walls as Amber led the others inside. The door slammed shut the moment Ashlyn stepped over the threshold. Darkness crept in on them, only broken by the torches set sporadically up the high walls.

"Well, Fire Princess," Kat said. "Was scaring the Nothingness out of the Protectorate necessary?"

"It was," Amber said. "If I hadn't stepped up, we'd still be out there arguing with them. At least I got us in."

"But what do we do now?"

Kym shifted uncomfortably. Aside from their little group, the entire tower was deserted. She squinted through the gloom, trying to see up the dark, grey walls. But aside from the stairs wrapping around them, they were just as bare as the ones outside. How was this place a prison? Didn't prisons need cells to hold the prisoners?

"Let's just leave her here. I'll pin a note to her shirt."

"Kat," Kym snapped. How could she say that? "We're not dumping her on the floor."

"I was only joking," Kat said defensively.

"This isn't the time," Tomark said seriously.

"If this place is a prison, where are the cells?" Jazin asked, looking at Xander.

"How should I know?" Xander demanded. "I stayed behind when they built it, remember?"

"What is the meaning of this?" A stern voice echoed through the tower.

Kym jerked her head upward, looking for the source of the voice. But she could only see darkness between the dim light of the torches. Who was there? She squinted at the stairs, tracking their progress as far up as she could, but still, she saw nothing.

"Who's there?" Tomark asked, his voice echoing through the dark. No one answered.

"This is stupid."

Ashlyn stepped in front of Kym. She invoked her Marks, and held her hands in front of her. A miniature sun bloomed between her fingers. It rose into the air, filling the tower with soft, yellow light. A woman stood on the stairs a few feet away. She wore dark green robes and had her hands held neatly behind her back.

"Why are you in my prison?" the woman demanded. "Only the enemies of the Rulers come here. Is that who you are?"

"We serve the Rulers," Kym said, her voice shaking. "We're their Vanquishers, and we're here to deliver a prisoner."

"Of course," the woman said bluntly. "Lady Evanna sent word of your arrival. The prisoner?"

Jazin stepped forward, heaving the girl off of his shoulder. He draped her in his arms, displaying her to the woman. Jazin didn't move as the woman stared down at the girl, who still stirred feebly in Jazin's arms.

Anger bubbled up inside Kym. Did Jazin have to present the girl like she was a prize he'd won? And why did the woman need to inspect the child? She was a ten-year-old girl. Why were they treating her like an animal?

"She won't be out for much longer," the woman said briskly. "Bring her. Time is short."

Kym and the others ran after the woman, already halfway up the first set of stairs. They climbed in silence, going higher and higher as the girl continued to squirm in Jazin's arms. The torches on the walls grew fewer the higher they climbed. Luckily, Ashlyn's miniature sun rose up the tower with them. But the higher they climbed, the less light it seemed to emit.

Kym expected to see cells as they climbed higher into the dark tower. But the walls remained blank as they walked round and round. Where was the woman leading them? They couldn't be going to the roof. Aside from being high in the air, that didn't offer much in keeping prisoners contained. Where were they going?

The woman stopped abruptly in front of a blank stretch of wall. Kym ran into Xander, who knocked Kat into the wall with his shoulder. The woman raised her right arm and placed her palm on the wall. Green Marks shone brightly on her arm as the woman stepped forward. Her arm passed right through the wall, and she rotated it like turning a key in a lock.

A loud thud emanated from the wall as the woman pulled her arm free. After moving several feet, she stopped, and Kym couldn't stop herself from staring. The wall before them shimmered like smoke, revealing a room behind it.

The room was small and square, with only a filthy sleeping pad on the floor. Chains lay curled in the corner, fastened to the wall with a thick, metal ring. The chains looked old, and the dark stone walls gave the feeling of being trapped far underground. Kym had to remind herself she was at least one hundred feet in the air.

"You two," the woman said, pointing at Jazin and Xander. "Bind her before she wakes up."

Jazin walked through the smoky door, Xander right on his heels. Jazin roughly placed the girl on the pad while Xander pulled over the chains. Jazin struggled to clamp the chains around the girl's writhing hands and feet. Kym opened her mouth to protest but stopped as the girl screamed once again.

"Get out," the woman ordered.

Jazin and Xander didn't need telling a second time. They leaped through the entrance as the woman placed her Mark-covered arm back into the smoky earth wall. She quickly rotated her arm back and forth, and another loud thunk filled the tower. The wall solidified, and the woman pulled her arm out of the stone.

A chill ran down Kym's spine, the girl's screams echoing inside her head. She was dangerous; Kym knew that. The girl had almost killed Kym and her friends, after all. But this, locking her away for the rest of her life, couldn't be the answer. How could this tower even hold her? The girl's death energy destroyed everything it touched.

"You sure that's strong enough to hold her?" Jazin panted. "Death destroys everything."

"Of course," the woman said. "Lord Phillip and Lady Zara made the chains themselves. No amount of death or life could possibly break them. And Lord Kai and Lady Melana reinforced the tower with their magic after the Earth Favored finished constructing it. They also enchanted my arm, making it the only key to the tower's cells. I was honored when they selected me as Tenbatter's Warden."

"What will happen to the girl?" Kym asked.

"Don't waste your energy worrying about that thing," the Warden said coldly.

"She's not a thing," Kym snapped, her anger reaching its tipping point. How could this woman be so heartless? "She's just a little girl who... She didn't know what she was doing!"

"Whatever you have to tell yourself," the Warden shrugged.

Kym's hands balled into fists. Her entire body trembled as she tried to keep herself from exploding. She wanted to unleash all her anger on this woman. Luckily for the Warden, Kym hadn't seen a drop of water since entering Tenbatter. She breathed deeply through her nose, trying her best to slow the pounding in her ears. It didn't work.

A hand appeared gently on Kym's shoulder. She jerked around, her mind blank, trying to shake it off. But Tomark didn't let Kym go. She stared into his dark green eyes, and slowly, her shaking slowed. He smiled down at Kym, pushing his dark, wavy hair out of his face.

"Kym's just worried about the girl," Tomark said politely to the Warden. "We all are."

The others all murmured in agreement.

"You have nothing to worry about," the Warden smiled. "The girl's in good hands."

"That's very good to hear," Ashlyn said. "When will she be released?"

"Released?" The Warden let out a laugh that was more like a bark. "Why the Nothingness would the girl be set free? Thed's presence inside her is clear. She betrayed her Rulers. This is what she deserves."

Kym's anger flared up again in an instant. How could this woman be in charge here? This girl didn't deserve to be locked away for something that happened to her. She didn't choose this, and the Warden didn't need to punish her for it. Locking her away for the rest of her life couldn't be the only solution.

This was just like what had happened to Kym's aunt and uncle when she was little. All they did was speak their minds, and the priests hunted them down and killed them for it. And now, the Rulers were punishing people for things that were clearly out of their control. If what happened to this girl happened to Kym's mom, the Rulers would lock her up without a second thought.

Melana was more of a threat to the Rulers than this little girl. Sure, the power of death had overpowered her, but Thed himself had possessed the Ruler of Darkness. Wasn't that a greater threat to the Rulers than a little girl or Kym's mom? If the Rulers wanted to end Thed's connection to Princirum, they'd have locked Melana in Tenbatter the second they built it. They'd have thrown in Phillip and Jazin too, the moment they saw them. But that, of course, never happened.

This time, it was Kat who grabbed onto Kym. She worked her hand into Kym's fist as they walked down the winding tower stairs. Kym tried to pull her hand out of Kat's. Kat used her free hand to punch Kym hard in the upper arm. Kat's sympathy only went so far.

The Warden stopped a few steps before the stairs ended. Kym and the others walked silently past her, and Kym tried her best not to look at the woman. She stared instead at the massive front door, which swung open with an ominous creak.

The outside world seemed overly bright as they stepped out of the dark tower. As they walked away, Kym glanced back over her shoulder. The Protectorate had their spears drawn once again, crossing them in front of the massive door. Kym looked away, shaking her head. She never wanted to see that place again if she could help it.

"Kym," Ashlyn said once they were out of earshot of the Protectorate. "I thought you were gonna slap that woman."

"So did I," Tomark said, although he didn't sound as entertained as Ashlyn.

"I thought I was, too," Kym sighed, her body no longer shaking. "I just…I couldn't let her talk about that girl like that."

"Kym, we know," Amber said impatiently. "This is exactly what happened at the first Summit you attended."

"What?" Kym said defensively. "No, it's not!"

"Kym, it kinda is," Ashlyn said.

"This is completely different."

Kym's mind raced back to that first Summit, the one that made her Vanquisher of Water in the first place. Melana had called the people who live in the city the 'detested,' and Kym had broken every rule the Favored were supposed to follow to tell her off. The way Melana spoke made her so angry she lost all sense. She'd wanted to attack Melana and make her see her way of thinking was wrong. Maybe her reaction to the Warden wasn't so different after all.

"Oh," Kym said sheepishly.

"I knew you'd get there in the end," Kat smiled.

"You have to be able to let these things go," Xander said. "It's going to get you into trouble one of these days."

"Sorry, I'm lost," Jazin said. "What did she do?"

"Oh," Amber said breathily. "Kym got…um…carried away when Lady Melana said something a little disrespectful at a Summit."

Personally, Kym thought that was the most underwhelming explanation of what happened. Melana wanted Kym's magic ripped from her after that outburst. But the way Amber told it, Kym may have coughed at the wrong time.

"You heard the Warden talking about the girl," Kym said defensively. "I had to say something."

"Of course you did," Amber said flatly. "You can't help but want to save helpless things."

"Amber, that was low," Kat snapped. "Even for you."

"What?" Amber demanded. "We all know it."

"She's just a little girl," Tomark said.

"Who committed a crime," Jazin said quietly. "She deserves to be locked up."

"So would you a month ago, mister Death Favored!" Kat shouted.

"I don't have death exploding out of me!" Jazin retorted. "And I know how dangerous death can be. Trust me. At least I'm using the power of death for good."

"For now," Kat snorted.

"Do you think the Rulers would let her go?" Ashlyn asked. "If we speak to them…."

"Ash, that's the most delusional thing you've ever said," Kat groaned.

"Kat's right!" Tomark shouted, forcing everyone to stop talking.

"The Rulers aren't going to let her go, no matter what we say. So there's no point in us arguing about it."

"Of course, they won't let her go," Amber drawled. "They're so paranoid they built a secret prison for their enemies."

Kym wanted to retort, to tell Amber and Jazin and the rest of them how wrong they were. But, as Amber's words washed over her, she knew Amber was right. The Rulers would never let the girl go, and there was nothing she could do to change that. The thought drove all the warmth from inside her.

"Well," Jazin said after several moments' silence, "I'd better get going. Lord Phillip's probably wondering what's taking so long."

"We should all leave," Tomark said quickly, apparently eager for the change of subject. "The Rulers don't want us talking to each other. Better not make them any madder than we have to."

"Or, we could stay out for a little while," Kat smirked. "Like old times?"

Kym's heart swelled at the thought. She could see them in her mind, back at their old meeting spot. Amber would light a fire while Kat made little earth stumps for them to sit on. They'd vent about the Rulers and other Favored, saying all of the things they never could back at the palaces. For once, they could finally be themselves.

"No," Xander said. "We're hanging on by a thread with the Rulers. Better not push our luck."

"He's right," Kym admitted, her heart falling.

"Fine."

Kat ran around the group, giving everyone her usual punch on the arm. Kym was sure Kat hit Jazin harder than the others. No one else winced. Smiling, Kat invoked her Marks and sank straight into the ground without a word. After quickly saying good-bye, both Xander and Amber warped away, vanishing in swirls of darkness and flame.

"Show-offs," Kym said, although ruining the effect by smiling.

"Hey," Tomark said, pulling Kym into a quick hug. "Keep your cool, okay?"

"Easier said than done, these days." Kym smiled as she pulled away.

Tomark invoked his silver Marks. He shot high into the air, causing Kym's hair to fly wildly around her. She smiled, watching him grow smaller as he flew gracefully through the air toward the bright sun. A few moments later, he vanished from sight.

"Kym," Ashlyn said, pulling Kym back to earth. "I can take you back to Wadita if you want."

"Hum," Kym said. Her mind was oddly blank.

"Do you want me to take you back to Wadita?"

"Oh, no. Thanks, though. Nila would flip out if I got back in a way that wasn't water-based."

"Are you sure? It would literally take a second."

"I'm sure. Termubra is full of rivers. It won't take me long to find one."

"Okay," Ashlyn said. There was a flash of light, and Ashlyn was gone.

This left only Jazin. Kym shifted back and forth on her feet, unsure what to do. Jazin seemed just as uncertain. He stared at the ground, kicking a particularly dirty pile of snow. Kym knew she should tell him good-bye, but what could she say? 'Thanks for disagreeing with everything I said' didn't seem right. Before Kym could make a decision, Jazin started walking away from her.

"Where are you going?"

"Back to Obsidian," Jazin said plainly. "But I need to find a place of death before I can go back."

"A what?" Kym repeated. She had no idea what Jazin was talking about, but she didn't like the sound of it.

"It's just a place where something has died," Jazin sighed. "I need to harness the energy to get back to Obsidian."

"Oh," Kym said uncomfortably. "That's...awful."

"Not always," Jazin said, smiling faintly. "The way I see it, it's a place where something found peace. That can't be all bad."

Jazin turned and walked off into the distance. Kym went in the opposite direction. She didn't care what Jazin said. No matter how he phrased it, harnessing the power of death just sounded wrong.

Kym invoked her Marks, closed her eyes, and concentrated. She focused on the calm feeling she always had whenever she was underwater, hoping it would lead her to the closest source. After a few moments, she felt something—a strange tingling inside her. She ran forward several yards, and the feeling intensified. She knew that feeling anywhere. There was water close by.

It took Kym twenty minutes to reach the river. Without breaking her stride, she jumped into the shallow water. Happy she wasn't fighting the current upstream, Kym rocketed downriver, trying to avoid the mucky riverbed as she swam toward the ocean. Luckily, Termubra was right next to Undarunci, so she didn't have to swim long before reaching her familiar beaches.

Kym launched herself out of the water when she reached Wadita, landing gently on the wet sand. The sun was high above her, and the air felt a little warmer. Luckily for her, today was a training day, so the beach and back garden were deserted.

In the entrance hall, the floor to the training rooms was open. Kym stopped, staring down the dark blue stairs. It couldn't be later than noon, so why was the floor open? She couldn't have been gone for too long, could she? If she could slip up to her room before anyone saw her—

"Kymbralyn," Nila's voice rang out through the hall.

Kym stopped dead in her tracks. She turned around. Nila glided toward her, the door to her private chambers closing silently behind her.

"You have finally returned."

"Yeah," Kym said sheepishly.

"Lady Evanna sent the Rulers a message when one of her Favored asked her for help after the battle. But we can all rest easy now that the girl is safe inside Tenbatter."

Kym's anger raged up once again. She wanted to scream at Nila and tell her how wrong she was about the little girl. But even as her anger stormed inside her, a quiet voice pierced through the chaos.

Remember to keep your cool.

"Yes," Kym said, fighting to keep her voice calm. "When were you gonna tell us about Tenbatter?"

"You would be told when you needed to know," Nila said. "And for you, today was that day. Which Vanquishers joined you at the battle?"

Kym's insides prickled. Of course Nila would avoid talking about the need-to-know prison. That wasn't important to her. What was important was who Kym spent the morning with. There was no way she could hide the fact that she'd seen her friends without outrightly lying. But, Kym was so angry at Nila she didn't care if she knew.

"Kat from Terradon, Tomark from Alfonburg, Ashlyn from Solaris." Nila's face grew sterner with every name Kym said. But she didn't shout out, so Kym carried on. "Amber from Inferon, Xander from the Great Fortress."

"Who?" Nila snapped.

"One of Melana—Lady Melana's—pupils. We learned his real name today."

"Very well," Nila spat, her voice full of icy fury. "Anyone else?"

"Yes," Kym said. "Jazin from Obsidian."

Nila's whole body tensed. Her nostrils flared as her hands shook at her sides. Rage flashed in her eyes, and Kym's first impulse was to back away several feet. After a few seconds of silent fury, Nila turned on her heel and stormed off without saying a word. When she reached a door on the other side of the hall, she wrenched it open, stepped through, and slammed it shut behind her, leaving Kym alone as the sound echoed around her.

CHAPTER SEVEN

YOUR
PLACE

Kym expected Nila to be angry. She'd been ready to get yelled at, and punished, and yelled at some more. However, she hadn't expected Jazin's name to be the thing to send Nila over the edge. He wasn't one of the people Nila feared would influence Kym's loyalties. Why was his name the one that sent her over the edge?

For the first time, Kym understood where Nila was coming from, and she didn't like it. It was a strange feeling, being on the same page as Nila. They'd been at odds since Kym's arrival at Wadita. She wasn't sure how she felt about agreeing with the woman who'd spent the past several months keeping her locked up. The thought made her skin crawl. Nila wasn't the best judge of character, after all. Should Kym give Jazin a second chance?

Sure, his ability to manipulate death was creepy, but oddly, that wasn't what Kym found unsettling about him. It was how determined he was to insert himself into the Vanquishers. Why did he know so much about them when he'd never met them before? And what did he have to gain by forcing himself into their group? It wasn't like being in it made Kym or the others popular with the Rulers. They'd punished them for their friendship, after all.

Kym shook her head, trying to clear the jumbled mess of thoughts from her mind. There was no point worrying about that now. Besides, it wasn't like she could stop Jazin from showing up if another death demon appeared. That is, if Nila ever let her leave Wadita again. After everything that happened, Kym doubted Nila would let her go as far as the beach.

Even though it wasn't night, all of the torches were lit. Kym shivered in her light training clothes. If she went down to train, Kenna and Aidan would certainly have something to say about Nila letting her leave the palace. She might as well go to her bedchamber. There, she'd be safe. Besides, now that she was back at the palace, she felt exhausted. Her mind drifted to her bed. Maybe, if she hurried, she'd be able to get in a quick nap before her maids showed up.

Kym opened her bedchamber door, and the air filled with a shriek of terror. Veronica and Isabel, their arms full of Kym's evening clothes, stared at her from the opposite side of the room. Slowly, they set Kym's clothes down on her bed before taking several tentative steps toward her, like they were approaching some wild animal.

"Oh, Pheil," Isabel breathed. She looked like she might faint.

"What?" Kym asked gingerly.

"You're filthy," Veronica stammered.

"What? No, I'm not."

Kym marched into the room, much to her maids' displeasure. She ignored their protests and walked into the enormous bathroom, looking into the large mirror on the wall. Kym's whole body, from her blond hair to her feet, was covered in mud. Tears covered her training clothes, and several twigs stuck out of her hair.

"Wow," Kym said, barely concealing her smile. "I've never looked better."

"This isn't a joke, Kym," Veronica snapped. "It'll be a miracle if we get you ready in time for dinner."

"What happened?" Isabel asked, helping Kym out of her clothes. "Where have you been? You were gone when we arrived."

"Oh…Nila sensed a death demon when she returned this morning. She sent me to battle it."

"Really," Veronica said, her eyebrows raised. "I thought that was no longer your responsibility."

"Well, Nila changed her mind," Kym retorted. "And let's be

honest; I've come back from death demon fights in far worse shape than this."

After removing her clothes, Kym relaxed in the swimming pool-sized tub. Her maids fussed over which soaps and oils would best remove the filth from Kym's body while she made marble-size orbs of water fly lazily around the room. Kym hoped they'd take their time. Maybe, if they took long enough, they'd let her eat dinner in her room? At least then she wouldn't have to face Nila's wrath in front of Kenna, Aidan, and the rest of the Water Favored.

But once again, Kym underestimated her maids' skill. They removed all the dirt from her body, dried and styled her hair, and dressed her for dinner with time to spare. Kym stared in the mirror, taking in the image of herself in the electric blue dress with golden accents. The whole thing seemed to shimmer in the candlelight. Sometimes, Kym thought her maids were the ones with magic, and not her.

When Kym and her maids entered the dining hall, nearly all of the tables were full. She scanned the room, looking for an open seat, and stifled a groan. There was only one place for her to sit. Kym walked silently over to Nila's table, joining Kenna, Aidan, and Ryland. She took the seat between Kenna and Aidan while her lady's maids stood behind her.

"Now that Kymbralyn has joined us," Nila announced contently to the room, though Kym could still see the anger in her eyes, "I will walk amongst you before we start our meal. I would like to hear how your training has progressed in my absence."

Nila rose from her seat and glided over to the next table, her maids trailing behind her. Kym's skin crawled uncomfortably, but she didn't look up from the blue tablecloth. Did Kenna, Aidan, and Ryland have to stare at her? She tried to ignore them, focusing on her reflection in the back of her spoon. Maybe, for once, they'd drop an excuse to grill Kym for whatever they thought she'd done wrong this time. But that didn't happen.

"What?" Kym snapped when she couldn't take it anymore.

"Nila told us what you did today," Kenna said.

"Of course she did," Kym said. "Why wouldn't she tell you everything I did in my life? She let me be the Vanquisher of Water again. So what?"

"We're not talking about you fighting a death demon," Aidan said. "We're talking about you being with those other Favored. The ones from the other palaces."

"What about them," Kym demanded, her temper already rising to danger zone.

Why did they even care if Kym saw her friends? It had absolutely nothing to do with them. She clasped her hands in her lap, squeezing them so tightly her knuckles turned white. She barely noticed the pain. She stared at the center of the table, Tomark's words playing in a loop in her head.

Don't lose your cool. Keep it together.

"The other Favored who showed up, they were the ones you used to hang out with, right?" Aidan asked. "The ones you talked to at the emergency Summit?"

"Why do you care?" Kym asked.

"Believe it or not, we're looking out for you," Ryland said.

"Sure you are, Ryland," Kym shot back. "I feel so looked after."

"Kym, we're in public," Kenna said bluntly.

"What the Thed! I don't care," Kym snapped. Didn't they understand how she felt? "We're not friends. Friends don't treat each other the way you've treated me. You've spied on me. You've made me miserable in training. And now you think you can tell me who I can and can't see?"

"Those Favored aren't loyal to Nila," Aidan said. "They could manipulate you into betraying her."

"*You* are the only people manipulating me," Kym responded through gritted teeth. Her head was pounding, and the sound seemed to be draining from around her. "Now, unless you want to start a fight right here, in the middle of the dining hall, you should shut the Thed up."

"You don't scare us," Aidan laughed, leaning back in his chair.

"Remember, Kym," Kenna sneered. "We trained you. Everything you know, you learned from us. Don't start something you can't finish."

Kym glared at Kenna. What would happen if she sent all of the water in their glasses flying at her? She doubted Kenna could stop her, even if she was more powerful. But Kym knew she couldn't. She closed her eyes, taking several breaths while the pounding faded from her temples. Something nudged her right shoulder, making her jump. Isabel, who stood behind Kym, winked. Kym turned back to the table. Her lady's maids may get on her nerves, but at that moment, she was happy they were there. At least they were on her side.

Kenna, who'd risen out of her seat, quickly sat down before Nila could ask questions. Nila thanked the gods for the day, and then everyone began to eat. Kym's stomach growled loudly as her maids placed plates of food in front of her. She hadn't eaten all day. The steamed crab, roasted fish, and creamy clam stew were as good as ever. Nila didn't take her eyes off of Kym through the entire meal, which only added to Kym's sense of urgency. She stood up the moment she finished, but Nila shook her head the tiniest amount.

"Do you need something, Lady Nila?"

"Sit," Nila said, her voice flat. "I wish to speak with you. We will wait until your fellow Favored have left."

Kym sat back down, but grudgingly. She didn't want to hear anything Nila had to say. She had Kenna and Aidan spy on Kym, and kept her away from her friends. Would she be able to keep her temper in check for long if left alone in a room with Nila? After her altercation before dinner, she doubted it.

It took another fifteen minutes for the dining hall to clear. Kym spent most of the time looking at the wall above Nila's head, not wanting to look her in the face. Finally, Nila, Kenna, Aidan, Ryland, and Kym were the only ones left.

"Leave," Nila said silkily to Aidan, Kenna, and Ryland.

"Are you sure, my Lady?" Aidan asked as Kenna and Ryland rose obediently from their chairs.

"Do as instructed, Aidan. I require a moment alone with Kymbralyn," Nila said.

Aidan stood up, wrapped his arm around Ryland's shoulder, and followed Kenna out of the dining hall. The door closed silently behind them, leaving Kym alone with Nila. She looked at Nila, who stared back at Kym with narrowed eyes. Kym watched Nila's maids back away, and the scuffling behind her told Kym her maids were doing the same. She was really on her own now.

"So," Kym said. She was surprised at how calm her voice sounded. "What do you want to talk about?"

"As you know," Nila said slowly, "the Rulers' Summit is tomorrow. In the past, I chose you as my companion to these Summits. However, to keep you from trouble, I have kept you here for the past several months."

Nila paused, apparently waiting for Kym to say something. What did she expect her to say? The fact that she'd been on Nila's bad side for months and confined to the palace wasn't a secret.

"Your insight," Nila continued when Kym remained silent, "into the matters we discuss at these Summits is valuable. However, if you are to accompany me, I must have certain… assurances."

"And what would that be?" Kym asked, although she could guess where this conversation was headed.

"Your loyalty," Nila said. "I need to be sure that if it comes to it, you will be with me. No matter what."

There it was—Nila's blind loyalty. Kym never understood why the devotion of her Favored was so crucial to Nila. It was something she'd resisted since arriving at Wadita. Now, Nila was offering her the thing she craved most. A chance to leave the palace again, even after seeing the friends Nila thought would test Kym's loyalty. But was it worth the cost?

"Nila," Kym said quietly. "You have to know me better than that by now. I'll side with what I feel is right. As long as our views are in agreement on that, I'll be with you."

Nila stared unblinkingly at Kym, making her skin crawl. She had to know what Kym's answer would be, but still, she asked. What would happen to Kym now? Would Nila confine her to Wadita for several more months or even years? Or was Kym's lack of loyalty too much of a betrayal for even that?

"Very well." Nila stood so abruptly Kym recoiled in her seat. She braced herself, ready for the explosion. "You will join me tomorrow. We will use water-construct horses, so we will leave at nine o'clock. Make sure you are ready."

Nila glided silently out of the dining hall, her gaggle of servants hurrying behind her. Kym gasped, taking several deep breaths. The explosion she expected never came. She hadn't promised Nila her blind loyalty, which she thought was a requirement for attending the Summit. But she was wrong. Nila was taking her to the Summit, without Aidan or Kenna there to watch her. Finally, she was free.

Slowly, Kym rose from her chair and walked out of the dining hall. Veronica and Isabel followed several paces behind her, which she appreciated. She wasn't in the mood to talk to them about what just happened. They always took Nila's side whenever she vented to them. They didn't understand that Kym and Nila saw things differently.

Back in her bedchamber, Isabel undressed Kym while Veronica pulled out something for Kym to sleep in. She dismissed her maids as soon as she pulled on the flowing blue nightdress. They bowed, wished her good night, and backed out of the room. Yawning, Kym extinguished the candles and crawled into bed, her body aching, ready for sleep.

Morning arrived too early. Kym stared up at the canopy, wishing she could stay in bed all day. There was a pit in her stomach; an odd, twisted feeling she couldn't place. Something was going to happen today. She didn't know if it was good or bad. She couldn't even figure out where the idea came from. But she felt it in her gut. Something was going to happen today.

She tried explaining it to her maids when they arrived, but they didn't take in a word Kym said as they whirled around her at top speed. They hadn't dressed her for such an important event in months, and Kym could tell they were more excited about the Prospect than she was. They put Kym in a tight-fitting dress covered in multicolored gemstones and draped a shimmering shawl over her shoulders.

"Finally, something other than training clothes," Veronica sighed.

Typically, Nila left for the Summits before her Favored were awake. However, since she'd decided on such a late departure, the entrance hall was packed with people. They stared at Kym as she stood near the large front doors, some even shooting her dark looks. It reminded Kym of her classmates staring at her after she'd been found as a Favored. She didn't care in the slightest. They could stare all they wanted. At least she was getting out again.

Nila emerged from her chambers after about five minutes. She swept past Kym without acknowledging her. Unfazed, Kym hurried out the front doors after her. The carriage stood waiting for them, the construct horses ready, a squad of Protectorate mounted on the outside. Nila glided up the carriage steps, and Kym struggled in behind her. She sat down, panting, and braced herself as the carriage lurched forward.

Kym and Nila sat in silence for a long time. Kym didn't mind. She stared out the window, watching the world pass by her in a whirl of color. She tried her best to forget the night before and everything Kenna, Aidan, and Ryland said. She'd gotten what she'd wanted after all. What was the point thinking about it now that she was out of the palace?

"Kymbralyn," Nila said. Her voice was cold, colder than usual if that were possible.

"Yeah," Kym said tentatively.

"Today, remember your place." Nila put a lot of emphasis on the last three words. "You will not speak unless instructed. If you leave the throne room, speak to no one. Am I clear?"

Kym nodded. Nila's meaning couldn't be clearer. If Kym put so much as a hair over the line, she'd be done. It was more important than ever that she kept herself in check, especially if her friends were there.

Kym turned back to the window, watching the varying shades of grey pass them by. They spent the rest of the trip in silence. After what seemed no time at all, the black mountain loomed out of the distance. Their carriage ascended the winding mountain roads, and before Kym knew it, they were in the front drive of Crystal Palace. Black, yellow, purple, and green carriages already sat on the graveled drive. The Rulers of Death, Light, Darkness, and Earth were already there.

Kym followed Nila silently out of the carriage. As Nila led the way up the steps, Kym ensured she was always a few feet behind her. She kept her head down, staring at Nila's shoes as she walked with her hands behind her back. They joined the other Rulers, their Favored and Protectorate guards in the entrance hall. No one spoke. Kym chanced a glance up and saw Nila's impassive expression reflected on the other Rulers' faces. She tried to see the other Favored, but they all stood hidden behind their Rulers.

They made their way to the throne room once Stailin and James arrived. The Rulers and Favored ascended the two curved staircases to the upper floors while their guards remained in the entrance hall. Kym followed Nila down the familiar corridors, staring at her shoes. Nila stopped without warning, and Kym almost ran into her. Why'd they stop? She chanced another glance up from the floor.

The doors to the throne room were closed, and the hall was entirely deserted. But why? They'd never waited outside at any of the Summits she'd attended. Why was Zara making them wait?

Kym could almost see the anger rising off Nila like heat. She, nor any of the Rulers for that matter, waited for anything. Standing in the hall, unable to enter their own throne room, must be torture for them. Kym fought hard to suppress her smile.

It took another ten minutes for the doors of the throne room to open. Zara glided out to meet them, looking even more irritated then the other Rulers.

"I apologize for the delay. The throne room needed to be

redesigned now that Phillip is among our number. We will enter together to see the new arrangement."

The Rulers murmured in assent. They rushed forward, stepping over the threshold before the doors were even completely open. Kym lifted her head slightly as she followed the Rulers inside. Out of the corner of her eye, she saw Ashlyn, Tomark, Xander, Amber, Kat, and Jazin take their places behind the Rulers' thrones. Kym's heart exploded with joy at the sight of them, and she fought to keep her excitement from her face.

The throne room looked just as it had a few weeks before. The thrones for the Rulers of Light, Darkness, Fire, Air, Water, and Earth still sat around the room's edge, forming a hexagon. The floor in the middle of the room still sat several inches lower than the perimeter. The skylight shone down to the middle of the room, illuminating Zara's lone throne. It was there, in the middle of the room, that Kym saw the change.

A raised circle of stone now sat in the center of the hall, half white, half black. Two thrones sat on the circle, matching the color it sat on. Black silk fell like water over the black stone chair, and Kym didn't need to guess who it was for. Phillip, closely followed by Jazin, joined Zara at the center thrones while the other Rulers took their seats.

"We now call this Summit of the Rulers to order," Zara said.

"I beg your pardon," Melana, the Ruler of Darkness, said silkily. "*We*, Lady Zara? I must say I do not—"

"Lord Phillip and myself," Zara said firmly, cutting Melana off. "Thed, god of death, shares equal status with Pheil, Goddess of Life. Therefore, it is only natural that Phillip and I have the same status. This decree comes from Rai, god of air and bringer of judgement, as did the ruling that stripped you of your authority in this throne room for another five months."

Kym tried hard to hide her smile. From her place behind Nila's throne, Kym could see all of the Rulers except for the Ruler of Fire, James. But she guessed James's reaction was identical to the others. They all looked at Phillip, who none of them liked, as if he'd taken their favorite toy. And in a way, he had. The Rulers loved their power more than anything, and the fact that Phillip, a newcomer, was above them must feel insulting. It was nice to see Melana get what she deserved, even if her punishment still didn't seem fair.

"If there are no further comments," Phillip said, a triumphant gleam in his eyes as he looked down at the other Rulers, "we should begin the Summit."

And so the Summit commenced. The very first thing the Rulers discussed was the little girl Kym and the others fought. The Rulers praised their performance and swiftness in stopping the girl before she reached the Palace of Light. They agreed locking her up for the rest of her life was for the best. Kym had to bite her tongue to stop herself from speaking out. How could they say that about a little girl?

"Could this have been an isolated incident?" James said. "Or should we expect more of her kind to rise, given the presence of death we witnessed in the cities?"

"I agree," Stailin said. "This girl is not the only one out there."

"She will merely be the first," Nila said grimly. "Thed's grip on the cities is already strong."

"No doubt more will come," Phillip said. "As support for Thed grows in Princirum, the people must adjust to the new order. Balance will reestablish itself, given enough time. Those who are too weak, or resist these changes, will surely succumb to this fate. We must strive to maintain balance while we experience this phase of the gods' plan."

Kym stopped her scream of fury in her throat. Were the Rulers really going to do nothing to stop Thed? How could they do this? It was their job to protect and guide Princirum for the gods. There was no way the gods wanted this to happen. A shudder ran through Kym's body. She felt the icy death that radiated from the girl and the cold touch of her mother's skin on her fingers. If the Rulers weren't going to do anything to save these people, Kym would.

Kym didn't cry out, although every fiber of her being wanted her to. She didn't run forward into the middle of the room. She didn't tell the Rulers how horrible they were. Instead, she took two steps forward and waited for Zara, or now Phillip, to allow her to talk. She'd speak for those the Rulers wanted to ignore, just like she did at her first Summit. She waited for someone to acknowledge her, but no one did. Fuming, Kym stepped back, her body shaking with rage. She didn't know how much longer she could keep her promise to Nila.

The Rulers moved on to discussing their protection. James, Melana, and Evanna thought they needed more Protectorate guards than they already had. Zara, however, shot this plan down. She reminded them if the Rulers kept taking Protectorate from the cities, there would be none left to defend the faith if the need ever arose.

Kym's hands balled up into fists. What was it the Protectorate did—defended the faith? Were they defending the faith when they killed Kym's aunt and uncle for asking questions, or attacked a helpless man for speaking to a Favored? No. They were ensuring the Rulers didn't find out someone questioned their authority. This was even harder to swallow than them keeping a little girl locked in a tower.

After that, no one had anything else to say. The Summit was over, and Kym couldn't be happier. If she didn't get out of there soon, she'd explode. She couldn't believe the Rulers wouldn't let her speak. Wasn't that why Nila brought her, to share her perspective? Clearly, Nila didn't care about Kym's opinion as much as she said. The Rulers stood, but Zara cleared her throat loudly. Everyone froze, their eyes trained on Zara. Kym stared up at the towering woman, her sheer, white dress almost floating around her. What else could Zara have to say?

"Before we part, there is one more thing I must tell you," Zara said. She looked around the room, and her usually stony expression faltered. Her eyes were alight with excitement, and Kym saw the ghost of a smile on her lips. "Yesterday, I received word from the four High Priests in the cities. The signs are clear. My friends, it is time."

Silence fell over the room. Kym stared at Zara, who looked like she'd just given the Rulers their hearts' desires. But why? She hadn't given them anything. What was she talking about? The Rulers all grinned, their eyes alight with greed, but more than that, it was a look of pure joy. They were excited, and the thought made Kym's stomach lurch. What could possibly make them this happy? Whatever it was, it could only be good for them.

CHAPTER EIGHT

A CHANGE OF HEART

"WE MUST MAKE THE ANNOUNCEMENT IMMEDIATELY," JAMES boomed, his voice bouncing around the throne room.

"If the priests are correct," Melana sneered.

"They have never misinterpreted the signs," Kai stammered, quivering slightly at the look on Melana's face.

"We will act quickly," Zara called over the Rulers' growing excitement. "Summon your Favored. We will begin tomorrow at noon.

"It seems foolish for you to depart now," Zara added as an afterthought. "Spend the night here if you desire."

Kym stared at Zara, her insides twisting uncomfortably. What could make the Rulers this excited? As far as Kym was concerned, it couldn't be anything good. And what were these signs the priest saw in the cities? Were they good? Bad? They must have happened before, since the Rulers clearly knew what Zara meant. And why did all of the Favored need to be at Crystal Palace for things to 'start'?

Kym glanced to her left, barely moving more than she knew she could. Kat stood beside Kai's throne, not bothering to look meek. She stared at Zara and Phillip, her arms crossed tightly across her chest, several lines creasing her forehead. That was odd. Normally, Kat said dropping a boulder on her foot was more helpful than paying attention at the Summit. Why was she acting so interested?

Apparently sensing Kym's eyes on her, Kat tore her gaze from Zara and Phillip. She looked at Kym, who raised her eyebrows, hoping Kat would know the question she couldn't ask aloud.

What are you doing?

Kat jerked her head toward Zara and Phillip in response. Kym actually took a step back. Why was Kat so interested in what Zara was talking about? She'd have an easier time finding the edge of the world than figuring out what the Rulers were up to.

"This Summit of the Rulers has reached its completion," Phillip said, bringing Kym back to her surroundings. "Everyone is dismissed."

Slowly, the Rulers made their way out of the throne room. Kym followed behind Nila, trying to stay on her best Summit behavior. Usually, Nila left the Summits as fast as possible, and Kym would have to run to keep up with her lengthy strides. But today, Nila walked so slowly Kym matched her pace with ease.

Kym stayed a few steps behind Nila, unable to take her eyes off her. It was so unlike her to walk so casually. What was going on? After a few minutes of silent walking, Nila led Kym down the stairs into the entrance hall. Kym opened her mouth to speak, but Nila was out the front door before Kym's lips formed the words.

"Are we going back to Wadita?" Kym asked cautiously as Nila approached their blue carriage.

"Leaving now would be a waste of time," Nila said. "I will send a message to the palace. Your fellow Water Favored must join us."

Nila raised her hands and directed them at the water construct horses harnessed to their carriage. She invoked her Marks, which shone through the sheer fabric of her sleeves. Water dripped silently off the bright blue horses like rain. Nila lifted her hands, and the glowing puddle rose into the air. She jerked her hands this way and that, and the formless blob of water began to change shape. Enormous wings bloomed on either side, while a long, slender tail wriggled from the back of the construct's flat body.

The glowing manta ray floated several feet above the ground. The hem of Kym's dress fluttered around her ankles as the construct flapped its massive wings. It was the most beautiful thing she'd ever seen.

Nila flicked her wrist, and the manta ray's glow intensified.

Kym lifted her hand in front of her face; her eyes stinging from the intense blue light. But she needn't have bothered. The constructs' glow returned to normal a moment later. It flapped its enormous wings and sailed through the sky, its brilliant blue color shining bright against the grey clouds.

"There," Nila nodded. "The construct will reach Wadita in a few hours. If Aidan and Kenna have the rest of the Favored in line, they should make it just in time."

Nila turned from the horseless carriage. Kym hurried after her, her mind racing. She knew very little about construct magic—Kenna and Aidan refused to teach it during their training sessions. They claimed Kym's group wouldn't be ready for several years. But she'd seen plenty of water constructs at Wadita, and even more outside of training, like when a fire construct arrived at Wadita to spy on Nila. But how were Kenna and Aidan supposed to know what to do when it arrived? Could constructs even deliver messages? She thought they could only perform a single task, like attack.

"So," Kym said tentatively as she followed Nila back up the palace steps. "What should I do for the rest of the day?"

"If you desire, I will permit you to spend the day with the Favored the other Rulers brought."

Kym stopped so suddenly her feet caught on the edge of the step. She slipped, falling hard to her knees. She barely noticed the pain pulsing through her legs. She stared at the back of Nila's head, who'd stopped walking, but didn't turn to face Kym.

This had to be some sort of joke. Why would Nila willingly let Kym be around the other Favored? All of the Favored who were there were the ones Nila didn't want her to see. It hadn't been twenty-four hours since Nila exploded at Kym for seeing them. There was no way Nila was okay with Kym being around them. There had to be a catch.

"Excuse me," Kym breathed, the shock she felt clear in her voice.

"The other Favored who are here." Nila turned to face Kym,

who was surprised to see the Ruler smiling. Nila never smiled. "They are your friends, are they not?"

"Yes," Kym said tentatively. "But I thought you didn't want me around them. You said they were a bad influence."

"So, you do not wish to see them?" Nila said, her smile growing even wider. It was the strangest thing Kym had ever seen.

"I do," Kym answered quickly. "I wanna see them."

"Then, I see no reason why you should not. Go. I will see you at dinner."

This had to be some sort of twisted test, Kym thought. Nila must be trying to test Kym's loyalty somehow. But why? She'd said Kym could be with her friends. Would she go back on her word if Kym actually went through with it? And testing Kym really wasn't Nila's style. It was something she'd expect Melana to do with Xander.

Slowly, Kym walked past Nila and through the front door. With each step, she expected Nila to call her back and demand Kym remain at her side. She never did. Kym glanced over her shoulder, but Nila wasn't there. Excitement bubbled up inside Kym. After months of wanting nothing else, Kym was going to see her friends, and no one could tell her no.

Kym found Amber and Ashlyn standing in the entrance hall. They stood quite a ways apart, and kept glancing at each other every few seconds. Their mingled looks of discomfort and excitement mirrored Kym's. She couldn't tell if the knot in her stomach was from happiness or fear.

"You look like you're gonna vomit," Amber drawled.

"You don't look much better," Kym said, raising an eyebrow. Amber's pale skin was a vivid shade of green.

"What's going on?" Ashlyn whispered. Did she think they were being watched? "James and Evanna said we could see each other."

"Nila said the same. It has to be some sort of test, like what Melana does to Xander all the time."

"I doubt it," Amber said. "James isn't one for playing games."

"So what is it then, she who knows the Rulers best?" Ashlyn demanded.

"I don't know," Amber snapped. "I've never seen them act like this before. Zara's never cryptic, and I've certainly never seen all the Rulers happy at once."

"I know," Kym said, thinking of Nila's twisted smile. "It was creepy."

Loud, slapping sounds echoed from somewhere above them. Kym looked around. Kat was running down the curved stairs, her dress pulled up to the knees, revealing her bare feet. Kym laughed. Clearly, she'd ditched her shoes the first moment she could. Kat skidded to a halt, bouncing off Ashlyn as she failed to stop herself.

"What did you do?" Amber groaned. "Throw your shoes at the first servant you saw?"

"Look, Fire Princess," Kat panted, clutching at her side. Kym saw Amber's nostrils flare. "I'm not in the mood."

"Is everything okay?" Ashlyn asked, rubbing the spot where Kat hit her.

"What? Yeah. We need to compare notes."

"Notes?" Kym asked.

"Kai just said he was completely fine with me seeing you guys, like he hadn't kept me locked in that green prison for months."

"Join the club," Kym said. "Our Rulers all said the same thing."

"Which means the boys won't be far behind," Amber said coolly.

Amber's prediction came true in under a minute. Tomark and Xander arrived, both wearing identical expressions of confusion and happiness, while Jazin merely looked confused. A jolt ran through Kym at the sight of him. Did he need to insert himself into their group every chance he could?

"Alright," Tomark said, "what's going on? Why are we allowed to see each other again? Stailin gave me this big speech before we left for the Summit about staying away from you guys. And now he's suddenly fine with us being friends?"

"Is it a trick?" Xander asked, his eyes darting this way and that. Kym knew he was thinking about the ways Melana tested his obedience in the past. "I knew something was off when Melana didn't bring the other two Pupils here."

"I don't think so," Kym said. "But they're definitely acting strange."

"I've never seen Stailin smile before," Tomark said, and Kym saw him shudder. "It was unsettling."

"It has to be what Zara said at the end of the Summit," Kat said. She looked at Amber. "What did she mean, 'it is time'?"

"I don't know!" Amber burst. Kym could see the fire flash in Amber's eyes. "Contrary to popular opinion, I'm not the resident Ruler expert, Kat."

Kym couldn't help but feel disappointed. If any of them could come up with an explanation for what was going on, it was Amber. Even if she didn't feel like it, Amber knew the Rulers better than anyone. She'd been James's right hand since she was little. She knew how he thought. She'd be able to see things the others may have missed. There had to be something else going on.

"Kat," Kym said, struck by a sudden thought. "Why were you staring at Phillip and Zara at the end of the Summit? You never pay attention in there."

"Well," Kat said in a mock business tone, "as all of you know, I feel like the Summits are more boring than dirt. But, didn't you notice how the Rulers all looked at the end of the Summit?"

"They were happy," Jazin said, lifting his hands in confusion. "What's wrong with that?"

"They're never happy," Tomark, Xander, and Ashlyn said at the same time.

Kym shook her head. There really was a lot about the Rulers Jazin didn't know. And what did he expect. He'd only been a Favored for five minutes.

"Before that," Kat pressed on, and Kym heard the irritation in her voice. "When Zara said the priests read a billboard or something, before the Rulers looked like they'd been hit with the happy stick."

Kym tried to think back. She'd been standing behind Nila's

throne, but she could still see most of the other Rulers. When Zara first said the word sign, it was like something flipped in the Rulers. Like they'd been given their hearts' desire.

"They looked greedy," Ashlyn said.

"Exactly!" Kat said, and Kym was surprised at how serious her voice was. "I want to know why."

"Sorry, what?" Xander said. "We know the Rulers are the greediest people in Princirum. Why is it such a big deal?"

"It's a big deal because we know they're greedy," Amber said slowly, her eyes widening. "We know they covet power above everything else. They've been at each other's throats for centuries. Melana wanted to start a war with the gods if it meant she'd get more power. And it's only gotten worse since the festival. The only thing that could make them forget all of that is the promise of power."

Kym stared at Amber, not wanting to believe her. But she knew Nila well enough to know Amber was right. All Nila cared about was power. She barely spoke to Kym when her magic was weak, and she always had her skilled Favored hide how powerful they were when the other Rulers were around. But how much more power could Nila get? From the way she wouldn't stop smiling, it had to be a lot.

"You're right," Tomark said. "They know what's going on. They know why the other Favored need to be here tomorrow. And whatever it is, it's made them excited."

"But we're still clueless," Jazin said. "We'll just have to wait until they announce it tomorrow."

"The Nothingness if I'm waiting that long, Death Boy," Kat said. "I wanna know what's goin' on."

"And how are you going to do that?" Xander asked. "We can't walk up to the Rulers and ask them."

"Says who?" Kym asked. "They're all in great moods, after all. Maybe they'll slip up and tell us something. I'm in."

"Me too," Ashlyn said. "Let's split up and see what we can find out."

"This is a horrible idea," Amber said.

"Completely," Tomark agreed.

"It is," Kat smiled. "Reminds me of the good old days when we did what we wanted and didn't care what the Rulers said."

They split up, agreeing to swap stories at dinner if they learned anything interesting. However, Kym had only walked a few feet when she noticed the massive flaw in Kat's plan. Kym had no idea where Nila was. She didn't even know where Nila slept when they stayed at Crystal Palace. Granted, the only other time that happened was during the Festival of Creation, and Kym never thought or even cared to ask. Now she wished she had.

With no real plan in mind, Kym turned right. She walked down the deserted corridor, unsure what to do next. The sound of shuffling feet echoed behind her. Kym dove to the side, pushed open a door at random and hurried inside. Her heart racing, she peered through the crack in the door. Six Protectorate in white-accented robes walked down the hall, their hands held behind their back. Kym held her breath, listening as their footsteps grew fainter.

Kym pulled open the door a fraction when she couldn't hear anything from the hall. There was no one there. She stepped out of the room, her heartbeat slowing with every step. Why were Zara's Pros wandering the halls? Nila never let hers do that, and Wadita was full of training Favored to look after. The only people at Crystal Palace were Zara and her servants. It made no sense.

And those weren't the only Protectorate Kym saw. They popped up in nearly every hall, wandering silently in groups of four or six. Kym ducked into empty rooms or onto balconies as they passed, praying they would leave her alone. A slight pounding bloomed in Kym's temple after her fifth run-in with the Pros. If she kept this up, she wouldn't find Nila for weeks. How many Pros did Zara have, anyway? She certainly had more than Nila.

Kym turned down what felt like the hundredth hallway, but it too was deserted. Two statues stood on either side of a door at the other end of the hall. Kym shrugged. Maybe she'd have better luck with the next corridor? Then she stopped. One of the statues at the end of the hall was moving. Kym stepped forward. It wasn't a statue at all. It was a Protectorate. A blue-robed Protectorate. Kym sighed with relief. This had to be where Nila was.

Kym half expected the Pros to spring into action the moment she approached. But, much to her surprise and delight, they remained motionless as she drew nearer. She smiled, reached out, and pushed against the ornate door. It swung inward at her touch, and Kym stepped inside.

A large chair inlaid with jewels sat in the middle of the room, facing a vast window. Kym closed the door carefully behind her, trying not to make a sound. Cautiously, she took a few steps forward before stopping. Nila's crowned head appeared around the side of the chair.

"Kymbralyn." She smiled widely. She looked like she was in pain. "This is a surprise."

"I...um..."

Now that she was here, Kym had no idea what to do. Could she just ask Nila what was going on? No, she couldn't. Nila was far too clever for that. She racked her brain. How'd Kenna and Aidan get information out of her to tell Nila? They did it all the time. It couldn't be that hard.

"Did you need something?" Nila snapped, much more like her usual self.

"Well," Kym began, choosing her words carefully, "it's about what you said out on the steps. Ever since the festival, you haven't wanted me around the other Vanquishers. They distracted me from being the best Water Favored I could be. If you don't mind me asking, why'd you change your mind?"

"Oh," Nila said, smiling again while she glanced around the room. "Recent events have made me realize I was too harsh on you. I am not blind. I have seen your demeanor since the festival. You are unhappy. You have isolated yourself from those who wish to help you. I was wrong, and wish to make it right."

Kym nodded, forcing herself to put on a thankful smile. Of course, Nila knew Kym was unhappy. This wasn't new news.

Kenna, Aidan, Ryland, and every other Water Favored told Nila that daily. But Kym knew Nila too. She'd lived at Wadita for over half a year, and she knew when Nila was lying through her teeth.

"Well, thank you for understanding," Kym said, although she knew Nila didn't understand at all.

"You are quite welcome," Nila said, continuing to smile awkwardly. "Is there anything else I can do for you?"

"Actually." This was it. But how to say it? "Sorry, it's stupid."

"Do not be ridiculous," Nila snapped. "What is it, Kymbralyn?"

"I'm excited about tomorrow," Kym beamed, trying her best to look as excited as possible without knowing what she was excited about. "I can't wait for the other Favored to get here and hear Lady Zara's news! It's wonderful, isn't it?"

"Indeed," Nila smiled, her voice as smooth as silk.

Kym held her breath. That was the best she could do without asking what was going to happen outright. She waited for Nila to say more, but she just continued to look down her nose at Kym. Had she pushed it too far? Nila waved Kym over to her. Kym walked up to Nila's chair, and she grabbed Kym's hand so tightly her fingers cracked.

"We better go," she smiled, not letting go of Kym's fingers. "It is time for dinner."

Nila released Kym and glided to the door. Fuming, trying to ignore the pain radiating from her fingers, Kym followed her. She had to give Nila credit; she wasn't stupid. She knew precisely what Kym wanted to know and didn't give away a thing. Kym hoped the others had better luck with their Rulers.

In the dining room, Nila joined the Rulers at the raised table set in front of a vast wall of windows. Kym sat with the other Favored at a table right in front of the Rulers. The Rulers thanked the gods, asking them to bless their meal as white-togaed servants carried it in on shining platters. The Rulers began chatting merrily with each other, which itself was an oddity. Kym seized the chance to have a whispered conversation.

"How'd it go?" she asked the table at large.

"It didn't," Jazin said. "I'm not surprised. I asked Phillip about tomorrow, but he said I needed to wait."

"Well, that was stupid," Kat hissed, loading her plate with food. "He wasn't going to tell you if you asked outright. I asked Kai every way I could think of, but he just smiled at me with that creepy grin. He did give me a load of crap about how sorry he is about keeping us apart. Please."

"Evanna said the same," Ashlyn sighed. "And all she told me was that the announcement would be exciting. Like we hadn't figured that out already?"

"Melana was really intense," Xander said. "She kept saying 'it is time' over and over again. But we already knew that, too. Zara said it in the Summit."

"Stailin couldn't sit still," Tomark huffed, "and said 'all would be revealed'."

"But we already knew that." Amber buried her face in her hands. "This is ridiculous. All we've learned is how to say 'you'll find out tomorrow' seven different ways."

"So James didn't let anything—"

"Since when were they so chummy?" Kat asked, cutting Kym off.

They looked up at the head table. The Rulers were no longer making polite chitchat. If Kym didn't know better, she'd have guessed they were making genuine conversation. Nila and Melana smiled contently while James laughed at something Stailin said. What was wrong with them? The last time Kym checked, which was the day before, the Rulers hated each other.

"I think I'm gonna hurl," Kat groaned.

"This is so weird," Xander said, shaking his head.

"I can't believe it, and I'm watching it," Ashlyn breathed.

"How can one little announcement do that?" Kym asked, nodding at the Rulers.

"Even I want to know what's gonna happen now," Jazin said, staring at Phillip and Zara, who seemed perfectly happy to be sitting next to each other. "All Lord Phillip's done since he became a Ruler is complain about Zara."

"I just don't understand why they're not telling us," Tomark said. "What do they gain by making us wait?"

"Watching us squirm is amusing to them," Amber said slowly, a little too much understanding in her voice. "How else can they feel superior?"

T H E
C A L L I N G

"How the Thed do you know that?" Kat scowled at Amber.

"Oh, c'mon, Kat," Amber snapped, rolling her eyes. "Even if I don't know their every waking thought, I know this. They raised me, as you well know," she added, squinting at Kat.

Kat opened her mouth to retort, and Kym didn't bother trying to stop her. Kat and Amber's relationship had always been uneasy, but Kym thought they'd put their past drama behind them months ago. Amber being closer to the Rulers than most Favored wasn't exactly a revelation. She was the Fire Princess, after all.

"But that doesn't explain," Ashlyn said, cutting Kat off, "why the Rulers are suddenly nice to each other."

"Maybe they finally put their differences aside?" Jazin said.

"You have a lot to learn," Xander chuckled. "The Rulers don't forgive, and they certainly don't forget."

"Can we drop it?" Tomark asked, staring at Kym and the others, his eyes narrowed. "Arguing about this is just gonna drive us nuts. Can't we just enjoy ourselves? We haven't been able to talk to each other for months. I'd much rather spend the evening with you guys. Why wonder about something we're gonna learn tomorrow anyway."

Kym felt oddly small. Sure, the Rulers acting happy was creepy, but was it that bad? They were so happy that they were letting Kym and the others be friends. But for how long? Tomark was right. They should use this opportunity to be together.

None of them mentioned the Rulers during the next four dinner courses. They ate, filling each other in on their news, which was admittedly very limited given all of their recent confinements. Amber tried, recounting her time spent as James's right hand.

"It's all very official. Anyone who wants to see Lord James for any reason must run it by me first. If I think it's appropriate, I step aside, and their audience is permitted."

"Wow," Ashlyn smiled, her over-the-top enthusiasm fooling no one.

"That sounds..." Tomark trailed off, unable to finish his thought.

"As dull as dirt," Kat droned. "Please, by the mercy of all the gods. I don't care which one at this point. Amber, you're a great Fire Princess, but if you don't stop right now I think I'm gonna die."

Kym laughed so much her mouth ached. And she wasn't the only one. Everyone else joined in the revelry, and even Amber's icy façade cracked. Kym's body felt lighter than air. It was just like when they'd sneak out on the weekends. After all of this time, and everything they'd been through, they were still the same.

The sound of scraping chairs from the Rulers' table forced Kym and the others into silence. Kym stood up, bowing to Nila as she and the other Rulers descended from their raised table. She was determined to keep Nila in a good mood, even if that meant bowing every time she moved a muscle. The Rulers stopped at the Favoreds' table, their odd grins still firmly in place.

"I think," Zara said, "it is time for us to turn in for the evening. You should be well-rested for tomorrow. It is a very important day."

The Rulers walked out of the hall. Kym exchanged hurried good-byes with her friends before they parted, each running off after their own Ruler. Kym caught up with Nila as she turned down the hall to her room. Once inside, Nila shot the white-togaed servants such icy looks Kym was surprised they didn't cry in pain. They backed away, bowing low, and closed the door behind them.

"Time for bed, Kymbralyn," Nila said. "You heard Lady Zara."

Kym wouldn't have thought about sleep for at least three more hours. But, disagreeing with Nila would be the easiest way to set her off, so she followed her into the next room. It was considerably smaller than Nila's, which meant it was still enormous by any other standard. A large bed sat against one wall, while the opposite one was made entirely of glass, providing an excellent view of the mountaintop trees.

Kym bid Nila goodnight and happily closed the door behind her. She walked over to the set of drawers by the bed and tentatively pulled one open. It was full of blue-colored sleeping clothes. Kym grabbed the top one and held it up to her chest. Kym stared down at the nightgown. How was there a drawer of clothes that fit her perfectly?

"Well, that's fancy."

Kym jumped. She spun around, and her feet caught in the hem of her dress. She crashed to the floor, falling hard onto her hands and knees. Fuming, her body aching, Kym looked up. Kat was leaning against the door, a sly grin on her face. But it wasn't the door Nila and Kym had used. It must be the door out into the hall.

"What the Thed?" Kym whispered, pushing herself to her knees. "Nila's right next door."

"Yeah," Kat smiled. She hurried over and offered Kym her hand.

"If she catches us…"

"Don't worry," Kat said confidently. "I have a plan."

Kym waited a moment, but Kat didn't say any more.

"Are you gonna phase back out if Nila barges in?"

"Can't." Kat shrugged, sitting down on Kym's bed. "This place isn't made of real earth."

"Then how'd you get in?" Kym slipped off her dress and pulled the nightgown over her head. "Nila's Pros are in the hall."

"Xander," Kat said plainly.

Kym glanced around the room. She couldn't see Xander anywhere. However, she knew from personal experience that didn't mean he wasn't there. She stared at the shadows cast around the room by the setting sun. They all looked, and acted, perfectly normal.

"Don't worry. He's not in here," Kat laughed.

"But then how will you—"

"He's standing guard in the hall. He'll come get me if we need to make a quick getaway."

Kym shook her head. Xander only did things for others if he got something out of it in return. Why would he help Kat sneak into her room? Wasn't he terrified Melana would find out? He'd never help Kat if he thought it would threaten his place as one of Melana's pupils.

"How'd you pull that off?"

"I nicely told him to come get me when we left the dining hall."

"And he did?" Kym couldn't believe it. "Just like that?"

"I asked nicely," Kat retorted. "Can't friends do nice things for each other?"

"Not Xander."

"Well, he did," Kat said quickly.

Kym stared at Kat. Normally, Kat was an open book—sometimes too open. Why wasn't she telling Kym the whole story? Could there be something going on between her and Xander? For all Kym knew, there could be. They'd spent so much time apart, anything could've happened. But if Kat wasn't ready to share, Kym wasn't going to keep pressuring her. After all, she must have a good reason for keeping it to herself, which was good enough for Kym.

"So, what's up?"

"Nothing really," Kat said. She seemed to relax at the change of subject. "I've just missed hangin' with you. And venting to you. We were together so often before the Rulers went all crazy paranoid. Things haven't been the same."

"I know," Kym sighed. The last several months flashed through her mind, and her always-prickly anger raged inside her.

"Kemmy and Baidan been as awful as ever?" Kat asked, flopping back on the bed.

"Yeah," Kym smiled, not even bothering to correct her. "I finally blew up at them yesterday. I couldn't take it anymore. They knew my mom was sick and didn't even tell me until after I visited her."

"Nothingness," Kat spat. "That's low. Even from what you've said they've done in the past. Have you heard anything new?"

"Nothing," Kym said. The bright glow her friends had lit inside her dimmed. "And I doubt anyone would me tell if there was any news."

"They have no right to keep that from you. She's *your* mom."

"But if Nila says 'don't tell Kym,' that's what they do."

"Them and everyone at Terradon. They keep saying 'Kai is right' and 'everything would be better if I listened.'"

"But you never listen," Kym smiled.

"I know!" Kat said, feigning surprise. "I don't understand why they can't grasp the concept."

This, Kym thought, was what she'd been missing. Kym always had to watch what she said at Wadita. Someone was always there, ready to run to Nila the second she did something she shouldn't. But Kat didn't care what Kym did or didn't do. She could finally be herself, and it was fantastic.

"Tomorrow," Kat yawned, stretching her arms above her head, "during Zara's announcement, the seven of us should totally stand together in front of everyone."

"Their brains would probably explode," Kym smiled, imagining the looks of horror on Kenna's and Aidan's faces.

"Sounds like a party to me."

Kym and Kat decided to call it a night. Even with the Rulers in good moods, they were pushing their luck. Kat walked over to the door, placed her hand on it, and tapped the wood with a single finger. The sound was so quiet Kym barely heard it, and she was standing right next to Kat. A human shadow slid under the door. It passed over Kym's shadow, and she instantly felt clammy and wet.

Xander's dark form stopped beside Kat, and he placed his hand on the shoulder of her shadow. Beside her, Kym saw the shoulder of Kat's dress wrinkle slightly. Her body, including her clothes, darkened and faded. Kat sank to the floor, where she joined Xander as a shadow.

"See you in the morning," Kym smiled, waving to pair of them.

Their shadowy arms waved back as they whipped under the door in a flash.

Kym ripped back the thick, white covers and crawled into bed. Her mind blissfully blank, she flopped down on the puffy pillows. She closed her eyes, breathed deeply, and felt herself instantly drift to sleep.

The snap of fabric filled Kym's ears. She opened her eyes but quickly shut them again as she buried herself under the covers. Her eyes watered in the bright morning light streaming in from the open windows. She heard feet moving around the room, as well as several drawers sliding open and closed. Trying to ignore the sinking feeling in her stomach, Kym peaked out from under the covers.

"Lady Nila would like you to wear these, Miss," said the white-togaed servant, bowing to Kym as she held a pair of tight pants, a tank top, and running shoes in Kym's face.

"Wha?" Kym asked groggily, still not quite awake. She missed Veronica and Isabel. At least they knew to wake her gently.

"Lady Nila needs you dressed, Miss," the servant repeated, placing the clothes on the bed before starting to tidy the already-clean room.

"What? Why?" Kym took off her nightdress and pulled on the clothes the servant provided.

"You're needed in the evaluation chamber, Miss," the servant said urgently. "Lady Nila said you were to move with haste."

The evaluation chamber? Kym hadn't set foot in there since her own evaluation, and that was months ago. That the first time she'd met Kat, Tomark, Amber, Ashlyn, and Xander. Warmth bloomed inside her as memories of that day flooded her mind.

"Lead the way," Kym said, shoving her feet into her shoes.

The servant led Kym into the hall, where Nila's Protectorate were nowhere to be seen. Kym followed the servant through the maze of hallways and stairs, and before she knew it, they were in the entrance hall. The servant opened one of the many doors around the round walls, and Kym stepped inside.

The prep room was just as she remembered it—rows of benches with a long table set along the back wall. Kat, Ashlyn, Amber, Tomark, Xander, and Jazin sat on the bench closest to the evaluation chamber door.

"What's going on?" Kym asked, sitting next to Ashlyn.

"No idea," Ashlyn shrugged. "All my servant said was I needed to get dressed and come down here."

They waited in silence for several minutes. Then, the door to the evaluation chamber opened. The Rulers glided into the prep room, smiling down at the Favored. But, after scanning the line of Rulers, something caught Kym's eye. Zara wasn't there.

"You missed training yesterday," James said bluntly, "and wasting another day would be pointless. We," he gestured to the other Rulers, "agree that the best course of action is for you to train together."

Kym stared at James. Train together? They'd never been allowed to do that before. Sure, they'd battled death demons more times than Kym could count, and when they'd sneak out at night, they'd sometimes share new skills they'd learned if they were particularly proud—but training together. It was unheard of. That must be why Zara wasn't there. She didn't have any Life Favored to train.

"We will divide you into two groups of two and one group of three," Melana said, her voice as silky as ever. Her narrow eyes raked over Kym and the others like she was trying to see inside them.

"You have two tasks while you train," the Ruler of Air, Stailin, said in a business-like tone. "The first, obviously, is to beat your opponent. The second, to try and push yourselves."

"You know each other well," Nila said sweetly. It was so out of character, it made Kym's skin crawl. "You have fought together. Try and do something that surprises your opponent."

"The groups of two are water and light, and air and fire," Kai said. "The group of three will be earth, darkness, and death."

"We will rearrange the groups after each match, giving you all the opportunity to work together," Evanna said.

"Remember," Phillip added. "The rules are the same as any sparring match. The path to victory can only be accomplished by yield or knockout. Do not hold back."

The Rulers stepped aside. Kym stood up, her skin tingling as the others rose around her. She knew from personal experience how intense sparring matches got. In her first-ever sparring match, she ended up breaking her opponent's ribs before it was over. Hopefully, none of them would take things that far. They were friends, and no matter what the Rulers said, Kym drew the line at hurting her friends.

Amber, of course, stepped forward first. Kym and the others followed her through the door and into the evaluation chamber. The room was domed, just like the training rooms at Wadita, but this room was much larger. A ring of stone enclosed the center of the room, while long spokes extended from the circle, dividing the space into thirds. Hard-packed earth covered one section, another contained several pools of clear water, while the final was bare.

Kym and Ashlyn walked into the section with the pools. They stood ten feet apart, their bodies turned sideways to each other. Kym's heart pounded in her throat. She'd seen Ashlyn do so many incredible things. During the Festival of Creation, Ashlyn fought Xander while moving at the speed of light. Kym took a deep breath, trying to calm herself.

An echoing bang rang around the room. Kym jerked her arms up, her blue Marks glowing. The water in the pools rose into the air. Kym shoved her hands in front of her, and the water shot forward. It combined into one large jet as it flew through the air, right at Ashlyn.

Ashlyn raised her hands over her head. The light from their section concentrated around her, forming a shimmering, yellow pillar. Stunned and momentarily mesmerized, Kym's concentration wavered. Her jet of water faltered, and splashed to the ground.

Droplets flew into the pillar of light, vaporizing the second they touched it.

A blast of glowing yellow light shot right at Kym. She jumped into the nearest pool, avoiding Ashlyn's attack, but felt the intense heat radiating from it. Kym formed a shield, and just in time. Ashlyn's light bolt exploded against Kym's shield, and she staggered back several feet. Panting, her heart racing, Kym splashed out of the water. She needed to do something. She couldn't lose this quickly.

Kym made a bolt the size of a beach ball. Focusing her energy on Ashlyn, she brought her hands together, then quickly pulled them apart. The large water bolt split, forming three smaller bolts. Not taking her eyes off Ashlyn, Kym flicked her wrists.

Her three bolts arched high into the air. But, even though she'd watched Kenna do this move countless times, she'd never actually learned it herself. The tracking bolts veered off course, and instead of honing in on Ashlyn, they merely flew in her general direction. Ashlyn threw a light bolt at one of Kym's, and it exploded in midair while she easily avoided the other two.

Kym staggered backward, trying to avoid the almost constant stream of light bolts flying from Ashlyn's hands. Kym needed to do something, or she was going to lose. A light swipe soared over her head, missing her by inches. She flailed her arms, her Marks still glowing, which caused several streams of water to rise momentarily into the air before splashing onto the already-soaked ground. Kym stared at the wet floor, then back at Ashlyn, who was readying another attack. It was a long shot, but if it worked…

Kym swung her arm around, her palm directed at the floor. The water covering the ground swirled around, skidding across the floor toward Ashlyn. She lifted her hand, a yellow bolt already hovering there, but she was too late; Kym's hands were already in the air.

A tube of water rose around Ashlyn. Kym watched through the warping water as Ashlyn threw her bolt. It exploded against the rising wall of water, vaporizing a hole, but more water quickly filled the gap. Panting, Kym's insides swelled. She'd won.

Ashlyn move frantically inside the water tube. Kym smiled. There was no way Ashlyn could get out of this. A circle of light appeared in the air, making Kym's eyes water. She looked from the ring to Ashlyn, whose hands dropped to her sides. The ring of light crashed down around Ashlyn, and steam filled their section of the dome.

Kym flew backward, unable to see. There was too much steam in the air. Where was Ashlyn? Kym heard a cough somewhere to her right. She needed to end this.

Kym formed a bolt, her heart pounding in her ears, and swung her arm as hard as she could across her body. The water swipe soared through the air, right at the height of Ashlyn's chest. There was a flash of yellow light, but Ashlyn must not have moved fast enough. Kym heard a grunt of pain, followed by a satisfying thud as Ashlyn landed on the hard floor.

The steam from their section of the room vanished. Kym doubled over, her hands on her knees, panting hard. Ashlyn lay sprawled on the floor twenty feet away. Kym hurried over to her, wiping sweat from her forehead. By the time she reached Ashlyn, she was already sitting up.

"Nice job," Kym said, offering Ashlyn her hand.

"Thanks," she panted, taking Kym's hand. "That water tube thing was clever."

"Thanks. Your light circle was the coolest thing I've ever seen."

They joined Tomark and Amber, who were already waiting in the ringed center of the chamber. It took Xander, Kat, and Jazin another ten minutes to finish their match. Finally, after an upset-looking Jazin was dragged out of the match, Xander dealt his final blow to Kat, making him the winner.

The rest of the morning consisted of some of the most amazing magic Kym had ever seen. Amber sent jets of flame at Kym, which wrapped around her when she got too close. Kat trapped Kym up to her knees in quicksand, ending their match in a matter of seconds. Xander tossed Kym around like a rag doll, grabbing her shadow and throwing it across the room, taking Kym with it. Kym even thought

Jazin did alright, given his limited training. He was able to keep Kym at bay by infusing her water with death energy before she overpowered him. Kym's final match was against Tomark, who never set foot on the ground while a tornado chased her around the chamber.

Lights flashed in Kym's eyes, and there was a steady pounding behind her forehead when the Rulers ended the training session. None of them held back during their matches, which seemed to make the Rulers even happier. They smiled down at the Favored, who all sat huddled on the ground, barely able to move. Kym hardly noticed their creepy smiles. She had more important things to worry about, like stopping the world from spinning around her.

Kym followed a servant back to her room. Her dress from the previous day lay ready for her on the bed. Even with how exhausted she felt, Kym managed a slight smile. According to Veronica and Isabel, wearing the same thing two days in a row was one of the worst things imaginable…after not having enough suitcases.

Kym stayed in the bath as long as she could, happily relaxing her sore muscles. But after only ten minutes, the servant burst into the bathroom to tell her the rest of the Favored were arriving. Kym finished washing, ran a brush through her damp hair, and threw on her dress.

The sight of Kym standing with the others at the top of the entrance hall balcony had the desired effect. Kym watched Aidan's hands ball into fists while Kenna's skin turned white. Nearly all the Favored had similar looks of shock and horror on their faces. Kym didn't care though. She just smiled down at everyone, happy to finally be with her friends.

Once the steady stream of Favored entering the entrance hall started to dwindle, Kym led the others down the curved steps. They separated when they reached the bottom, joining the Favored from their palaces. Kym, eager to make Kenna, Aidan, and Ryland as uncomfortable as possible, stood right next to them. She could almost hear the air crackling around Kenna. Smiling, Kym took another step closer to her.

The front doors closed, and silence fell over the crowd. Zara appeared on the balcony overlooking the entrance hall, her flowing white dress shimmering in the torchlight. The other Rulers joined her, and a wave of muttering flew through the gathered Favored. Kym looked around. Why were they all staring at the Rulers? Zara hadn't even made her announcement yet. Kym looked closer. They weren't looking at the Rulers. They were looking at Phillip. Of course. Most of them hadn't seen him before, standing on Zara's right side. Zara raised her hands, and the Favored stopped their muttering.

"Thank you for joining us," Zara said, her voice ringing around the room. "I know you had little warning, but I assure you; your journeys were well worth it. Today, I am pleased to announce that the time has come. The high priests from the cities have seen the signs. The gods' will is known. The Calling is upon us once again."

Zara paused, allowing her words to sink in as excited mutterings rippled through the crowd. Something stirred deep in Kym's memory. She'd heard of the Calling before. Someone must have mentioned it to her a lifetime ago. But she had no idea what it was, or why everyone was so excited.

"The Calling is the greatest test a Favored will face in their lifetime. Four Favored will represent light, fire, air, water, and earth. The three Darkness Pupils will all participate, and the singular Death Favored is obliged to represent his element. These Prized Favored will compete in five trials, during which they must prove their might to the gods. The winner will receive the honor of a lifetime—a divine audience, during which the gods will grant the winner one request. The First Trial of the Calling will begin in forty days."

CHAPTER TEN

WHY
NOW?

A SINGLE CLAP ECHOED AROUND THE SILENT FAVORED, THEN A second, then a third. Thunderous applause filled the entrance hall as the Favored celebrated Zara's announcement. And they didn't stop there. Many hooted, and some jumped up and down, unable to contain their excitement for the Calling.

Kym clapped with the rest, but only halfheartedly. A thought stirred in the deepest parts of her mind. She had heard of the Calling before. She was sitting on a broken chair in the back of her religious studies class, a requirement for all students when they moved from the lower levels of education. Her teacher's voice, in all its monotoned glory, clawed its way to the forefront of Kym's thoughts.

This battle between the first Favored established the Calling. Twelve contests for the gods' glory have taken place in Princirum's long and wondrous existence. The physical and planal elements have each proven their worth at least once. Maybe, if the gods deem it worthy, you'll experience a Calling in your lifetime.

Of course, Kym hadn't known, or cared, what the 'physical' and 'planal' elements were at the time. Back then, when she was an outcast, she wanted nothing to do with magic. But now, she understood. One Favored from each of the elements had won the Calling at least once, except for life and death. And there'd only been twelve of them. This must be why the Rulers were excited. The Calling was something rare.

"Settle down," Zara called over the buzz filling the hall, and everyone fell silent at once. "I am glad you are excited about this historic event. We," Zara spread her arms to indicate the other

Rulers, "share in your enthusiasm. However, there are two things I must address before we part. First, each Ruler has the responsibility and pleasure to choose which Favored will represent each element. They will select their Prized within the next forty days.

"Secondly, if you are unsure whether you wish to submit yourself to the Calling, I offer you this incentive; winning does not only benefit the victor but the people of Princirum as well. Whichever Prized wins the Calling, the gods will reward those devoted to the winning element with seven years' good fortune. So, if a Light Favored emerged victorious, then those who declared Thilg, the Goddess of Light and Wisdom, as their patron will experience seven years of good fortune. Nothing could do more good for the people of Princirum. We must all play our part in the gods' plan."

Anger boiled deep in Kym's stomach. How could winning a contest be the best thing for the people of Princirum? While death crept in from every direction, making people sick, how could this be the right time for a magical contest? She was the Vanquisher of Water. Her job was to fight death demons and protect Princirum. This couldn't be the gods' plan. How could winning a contest stop the powers of death?

"I will see you in forty days for the First Trial," Zara said, once again calling the room back to attention. "May the worthy among you answer the call."

Excited chatter filled the entrance hall as the Rulers, minus Zara, descended the curved stairs, each accompanied by their Protectorate. Kym could feel Kenna and Aidan practically bouncing with anticipation on either side of her. No doubt they wanted to tell Kym how perfect they were for the Calling. They did the same thing when Nila put them in charge of the Water Favored's performance for the Festival of Creation. Participating in a magical contest was what they'd been training for.

Kym stepped away before they could speak. Hopefully, their excitement would wear off by the time they returned to Wadita, and Kym wouldn't have to hear about it. She spotted Kat and Tomark in the middle of the entrance hall. Kym pushed her way through the crowd, as did Ashlyn and Xander, while Amber and Jazin emerged with a little more ease.

"Well, that was informative," Kat said dryly.

"I guess we know why they're so happy," Tomark said.

"This couldn't have come at a better time for them," Ashlyn agreed.

"What are you talking about?" Jazin asked. "Isn't it good for all of us?"

"The Rulers love to show each other up," Xander said. "And from the sound of it, this Calling is the final say in which element, and god, and Ruler, is the best."

"And, having 'good fortune' for seven years sounds like something they'd all kill for," Tomark added.

"Nothingness, this is gonna be a nightmare," Kym sighed. Before the Festival of Creation, Kenna and Aidan pushed every Water Favored to their breaking points to perfect their performance, which they never ended up performing. She didn't wish to relive the experience.

"I wonder what the five trials are?" Kat said excitedly.

Everyone looked at Amber, who stood between Jazin and Ashlyn. For a moment, she stood there, her eyes darting around their circle. Then, she threw her hands in the air.

"Why are you looking at me?"

"Well, don't you know what the five trials are?" Xander asked eagerly.

"How the Thed would I know that?" Amber snapped.

"You know everything," Kat said flatly.

"How many times do I have to tell you I'm not an all-knowing magical archive? I know nothing about the Calling, except that it's a contest between the Favored. There hasn't been one in our lifetime, so how would I know anything about it?"

All around her, Kym saw disappointment on the others' faces. They'd expected Amber to know more than she did. Kym rolled her eyes. Why were Kat and Xander so interested in knowing what the trials were? Did they actually want to compete in the Calling? But why? It was a test to see who the best Favored was, and Kym's group didn't exactly act like typical Favored. They constantly fought against all the rules and expectations. To Kym, the Calling sounded like a waste of time.

"We're sorry," Ashlyn said, smiling at Amber. "It's just you always know so much more about all this stuff than we do."

"Welcome to Club Clueless," Kat walked over to Amber and swung her arm over her narrow shoulders. She was so tall Kat barely managed it standing on her tiptoes.

"I like it," Tomark smiled. "We're all on the same level now."

"If the Rulers pick us," Amber said pointedly.

"They have to," Jazin smiled softly, nudging Amber in her side. "They'd be stupid not to."

Kym fought every instinct she had not to roll her eyes again. Amber was the last person in Princirum who needed her ego stroked. Why did Jazin keep doing it? And was Amber's giggling that necessary? Kat didn't seem to think so. She pulled her arm from Amber's shoulders so quickly it was like Amber shocked her.

"Guys," Xander said abruptly.

For a moment, Kym thought he was talking to Amber and Jazin. But he wasn't looking at them. His eyes were darting wildly around the room. Kym looked around. The entrance hall was almost deserted.

"We'd better go," Ashlyn said. "We shouldn't keep everyone waiting."

"Why not?" Kat laughed.

Only one of the blue carriages had its door open, leaving Kym with no other choice for where she'd spend her journey back to Wadita. Kenna, Aidan, and Ryland, all looked extremely angry as she stepped inside. She shut the door, trying her best not to look at them. She took her seat, and the carriage moved slowly forward. This carriage must have real horses pulling it. She was in for a long ride.

"You should be ashamed," Kenna snapped, not wasting a moment.

"What did I do now?" Kym asked, trying to sound innocent.

"You were with those other Favored," Aidan said, his forehead covered in lines as a vein popped in his neck.

"So? What's wrong with that?" Kym asked. They didn't know Nila allowed Kym to be with them.

"You're not supposed to be around them!" Ryland said.

"Yes, I am."

"Liar," Kenna retorted. "Lady Nila forbade you from seeing them months ago. And then you go and disrespect her like that."

"She changed her mind," Kym smiled.

"I doubt that," Aidan said, shaking his head.

"She did," Kym assured him, nodding enthusiastically. "If you don't believe me, ask her when we get to Wadita. I'm sure she'll tell you all about it.

"And," she added, relishing the shocked looks on their faces, "if you don't want to bother her, ask Evanna, or James, or Melana, or Phillip, or Kai, or Stailin. They're all fine with us being friends. So you can stop worrying about it!"

This statement had the desired effect. Kenna, Aidan, and Ryland all looked like she'd hit them in the face. They tried to recover, smiling so broadly Kym was sure it hurt. The veins receded from Aidan's face, and Kenna's eyes softened as she leaned back in her seat. It was like Kym's words literally turned off their rage.

"Oh," Kenna faltered. "Well…um…that's…"

"Great," Aidan smiled.

"Thanks," Kym said. Then, deciding to throw caution to the wind, she added, "I'm thrilled."

Aidan opened his mouth to speak, but Ryland leaned back against him, covering Aidan's mouth with his hand. Kym pretended not to notice and turned to look out the window. Maybe they, and the rest of the Water Favored, would stop treating her like an enemy. If Nila okayed Kym seeing her friends, it should be good enough for them.

They sat in silence for a long time before any of them spoke again.

"You've missed a lot of training the past few days," Kenna said, and Kym could tell she was trying to keep her voice conversational. "But I'm sure you'll make it up after a few extra sessions—"

"I only missed one day," Kym said. How much could she have missed? Kenna and Aidan rarely taught anything new.

"Well, you fought a death demon, then you had the Summit, and of course you missed today," Aidan said, pushing Ryland's hand away as he tried to cover his mouth again.

"We all missed today, you goof," Ryland said, swatting Aidan's hand away.

"I didn't," Kym said.

"What?"

"The Rulers said we'd missed too much training. So they had us train together."

"Oh…well, that's good to hear," Kenna nodded, grinning a little too forcefully.

Kym waited for them to say more, but none of them did. She turned back to the window. She had to admit, she was impressed. They were acting like everything was perfectly normal. She remembered everything they'd done to her, but the thought of the last couple of days eclipsed it, reducing her fiery anger to no more than a tingle. Being mad at them was pointless. In their minds, they were just doing what Nila told them. To them, they'd done nothing wrong.

The sun settled behind a particularly dark patch of clouds. Kym pulled several blankets down from the small rack over her head. Without construct horses, they weren't going to arrive at Wadita any time soon. She held a blanket out to Kenna, who stared at it like she'd never seen one before. Then, a small, genuine smile on her lips, she took it. Kym tossed another to Aidan, who draped it over himself and Ryland.

The sky was dark when the carriage pulled into Wadita's sandy front drive. Kym threw off her blanket and climbed out of the door the moment the carriage stopped. She wasn't in much of a talking mood, and neither, it seemed, were her companions. They let her leave in silence, and Kym felt lighter than air. For the first time in months, no one was following her.

Her muscles screamed in protest as she stepped onto the sweeping stairs. She'd been so preoccupied with the Calling announcement, and everything that happened in the carriage, she hadn't realized how sore she was. That training session earlier had been unlike anything she'd ever experienced, and now she was paying for it. The pain doubled every time she stepped, shooting through her body like fire.

It took Kym nearly twenty minutes to hobble her way up the steps and through the many hallways to her bedchamber. When she finally reached the door, she stopped, pressing her forehead against the wood as lights popped in her eyes like fireworks. She had no idea what time it was, but the loud growling in her stomach told her one thing. It was time to eat. But before that, a nap in her own bed sounded like the best thing in the world.

Veronica and Isabel waited inside Kym's bedchamber. They rushed over to Kym the moment she opened the door, their dazzling smiles in place. The room spun around her the second she stepped over the threshold. Veronica and Isabel each slipped an arm under Kym's arm and half led, half dragged her to her bed.

"You're exhausted, my dear," Veronica said, helping Kym to lie down.

"And you're shaking," Isabel said. "Have you eaten?"

Now that she thought of it, Kym hadn't eaten all day. The last thing she remembered eating was dinner after the Summit. No wonder she felt like a pile of crap.

"No."

"Oh, Pheil," Veronica sighed. "It's a wonder you can even take care of yourself without us."

"Hey, I did fine," Kym said, though she ruined the effect by not being able to hold herself up.

"I'll get you some food," Isabel said. "Dinner isn't for another few hours."

Isabel returned minutes later with a tray covered in crackers, fruits, cheeses, and a large water pitcher. Her stomach rumbling loudly, Kym grabbed everything she could, barely even noticing what she shoved in her mouth. The pounding in her head grew fainter with every bite. Kym started to feel like herself.

Veronica and Isabel helped Kym out of her dress, only muttering a few choice words about Kym's fashion disaster. They left Kym alone in the bathtub, where she continued to eat and drink. Rose-scented steam drifted around her, making her mind go blissfully blank. She'd stay there forever if she could. Veronica, however, had other plans.

"Miss, if you want to be on time for dinner, you really need to get out of the tub now."

"Do I have to?" Kym pleaded. The water was so relaxing.

"Yes," Veronica answered sternly. "If you don't, you'll be pruney for dinner."

"Well," Kym smiled, "we can't have that, can we?"

"No, we cannot," Veronica answered seriously.

Kym climbed out of the tub. She dried herself off and walked back into her room, where Isabel handed her a simple blue robe. Kym slipped the shimmering material on without complaint. At least she didn't have to put on another gown right away. She flung herself onto her bed and heard Veronica and Isabel sigh behind her.

"How long until dinner?" Kym asked. She hung her head off the edge of the bed, watching her maids upside-down. "And do I have to go? Can't I just eat up here?"

"Of course you have to go," Isabel said, busying herself with straightening the pillows on Kym's couches. "Why wouldn't you?"

"Are you still not well?" Veronica asked. "Do you need anything more to eat or drink?"

"No. It's not that. I feel fine. It's just been a long day."

"What happened?" Isabel asked. "Why did Lady Nila summon everyone to Crystal Palace? No one told us anything."

"Oh, that," Kym shrugged, sitting up straight. "Zara received word from the high priests. The Calling is happening."

Veronica's hands shot up to her mouth while Isabel nocked

several pillows to the ground. They looked like Kym just granted their greatest wish.

"I can't believe it," Veronica said breathlessly.

"I never thought I'd live to see one. Thank Pheil!" Isabel said, wiping the tears from her cheeks with trembling hands.

Kym, who'd grown used to her maids' over-the-top reactions, hadn't expected them to act this excited. Why were they interested in a magic contest? It had nothing to do with them. Then it hit her. They'd spent their lives in the temple. To them, The Calling was a sacred event—proof that the gods' plan was in motion.

"Well then," Veronica said, composing herself. "There's no question of you skipping dinner now."

"What? Why?"

"If the high priests declared a Calling, then the time frame for Lady Nila to select her four Prized has already started."

"Zara said they have forty days," Kym groaned. She'd hoped Zara calling the chosen Favored Prized had been a one-time thing. Clearly, it wasn't.

"Lady Nila will probably give her instructions at dinner," Isabel said. "You can't miss that."

Kym considered putting up a fight but knew it would be pointless. She gave into her lady's maids, and they started dressing her at top speed. Now that she thought of it, she'd never actually gotten her way whenever she had conflicting ideas with them. The thought made Kym laugh. Even though they served Kym, they were really the ones in charge.

Kym walked into the dining hall, which was already full of people and excited conversation. She spotted Kenna, Ryland, Jean, Jax, and Aidan, all sitting at a table near the back of the room. Kym sighed and walked over to join them. She guessed letting things go meant willingly sitting with them at meals.

Much to Kym's annoyance, all they wanted to discuss was the Calling. However, none of them knew more than Kym did herself. Even Aidan and Kenna, after all their private time with Nila, had no idea what the trials of the Calling could be. So, when Nila joined their table and tapped her knife gently against her glass, the room fell immediately silent.

"I am delighted you are excited for the Calling," Nila began. "As you know, the Calling will begin in forty days' time. Before then, it is my honor to select four of you who will represent the great element of water and the goddess, Reta, in this Calling as our Prized. My assessment will begin at sunrise in six days. Until then, formal training is canceled. All of the training rooms will be available for your use to prepare for my assessment. I strongly advise you prepare on your own.

"I shall select my Prized in three stages, narrowing you down to the final four who will be our representatives in the Calling. After the assessment is complete, the Prized will use the remaining time until the Calling to train and prepare themselves."

Nila sat back down while everyone else stood, making their way out of the dining hall. Kym stood too, yawning as her eyes drooped. She could already feel the soft fabric of her sheets against her skin. Maybe she'd sleep in a little. She might even blow off training. She had no intention of competing in the Calling, after all.

"Kymbralyn." Nila's voice caused Kym's fantasy to crash around her. "Stay here. I need to speak with you."

Kym stifled a groan. What could she have possibly done this time? For once, could she eat dinner and go to bed in peace? She wracked her brain, trying to figure out what possible reason Nila had for keeping her back. But she'd done nothing. She'd done everything Nila asked. She followed the rules at the Summit and even double-checked Nila was alright with Kym speaking with her friends.

"Kenna." Nila's brisk voice cut through Kym's thoughts like a knife. "Stay as well."

Now Kym was really confused. Why was Kenna staying behind too? She never got in trouble. She did everything Nila wanted without question. Slowly, Kym sat down beside Kenna.

"This does not concern you," Nila said, waving her hand at the rest of their table. "Leave us."

Aidan, Ryland, Jax, and Jean all left the dining hall, looking just as confused as Kym felt. Nila's Pros and servants backed away as they waited for the doors to close behind the final Favored.

"Be in my chambers tomorrow morning at sunrise," Nila instructed, her voice uncharacteristically urgent.

"What?" Kym asked. Clearly, she wasn't going to sleep in.

"Why?" Kenna asked, leaning forward in her seat.

"You will learn in the morning," Nila said mysteriously, like she was planning some big surprise and didn't want to spoil it. "Remember: be there at sunrise."

Even more confused than she'd been before, Kym followed Kenna out of the dining hall. Neither of them spoke as they climbed the stairs to the bedchambers. Kenna looked positively giddy, but Kym didn't bother asking why. She knew Kenna had no idea why Nila wanted them, and was just happy Nila picked her over everyone else. Kym didn't even bother trying to deduce Nila's motives. If she'd learned anything over the past few days, it was that if Nila wanted to keep her in the dark, there was nothing she could do about it.

CHAPTER ELEVEN

THE MASTER OF MASTERS

"Time to get up, Miss Kym."

Kym groaned and buried her face in her pillow. She'd barely opened her eyes, but that was enough for her to know one important thing; it was still dark outside. Why did she need to get up so early? Nila wanted to see her at sunrise. She'd said nothing about needing to be dressed in her best clothes for the occasion. She still had no idea why Nila wanted her.

Isabel practically dragged Kym out of bed. She knew it was pointless to resist, but Kym tried her hardest to be of no help to her maids. She didn't lift her arms or turn her face when they asked. But it was futile. They cleaned and dressed her in a simple blue gown in record time. Kym left her bedchamber before the dark sky was even tinged with red.

She stopped when she reached the deserted entrance hall. Where was Kenna? If Kym, who didn't want to be there in first place, could make it on time, why couldn't Kenna? She always harped on Kym whenever she was more than five seconds late for training. But Kym knew better than to bring it up to Kenna's face. She needed Kenna, who was one of the few people at Wadita who actually knew where Nila's private rooms were. Sure, Kym always assumed they were behind the door Nila always seemed to be going and coming from, but Wadita was massive. Her rooms could literally be anywhere.

Kenna arrived a few minutes later. She didn't say anything, although Kym noticed the absence of her usual appraising look.

Since Nila wasn't worried about Kym anymore, Kenna didn't seem to be either. It was like a weight lifted off of Kym's shoulders.

Kenna led Kym to the door she'd seen Nila enter countless times. She reached out and grabbed the round knob, but she didn't turn it. She stood there, the knob hidden beneath her outstretched hand, before releasing the handle and stepping back. Nothing happened.

"Um…"

Kym stared at Kenna. What was going on? Why didn't she open the door? She hadn't even turned the handle before stepping back. How were they supposed to go see Nila if Kenna wouldn't turn a doorknob? There had to be something Kym hadn't seen. But no, all Kenna did was touch the handle, then step back.

The door swung open of its own accord. Smiling, Kenna stepped through into the next room. Kym followed, trying hard not to roll her eyes. The door closed behind them, plunging the room into total darkness. Kym looked around. There had to be a torch or candle somewhere. The walls around them bloomed into life, glowing blue like the fading embers of a fire. It reminded Kym of her magic.

They were standing in some kind of antechamber. The room was round, with walls covered in doors that could lead to anywhere. Shallow basins of water sat on the floor between the doors, reflecting the walls' blue light. It looked like a smaller version of the entrance hall.

Kenna approached the door in the very center. When she was about three feet from it, a high-pitched ringing filled the room. Kym clapped her hands over her ears, trying to block out the painful sound. The water in the basins on either side of the door glowed, and two water construct guards bloomed into being. They held shining blue swords, which they crossed in front of the door.

"You are not permitted—" one of the constructs said. Its booming voice made Kym's insides quiver.

"We are here at Lady Nila's invitation," Kenna cut across the construct. Clearly, this wasn't her first visit to Nila's chambers. "Let us pass."

Nothing happened. The constructs stood where they were, barring their path while Kenna stared them down. Kym suppressed a snort. What did Kenna expect? Kym knew very little about constructs, but she did know they were infused with a single thought or purpose. If Nila created these constructs to keep people out, there was nothing Kym or Kenna could do.

"You are not permitted here," the second construct boomed as Kenna's body tensed. Kym stifled a laugh. "Leave the way you came."

"We are here," Kenna repeated, her teeth clenched, "at Lady Nila's—"

"You are not permitted here."

"What is wrong with you?" Kenna exploded, throwing her arms in the air. "Let us through!"

"Leave the way you—"

The door the constructs were guarding burst open. Nila glided into the antechamber, her eyes narrow as she took in the scene before her. She waved her hand lazily over her shoulder. The construct guards dissolved and rained back into their respective basins.

"Come," Nila ordered, walking back the way she'd come. "Time is short."

Kym followed Nila into the next room, and her mouth fell open. A giant blue throne sat on a raised platform in the center of the large, round room, illuminated by a single skylight. Tall, crystal urns full of clear water sat on either side of the throne. Magnificent tapestries covered most of the walls, while the solidified water floor was left bare. Nila's throne room bore a remarkable resemblance to the throne room at Crystal Palace. However, it didn't escape Kym that here, Nila's throne was in the center, not unlike Zara's and Phillip's thrones. In this room, Nila was in charge.

"So," Nila said, stepping up onto the raised platform and sitting down. "I am sure both of you are wondering why I summoned you here at this hour. I have a task for you."

Nila looked down at Kym and Kenna, apparently expecting them to react. Deep inside Kym, the tiniest sparks flickered to life. Was she sending Kym and Kenna to fight a death demon? No, she couldn't be. If she knew about it the previous night, she'd have sent them then. And if it wasn't a death demon, what did Nila want? Kym hoped she'd at least get to leave the palace.

"As Zara explained yesterday, I have the great honor of selecting the four Prized to represent the goddess Reta during this Calling. For some elements, like darkness, the Prized are merely the current palace residents. I, on the other hand, want the best to represent water. As I have done with past Callings, I will select my Prized from all living Water Favored; this includes Wadita's current residents as well as the Masters."

"Nila—Lady Nila," Kym corrected herself. "I'm sorry, but what do you want us to do?"

"When a Water Favored masters their magic, they are granted an estate in Undarunci. You and Kenna will travel to these estates and personally invite the Water Masters back to Wadita on my behalf. They must arrive the night before my assessment begins, and we will mark the occasion with a feast. You have five days to complete your task."

Nila passed Kenna, her eyes alight with excitement, a large scroll of parchment. Kym, on the other hand, tried not to let her disappointment show on her face. Her views on the Calling hadn't changed overnight. She'd rather use her magic to do something useful, like keep death out of Princirum, than compete in a magic contest. But maybe, if she did what Nila asked and gathered the Masters with Kenna, she'd let Kym skip the Calling? It was worth a try.

"Your carriage is ready," Nila continued. "I have provided construct horses, so speed on the road will not be an issue. Show the scroll to the horses, and they will know where to take you."

Nila waved her hand at the door, which swung open. Realizing this was their cue to leave, both Kenna and Kym bowed to Nila, backing out of the room. They raced through the antechamber and into the entrance hall, which was now full of early morning light. Their carriage stood waiting for them like Nila said. The construct horses stood still as statues, already harnessed into place.

"How many estates are there in Undarunci?" Kym asked, trying to pass her annoyance off as interest.

"I've visited several of them," Kenna said importantly, unfurling the scroll. "But I have no idea how many there actually are."

On the parchment was a detailed map of Undarunci. Wadita, of course, was at the very bottom by the coast. Tiny dots peppered the rest of the map, indicating a Master's estate. Kym's heart fell. There were easily one hundred of them.

"How are we going to do this in five days?"

"I have no idea," Kenna said, holding the map in front of the horses. They sprang to life, pawing at the ground as they shook their heads. "We'll have to be quick at each one if we stand a chance of making it in time."

They both climbed into the carriage, which lurched forward the second Kenna closed the door.

"Why couldn't Nila send the Master Favored construct messages?" Kym asked, thinking back to how Nila had summoned Kenna and the others to Crystal Palace.

"Just Masters, Kym," Kenna sighed, shaking her head. "And not even Lady Nila could manage that."

"I thought once a construct was made you didn't have to think about it anymore?"

"You don't, but your energy still fuels it. Remember, your energy is finite. Even Lady Nila doesn't have enough energy to create over a hundred constructs, let alone infuse them with a message. You should know that."

Kym wanted to say the reason she didn't know that was because Kenna, her teacher, never taught it to her. But she stopped herself. There was no point in starting a fight right now. They were about to spend five whole days together.

"So, where are we going first?" Kym asked, eager to change the subject.

"Not too far, I think," Kenna said, examining the map. "With how fast these constructs go, we should get to the first estate in about thirty minutes."

The carriage sped forward before turning suddenly right. They bumped up and down along the new, uneven road. Before too long, Kym's body started to ache. She was relieved when the carriage finally stopped.

Kym climbed out first. They were standing in front of a vast, snow-covered field. Kym could see the first estate off in the distance; a massive blue house surrounded by snow-covered trees. At the front of the carriage, the horses were once again as still as statues.

Kenna started walking toward the house, trudging her way through the knee-high snow. Kym followed her, and the hems of their gowns were soaked in minutes.

"Can't we just move the snow?" Kym asked, her teeth chattering.

"I wish," Kenna trembled. "I've only been able to control water when it's liquid. I've tried when it's ice and steam, but it never works."

"That makes no sense," Kym said. Ice, steam, and snow were water, after all.

"I know," Kenna groaned. "Why couldn't the priests have seen the signs for the Calling in the summer?"

To Kym's surprise, she laughed at Kenna's comment. She couldn't remember the last time Kenna made her laugh. When Kym was the weakest Favored at Wadita, Kenna helped train her when no one else would. They'd even spend their free time together. They used to be so close before Kym met Kat, Tomark, Amber, Ashlyn and Xander. After that, it was like something broke between them, something neither of them could fix.

Kym couldn't feel her feet when they reached the estate. Kenna hammered continuously on the vast double doors, her fist trembling.

The door opened in seconds, and Kym practically fell inside. A blue-clothed servant stood before them, a tray of steaming mugs balanced on his hand. Kym took one gratefully. The piping hot liquid burned her insides, jolting her back to life.

"Miss, and Miss," the servant said, inclining his head to Kenna and Kym's soaked dress hems, "if you wouldn't mind. The mess."

"Alright."

Looking slightly annoyed, Kenna directed her hands at her and Kym's dresses and water seeped out of the wet portions. Their dresses now dry, Kenna sent the water into an empty urn beside the door. Satisfied Kym and Kenna were no longer a mess risk, the servant led them into the next room.

It was large, with a fire crackling merrily in the fireplace. An older woman dressed in blue silk pants and a simple white shirt sat on one of the many overstuffed sofas, her long, greying hair resting loosely at her waist. She studied Kenna and Kym as they approached, her eyes narrowed and her lips pursed. She directed them to the sofa next to her, a wide grin spreading across her lips.

"So," the old woman croaked as Kenna and Kym took their seats, "it's not every day I get visitors from Wadita. What does Lady Nila need?"

"The priests have seen the signs," Kenna said, sitting up a little to deliver their official news. "It's time for the Calling."

"When?" The woman straightened up as well, her eyes widening.

"Thirty-nine days," Kym answered. "Nila's selecting her Prized in six days. She'd like you at Wadita the night before for a welcoming feast."

"I'll leave at once." The woman stood with surprising speed for someone so old.

"Thank you for your hospitality," Kym said, standing too. Kenna did the same next to her. "But we'd better get going."

"Yes. Of course."

The woman led them out of the room. The servant who'd

greeted them stood by the front door, his hand already resting on the handle.

"Have you ever witnessed a Calling?" Kenna asked bluntly.

Kym wanted to cover Kenna's mouth with her hands. Did she just ask how old the woman was?

"I have," the woman said. She didn't sound upset. On the contrary, she sounded proud. "When I was five. Fire proved worthy that year."

Kym pushed Kenna out the front door before she could say anything more. They trudged their way back to the carriage in silence. Kenna showed the constructs the map while Kym pulled the water from their soaked gowns. It was only once they were safely inside the carriage and off to their next destination that Kym gave Kenna a stern look.

"What?"

"That last question was a little rude."

"No, it wasn't," Kenna said, waving Kym off.

"It was. You basically asked how old she was."

"Oh, Nothingness. She didn't care, Kym. And it's an accomplishment, being alive for two Callings."

The next four days passed in a blur of houses, polite conversation, and restless nights as they tried to sleep on the long journey. The horse constructs always took them to the next closest estate, so they were never in the carriage for more than an hour. Half the time, they'd arrive in the dead of night. Luckily, the estates were heavily staffed, so someone was always there to let them in. The Masters were understandably annoyed at being woken at such strange hours. Kym didn't blame them. But everything changed when they heard Nila's message. All were eager to answer their Ruler's summons and return to Wadita.

Kym expected the Masters to be older, like the first woman they met. She was wrong. In fact, the Masters' ages varied greatly, from early thirties to late seventies. Kym had never given any thought to what happened when she finished her training. She didn't even know how much longer she had. She thought of the Favored at

Wadita. None of them were older than thirty. It seemed stupid to think all of the Masters were old.

By the fifth day, Kym and Kenna started to worry. They'd easily reach the last estates by the end of the day, but that wasn't what concerned them. The final estate was at the opposite end of Undarunci as Wadita, almost at the border of Zara's realm. Even with the water-construct horses pulling them at their incredible speeds, they might not make it back to Wadita in time for the welcoming feast. If Kym wanted to stay on Nila's good side, they'd have to find a way.

They pushed their way through falling snow to the final estate, and something odd caught Kym's attention. All of the estates they'd visited had been very quiet. Of course, they'd been full of servants, and it had been the middle of the night half the time, but overall, the Masters seemed to live quiet lives. So Kym didn't expect to see at least ten carriages and several cars parked in front of the final estate.

Music wafted out into the cooling air through open windows, along with the unmistakable sounds of a party in progress. Kenna knocked on the door, and Kym saw a light in her eyes that usually only shone when she'd won a sparring match. She did say she'd been to see some of the Masters before. Did she know who lived here?

The front doors opened, and Kym and Kenna stepped quickly over the threshold. They dried their dresses, now a habit, and followed the servant through a second set of double doors. The room was full of people. Some wore the unmistakable robes of the Temples, while others wore gowns and suits. After wearing the same clothes for five days, Kym and Kenna's clothes were easily the most opulent. Even those who'd managed to get their hands on a few jewels were out of Kym and Kenna's league. Kym felt a sudden surge of pride for her lady's maids' work.

A band sat in a far corner, while more servants than Kym expected weaved through the dancing crowd, carrying trays covered with food. But the most spectacular aspect of the room was happening above them. Sheets of water, large as blankets and thin as paper, drifted gracefully through the air. One descended into the crowd, winding its way through the dancers like liquid glass. It swirled around Kym and Kenna before gliding back to the air above. It was the most fantastic thing Kym had ever seen.

It took a few moments for the partiers to register Kym and Kenna's arrival with everything going on. The music faded away, and people bowed their heads. Those dressed in the Temple robes bowed the lowest, dropping to their knees and laying their heads on the floor.

A shiver ran down Kym's spine. At Wadita, she'd grown accustomed to the servants always bowing whenever they saw her. Veronica and Isabel, knowing how much Kym hated it, actually stopped doing it for the most part. But to see complete strangers do it made Kym want to run from the room.

"What's going on?" A very tall, very tan man walked toward them. His shirt was covered in glittering blue gemstones and strained against his massive arms. His light, golden hair bounced on his forehead with every step he took. "Why has the party stopped?" he asked, his voice low and smooth.

"Master Lance," the servant who'd brought Kym and Kenna into the ballroom bowed low to the man as he drew nearer. "These ladies just arrived unannounced."

Something stirred in Kym's memory. Lance. She'd heard that name before, and it had been Kenna who said it. But she couldn't quite place it. She stared at his face. He was by far the youngest Master they'd visited. The memory rushed back to her in an instant. She was sitting in the Wadita dining hall as Kenna, Aidan, and Ryland discussed Lance, who'd mastered water magic in four years, the fastest ever to do so.

"Where are your manners?" Lance asked coolly, his dark blue eyes moving slowly from Kenna to Kym. "Water Favored are always welcome in my home."

"Please, Miss and Miss." The servant bowed so low his back was parallel with the floor. "Please forgive my ignorance?"

"Music!" Lance called before Kym or Kenna could answer. He

snapped his fingers, and music filled the air. The party resumed around them.

"La—Lance," Kenna stammered. Kym knew Kenna idolized him. "We have a message for you from Lady Nila."

Lance raised a finger to his lips, silencing her. He inclined his head to a door to his left and started walking toward it. Kym and Kenna followed, Kenna a little too close for Kym's liking. Could Kenna be any more obvious? Lance led them into the next room, which was dark except for the fire crackling in the fireplace.

"Nice party," Kym said, happy to be away from so many watching eyes.

"That?" Lance jerked his head back at the door. "That's nothing. Lady Nila likes me to keep in touch with all the prominent people in the cities. So she can stay informed."

"That's such a responsibility," Kenna gushed, taking a step toward Lance. Kym bit her tongue to stop herself from laughing.

"So," Lance said, looking at Kym. "Your message from Lady Nila?"

"The high priests have seen the signs. The Calling is happening."

Like all the other Masters, Lance's eyes lit up. A wide smile spread across his face, revealing perfectly white teeth.

"Excellent. When is—"

"Thirty-five days," Kenna said in a rush. "Lady Nila is hosting a welcome feast at Wadita for all returning Masters tonight."

Lance's eyes darted to Kenna before falling back on Kym. "Tonight? Cutting it a little close, aren't you?"

"We had a lot of messages to deliver," Kym said flatly. Why was he only looking at her?

They stood in silence. Kym could practically feel the excitement radiating off Kenna. Lance, however, looked as calm as could be. He bit his lower lip, and his brows furrowed. He was thinking about something, but Kym couldn't see what. Even with the construct horses, they couldn't make it back in time. The feast started in two hours. Personally, Kym wouldn't mind if they missed it.

"Well," Lance said finally. "There isn't a moment to waste then, is there?"

He walked to the closest table and rang the little bell sitting on it. A servant walked in with a long, blue coat draped in his arms.

"I'm leaving for Wadita," Lance said as the servant helped him put on his coat. "Miss…"

"Kenna!" she practically shouted.

"Kym."

"Right," Lance smiled. "Miss Kym and Miss Kenna will join me. See that my guests enjoy themselves and send my manservant on after us."

"We'll never make it," Kym said. "Even with Nila's construct horses."

"We're not taking the carriage," Lance laughed. "Don't worry. My manservant will bring the carriage when he comes to join me."

"But if we're not traveling by carriage," Kenna began breathlessly. "How are we getting back? There aren't any rivers near here for us to swim in."

"We still wouldn't make it in time," Kym shrugged. "Even if we used rivers."

Lance didn't answer. Instead, he grabbed each of them by the hand and led them out of the room. The partiers bowed as they passed, but Lance ignored them. He pulled Kym and Kenna through the crowd and out into the garden outside of the ballroom. It was nice, surrounded by hedges with an enormous fountain in the center.

Kym tried to pull her wrist from Lance's grip, but his hold on her was extremely firm. Did he really need to drag them out here? How was this going to get them to Wadita? He stepped right into the fountain's pool, not letting go of Kym's or Kenna's hands. Kym, caught off guard by stepping into a fountain, nearly lost her balance.

"What the Thed—"

"Shh," Lance said.

He invoked his Marks, which shone like neon blue strings as the sun sank behind the horizon. The sound of churning water filled the air, and Kym looked down. The fountain's water swirled around them, forming a cyclone that reached her knees. She looked at Kenna, who looked simultaneously stunned and mesmerized. What was Lance doing?

The swirling water reached above their heads, spinning faster and faster. Lance turned on the spot, pulling Kym and Kenna along with him. Kym's feet left solid ground, the bright light from Lance's estate streaking before her eyes. Water rushed around her, compressing everything inside. There was a flash a of brightest blue, and then everything was gone.

T R Y I N G   T O
F A I L

KYM COULDN'T SEE. SHE SPUN SO QUICKLY HER BODY FELT LIKE IT was on the verge of exploding. She had no sense of space. Lance's hand was in hers, but also not. She knew Kenna was there, but she felt miles away. The sound of rushing water was the only constant in the void around her.

Kym's feet slammed into something solid. Her knees buckled, and she collapsed as a mass of blues, browns, and deep reds assaulted her vision. Lights popped in her eyes, and everything wobbled as her stomach lurched. She squeezed her eyes tightly shut, breathing deeply through her nose. She wouldn't be sick. She wasn't even sure where she was.

Slowly, carefully, Kym pushed herself off the cold ground. She looked up at the building and couldn't believe her eyes. Wadita. Carriages parked in neat rows lined either side of the long drive. The windows were alight with activity, as shadows ran this way and that across the many floors.

"What did you do?" Kenna stammered. Her face was green, and it looked like it was taking all of her will power to remain standing.

"Since when could Water Favored warp?" Kym asked before Lance could answer. Both he and Kenna looked shocked, but more than that, Lance looked impressed.

"How do you know about warping?" he asked, his eyebrows raised.

"Friends of mine can do it." Kym said. Why was he acting like warping was some big secret?

"Not Water Favored," Lance said confidently. "I only developed the skill a few—"

"They're not Water Favored," Kym said plainly.

"Really," Lance said slowly. "They must be powerful if they're able to warp. How'd you become friends with non-Water Favored anyway?"

Kym didn't know where to begin. It was such a long story, and she wasn't sure how much of it she was allowed to tell. Sure, Nila and the other Rulers gave Kym and her friends their blessing, but that didn't mean other Favored would understand. They disliked each other on principle and never tried to know the Favored from the other elements.

Besides, she hadn't told anyone at Wadita the whole story behind her friendship with the Vanquishers. Why would she tell Lance? She'd just met the man not ten minutes before. Why was he so interested in her friends anyway? He was the embodiment of what a Favored should be, and her friends were, well, not. Kat was easily a good foot and a half shorter than him, and she'd eat him alive.

"We should get inside," Kenna said quickly.

Kym and Lance followed Kenna up the sweeping front steps. There were more people than Kym had ever seen packed into the entrance hall. Some of the younger Favored were there, but for the most part, the crowd consisted of Masters. All were dressed in their finest clothes, chatting excitedly as they waited for the feast to start.

"We need to change," Kenna said, elbowing Kym in the ribs.

"Yeah," Kym nodded, although she didn't mean it. Sitting through a feast with all of these people was the last thing she wanted to do after traveling for five days.

"Luckily for me," Lance smiled, glancing down at his clothes, "you found me dressed for a party. I'll see you later."

"Bye," Kenna laughed, unable to hide her nerves.

Kym grabbed Kenna's wrist and dragged her to the bedchamber doors. She never understood why girls acted so strange around guys. Lance was at least five years older than Kenna. What did she think was going to happen? Kym pulled open the door and shoved Kenna through. She turned to close the door and saw Lance staring at her from the edge of the crowd. He raised his hand, a trace of a smile on his cool face.

Kym and Kenna ran up the stairs. Kym guessed they had no more than an hour to get ready. Kenna didn't say anything when they parted on her floor. No doubt they'd be sitting together at the feast. And after five days together, Kym didn't have anything left to say to her.

Kym found her maids on their knees in her bedchamber, tears glistening in their eyes. Kym froze in the doorframe, the bottom falling out of her stomach. She'd never seen her maids in such a state. It was like someone died.

"Please, Miss," Isabel sobbed.

"We beg your pardon," Veronica cried.

"What the Thed happened?" Kym looked around the room, her heart racing. Everything seemed normal. "Are you all right?"

"Five days," Isabel lamented, still on her knees.

"If we'd known," Veronica wailed.

Frustration instantly replaced Kym's worry. They weren't hurt. Nothing was wrong. They were traumatized by Kym wearing the same dress for five days.

"You," Kym said, trying and failing to keep her voice calm. She marched over to her maids and pulled them to their feet. "Are not allowed to be hysterical unless it's for something important."

"This is important," Veronica stammered, trying to regain her composure. "You deserved better."

"I was fine," Kym said hotly. "I was just at a party at a Master's estate, and I promise you I was the best-dressed person there."

This seemed to calm them, but only slightly. Luckily for Kym, Veronica and Isabel had another crisis to deal with at that moment, so they let Kym's fashion mishap slide. They had under an hour to get Kym ready for a feast, and she'd been stuck in a carriage for five days.

They wasted no time. They stayed in the bathroom while Kym

washed, reminding her every thirty seconds to speed up. She tried ignoring them, but after their fifth reminder to get out of the tub, they took matters into their own hands. Isabel had Kym dried and robed in record time. She brushed Kym's damp hair, unsure what style would best suit the dress.

"I need to see you in it before we commit."

Isabel handed Kym over to Veronica, who had Kym's new dress waiting for her. It was sleeveless and started as dark, midnight blue at the top and slowly faded to a light sky blue at the end of the long train. Tiny, clear gemstones covered the dress, which sparkled with the slightest movement. Kym thought she looked like a mixture of the sky during day and night. Veronica gave Kym a pair of white gloves that went past her elbows as she slipped Kym into some high heels.

Isabel contemplated Kym's blond locks for several minutes, running her fingers through it, lifting it up and down. Finally, she went to work. She brushed Kym's hair one last time, then Isabel did something Kym wasn't expecting. She took all of Kym's hair and draped it over her left shoulder. Kym stared at Isabel, stunned.

"Simplicity can often be the most beautiful thing," Isabel smiled, leading Kym to a full-length mirror. She couldn't help but agree.

The entrance hall was more crowded than when Kym left it. Of course, all of the training Favored and Masters were there, but so were their servants. With so many people, the massive entrance hall felt oddly small. Kym stayed near the edge of the crowd, waiting for the dining hall doors opened. The sooner this feast was over with, the better.

Kym barely recognized the dining hall. Blue silk banners emblazoned with a giant wave, the symbol of water, hung from the walls. Shimmering white cloths covered the tables, which had little name cards on them. Kym looked around for her name. Where'd Nila put her? She looked at the head table; Nila was there, of course. So were Kenna and Aidan, but there were others there as well. The older woman Kym and Kenna visited first was at the very end of the long table, while Lance sat on Nila's right. A single chair remained open between the older woman and Lance. Kym stifled a groan. She didn't need to see the card to know where Nila wanted her to sit.

"Welcome," Nila called after everyone had taken their seats. "It is lovely to see these familiar faces among the new. We give thanks to the gods," Nila raised her hands, her head turned to the ceiling, "for blessing us with this gift. May you find these Favored worthy, and may they answer your call. Greatest Reta, goddess of water, bringer of purification, may your chosen Favored fight for your honor and glory."

Nila sat, and everyone began to eat. Veronica and Isabel brought Kym trays of beautifully prepared food, far fancier than the usual fare at Wadita. Nila was pulling out all the stops. Kym turned and started talking with the older woman, Roetta. Roetta mastered water over seventy years before, making her the oldest living Water Favored.

"That match went on for nearly three hours," Roetta croaked. "After I won, no one saw him for six and a half weeks."

"That's incredible." For the first time in several days, Kym relaxed. With Masters like Lance and Roetta, Kym's chances of being a Prized were very slim.

"I'm curious," Lance said slowly, pulling Kym away from Roetta. "How does someone with so little training know such advanced magic?"

"Kymbralyn is the Vanquisher of Water," Nila said, nodding significantly at Kym. Kym shifted uncomfortably in her seat. "She has spent most of her time roaming Princirum, keeping the powers of Thed at bay."

"After less than a year?" Lance asked, his eyebrows raised.

"It is extraordinary. Her speed and progression rival your famed experience, Lance."

Kym's face grew hot at Nila's words. Not only were they flattering, but they were, from Kym's perspective, completely inaccurate. What happened to those first months when she was the worst Favored at Wadita? And what about when she fell out of favor and

Nila confined her to the palace for months? According to Nila, those things never happened.

Lance looked sideways at Kym, his chin resting on his palm and his bottom lip pressed between his teeth. He didn't say a word. Kym tried to not fidget in her seat. Why did he have to stare at her all the time? It made her skin crawl.

"I hope," Nila began once everyone finished eating, "you have enjoyed meeting each other during our wonderful feast. Tomorrow, I begin my assessment of all Water Favored to select our four Prized. Over the next ten days, you will participate in three different assessments. All but twenty of you will be eliminated at the end of the first. The second will bring that number down to ten. The final ten will face one last test before I select our Prized for the Calling.

"I suggest you get a good night's sleep. You will need it to stand a chance tomorrow."

Nila stood, as did everyone else in the hall. Kym bid the others at her table goodnight and made her slow way through the crowd, thinking only of her bed. The last several days were catching up with her, and all she wanted was to collapse on her own pillows. It would be a nice change after the carriage bench.

Veronica and Isabel helped Kym undress. Veronica took her feast clothes into the closet, while Isabel brought Kym a pair of short shorts and a tank top.

"No nightdress?" Kym asked, although she wasn't complaining. She couldn't remember the last time her maids let her wear something like this to bed.

"I figured you'd want something comfortable," Isabel winked.

Kym threw the decorative pillows from her bed haphazardly on the floor. A loud bang boomed from her door, making Kym jump. Who could be there this late? The only person who visited her late at night was Kenna, but she hadn't done that in months. The banging persisted as Kym ran over to the door. If Kenna kept this up, she'd wake the whole palace. Kym wrenched open the door, ready to tell Kenna off. But it wasn't Kenna standing in the hallway.

"Hi," Lance smiled, leaning against the doorframe. "You gonna invite me in?"

Kym saw Veronica and Isabel retreat into the closet out of the corner of her eye. She wished they hadn't. She didn't want to let Lance in, but would it cost her? He was Nila's favorite Favored. If she didn't let him in, and he told Nila, it could undo all the work she'd done to get back in Nila's good books. So, reluctantly, Kym stepped aside.

"Do you need something?" Kym asked, trying to keep her voice as friendly as possible.

"I find you fascinating, Vanquisher of Water," Lance said, perching himself on the edge of one of Kym's sofas.

"My name's Kym."

"I know," he smiled. "I've never met a 'Vanquisher' before."

"We're new," Kym said flatly.

"We?"

"There's one for each element. We fight death demons together."

"Your friends?" Lance nodded. "The ones who can warp?"

"That's them."

"You must have seen some incredible things."

"I've seen my fair share."

Kym wasn't sure what else to say. Lance didn't seem to want anything in particular. Why was he in Kym's room when he should be preparing for Nila's assessment? He didn't seem like the type to disobey Nila's instructions, no matter the circumstances. Had Nila sent him here to check on her? But why send someone who barely knew her?

"You know," Lance said. He stood up slowly, rubbing his neck with one hand. "We could help each other."

"What?" Kym hadn't expected that.

"C'mon." He took a step toward Kym. "The Vanquisher of Water. The Master of Masters. We could show each other things the other never imagined."

"Master of Masters?" Kym didn't like the sound of that.

"Lady Nila's most trusted Master," Lance clarified. "Who'd love a lesson from the Vanquisher of Water."

"You're a Master," Kym said, taking a step back while Lance drew nearer. "What could I teach you?"

"Like you said," Lance was right in front of Kym. She stepped back, but ran into the wall. "You've seen your fair share."

Lance pressed his lips against Kym's. Her face burned white-hot, and she reacted instinctively. She raised her hand and the water from a vase of flowers on the table next to her shot into the air. It hit Lance right in the face, pushing him away from her. He stared at Kym, his eyes wide with shock. He waved his hand, and the water flew off his face. His dark blue eyes roved over Kym, and all the warmth he'd exuded vanished from their depths.

"See you in the morning."

Lance left the bedchamber, leaving Kym leaning against the wall. She stayed where she was, unable to process the past minute. Why had he kissed her? She never indicated that she even liked him. She barely knew him. And what was that whole thing about them teaching each other? She knew for a fact there was nothing she could teach him that he didn't already know.

Veronica and Isabel walked out of the closet and left the room without saying a word, but Kym hardly noticed. After a while, she extinguished the candles and crawled into bed. She closed her eyes and tried to forget what happened. But she knew she never could. She'd just had her first kiss with the most talented Water Favored who ever lived, and she wished it never happened.

The Favored gathered in the entrance hall early the next morning. Kym stood with her back pressed against the wall, trying not to think about the night before. What good would it do her? Today, she needed to focus on Nila's assessment. Hopefully, the more experienced Favored and Masters would outshine her, and she'd be eliminated early.

Kenna, Aidan, and Ryland joined her, their faces varying shades of green. Kym waited for them to say something, but none of them seemed able to do more than blink rapidly. She smiled. Since she wanted nothing to do with the Calling, she wasn't nervous at all. Yet another reason why she couldn't wait to get this assessment over with.

"Mornin'."

Kym looked around. Lance stood next to her, smiling his dazzling smile. Kym smiled back, trying her best to hide her confusion. Why was he acting like the previous night hadn't happened? He'd kissed her, and she'd smacked him with water. Why was he acting like they'd been friends for years? Next to her, Kenna's confusion was clearly etched on her face.

The door to Nila's chambers opened, and she drifted out into the entrance hall. The crowd parted as she raised her hand. The floor split open, and everyone followed Nila down to the training rooms. They'd only descended halfway down the stairs when Nila opened a door.

A giant sphere half-filled with water, it was the largest sparring room in the palace. A ring of solidified water stuck out about a yard around the edge of the sphere for people to stand on. It took several minutes for everyone to file inside. They stood along the outside edge, barely uttering a sound.

"As I said last night," Nila began, standing on the water in the middle of the room. "This first assessment will narrow you down to the top twenty. You will spar with each other at random, with the winners moving on to spar again. You will continue to spar until twenty of you remain. This will take two days and will eliminate those who lack the basic combat skills the Calling requires."

Nila looked up to the ceiling, her arms extended. "Ever watchful gods, hear me. Guide these chosen few, your Favored, as they display the skills required to become one of your Prized. Reta, goddess of water, bringer of purification, let your will be known."

Kym's sparring match was the shortest of the first day; it only lasted seven seconds. She couldn't help it. Nila paired her against a girl who was still learning basic combat skills—something Kym mastered months before. If Kym didn't win, Nila would know she wasn't even trying. Kym flicked her wrist, blasting the girl into the air with a large jet of water. She flailed through the air, then splashed back into the water below.

The next morning, Nila paired Lance with Matt, who Kym trained with when she first came to Wadita. He, along with other Favored, would bet on how badly they thought she'd do. She knew Matt wouldn't last against Lance, and was happy to see him get beat. Matt had enough time to make a water orb before two energized water tentacles rose out of the water on either side of him. They coiled tightly around Matt and threw him across the room, where he crashed into the wall. Kym gladly cheered with the rest of the crowd.

Kym had two different sparring matches that day. Both of her opponents had been at Wadita longer than her, but they just stood in the same spot while attacking constantly. Kym tried to let them hit her, but she would've needed to stand completely still for that to happen. She beat them without breaking a sweat, but she wasn't too worried. She still had plenty of time to get eliminated herself.

Finally, there were only twenty Favored remaining. Looking pleased, Nila announced the next part of the assessment, which would take three days to complete. They'd each have one more sparring match, with the winner moving on to the final round. Kym's match was against a Master in his late fifties. This was it. She'd let the Master beat her, and she'd be out of the Calling for good.

Pillars of water rose around Kym, caging her in. She threw a swipe at the pillars, cutting them in half. A bolt soared right at her, and Kym dove to the side, narrowly avoiding it. She threw a bolt at the man's feet, and he stumbled back.

No. Kym stopped herself before her next bolt left her hand. This isn't what she wanted. She needed to give him a chance to hit her. She clapped her hands together, and then jerked them apart. The bolt split, and she flicked her wrist. Hopefully, just like when she'd trained with Ashlyn, these tracking bolts would veer off course.

However, this Master wasn't Ashlyn. Like the others she'd fought, he seemed reluctant to move, insisting on attacking from one spot. He made a small shield, deflecting Kym's first bolt. However, the other two hit the water on either side of him. He flew backward, sliding across the surface of the water and into the wall behind him. Kym waited for him to get up, but he remained motionless. Kym's heart fell. She'd needed him to win. Even trying to fail, she'd made it to the final round.

Kym sat around the sparring room for the next several days, praying Favored and Masters more powerful than her would win. Of course, Kenna and Aidan won their matches; they'd fought Favored who'd been at Wadita as long as they had, but those Favored weren't Nila's favorites. They were no match for Kenna and Aidan. Jean and Jax, two Favored from Kym's training group, and Ryland also won their matches.

Lance always appeared next to Kym whenever she wasn't expecting it—to watch matches, during meal times, and even once when she escaped for a few minutes of peace in the garden. He never tried to kiss Kym again, or even speak to her. He'd just stand near her, glancing in her direction every so often. Kym wanted to say something but held her tongue. Lance would undoubtedly make it into the Calling, and once Kym was out of the running, she wouldn't need to see him again.

The only problem was, other people noticed Lance hanging around Kym. She caught them staring between sparring matches, or in the dining hall, or anywhere, really. And the strangest thing was, they were all smiling. But why? Ever since the festival, all she'd gotten from people were dark looks. Why were they smiling all of the sudden? She couldn't figure out why until the middle of the third day. Lance finally left her alone to do his sparring match, and Kenna quickly took his place beside her.

"Hi," Kym said tentatively. Kenna had barely said anything to her since they'd returned from collecting the Masters.

"So," Kenna said flatly. "Lance has been hanging around you a lot."

"Yeah." Kym didn't have much to say about him after he kissed her out of nowhere.

"Well," Kenna said, "he's clearly wasting his time on you. You're so ungrateful."

"What?" Kym demanded. What did people think Kym and Lance were doing? And what did she have to be grateful for, exactly?

"It's a perfect fit, and you, of course, don't even care. He's Lady Nila's Master of Masters, the best there is, and you're the first Vanquisher of Water. I'm sure Lady Nila's thrilled you two connected. The gods couldn't have planned a more perfect match."

Kenna's words swirled around Kym's head. Could Nila really be happy that Kym and Lance were together, even though they weren't? Nila always wanted her powerful Favored to get along. Wasn't this the next logical step? She'd talked Kym up to Lance during the welcome feast. Maybe, if seeing them together made Nila so happy, she'd let Kym fight death demons instead of doing the Calling? If only he didn't make Kym's skin crawl.

When Lance won his match, he sat down beside Kym, Kenna mysteriously moving several feet to the side, her face downcast.

"Well," he said smugly, wiping the sweat from his forehead. "What'd you think?"

Kym took a deep breath. "You did great," she said, trying not to roll her eyes.

"The ten Favored moving on to the final round are," Nila announced at the end of the third day, "Kenna, Jax, Kymbralyn, Lance, Aidan, Jean, Roetta, Peira, Larus, and Ryland. The final assessment will take place tomorrow night. You will not know what the assessment is until that time. Take tomorrow to prepare."

Kym spent the next morning out in the back garden. It was uncommonly warm out, with the bright blue sky making a rare appearance. She'd move some water around whenever someone passed, but other than that, she didn't bother preparing for Nila's assessment. With all those Masters, Kenna, Aidan, and the others from her training group, her chances of making it were very slim. She just needed to fail whatever the test was, and she'd be free of the Calling for good.

At dinner, Kym sat with the nine others who'd made it to the final round. Of course, Lance took the seat next to her, which made everyone else in the hall point and stare. Kym could feel Lance basking in the glow of all the attention. She focused on her food, barely speaking to him or anyone else. At the appointed hour, Nila led everyone back down to the training room in silence.

"You will perform the final assessment together," Nila said, addressing the ten remaining Favored. "Your task is simple—be the last one standing. Fight until you cannot go on. You may not engage with each other. Take your places."

Kym's mind buzzed with questions as she stepped onto the surface of the water. Everyone invoked their Marks, ready for a fight. But what were they fighting? Nila, who Kym thought spoke too vaguely normally, must have forgotten something. How were they supposed to be the last one standing if they didn't know what to do? She couldn't get herself eliminated if she didn't know what she was fighting.

Something huge slammed into Kym's back. She slid across the water, the cheers of the crowd fading around her. She looked wildly around, pain blooming in the small of her back. What hit her? Then she saw it. A human-shaped water construct ran right toward her, a large mallet in its hands.

Kym threw a water bolt, hitting the construct directly in the middle. It vanished in a flash of blue light. Her back aching, Kym pushed herself up from the ground. She looked around for the others, but what she saw made all thought vanish from her mind. Three more constructs were running right for her, their swords raised.

Kym swung her arm and her water swipe cut the trio cleanly in two. They vanished as well, but not before five new constructs stepped forward to take their place. Kym spun around, her heart pounding, ready to run. But there was nowhere for her to go. She was at the edge of the pool.

Kym went on the offensive, throwing attack after attack at the neverending wave of constructs. Cries of pain filled the air as more flashes of blue light exploded around her. What was going on? The constructs couldn't be hurting the others, could they? If they were, it was because Nila made them that way. Kym prayed she was wrong.

No less than ten constructs were closing in on Kym, their weapons ready. Kym pulled as much water as she could from the pool below. Her compact bolt quivering in her hand, she sprinted around the group of constructs. She threw the compact bolt at the closest one, which was about a foot away. The explosion blew the constructs apart, but sent Kym flying through the air.

Kym slammed into something solid. Lights popped in her eyes as ringing filled her ears. She rolled onto her stomach, the world spinning around her. Her stomach lurched, and Kym clamped her mouth shut. She wasn't going to puke—not with everyone watching. Slowly, she pushed herself back to her feet. Constructs closed in on her from every direction. There were too many for her to fight.

Sweat pouring down her face, she directed her hands at the water and spun in a circle. A ring of glowing water appeared around her. She raised her arms high over her head, and the glowing ring followed, sealing her inside a dome of energized water. Kym braced herself as the constructs lunged, bouncing off the water dome as even more constructs surrounded her. How was she going to do this?

A jolt rushed through Kym's body that had nothing to do with the attacking constructs. Why was she even trying to stay in this fight? The constructs appeared so quickly, and she did what Nila trained her to do—fight. But she didn't want to fight. If she did, she could be in the Calling. She didn't want that. She wanted out.

Cracks spread through her water dome like spider webs, but Kym did nothing to stop them. She let her mind and body relax, stopping her energy from flowing into the powerful shield. Her Marks vanished, and the water beneath her grew unsteady. The dome shattered like glass as three constructs pierced it with their swords. She closed her eyes, breathed in, and the water below gave way.

The moment Kym sank beneath the surface, the constructs

rushed off in different directions. She swam to the edge of the pool, and pushed herself out onto the ringed ledge. Panting, her heart pounding in her ears, she looked over her shoulder. Kenna, Aidan, and Jean were all climbing out of the water. Lance, the Master of Masters, was the last one standing.

Once Kenna's foot left the water, the constructs surrounding Lance dissolved, leaving him alone in the middle of the pool. Without the crashes and cries of battle, the room felt oddly empty. Lance walked over to the edge of the water, his hands raised over his head in triumph as the crowd cheered. He joined Kym on solid ground, smiling cockily as he waved to the crowd.

"Good job," he panted, wiping the sweat from his head.

"Thanks," Kym said, trying to look pleased with herself. Hopefully, she hadn't done as well as Lance thought.

Nila walked to the middle of the pool, the water glowing brightly beneath her feet. Kym's heart raced somewhere near her throat. She'd stayed in the assessment a long time before dropping out. She had no idea how many of the others were eliminated before her. Was Nila going to pick her?

"Well done. All of you. However, only four of you can be our Prized for the Calling. After reflecting on your performances in all three assessments, my choice is clear. The four Prized of Reta are: Lance, Kymbralyn, Aidan, and Jean."

"What?" Kenna's shriek of horror echoed around the room. "I lasted longer than Jean! I deserve this highest honor!"

Kym's mouth fell open. Kenna had always been Nila's most vocal supporter. She'd never seen Kenna do anything to upset her. But here she was, in front of every Water Favored, disrespecting her. Kym couldn't believe it.

"Yes, you lasted longer than Jean," Nila said, her voice icy and dripping with venom. "But your magical style is too similar to Aidan's. We need a variety of skills to win. And you," Nila paused, and Kym saw tears running down Kenna's cheeks, "you are not unique enough."

It was so quiet Kym could hear Lance and Ryland panting on

either side of her. Her eyes darted between Kenna and Nila, waiting for one of them to do something—anything. Nila demanded absolute loyalty from her Favored, and Kenna had broken hers. Kym watched Kenna, her whole body shaking, wipe the tears from her face. She turned her back on Nila and stormed out of the chamber, slamming the door behind her.

CHAPTER THIRTEEN

THE
CHOICE

"Well." Fury dripped from Nila's silky voice, although she maintained her regal composure. "I expected more. I thank each of you for your devotion, as selecting the Prized is not an easy task. Congratulations to our four incredible Prized. The rest of you will resume your regular training schedules."

Applause boomed around the room, but Kym didn't hear any of it. There was too much anger swirling inside her like fire for her to care. She was one of Nila's Prized, and she had no one to blame but herself. Why had she been so stupid? She should've gotten herself out of the running in the first assessment, like she'd planned. There were other Favored, like Kenna, who saw this opportunity as an honor. They wanted it. They deserved this more than Kym.

Everyone except Kym, Lance, Aidan, and Jean filed out of the room. Slowly, Kym pushed herself to her feet. Next to her, Aidan stared so intensely at Nila Kym was surprised she didn't flinch. Aidan and Kenna had been at Wadita together since the beginning. They were best friends. Would he speak for her? Kym doubted it. Nila chose him as a Prized. He wouldn't risk losing that chance, even for Kenna.

"Well done," Nila said. "You should be proud of what you accomplished. There is just over a month until the First Trial. During that time, you will dedicate yourselves solely to training."

"What's the First Trial?" Jean asked excitedly.

"I do not know," Nila huffed. "Lady Zara, who has no Favored and is therefore impartial, designs the trials. I will not know what you are facing until the day it happens."

"How're we supposed to prepare for the trials if we don't know what they are?" Aidan asked.

"I can tell you this. You will complete the first two trials as teams. Over the next month, you will hone your skills and learn your partner's strengths as you work together."

"Who are our partners?" Jean asked.

"Your partner is Aidan," Nila said. She turned to Aidan. "She is no longer your trainee, but your equal. That leaves Lance with Kymbralyn."

Kym stifled a groan. Out of all the Water Favored, she'd rather be paired with anyone but him. But, after all the whispering and stares, Nila putting them together wasn't a surprise. Even Kym could see the appeal; Nila's Master of Masters and the Vanquisher of Water were a formidable pair. There was only one problem. Kym didn't want to do it.

"Remember that while the Calling tests your magic, it will also test you," Nila said. "I will see you here tomorrow morning to begin your training."

Lance, Aidan, and Jean left the training room, identical expressions of joy on their faces. Kym, however, stayed where she was. She needed to tell Nila how she felt, and she didn't see any reason putting it off. They were both there. At least once she told Nila, she'd have plenty of time to pick Kym's replacement.

"Is there something you need, Kymbralyn?" Nila asked coldly.

"I'm…" Kym's stammered, her mouth turning suddenly dry. How could she say what she wanted without making Nila angry? "I'm honored you chose me. But I don't want to be a Prized."

Nila seemed to grow ten feet as she drew closer to Kym. She stared down her nose, her face blank and impassive. Kym, to her credit, didn't cower under Nila's gaze. She stared determinedly back up at Nila, trying to keep her face calm while her legs shook violently and her palms grew sweaty.

"Oh," Nila said, her voice as cold as ever. "Then what do you want?"

"I'm sure being a Prized in the Calling is a great honor, but I don't want to compete in a contest. I want to protect Princirum. I want to fight death demons, and Thed, like you taught me to. Let me keep being your Vanquisher of Water."

Kym braced herself, not taking her eyes off Nila. What would she say? But her face was just as impassive as ever. Her eyes didn't narrow, and no lines appeared on her forehead. All Kym could see was the slow rise and fall of Nila's chest.

"It seems," Nila said slowly, "you have a choice to make."

"I get to choose?" Kym asked, taken aback. It never occurred to her that being in the Calling was her choice to make.

"Oh, yes. Being in the Calling is not a punishment. All Prized have the choice to compete or not."

Kym couldn't believe her ears. She didn't have to be in the Calling after all. While Lance, Jean, Aidan, and whoever took her place were off competing in a ridiculous contest, she, Kym, would be doing something worthwhile. She'd fight for Princirum the right way—by protecting it.

"Okay," Kym smiled. "Then I choose to—"

"I hope you make the right choice," Nila said, taking a step closer to Kym. "For your mother's sake."

The water seemed to vanish beneath Kym's feet. All the happiness she'd felt over the last few seconds disappeared in a flash. She couldn't breathe. She must have misheard. What was Nila talking about?

"Wha—what?" Kym stammered.

"Tell me, Kymbralyn," Nila said, walking slowly around Kym. "When I permitted you to visit your dying mother, who did the doctors say sent them?"

Kym tried to remember, but her mind was like a pile of rocks. She couldn't think. Why was Nila talking about her mother, or doctors? It made no sense. They were talking about her being one of Nila's Prized. What did doctors and her mom have to do with that?

"Who sent the doctors, Kymbralyn?"

Kym closed her eyes, breathing through her nose. She could see the doctors staring at her around the kitchen table, looks of terror on their faces. But why? Kym hadn't exploded the glasses yet. They just kept asking Kym to tell *her.*

Please! Tell Lady Nila we've done everything she asked.

"You." Kym's voice was no more than a whisper.

"Me," Nila said, continuing to circle Kym. "I have tried, Kymbralyn. I allowed you to resume your friendships with the Vanquishers. I took you to the Summit. I reinstated you as Vanquisher of Water. I overlooked your negative behavior and let you leave this palace. I let you visit your dying mother, whose doctors have continued her care at my request. All of this and still, when I grant you this highest honor, you betray me."

"Nila," Kym said. She didn't know what to say. "I—"

"You are unlike any Favored I have encountered. Water has not won the Calling for centuries, but with you, water will reign supreme. Finally, I will reap the benefits of the seven years' good fortune the gods will grant me when you win."

"But…Nila…if Thed is—"

"Your victory in the Calling," Nila cut across Kym, "will prove death's inferiority. You will battle death but in the Calling, as you fight against the only known Death Favored, Jazin. When you win, you can waste your divine request on you mother and ask the gods to heal her. If you choose not to compete, I will order your mother's doctors to leave her side. If you lose a trial, your mother's life will hang in the balance. If your true motives for competing in the Calling come to light, your mother will descend into Nothingness, forced to wander for all eternity."

Nila walked toward the door, leaving Kym alone. Her insides turned to ice as Nila glided past her. No matter the choice, Kym would never put another person in danger. Was winning the Calling so important that Nila needed to threaten Kym's mom to make her do it? Kym looked around, hoping a solution would rise from the water.

"The choice is yours to make, Kymbralyn," Nila said smoothly as she left the room. "Choose well."

Kym didn't sleep that night. She stared at the canopy, a war raging inside her heart. Would she be the Vanquisher of Water, or the Prized of Reta? To be one meant her freedom from the palace, but promised certain doom for one of the few people who'd never turned their back on her. How could she take her chance at freedom when it would cost her mom her life? She couldn't. Her mother's life was worth far more than her freedom. She'd fight to save her, no matter the cost.

Kym got out of bed when her maids arrived that morning. She dressed in the clothes they gave her, and left for the entrance hall without saying a word. Jean and Aidan were already there when she arrived, both wearing massive grins. Lance appeared a few moments later, right next to Kym. She wanted to step away, but she resisted. Lance was her partner now, no matter how much she couldn't stand him. If she was going to save her mother, she needed the Master of Masters.

The entrance hall floor split open, and Kym and the others went to the largest training room. Nila was already there, standing on the middle of the water. Kym stepped onto the surface, which glowed peacefully beneath her feet. Nila waved her hand, and the door slammed shut behind them.

"Today, you will familiarize yourself with your partner's fighting style. I picked each of you because, as a group, your styles are diverse. Watch your partners, and learn how to work as effective teams."

Kym and Lance stood on opposite ends of the pool. She stared at him, bouncing slightly on the balls of her feet. From what she'd seen in the assessments, she had her work cut out for her. She didn't even know how to do half the moves she'd seen him do.

At Nila's signal, Kym's bolts zoomed into her hands. Across the pool, two large orbs of water encased Lance's hands. They grew, stretching into wriggling arms of water as they started to glow. Kym threw her bolts, and Lance swung his arms, whipping the water extending from them. They hit Kym's bolts in midair, which exploded while Lance's tentacles remained intact.

Lance shoved his arms forward, and his tentacles shot right at

Kym. She dove to the side, narrowly avoiding the wriggling arm. The other appeared on her other side, and Kym scurried back. How did they move so quickly? She needed to get out of Lance's reach, and she couldn't do that standing on the water. Kym exhaled and let her energy flow stop. The water beneath her gave way, and she sank beneath the surface before Lance's tentacles wrapped around her.

Kym swam through the water, stopping right beneath Lance. Concentrating her energy on herself, she launched out of the water, making a bolt as she went. She threw it down at Lance, who reacted just in time. His tentacle blocked Kym's attack, but broke apart in a flash of bright blue in the process.

Kym landed gracefully on the surface. She turned to face Lance and lunged to the left as his remaining tentacle darted at her. She needed to get rid of his other tentacle. Her heart pounding in her ears, she threw a swipe in Lance's general direction. She missed, hitting the water a few feet in front of him, disrupting its smooth surface.

"Ah!" Lance flailed his arms, trying to steady himself on the wobbling water beneath him.

A light went on in Kym's head. She directed her hands at the water and whipped them as fast as she could. Waves danced across the surface toward Lance, who continued to wriggle like a fish out of water. Kym made two more bolts and threw them at Lance. He deflected both attacks with his remaining tentacle, but staggered back to the edge of the pool on the uneasy water.

Kym raised her hands. A wall of water rose from the pool, trapping Lance at the edge. Kym smiled. She'd trapped Ashlyn the same way back at Crystal Palace. Through the wall, Kym saw Lance create two bolts. He shoved his hands, and the first bolt blasted into the other. The blast, larger than any Kym had seen, ripped through her wall of water. Kym focused on the gash, and more water rose to fill it. No matter how much water Kym put into the wall, Lance would force his way out in a manner of seconds. She needed a new plan.

Kym lowered one of her hands, and two water orbs rose next to her. She took a deep breath and dropped the hand holding the wall. Water crashed down around Lance, who'd just shot another massive blast. He staggered back, his blast flying wildly off course. Kym threw her two bolts at him. He deflected the first, but wasn't fast enough to stop the second. It hit him right in the chest, and he flew back, slamming into the wall.

Kym doubled over, her heart pounding in her chest. Panting, she walked over to Lance, his back pressed against the wall. His nostrils flared as Kym offered him her hand. He shoved it aside.

"What," Kym asked. Was he mad about losing?

"Why'd you do that," he asked, rubbing the small of his back.

"Do what?"

"Fight that way. All you did was make me lose my focus. Why didn't you attack more?"

Kym fought the urge to kick him in the shin. He wasn't mad that he lost. He was angry at the way Kym won. So what if she didn't spend all of her time throwing attacks at him. Sure, that was the way Aidan, Kenna, and Nila taught her to fight. But after fighting so many death demons, she'd learned that just attacking wasn't always the best strategy.

"What difference does it make?" Kym retorted, trying to keep her tone neutral. "I won in the end."

"The Calling is a test of magical power," Lance sneered. "You'd better show some if you want to stand a chance."

Kym and Lance walked off the water, leaving space for Aidan and Jean to take their turn. Kym stood next to Nila, and every fiber of her body wanted to attack her. But, instead, she stared straight ahead and watched Aidan spar with Jean. She couldn't let her anger get the better of her. Not with her mother's life on the line.

"You chose well, Kymbralyn," Nila whispered silkily.

Kym and Lance spent the next several days sparring with each other, only stopping when it was Aidan and Jean's turn. She kept trying to get Lance off his game, which meant attacking him in ways he wasn't expecting. Like most Favored, he liked to stay in one place, so she never actually aimed any of her attacks at him.

Once she got him moving enough, he'd lose his cool, and she'd strike.

But Lance was the Master of Masters. Even with Kym trying to underfoot him, he beat her more than she did him. He threw her around with water tentacles and blew her shields away with what he called alignment blasts. He'd line up two or more blasts and fire them into each other, and the energy from the first would fuel the second. He also made bolts that zoomed around him and attacked Kym if she got too close.

After about two weeks of sparring against each other, Nila had them fight together, and it was clear that Kym and Lance's styles did not mix well. Lance preferred to attack head-on, overwhelming his opponent with sheer power. This left little room for Kym, who preferred not hammering her opponent into submission. However, if she was going to win the Calling, she needed to make fighting with Lance work. So, she attacked first and got their opponent, who was always a random Water Favored, off balance, leaving them open for Lance to take them out.

Aside from complaining about Kym's fighting style, Lance's favorite topic was advanced magic. He'd boast about all the things he could do that Kym couldn't, but she didn't mind. To show how advanced the skills were, Lance explained how he did them. After two short weeks, Kym's tracking bolts were more accurate, her constructs held a defined shape, and she'd even managed to copy his tentacle arms, although it resulted in a massive headache. Lance was shaping up to be the best teacher she'd had.

Kym and Lance trained long after Aidan and Jean quit for the day. Lance insisted she needed the extra practice. Kym went along with it, although she wished she could be anywhere else. Lance wanted her to work on her defensive strategies, which she thought were far superior to his. So she decided to have a little fun.

Kym dodged this way and that, avoiding every one of Lance's attacks, just like he wanted. However, she never used magic once. Her insides swelled as she watched Lance's eyebrows creep closer together.

"Hold still," he said through gritted teeth, sweat shining on his forehead. "And get with the program."

"C'mon, Master of Masters," Kym panted. It was worth nearly getting beat to see Lance loose his cool. "What's the matter? Can't hold me down?"

Lance reached out, his face full of rage. Kym laughed and stepped to the side, although she didn't know why she bothered. He didn't have an attack in his hand. Every fiber of her body turned to stone as her muscles tensed under her skin. Kym tried to move, but there was something wrong with the connection between her mind and body. Her body rose motionless off the water. Kym gasped as pain coursed through her frozen body. What was going on? How was Lance holding her in the air?

Lance swung his arm and Kym's insides jerked backward. She flew through the air and slammed into the curved training room wall, lights popping in her eyes while her body shook uncontrollably. She stared up at Lance, who was walking toward her, a triumphant smile on his face. Rage stormed inside her at the sight of him.

"Looks like I can hold you down after all."

"What'd you do to me?" Kym stammered, fighting the urge to attack him where he stood.

"It's called the Cladium. Light, darkness, fire, air, earth, and water each have one. The Masters have always pushed the limits of what magic is capable of. Most of the time, our discoveries are widely accepted, like warping. Other times, we take things too far."

"What did you do to me?" Kym demanded again, pushing herself up.

"Isn't it obvious?" Lance asked. But when Kym didn't respond, he pressed on. "I controlled the water in your body."

Kym's mouth fell open. Why would Water Favored want to reach inside a person? Who would want, or even need, to control another human being? It was sick and wrong, and evil. Why would Lance use it on her without even explaining what it was, and when she wasn't expecting it? He should have at least asked her permission before controlling the water inside her body.

"That's disgusting," was all Kym could bring herself to say.

"That's balance," Lance countered. "The gods created Princirum to be the epitome of balance. Everything has an opposite. The same goes for magic. There is a pure side to it, but there is also a bad side, a vile side."

The final weeks of training passed in a blur. Lance didn't show Kym any more advanced or vile magic, and she tried her best to keep him in a good mood. If she was going to save her mom, they needed to work together, which wouldn't happen if she punched him every time she looked at him. They followed their strategy, never losing a match as they sparred against groups of Water Favored.

Kym retreated to her bedchamber in the evenings, where Veronica and Isabel tended to her aching body. She didn't dare go into the dining hall for dinner. She tried it the first night, but barely ate a bite as everyone kept staring at her. At least being trapped in her room gave her a break from Lance, who never missed a chance to walk around Wadita with a smug look on his face.

"Well done," Nila said on the final day of training. Her eyes were alight with glee as Jax, Ryland, and three other Favored were carried unconscious from the room after sparring with Kym and Lance. "You are ready. Tomorrow morning, you will gather in the palace Temple to receive Reta's blessing. Then, you will depart for Alfonburg, the Palace of Air, for the First Trial."

Kym's stomach did a backflip. Her throat closed as her palms filled with sweat. She shook her head. She didn't care what the First Trial was. It didn't matter. The only thing that mattered was her mom. She had to win.

Her maids had a bath ready for Kym when she entered the room. She sank beneath the sweet-smelling surface, trying to let her overactive nerves quiet in the warm water. It didn't work. She crawled into bed and stared at the canopy while her maids raced around the room, putting the final touches on more gowns than Kym could count. Slowly, her mind racing, she fell into darkness.

~

Kym didn't know where she was. Everything around her was undefined, like a painting before the details were added. Nothing made sense. How'd she get here? She turned on the spot, trying to get her bearings, only to see the same dark grey in every direction. Where was this place?

She stepped forward, and a crackling sound filled the air. It was like the last popping embers of a fire, or the crunch of dead leaves. Kym looked down. Cracks grew like spiderwebs through the dark expanse beneath her. She stepped again, her heart pounding in her ears, and more cracks appeared. The whole place was collapsing. Kym sprinted forward, the sound of cracking, breaking things filling her ears.

~

"It's time, my dear."

Kym's eyes drifted open at Veronica's words. It was still dark outside, but after a month of waking before the sun rose, Kym was used to it. She climbed out of bed and saw Veronica with a dress draped in her arms. No doubt it was one of the ones they'd been working on the night before. Veronica handed it to Kym, who was surprised at its simplicity. No jewels, no metallic trims, no flowing sleeves. It really was just a dress.

"The ceremony this morning calls for humble clothes," Veronica said, seeing the expression on Kym's face. "You're asking the gods to bless your endeavor as you answer their call. And then, of course, you have your journey to Alfonburg right after. This dress will suit both occasions."

"Then, what's all that?" Kym yawned. Isabel had just walked out of Kym's closet, her arms full of Kym's gowns.

"They're for after the trial." Isabel strained under the gowns' weight. "They will, of course, have an outfit ready for you to compete in. But we weren't sure what would suit you best. I guess we'll find out when we arrive."

"Wait? You're coming?"

"Don't be ridiculous, my dear," Veronica smiled gently. "Of course we're coming. The Calling is a glorious celebration of the gods'. We wouldn't miss it."

"And," Isabel added, "you won't return to Wadita between the trials. This way, we'll be there to look after you."

Warmth spread through Kym like fire. She had a feeling Isabel was referring to more than just dressing and serving her.

Kym had only been to the palace Temple a few times. After her first sparring match, when she'd broken Chloe's arm and bruised her ribs, she'd gone to the Temple to ask Reta for forgiveness. It was a dark room, with two sets of benches facing a large altar in the center. A statue of a woman with a kind face stood in the middle of the altar's pool: Reta, the goddess of water and purification. Several smaller shrines to the other gods sat in niches around the back wall. At Wadita, they rarely saw any use.

Kym knelt before Reta's altar between Lance and Jean, trying her best to stay still. She stared up at the kind face, and a shiver ran down her spine. Even back home, Kym felt like the gods' statues were looking right through her.

"Great Reta," Nila called, her arms open wide as she looked into the statue's face, "bringer of water's purifying touch, we call on you. Your Prized kneel before you, ready to answer your call as you have planned. May your waters purify them, and let them rise, cleansed by your touch. Lead them on their path to victory in your name."

Nila turned her hands to Kym, Lance, Aidan, and Jean. Four orbs of water rose out of Reta's pool and hovered over their heads. Nila flicked her wrist, and the water rained slowly down on them. Kym gasped as the first drops hit her skin. It was warmer than she expected. But, as it trickled down her back, it cooled rapidly. It took ten minutes before the orbs ran out. Kym's knees ached after the first two. It would've been much faster if Nila dumped a bucket on them.

"It is time," Nila said when the orbs finally ran out and the rain stopped. "Your carriages await you outside. I will not see you until the trial is over. Make me proud, and may you answer the gods' call."

The Temple doors opened, and Kym, Lance, Aidan, and Jean got to their feet. They walked out to the front drive, not even bothering to dry themselves. Two carriages sat waiting for them, each with construct horses hitched to the reins and four Protectorate standing guard. The air was warmer than it had been in months, and rays of sunlight pierced through the grey clouds above. Aidan and Jean climbed into the first carriage, and Kym, secretly wishing she could join them, followed Lance into the second.

"What?" Kym snapped as the carriage lurched down the front drive. Lance wouldn't take his eyes off of her. Why'd he have to stare all of the time?

"I want to make sure we're on the same page before we get to Alfonburg."

"We are," Kym huffed. "We've been training for weeks. I know what I need to do."

"Look," Lance said. "Clearly, we don't see eye to eye."

"Clearly."

"But when we get to Alfonburg, we need to act like a team. It's what Nila would want."

Kym wanted to tell him that teammates didn't perform vile magic on each other, or kiss them after only knowing them a few hours. But she held her tongue. He was right, but not for the reasons he said. Kym didn't care what Nila thought. Nila could fall off the edge of the world for all she cared. She needed to win the First Trial, and to do that, she and Lance needed to work together.

"Alright."

CHAPTER FOURTEEN

THE
FIRST TRIAL

"KYM," A VOICE CALLED, A MILLION MILES AWAY.

She didn't want to listen. Didn't the voice know she was happy where she was? Everything around her was still, a place where time didn't exist. Here, she wasn't going to the first part of a competition she wanted nothing to do with. Her mother's life didn't hang in the balance. She had no worries in this place. She would've done anything to stay.

"Kym!" the voice shouted, louder and more distinct than before. "Get up. Now."

Kym's eyes snapped open. Lance sat on the bench across from her. He was bent forward, apparently ready to yell in her face if she hadn't woken. Kym sat up and slid across her bench to the window. Trees taller than any she'd seen zoomed past, glittering and white like something from a dream. Was she still asleep?

"When'd I pass out?" Kym asked, tearing her eyes from the wonderous view outside.

"Not sure," Lance shrugged. "Couple hours ago, maybe."

"Did you sleep? You may need it."

"I'll be fine," Lance said smugly. He glanced out the window. "With any luck, we'll have some prep time before the trial starts. Don't be nervous," he added.

"I'm not," Kym said defiantly, although her insides felt like one twisted knot. "Why would I be nervous? I spend my days fighting death demons."

"Well, get it together," Lance said. "We're here."

Kym looked back out the window. Trees, at least two hundred

feet tall, lined Alfonburg's front drive. The palace was identical to Wadita, with massive tall towers, many floors, and sweeping front steps. The only difference were Alfonburg's silvery-grey walls, covered in delicate, swirling patterns.

"It looks like clouds," Kym said as the carriage jerked to a halt. "Very dense clouds."

The door to their carriage opened before Kym or Lance touched the handle. A servant dressed in silver stood on the graveled drive, his eyes trained on his shoes, and his hand held out. Kym took it, smiling at the man, but he didn't lift his black-haired head. Lance, Aidan, and Jean exited the carriages, and the servant led them and their squad of Protectorate inside. The rounded entrance hall was giant, with doors covering the far walls and tall, slender windows on the other. Kym sighed. It was like they'd never left Wadita. The servant led them through one of the doors into a room with a large pool in the middle.

"You're to wait here, Master, Mister, and Misses," the servant wheezed in a singsong voice, "for the trial to begin. I will return shortly with your prepared garments."

The servant backed out of the room, leaving Kym, Lance, Aidan, and Jean alone with their Protectorate. They melted into the walls, and Kym silently wished they'd stay there. Kym kicked off her shoes and stepped onto the surface of the pool before Lance could tell her what to do. She made an orb of water rise from its glassy surface; it drifted lazily through the room. It wasn't much, but it was all she could manage since her hands wouldn't stop shaking.

The servant returned an hour later, four packages held in his arms. Kym took her oddly squishy bundle, her heart pounding in her ears. She ripped off the brown paper, revealing a pair of tight pants, running shoes, a shirt, and a jacket. All of Kym's clothes were royal blue, the same color as Lance's. Aidan and Jean's clothes, though identical, were a lighter shade of blue.

"Your personal staff provided your sizes," the servant said. "I will retrieve you for the trial shortly."

Kym sat by the edge of the pool, absentmindedly stroking her new clothes with trembling hands. Why wouldn't they stop shaking? Being a bundle of nerves wouldn't do her any good. She breathed deeply, and the pounding in her veins lessened slightly. She stared at the water, which didn't move an inch as Aidan paced across it.

The servant returned sooner than Kym expected. None of them spoke as they followed him out into the entrance hall. The servant directed them to a door flanked by grey-robed Protectorate. Even with her mounting nerves, Kym still felt a twinge of annoyance at the sight of them. They stood aside and bowed their heads as Kym and the others stepped into the next room.

It was massive, much larger than the one with the pool. Groups of chairs sat around the silver walls, which were covered with enormous banners emblazoned with the elemental symbols. Lance took the lead, steering their group to the giant blue wave. Other Favored already sat beneath the yellow sun of light, the red flame of fire, the silver twister of air, and the green boulder of earth. No one sat beneath the purple shadow or the bleed, a half white, half black circle whose two halves seeped into each other.

Lance drew closer to Kym, slipping his hand into hers. Kym tried to jerk her hand away, but Lance's grip was so firm her fingers hurt.

"What are you doing?" Kym asked, trying to free her fingers.

"We're a team," Lance hissed. "Remember?"

"Since when did that mean holding hands?" Kym groaned. Jean and Aidan had their elbows locked on Lance's other side. Why couldn't they do that? They'd look united, and Kym's fingers wouldn't be on the verge of popping off.

Kym glanced around the room, not wanting to look at Lance. Joy surged through her like an electric shock. Kat, Tomark, Amber, and Ashlyn were there, sitting with the Favored from their elements. Kym had expected to see Amber there. How could the Fire Princess not be in the Calling? But seeing Kat, Tomark, and Ashlyn was enough to make Kym forget about Lance.

The door to the room opened, and Xander, Jazin, and the two other Darkness Pupils walked in. Kym wasn't surprised to see them. Zara said Xander and Jazin were guaranteed spots since the Darkness and Death Favored were so limited. Kym's heartbeat quickened as she looked at Jazin, his pale, slender arms hanging loosely beside him. It didn't matter who else was there. If Kym wanted to keep her mom alive, she couldn't let Jazin win.

Kym tugged her hand free from Lance and walked into the open center of the room before Lance could say anything. The others did the same. Their clothes were identical to Kym's, with the only difference being the color.

"So," Kat said. "We all made it."

"Are you surprised?" Amber asked in full Fire Princess form. "The Rulers made us Vanquishers. Of course, they'd select us as their Prized."

"Sure," Xander said. "Because the Rulers love us, and we never get on their bad sides."

"Who are your partners?" Kym didn't recognize any of the other Favored in the room.

"Well, Xander's my partner," Jazin said.

"Melana and Phillip let you be partners?" Ashlyn asked.

"I'm surprised too," Xander admitted.

"Really? I'm not," Jazin said in a tremulous voice.

Kym's spirits rose a little at the sound. Nila's voice forced its way to the front of Kym's mind, full of anger and determination. *You will battle death but in the Calling, as you will fight against the only known Death Favored, Jazin.* If Kym wanted to stop death from spreading, and keep her mother safe and Nila happy, beating a nervous Jazin sounded like an easy solution.

"Well, I'm with the old guy," Kat waved her hand over her shoulder. The man looked at least eighty, and his left arm was made entirely of stone.

"What happened to his arm?" Tomark asked.

"He lost it fighting, I think," Kat shrugged. "But Kai made him that thing so he's not totally useless. I really didn't listen when he talked about it."

"Well, my partner is worthless." Amber glared at a tall teenager sitting with the other Fire Favored. Kym thought he looked on the verge of passing out. "He can't do anything useful."

"Um, you thought we were worthless too, once," Ashlyn said, smiling.

"I never," Amber snapped, although Kym saw the corners of her mouth twitch.

"Tone it down, Fire Princess," Tomark whispered. "My partner's good," he added in a regular tone. "She's an Air Master."

"That's great!" Ashlyn smiled. She pointed to a tall, black-haired man sitting by the yellow banner. "My partner's a Master too."

Kym opened her mouth to speak but stopped as an arm draped itself across her shoulder. She spun around. Lance was smiling next to her, his dark blue eyes raking over the others. Did he need to do this in front of her friends? Talking to them without him didn't make them less of a team.

"Who the Thed are you?" Kat demanded. She glared up at Lance, who was at least a foot and a half taller than her.

"You must be Kym's Vanquisher friends," Lance said smoothly. "She'd mentioned you."

"Well, she hasn't said a word about you," Kat shot back.

"This is my partner, Lance," Kym said quickly. As much as she wanted Kat to put Lance in his place, she needed him in a good mood for the trial.

"Lance?" Amber perked up at the sound of the name. "Lady Nila's Master of Masters? Your skills are legendary, even among the Fire Favored."

"As is your reputation, Fire Princess," Lance said, inclining his head to Amber.

The door to the room opened, and Kym was grateful that it did. Lance turned to see who entered and missed Ashlyn and Xander's snorts of laughter, Tomark's shocked stare, and Kat's excellent impression of vomiting. Kym tried to keep her face calm. Laughing at Lance right before the trial wasn't going to help her win.

Stailin and Melana drifted into the room, which fell silent almost instantly. Kym followed Lance back to the Water Prized area, while Kat, Amber, and the others went back to their respective sections. Stailin and Melana stopped in the center of the room. Stailin raised his hand, and waved, indicating the Favored should gather around him and Melana.

"Congratulation," Stailin said. "As Prized, you have come to answer the gods' call and battle for their honor and glory. May the gods' will be known through your victories and accomplishments."

"You will complete the first two trials of the Calling as teams," Melana said flatly, "Combat between the Prized during these trials is strictly prohibited."

Kym stared at Melana. They weren't allowed to fight each other? All Kym had practiced for the past month was fighting other Favored. Wasn't that the point of the Calling? And how were they supposed to use their magic if it wasn't for fighting? Fighting was all they knew how to do.

"With that out of the way," Stailin said, rubbing his hands together, a gleam in his eye, "it is time for the First Trial. Your goal is simple: Locate the chest that corresponds with your element's color and bring it back to the starting line. Any questions?" Before Kym could even think of a question, Stailin continued, "Good. We will escort you to the starting point."

Stailin and Melana led the Prized through a door on the other side of the room. The knot in Kym's stomach lessened as she followed the Rulers into a dimly lit tunnel. But only slightly. Her mother's life depended on Kym finding a box and bringing it back. That couldn't be too hard, could it?

They walked down the torch-lit tunnel for several minutes before stopping. Kym squinted through the gloom, trying to make out the Rulers at the front of the group. Why'd they stop? She stood on her tiptoes and found her answer behind Stailin and Melana. They'd reached a dead-end.

"I will shroud your sight with darkness," Melana said, invoking her purple Marks, "When your sight returns, the trial will begin. Line up beside your partners. Prepare yourselves."

Kym quickly got into position. Lance stood on her left, ready to run, while a pair of Light Prized stood to her right. Kym didn't bother looking at Lance. He didn't matter. All that mattered was winning. The edges of Kym's vision blackened, and then all she could see was darkness. Gingerly, she lifted her hand. She couldn't even make out her fingers.

The sound of scraping stone filled the air, and Kym's legs tensed. Warm, fresh air rushed over her face, contrasting the cold, damp air of the tunnel. The dead-end must have opened. The trial was about to start. The darkness in her eyes began to fade. At first, all she could see were shapes. Then, slowly, Kym saw the world before her.

Outside the tunnel was a beautiful summertime forest. Blue and yellow birds zoomed by, chirping happily as butterflies fluttered peacefully through the air. Somewhere in the distance, Kym heard a rushing sound; there must be a river nearby. The sun was high in the sky, even though Kym knew it must have set by now.

Kym sprinted forward, Lance right on her heels. They raced out of the cave opening and, luckily, weren't the last to leave. Lance, his legs much longer than Kym's, overtook her and headed straight into the trees. Kym followed, not even bothering to look back as she darted between the tall, thick trunks. They ran for at least ten minutes before stopping in a grass-filled clearing.

"Now what?" Kym looked around, clutching at a stitch in her side. Every way she turned, all she saw was forest.

"Give me a minute," Lance snapped. He closed his eyes and invoked his Marks. "There's water nearby," he said, opening his eyes. "It feels like a stream."

"Good," Kym sighed. "We'll need it before too long."

It took them twenty minutes to reach Lance's 'nearby' stream. It was decent-sized, about seven feet across and full of clear water. Kym, clutching at the massive stitch in her side, didn't care. How was this 'nearby'? They needed to hurry up. They'd wasted so much time already.

"We should follow the stream that way," Kym jerked her head in the opposite direction from where they'd come.

"Why?" Lance panted.

"Because," Kym said, fighting to keep calm, "it leads away from the cave and deeper into the forest."

Lance nodded, though reluctantly. They walked along the bright blue stream lined with wild flowers, but saw no sign of the chests or any of the other Favored. Kym's stomach churned. Were they even going in the right direction? It was nice to have water close by, but if they didn't find the chests, they were screwed.

"Why haven't we found it yet?" Lance burst out. He stopped walking, sitting on a fallen tree trunk.

"How should I know?" Why was he yelling at her? It wasn't like he was offering any new ideas. "But yelling isn't going to solve anything. Neither is sitting."

Lance opened his mouth to retort. A high-pitched scream filled the air. There was the unmistakable sound of an explosion, and the birds in the trees took off in fright. Panic surged through Kym, turning her muscles rigid as stone. Lance sprang to his feet. He ran in the direction of the scream, Kym right behind him.

They found the source of the scream, and the explosion, after only running for a few minutes. Two Fire Favored, not Amber and her partner, were surrounded by a shimmering wall of light. The wall moved toward the girl, a bright red chest held under her arm. Her partner threw a firebolt at the wall of light, but it soared right through it like the wall wasn't even there.

Lance started running the way the Fire Favored had come from, but Kym couldn't move her feet. Another wall of light rose behind the girl. She screamed again as her skin touched the shining yellow light. Kym stepped forward. Maybe, if she blasted it at the same time as the other Fire Favored…? Lance's hand closed tightly around Kym's arm. He marched away from the Fire Favored, dragging Kym behind a particularly thick tree trunk.

"Let me go," she demanded, trying to wrest her arm from his grip.

"What's wrong with you?" he hissed at her. His voice was barely more than a whisper.

"They needed help," Kym gasped, finally managing to free herself. "You saw them. They have no idea what to do."

"So what?" he snapped. "You can't help other Prized if we want to win, Kym. If they can't handle it, that's their problem. And that's good for us."

Kym shook her head. How could she be so stupid? She had a job to do, and helping other Prized win wasn't going to save her mom. The Fire Favored's screams filled the air once again. A shudder ran through Kym's body. She couldn't turn back.

Apparently, the Fire Favored weren't fans of the narrow forest paths. They'd burned their own, much wider trail, which gave Kym and Lance something to follow. After only walking for a few minutes, Kym saw the table. It was massive, draped in white silk, and surrounded by tall, white stone pillars. The chests formed a line down the middle of the table. Kym drew closer, counting the little boxes. Three of the twelve were missing.

Kym sighed. They weren't the last to reach the chests after all. And if they hurried, they could still win the trial. Kym stepped forward, her hand outstretched, but stopped as she looked more closely at the pillars.

"What are you waiting for?" Lance demanded. "We need to go!"

"We need a plan before I just take it," Kym snapped. She'd seen those pillars before. During her evaluation at Crystal Palace, the Rulers used stone pillars to fire attacks at her. Could these be the same things? "I recognize the pillars. I think they're from the evals."

"I know."

"What if they attack us if we get too close to the chests?"

"We don't know they will," Lance retorted.

"Nothingness! You're infuriating. The Rulers wouldn't just put these pillars here for fun. And what if those walls surrounding the

Fire Favored show up? I bet they're supposed to stop us from getting back. *So*," Kym put a lot of emphasis on the word, "we need a plan."

"Fine," Lance spat. He looked wildly around for a moment, then said, "I'll cover you from back here while you grab the chest. We'll run for the stream and follow it back to the tunnel. That way, we'll have all the water we need."

"That's a terrible plan," Kym said. They'd probably get stopped before they reached the stream. "You should draw their fire from over there," she pointed to the opposite side of the table, "and then I'll get the chest."

"Nothingness, just take it!" Lance burst, his face turning red. "You're wasting time!"

Every part of Kym screamed that she was making a mistake. But Lance was right about one thing. She was wasting time. So, going against every fiber of her being, she stepped passed the circle of pillars and lifted a blue chest from the table. Nothing happened. Kym sighed and stepped back. Walls of earth and flame shot up on either side of her as bolts fired out from the niches in the four closest pillars.

"Run!"

Kym didn't need Lance to tell her twice. She invoked her Marks and let her energy flow out from her. She felt the tug of the stream and made a beeline for it, silently cursing Lance as she ran. This was the worst plan ever.

A wall of darkness bloomed in front of her. She skidded to the side, slamming to the ground right in front of it. Her heart racing, she scrambled to her feet. A wall of flame grew to her right, but the left was still clear.

"The stream's that way!" Lance yelled as she ran away from the walls of fire and darkness.

"I know that!" Didn't he see the walls blocking her way?

Kym could feel the droplets of water flowing down the stream. She was so close. She let her energy out, praying she was close enough. A jet of water soared through the air, and relief flooded through Kym's body.

Kym energized the water and threw a swipe at the wall barring her path. The swipe exploded in a flash of blue against the wall of darkness, but the wall remained where it was. A bright purple swipe shot out from the wall right where Kym's hit it. Kym dove to the side, her blond hair flying around her as the swipe soared over her head. Panic coursed through Kym like fire. These walls weren't just to stop them; they could attack as well.

"Stay down!" Lance yelled from behind Kym.

Kym looked up. Lance had his arms crossed in front of his chest, a ring of energized water floating in front of him. He pulled his arms apart, and the ring split into several large bolts. Lance waved his hands, and the bolts lined up in front of him. He shoved his hands forward. The first bolt blasted into the second, which fired a bigger blast into the third. The final blast exploded from the sixth orb with the force of a cannon and was thicker than a tree trunk. It blew straight through the wall of darkness, which faded away.

"Get up," Lance ordered, pulling Kym to her feet with her free hand. "If we lose because you can't handle yourself—"

"I can handle myself just fine," Kym said defensively, although she was secretly grateful for Lance's save. "We just need to get the chest back to the tunnel."

They ran along the surface of the stream toward the tunnel. Kym threw more attacks at the walls that appeared around them, but they reflected every move she tried back at her. Lance's alignment blast was the only thing that damaged them. But as they continued, Lance's panting grew louder and louder as his pace slowed. At this rate, he'd use up all his energy before they made it back.

Slowly, the trees around them thinned. The pounding in Kym's head lessened. They were at the edge of the forest. The tunnel, and the end of the trial, was so close. They just needed to make it a little farther.

Kym stopped dead in her tracks. Walls of fire, light, earth, darkness, and air filled the gaps between the final trees, blocking their access to the tunnel. Pillars sat every ten feet along the tree line, their elemental niches directed at Kym and Lance. Countless crashes filled the air as more walls appeared behind them. Kym tensed as she took in her surroundings. There was nowhere for them to go.

Lance spun on the spot. Four glowing blots rose from the water, orbiting around Lance like tiny moons. The bolts burst into one million pieces, which shot off in every direction. Kym directed her free hand at the water below her, spinning in a circle as well. A glowing blue ring appeared around her and Lance. She raised her hand, and a glowing blue dome rose around them as Lance's reflected attacks rained down on them.

"What the Nothingness?" Lance demanded as attacks slammed into the shield. "We're sitting ducks now."

"Me?" Kym panted. "You're the one who just provided the walls with attacks to reflect."

"We only have fifteen feet until we clear the trees," Lance said, clearly not listening to Kym. "People are already beating us back by now."

"Probably because they didn't send attacks into the attack-reflecting walls," Kym retorted. "We need a better plan."

Cracks spread like spiderwebs across Kym's dome. It wasn't going to last much longer. If only there was a way for them to get through the barriers without attacking. Kym scanned the wall of elements in front of her. There had to be a gap. How else were they supposed to get through?

"There!" Kym said, looking at a section of wall about one hundred feet to their right.

"What?"

"Over there. Is that section of wall made of water?"

Kym stared at the rippling space between the trees. Yes. That was a wall of water. That had to be their way out. All they had to do was get there without any other walls appearing to block their path.

"Don't attack unless it's absolutely necessary," Kym said,

lowering her shield. "We don't want those pillars attacking us too, if we can help it."

"Fine," Lance huffed. Four large water orbs rose from the stream, floating around him like clear moons.

They both took a couple of steps toward the water section. Nothing happened. Her confidence rising, Kym took a few more steps. A wall of fire burst in front of her as bolts and blasts flew through the air from the pillars. She dove to the ground as Lance's alignment blast rocketed over her head, destroying the wall.

Kym rushed forward, trying to ignore the ringing in her ears as attacks flew around her. They needed to make it back to the tunnel. If they could do that, this mess would be over. Something exploded against her side as sweat poured down her face. Kym fell to the ground, pain radiating from the spot. She ignored it, pushing herself up as she stared at the wall of water. Just a bit farther.

Kym held the chest out in front of her as Lance blasted another earth wall from their path. Kym lunged forward, and her hands passed through the wall of water. She closed her eyes and stepped through the rest of the barrier. A splash next to her meant Lance did the same. There was a flash of bright blue, and Kym opened her eyes. They were back inside the tunnel. They'd finished the First Trial.

Kym would've felt proud if every part of her body didn't feel like it was on fire. She laid on the dark, soft earth, hoping the pounding in her head would go away. After a while, Kym lifted her head a fraction. She and Lance weren't the only ones in the tunnel. Tomark and his partner, a woman about a foot taller than him, sat a few feet away, looking just as tired. Xander and Jazin were also there, but neither of them looked tired at all.

"Why aren't you exhausted?" Kym panted, barely able to keep herself up.

"We didn't waste time running," Jazin said, his quiet voice ringing through the silence.

"What?"

"Once we got our chest, I warped us back here," Xander said

plainly. "It seemed like the obvious move."

The bottom fell out of Kym's stomach. It was the obvious move, and Kym felt like an idiot for not thinking of it. Lance could even warp. They could've returned to the tunnel the moment they found the chest. Would that have made them the first ones back? She hadn't beaten Jazin, like Nila wanted her to. Would her lack of judgement cost her mother everything?

It took another twenty minutes for all of the Prized to return. Kat, Amber, Ashlyn, and their partners all made it back around the same time. Both Kat and Ashlyn looked pleased, but Amber looked like she was on the verge of setting her partner on fire. Aidan and Jean, covered in really nasty cuts, were the second to last to arrive. The tunnel closed once the last pair appeared inside. Slowly, everyone got to their feet and started the long walk back through the tunnel. When they reached the room with the elemental banners, they found the Rulers there, waiting for them.

"Congratulations," Lady Zara said, "on completing the First Trial of the Calling. The winners, by a clear three minutes, are the Prized of Kensrad, Xander, and the Prized of Thed, Jazin."

"How's that possible?" demanded one of the Air Prized. "We got to the table way before they did."

"Once they retrieved their chest," Zara said calmly, "Xander darkness-warped himself and Jazin back to the tunnel entrance. This was not engaging in combat with another Favored and did not violate the rules. Their win is legitimate, and very well earned."

Kym's body felt like lead as Zara's words sank in. Her breathing quickened, but she barely took in any air, and her insides turned to ice. She hadn't won the trial. Nila said she'd tell the doctors to leave her mom if she lost. What was she going to do?

"Three teams of Prized," Zara continued, "will be eliminated based on their performance in the First Trial. These teams were the last to return with their chest. Therefore the Darkness Favored, Pupil and Pupil, the Water Favored, Aidan and Jean, and the Air Favored, Heiro and Stekar, have failed to answer the gods' call. You are unworthy of their divine wisdom."

CHAPTER FIFTEEN

SIMPLY
EXHAUSTED

KYM WATCHED A SQUAD OF PROTECTORATE LEAD AIDAN, JEAN, AND
the others away, their heads hung low. But their shame was nothing
compared to Nila's anger. Her face was colorless, and her eyes were
wide with fury. And she wasn't alone. Kym noticed Melana and
Stailin both looked equally murderous.

Kym's body shook with suppressed nerves. No one said Prized
would get eliminated after each Trial. She'd thought they'd do all
five trials, and whoever did the best in all five would win. If she
messed up in one trial, she'd have another one to make up for it. But
no. There was no messing up, no do-overs. To save her mom, she
needed to win.

"The Second Trial," Zara said as the doors closed behind the
eliminated Prized, "will take place in five days at Terradon. Your
Rulers will determine when you will depart Alfonburg. Lord Stailin
has kindly offered his hospitality to all Prized who wish to prepare
for the Second Trial here. Now, you must rest. May you all be
worthy of the gods' call at the Second Trial."

Zara glided out of the room, the other Rulers right behind her.
Kym looked to Nila, hoping to see some sign that she'd done well
enough to keep her mom safe. But all she saw was the swish of
Nila's glittering blue hem as she left the room. Kym's heart fell.
Things couldn't get any worse.

The door barely closed before it opened again. A wave of
servants burst into the room, lugging enormous trunks and
numerous garments in their arms. Veronica and Isabel made a
beeline for Kym. She walked over to them, not saying a word to

Lance. She was actually happy to see them, a thought that both shocked and amused her.

"Oh dear," Veronica said, her eyes raking over Kym as she and Isabel led her to a lonely corner of the room. "You're in a right state."

"Come now, Veronica," Isabel smiled. Kym noticed a twinkle in her eye. "This isn't the worst we've ever seen her."

Kym laughed for the first time in what felt like years. Her body shook uncontrollably and her legs gave way beneath her. But she didn't care. She never thought of her maids as funny. Annoying—yes. A little overbearing—absolutely. But funny? And to top it off, they'd even used Kym's own joke.

"We're so proud of you, my dear," Isabel said, beaming at Kym as she helped her back up. "You did so well."

"You watched?" Kym thought only the Rulers watched the trials.

"Oh, yes," Veronica said excitedly. "It was exhilarating. At first, I was worried you weren't going to find your chest, and when you did, you had even more trouble getting back. I was…"

Veronica trailed off, her eyes darting in the direction of the blue water banner. Kym turned and saw Lance standing there with his manservant. She took a deep breath, trying to keep her face calm, which was difficult. His inability to think ahead could have lost them the trial multiple times. She'd have slapped him if she knew it wouldn't upset Nila.

"You recovered well," Isabel whispered.

"Thanks," Kym sighed. "But how'd you watch the trial? There weren't any stands or—"

"Lady Zara set it all up," Veronica said, wrapping a bandage on Kym's sore middle. "The forest was full of cameras. We watched the whole thing on massive holo-screens."

"Really?" A lifetime ago, Nila told Kym technology didn't work at the palaces because of all the magic. Clearly, that was just another lie.

"We were in the back, of course," Isabel said, handing Kym a fresh set of light blue clothes. "The Rulers reserved the front for their personal guests; the high priests, city mayors, and other people of influence from the cities were all there. They all seemed to be very interested."

Veronica and Isabel left Kym five minutes later, fully dressed and ready for an evening of relaxation. She stayed where she was, perfectly happy in her corner of the room. Over by the wave banner, Lance was still being pampered by his servants. Kym had no desire to be anywhere near that. So, she sat on the floor, her back and head pressed against the cool wall, and closed her eyes.

"Whatcha doin'?"

Kym opened her eyes. Ashlyn was bending over her, her long, red hair swaying in front of her. Kym smiled. She shifted along the floor, making room for Ashlyn to sit. She lowered herself down, smiling warmly back at Kym.

"So," Ashlyn said.

"So…what?" Kym asked.

"Your partner?"

"What about him?" Kym huffed, unable to keep the frustration from her voice.

"Well," Ashlyn said slowly, like she was working herself up to saying something unpleasant. "He came over. He put his arm around you."

"Yeah," Kym said evasively.

"You looked like you wanted to punch him."

Of course, Ashlyn was right. Kym wanted to punch Lance at least twelve times on a good day. She opened her mouth, ready to tell Ashlyn what an arrogant piece of work Lance was and that she only tolerated him because she needed to save her mom. But she couldn't. The room was full of people, and the last thing she needed was Nila finding out she told about her mother. And if Ashlyn had noticed, who else had?

"He surprised me," Kym said finally. "I guess I was too focused on the trial."

"Uh-hum," Ashlyn said, "and that's it?"

"What else do you want to know, Ash?" Kym snapped.

"Kym," Ashlyn said gently, shifting her body to face Kym, "I know you. Something was off when he put his arm around you. And something's off now. You look exhausted."

"I'm…" Kym trailed off. What could she say? She couldn't tell the whole truth, but maybe part of it? "It's the Calling. Nila's putting all this pressure on me to win so she can get the good fortune. I think it's starting to get to me."

"All of the Rulers want their Prized to win," Ashlyn said. "We knew that would happen when Zara announced it. This competition is what they've been waiting for to prove who's best."

"No one else is a nervous wreck."

"We're all nervous," Ashlyn said, taking Kym's hand. "I never thought Evanna would pick me. I've been a source of too much trouble. But this is my chance to prove what I can do. I'm the Vanquisher of Light, and now, I'm a Prized of Thilg. No matter what happens, Evanna can't take that from me."

Kym looked into Ashlyn's soft, green eyes, shining with their own gentle light. She wanted to tell Ashlyn about Nila threatening her mother to force her into the Calling, which she never wanted to be in. But she knew she couldn't. Ashlyn had spent her whole time as a Favored trying to stand out, her first chance to do so as the fifth of seven sisters. Of course, the Calling was her ultimate chance to show how unique she was, even among the Light Favored. This was Ashlyn's chance to shine. Kym couldn't spoil it for her.

The door to the chamber opened. Several servants dressed in grey entered the room, balancing trays of food on their hands.

"C'mon." Ashlyn stood up, pulling Kym along with her. "Let's eat."

The servants stood their ground, smiling happily as eighteen very hungry Prized bombarded them. Within five minutes, everyone was on the floor, sitting in small groups, eating and talking. Of course, most of the Favored stayed with their own element. Kat, Amber, Tomark, Xander, and Jazin joined Ashlyn and Kym in her corner. Kym glanced over at Lance, whose servant was busy serving him food.

"That trial was exhausting," Jazin sighed. "I can't imagine what the next four are going to be."

"Why are you tired? You didn't do anything," Kat smiled. "Personally, I haven't been this tired since Xander and Lady Melana tried to kill us."

"Oh, haha," Xander said. "I guess I have a reputation to uphold, isn't that right, Fire Princess?"

"Shut up, Xander," Amber snapped.

Kym's eyes darted between Amber and Xander. They all knew how Amber felt about being the Fire Princess. But she hadn't exploded at any of them when they called her that for months. To Kym, Xander, and the others, calling Amber Fire Princess was a joke. They knew Amber didn't like being someone who looked down on everyone like dirt. Why was she snapping at them?

"Amber, he was teasing," Ashlyn said gently.

"No, he wasn't."

"I was, and you know it," Xander said defensively.

"Not you." Amber's golden-brown eyes flashed at Kym, who fought the urge to flee several miles. "Lance."

"I'm sorry," Kym said, and she meant it. First, Lance made Kym uncomfortable, and now he'd upset Amber by calling her Fire Princess. Why'd he even come over in the first place?

"Amber, we know that's not who you are," Tomark assured her.

"I need some air."

Amber stood and left. Jazin put his plate on the ground and ran after her. He caught her when she was at the door, grabbing her shoulder as they left the room.

"When'd they get so close?" Kym asked the group, staring after Amber and Jazin, unable to close her mouth.

"I dunno," Kat shrugged, clearly disinterested.

"They barely know each other," Xander said, his eyebrows raised.

"Just like you and Lance, I guess," Tomark huffed.

Kym turned to Tomark, who was already on his feet. She opened her mouth to speak, but he was handing his empty plate to a servant. The warmth inside her faded as she watched him leave. Did he think she and Lance were...? There was no way. Even if she liked him, he was at least seven years older than her. Kym's stomach gave an uncomfortable lurch at the thought.

No longer in the mood to eat, Kym wandered around the room. It took Lance another hour to dismiss his servants. Kym walked over to him, trying her best to smile, but Tomark's comment rang in her ears. Her smile ended up more like a grimace. However, Lance's sneer wasn't much better.

"What?" Kym demanded.

"Nothing," Lance said slowly before adding, "trouble in paradise?"

"Why do you—" Kym stopped herself mid-sentence. She was tired, and the last thing she needed was another fight with Lance. "Everything's fine."

"Really," Lance said. His eyebrows traveled so far up his forehead that they were in danger of disappearing in his golden hair. "I thought I saw—"

"We're fine," Kym cut across him. "We should sleep. It was a long day."

Kym and Lance's rooms were connected to their practice room. When Isabel shook her awake, Kym's body ached so badly she could barely move. Why were they getting her up so early? The next trial wasn't for four days. Didn't she deserve to sleep in after getting through the First Trial?

Nila and Lance were already in the pool room when Kym walked in. Nila's eyes narrowed, and she looked taller than usual as she stared down at them.

"Aidan and Jean failed me," Nila said, her voice cold. "They lost the trial while you succeeded. You two are the last chance water has to experience the gods' good fortune for seven years. Do not fail me."

Nila looked at Kym and gave her head the smallest of nods.

Some of the tension inside Kym vanished. So, even though she didn't make it back first like Xander and Jazin, she hadn't lost. For now, Kym's mom was safe, and she needed to keep it that way. In the next trial, she needed to do better.

"We won't let you down, my Lady," Lance said quickly, bowing to Nila. Kym did the same, fighting her ever-growing urge to kick Lance in the shin.

"Good," Nila said briskly. "You will train for three hours this morning before your presentation at midday."

"Presentation?" Kym's stomach did a backflip. Why were she and Lance being presented?

"You will depart for the Palace of Earth this afternoon," Nila continued, ignoring Kym's question. "Do not overexert yourselves. You will train more at Terradon."

Kym and Lance didn't speak the whole time they trained, which she didn't mind in the slightest. Lance threw attacks at his Protectorate, who actually did a decent job dodging them, while Kym decided to practice something Lance showed her a few weeks before. She placed a single drop of water on the silvery grey floor. Slowly, she pulled her hands apart, letting energy expand around the water. The droplet grew, forming a large puddle. Kym sent all but a single drop of the water back into the pool, then started again.

At noon, Kym and Lance's Protectorate escorted them into the entrance hall. It was packed with people. Aside from the Prized and their Protectorate, Kym didn't recognize a single person. Who were all of these people? And why were the Prized standing on the raised platform in the middle of it?

The crowd descended on the Prized, pushing their way to the platform as they tried to be the first ones there. Kym's first instinct was to back away, but her two Pros stood right behind her, allowing her no means of escape. A woman in her mid-thirties approached Kym and Lance, twisting her shimmering blue shawl tightly in her fingers. Kym stared at her. Why did she look so nervous.

"Thank you, Blessed Ones," she breathed, bowing so low she almost kissed Lance's feet. "You do the people a great service. I pray to the Great Purifier for your continued success. Because of you, Reta's waters will drive death from the land."

"Rise," Lance said, and Kym heard the smugness in his voice. "Your prayers are well placed. I assure you, under my guidance, water will claim victory. It's the gods' plan."

Kym suppressed a snort as the woman backed away, tears of joy in her eyes. If Lance had his way, they'd be eliminated from the Calling already. And if the Calling was somehow part of the gods' master plan, then it was the worst plan ever.

They continued in this way for nearly an hour. When her line of well-wishers dwindled, Kym's eyes drifted around the room. Everyone else was at the end of their lines, but Jazin still had at least twenty more people to go.

"You usher in a new age," Kym heard an elderly man stammer as he stared at Jazin. "Soon, others will see."

"Death isn't a curse," Jazin said. "Thed claimed my brother and sister when we were born, and held me in his arms ever since. But now, I see he was only preparing me to show Princirum a different way."

Kym watched the man walk away, her insides squirming. She knew Jazin had been sick, but he never said anything about his brother and sister dying. And the way he talked about death…had she misjudged him? Kym shook her head. What was she thinking? She needed to beat Jazin to save her mom. Nothing else mattered.

When the hall finally cleared, Kym and Lance followed their guards out to their carriage. It sped off the moment they stepped inside, barely giving the Pros time to hop on. Kym wedged herself in the corner, her head pressed against the curved wall. Terradon was on the opposite side of Princirum. She and Lance were in for a long ride.

The sun disappeared behind the mountains as they approached Terradon. Kym watched the grass-green walls grow larger as they approached, unable to hide her disappointment. It looked just like Wadita and Alfonburg. But while Alfonburg and Wadita looked like clouds and waves made solid, Terradon just looked like shining stone.

Back at Wadita and Alfonburg, there was a hint of spring in the air, but not at Terradon. Kym pulled her cloak more tightly around her as the cold mountain air seeped into the carriage. Kym and Lance didn't wait for someone to escort them inside. They got out of the carriage and ran into the entrance hall as fast as possible, trying not to freeze.

The next three days blended into a neverending nightmare. There was another training room ready for Kym and Lance, which Nila refused to let them leave. They trained from the time the sun rose until it sank behind the mountains; throwing attacks at their Protectorate, dodging drills, and daily sparring matches became the norm. The room started to spin around noon each day, and by the evening, the pounding in Kym's head was so intense she didn't register what Veronica and Isabel gave her to eat.

But Kym didn't complain. She did whatever Nila asked without hesitation. She didn't have time to worry about how tired she was. It was nothing compared to how her mother would feel if she failed in the next trial. She didn't even have enough energy to be annoyed with Lance, but luckily, neither did he. Apparently, their partnership worked best when they were too tired to speak.

Kym wasn't sure when the other Prized arrived at Terradon. Nila only let her go to her bedroom, which was right next to the training room. Secretly, she hoped all the Rulers were as determined to win the Calling as Nila. That way, the Prized would all be equally exhausted. On the morning of the Second Trial, Kym's maids woke her with the best news she'd heard in her life.

"No training today," Veronica smiled. "Lady Nila wants you to rest before the trial."

Finally free of the training room prison, Kym spent the morning lying on the grass in Terradon's massive garden. Warm air drifted around her as Kym lay under the bright sun, which had broken through the grey mass of clouds once again. The cold weather they arrived in must have been a fluke. It would have been a perfect day if her Pros hadn't followed her around like shadows the whole time. Kym pretended they weren't there. She was determined to enjoy her little slice of freedom, no matter how brief.

"Look who finally showed up."

Kym sat up. Kat stomped across the grass, her arms folded over her chest. She plopped down next to Kym, who saw the corner of her mouth inch upward.

"What are you talking about? I've been here for days."

"Since when?" Kat demanded.

"Nila's kept us locked in our training room. She really wants us ready for the trial."

"Should be a blast." Kat smiled.

"Really?" Kym raised her eyebrows.

"Totally. I haven't been able to cut loose since the whole festival debacle. I don't care about getting Kai his good fortune or '*battling for the glory of earth,* '" Kat said in a passable imitation of Kai. "It's nice to have fun again, yeah?"

"Yeah, fun," Kym said halfheartedly. She'd call her current situation many things, but fun wasn't one of them. And since when was Kat's idea of fun doing what the Rulers wanted? Last she checked, Kat's idea of a good time was doing the opposite of what the Rulers asked.

"Are you okay?" Kat asked. "You seem off."

"I'm fine," Kym said, throwing a smile on her face. "Just tired. Nila's been working me and Lance like crazy."

"You said that." Kat's brows inched together. "Are you ready?"

"As I'll ever—"

"Of course we're ready," a deep voice cut across Kym.

She turned around. Lance stood a few yards away, flanked by his Protectorate. His arms were folded across his chest, and there were several lines across his tan forehead. Kym suppressed a groan. What was he even doing out here? He said he wanted to spend their free time inside.

"Thanks for answering, *Kym*." Kat glared at Lance.

"Lance is right," Kym said quickly. She could practically see the smoke issuing from both of their ears. "We're good to go."

"Well, you're a little spitfire, aren't you?" Lance said, looking down at Kat.

"And proud of it."

Kat sprang to her feet before Kym could say a word and walked right up to Lance. He towered over her, his arms as thick as her head. But Kat didn't back down. She stared right back into his face.

"Let's go inside," Kym said, stepping between them. She shoved Lance back toward the palace. "Nila wants us to relax. Remember?"

"You're right," Lance said, regaining his composure. "We should start getting ready."

He slid his arm around Kym's shoulders. A shudder ran down Kym's spine as she tried not to pull away. She needed him in a good mood for the trial, which meant not punching him in the nose. So they walked back to their training room together.

"Some friend you got there," he scoffed as one of their Pros shut the door behind them.

"She's an acquired taste," Kym said. She wanted him to drop the subject, and it was true that Kat took some getting used to. "C'mon. We gotta get ready."

Veronica and Lance's servant arrived a short while later with their clothes for the Second Trial. But instead of the small package they received for the First Trial, they each carried a large trunk. It looked just like the chest from the First Trial, only bigger. Tentatively, Kym opened hers. It was full to the brim of every type of clothing imaginable. There were clothes for summer, winter, rain, shine, and every other kind of weather.

"What's this?" Kym asked.

"These are from the Rulers," Veronica said excitedly. "They're your clothes for the Second Trial."

"You're to pick your outfit from the clothes the Rulers provided," Lance's servant drawled. "Be sure to choose wisely."

Veronica and Lance's servant left the room. Kym examined the clothes. Why were the Rulers letting them pick their outfits now? They'd had no say in the matter for the previous Trial. A light went off in Kym's head. This was part of the trial somehow. But before Kym could even think what to wear, Lance's hand plunged into her trunk and pulled out a tank top, shorts, and a pair of running shoes.

"Put those on," he said, throwing them at her.

"Seriously," Kym said indignantly. Did he really just tell her what to wear?

"They're the best clothes for combat," Lance said matter-of-factly, pulling similar clothes from his trunk. "The others are too restrictive."

"Okay." Kym let go of the clothes Lance gave her, and they fell to the floor. She pulled a light jacket and sweatpants from her trunk. "That doesn't mean we shouldn't wear other things on top of it."

"We won't need that," Lance said defiantly.

"Really? So you know exactly where they're gonna stick us for the Second Trial? We'll be screwed if they dump us somewhere cold."

"We'll be screwed," Lance retorted, "if we can't fight because we have on the wrong clothes."

"For Nothingness' sake!" Kym threw her hands in the air. Was he going to be this difficult about clothes? "We can take off the extra layers if we need to. I'd rather have them than not."

Lance opened his mouth but closed it quickly, his eyes narrowed. Kym smiled to herself and dressed in the fighting clothes Lance wanted, then pulled the pants and jacket she picked over them. When they were fully dressed, they each walked to opposite ends of the training room pool, where they sat with their backs to each other.

They didn't have to wait long before a green-dressed servant came to collect them. Kym and Lance followed the little woman out into the green entrance hall and through another door. The chamber looked identical to the one at Alfonburg, with elemental banners on the walls and chairs clustered around the room.

However, unlike the First Trial, all of the Prized stood in the middle of the room. Every pair's outfit was different from the next. One looked like they were going to the beach, while another was dressed for a blizzard. Kym looked down at her outfit selection. Compared to some of the others, it was actually very practical. She glanced sideways at Lance, barely bothering to hide her smugness.

She saw Jazin and Xander standing together. Out of everyone, they looked the calmest. Kym shook her head. She couldn't lose to Jazin again. This time, for her mother's sake, she needed to win.

The door to the chamber opened, and the minimal chatter died away. Kai glided into the room, his brow gleaming, with Melana right behind him. Kym suppressed a laugh. Kat had told her Melana terrified Kai.

"It is time," Kai said, his voice trembling slightly, "for the Second Trial of the Calling. Lady Melana will explain the trial's expectations."

"Like the First Trial," Melana drawled in an emotionless voice, "you will not engage in combat with any other Prized. You are, however, free to use magic against anything you encounter."

"The goal of the Second Trial is," Kai pressed on, "to be the last. If you feel you can no longer participate, shoot a blast into the air. If one person withdraws, the whole team is withdrawn. Come this way."

Kai and Melana walked between the Prized to a door on the other side of the room. They led them into a tunnel similar to the one from the First Trial. However, while the previous tunnel had been relatively flat, this one sloped steeply downward. The floor leveled out after a little while, where they reached a dead end.

Kym looked up. They were standing at the bottom of a massive hole. At least, she thought it was a hole. She squinted up, trying to see a sign of light through the darkness above. But all she could see was blackness.

Kym looked down. Everything around her was just as black as the space above. Melana must have darkened her sight again. Kym took a deep breath, her heart racing as a chill ran across her skin. All they needed to do was be the last ones standing when the trial finished. Before the Calling, she'd have thought that an easy task. But with Lance attacking first and thinking never, this wouldn't be so simple. What if his attacking got them eliminated too soon?

The stone floor beneath Kym trembled. A shudder ran through her legs as the earth pushed against her feet. The floor was moving. On and on they rose; the hole above them really did stretch forever. Kym's hair whipped around, hitting her in the face. The scent of clear air filled her nose, and the ground beneath her turned still and silent.

CHAPTER SIXTEEN

THE
SECOND TRIAL

Tiny lights bloomed in Kym's eyes, twinkling in the distance
as her hair flew around her face. She spun around, trying to take in
her surroundings as she squinted through the gloom. Why was it
staying so dark? She looked up. A ghostly sliver of a moon drifted
behind thin, wispy clouds. There were no trees, no bushes, not much
of anything as far as Kym could tell. Just a lot of sand.

It drifted over her shoes, carried by the warm, light breeze. Kym
pushed her hair out of her face. Around her, the Prized were still as
statues, staring at the vastness before them. They all could see, so
the trial must have started. So why wasn't anything happening?

Lance grabbed Kym's wrist and pulled her away from the
others. The sound of feet scraping against sand filled the air.
Everyone must be going off in a different direction, but no one
seemed to be in any real hurry. Kym didn't see the point. There
wasn't anything around, and if something did get close, they'd see it
coming for miles.

Kym wormed her wrist out of Lance's fingers. They walked for
at least ten minutes before Lance stopped. He looked around,
turning slowly on the spot, then sat down on the sandy ground. Kym
stared at him.

"What are you doing?"

"I'm bored," Lance shrugged.

"Well, good for you," Kym said. "I don't think we should—"

"Stop?" Lance finished, cutting her off. "There's nothing out
here. The Rulers said we're not allowed to fight each other. There's
nothing chasing us. We're not doing anything."

"You'd rather the Rulers sent something to chase us? Good plan."

Kym couldn't believe him. How could Lance be so calm? They couldn't survive in a desert without water, but they needed it for magic too. What if the Rulers sent something to attack them? Out here in a desert, she and Lance were at a severe disadvantage.

"We need to find water," Kym said, fighting to keep her voice calm.

"What?" Lance asked thickly, clearly not paying attention.

"Water," Kym said slowly. "We need to find some before the Rulers throw something at us."

Kym invoked her Marks, letting her energy drift out from her. She closed her eyes and could almost see the glistening water in her mind. All she had to do was find it. Her energy stretched farther away, and Kym's skin felt like it was being pulled in a million directions. She gritted her teeth, trying to ignore the pain. The Rulers wouldn't put them somewhere they couldn't do magic for a magical contest. She just needed to find it.

It was like a needle pricked Kym's finger. The tiniest feeling, almost indistinguishable from the other pains, but it was there. Kym relaxed, opened her eyes, and her body stopped aching. She turned right, facing the open expanse of desert in front of her. There was water somewhere in that direction.

"Get up," Kym said, kicking Lance's dust-covered shoe. "I found water."

"Good," he said, pushing himself up. "Now we're ready for a fight."

The wind increased as they walked, pelting them with sand. Kym pulled her hood over her head, as did Lance. She shook her head. She'd been right about the clothes, after all. She invoked her Marks every few minutes, making sure they were moving in the right direction. They were, but the water was still quite a ways away.

Kym's feet dragged as her body slowly turned into a furnace. It was so warm Kym's lips started to chap, and her tongue felt like sandpaper in her mouth. If only she could take her jacket off. But the wind was stronger than before, producing a constant storm of sand around them.

"Nothingness! This sucks," Lance yelled over the rush of the wind, and for once, Kym agreed with him. This did suck.

Kym's connection to the water intensified. It was no longer a prick on her finger but a pull in her gut. They were close. They had to be—just a few more minutes.

The pond was so small Kym didn't see it as she squinted against the whirling sand. Luckily, she stepped in it. Water seeped into her shoe, and a shiver ran up her spine as the hairs on her arm stood on end. Her heart racing, Kym looked down at the little puddle. It was empty.

"What the Thed! You're an idiot, Kym," Lance growled.

"We can make more," Kym fumed through clenched teeth.

She pointed her hand at her soaked shoe, and the water drifted out of it. The ball of water was smaller than an apple, but it was enough. She concentrated her energy on the water, which grew to the size of a large ball. Panting, she waved her free hand toward her face. A stream of water flew through the air and into Kym's open mouth. She swallowed, and a shudder ran through her body. The water was icy cold.

"Take some if you're thirsty."

Lance didn't need Kym to offer twice. He sent two large streams into his mouth while Kym re-increased their water. When they'd had their fill, Kym compressed the water as much as she could before holding it close to her chest.

"I'm sick of this wind," Lance said.

"We should try and find shelter," Kym said, looking around.

"What shelter?" Lance asked, sounding irritated. "There's nothing out here."

"There's that," Kym answered, pointing with her free hand.

A structure made of black stone sat a hundred feet away. Kym didn't wait for Lance to answer before breaking into a run, the water floating in her hand. This must be part of the trial. They needed to find this shelter to wait out whatever crazy weather the Rulers were creating. It was even near a water source. Kym dashed through the empty doorway, and a smile spread across her face.

"I should've known I'd find you at home."

Kat and her partner, the one with the earth arm, sat on stone stumps in the middle of the room. There were two bunks set into the far wall of the house, one on top of the other. But aside from that, the tiny house was empty.

"Welcome," Kat said, sounding oddly like Kym's maids. "Please come in. Would you like to sit on dirt or dirt?"

Kym laughed. Lance, panting loudly, entered behind her. She glanced over her shoulder. His eyes were narrowed, and he was glaring at Kat.

"Do you mind if we crash here?" Kym directed her question at Kat's partner. She already knew Kat's answer.

He looked Kym up and down, rubbing his chin with his earthy hand. His face was heavily lined, and he had very little hair left on his head. But, Kym noticed an alertness in his chocolate eyes as he looked her over. Slowly, he rose from his earth stump.

"You can stay so long as you don't bounce when trouble comes." His voice was worn, gravelly, and deep. He jabbed Kym hard with one of his earthy fingers. "And trust me, it's comin'. You gonna share that?" he added, looking at the ball of water floating in Kym's hand.

"Sure," Kym smiled.

She and Kat moved without speaking. Kat pointed her hand at the ground, which caved in as Kym lowered the water into the hole. Kym took a couple more steps inside. Lance remained by the door, his arms folded across his chest. Kym groaned. Did he need to make everything so complicated?

Kym waited about three seconds before grabbing Lance's arm and dragging him inside. She expected him to resist. He'd refused to come in on his own, after all. But other than dragging his feet a little, he didn't object. Kym sighed. Finally, something was going her way.

"The place only came with two bunks," Kat jerked her thumb over her shoulder, indicating the two rectangular holes in the wall. "I guess the Rulers weren't expecting us to share."

"Clearly," Lance breathed next to Kym.

"That's fine," Kym said quickly, hoping no one else heard Lance. "Some of us should stay up while the others sleep. In case something happens."

"We'll stay up," Kat nodded to Kym. "Lance and Lennax can sleep, then we'll swap. Trust me. You boys could use some beauty sleep."

"You wish you had my looks, Little Kat," Lennax said, climbing into the bottom bunk.

"Kym," Lance said quietly. He jerked his head to the corner of the room.

Confused and slightly annoyed, Kym followed. What could it possibly be now? Did he want them to leave? This was the only shelter they'd found since the trial started. How would they survive out there in the open? Kym could still hear the wind howling outside.

"What?" Kym asked impatiently.

"This is a bad idea," Lance whispered.

"We have no other options," Kym said. "It's either stay here or get pummeled by the weather out there."

"We should be the ones staying up together. We're a team, and if something happens, you'll be alone without help." His eyes darted toward Kat, sitting on one of the earth stumps.

"I won't be alone," Kym said, fighting not to roll her eyes. "Kat's here, and I trust her. Go sleep."

Kym turned away before Lance could answer. Why was he worried about Kym being with Kat? If combat between the Prized was allowed in this Trial, Lance might have a point. But the Rulers told them specifically they weren't to fight each other. He was worried about something that couldn't even happen. Was it really so hard for him to accept help from someone when they offered?

Kym sat down beside Kat as Lance climbed into the top bunk. It only took a few minutes before Lance and Lennax's heavy breathing filled the little room. For a while, Kym and Kat sat in silence, Kym occasionally sending streams of water into her and Kat's mouths. Sweat continued to fall down Kym's face and back. She pulled off her dust-covered jacket and threw it in a corner.

"Lennax is…interesting," Kym whispered to Kat, wiping the sweat from her forehead. "How'd you two get paired together anyway? You're so alike."

"I'm glad you see me as a cranky old man," Kat smirked.

"Well, I don't think you're old," Kym smiled.

"Oh, haha," Kat laughed. "Would you believe we're paired together because of our superior magical abilities?"

"Nope."

"Fine," Kat smiled. "Kai said I was the only Earth Favored capable of putting up with his belligerent attitude, and he's the only person I haven't offended yet."

"Really?" Kym knew none of the Earth Favored could stand being around Kat for more than five minutes. But after a month with Kat, Lennax was still there.

"And I've tried everything," Kat said, feigning distress. "Insults. Ignoring. Punching. But nothing puts him off."

"The gods couldn't have planned a better match," Kym grinned.

"I guess." Kat rolled her eyes. "What about you and Master Moody over there."

"What about him?" Kym groaned. Lance was the very last thing she wanted to talk about.

"Well," Kat said, her tone about as subtle as a hammer, "he's a jerk."

"He likes things his way," Kym said slowly, trying to say it the nicest way she could.

"So why is he all over you?" Kat demanded. "It's kinda creepy."

"Nila wants us to be a team."

"So does Kai, but you don't see me skipping through the halls with Lennax, looking like I want to punch him in the nose. Seriously, ever since the Calling started, you've looked like you're gonna vomit."

Kym opened her mouth to speak, but quickly closed it. Kat knew her better than anyone. Of course, she picked up on how Kym was acting. Her first impulse was to tell her everything like she used to when they'd sneak off all the time. Back then, there were no secrets between them. She may not be able to do anything to help Kym's mom, but at least Kat would know.

"Kat, the reason I'm—"

"Please tell me you've punched him?" Kat cut across her.

"What?" Kym asked, taken aback

"You don't have to fill me in if you don't want to," Kat said, and she sounded serious. "But at least tell me you haven't let him get away with this crap."

Kym looked past Kat to where Lance lay sleeping in his bunk. For the most part, she'd let Lance do whatever he wanted. She needed him on her side to win the trials, which meant keeping her mouth shut when he randomly acted like they were friends or touched her unexpectedly. She thought of that night he kissed, the night she'd water-slapped him in the face. Kym turned back to Kat and nodded.

A grin spread across Kat's lips. All warmth vanished from the air as clouds of mist burst from Kym's mouth. Goosebumps rose all over her skin as her body trembled. She quickly slipped her jacket back on, and as she looked down at the ground, ice grew around the edge of the water hole.

"You know what would be really nice right now?" Kym asked, her voice trembling. "Amber."

"I'd prefer a blanket."

"Really?" said Kym. "Not a fire?"

"The fire," Kat said. "comes with Amber complaining about the cold. That's the last thing I need right now. Why'd the Rulers make it so cold anyway?"

"Probably to make some of the teams drop out," Kym said.

They stayed awake as long as they could, but after an hour of yawning and poking each other in the side to stay awake, Kym and Kat gave in. Kym shook Lance awake while Kat pushed Lennax out of the lower bunk. Once Lennax and Lance walked away, Kym climbed in with Kat and closed her eyes. She didn't care that Lance, or even Nila, wouldn't like it. Her job in this Trial was to last the longest. She stood a far better chance of doing that with Kat keeping her warm.

A deafening crash boomed around them. Kym sat bolt upright, smacking her head on the top of the stone bunk. Next to her, Kat flailed around, smacking her in the side. Kym fell out of the bunk, landing awkwardly on all fours. Her head and side aching, she pushed herself up. Something large and heavy fell onto her back, forcing Kym back to the ground.

Kym pushed the still flailing Kat off of her. She scanned the room, looking for Lance and Lennax. They were gone. Kym stood up, panic replacing the pain in her body. Where'd they go?

"Wha's goin' on?" Kat asked thickly.

The ground shook violently. Kym flailed her arms, determined not to fall a third time. Next to her, Kat did the same. However, she didn't seem to share Kym's panicked expression. In fact, she looked almost bored.

"Well, Lennax's doin' somethin'."

Kat sprinted out the door. Confused, Kym raced after her. What could Lennax be doing to cause that much shaking? Outside the little structure, Lennax and Lance were locked in battle. Constructs, at least twenty feet tall, were closing in on the tiny house. Three bolts floated around Lance, firing blasts at the constructs while Lennax slammed his earthly fist on the ground. Spikes of earth burst from the ground, piercing the approaching hoard.

"Why the Thed didn't you wake us?" Kat spat at Lennax.

She invoked her Marks and quickly whipped her hands above her head. A wall of earth rose around them and the house, blocking the constructs' path. Lennax and Lance turned to look at them, their faces downcast. Were they really upset Kat stopped them from fighting?

"You needed your beauty sleep," Lennax taunted over the crashing from the other side of the wall.

Kym glared at Lance. He had his tentacles around his hands, and his face shone with sweat. How long had this battle been happening? If Lance got them eliminated while Kym slept…her blood boiled at the thought. So much for them being a team.

"Pool," Kym said to Kat.

Kat flicked her wrist, and a cloud of dust rose into the air. Kym invoked her Marks and directed her hand at the house. Their water soared through the doorway, and as it drew nearer, Kym wanted to scream in fury. It was barely larger than a grape. Why hadn't Lance replenished it? Couldn't he think ahead, just once?

"Cover me," Kym spat at Kat, who nodded.

Fuming, Kym started increasing the water, trying to fill the pool as quickly as she could. Around her, the crashes from the constructs grew louder as they smashed through Kat's wall. Kym heard Kat grunt as pieces of earth rained down around her. But, not one piece made it near her. Kat must be redirecting them.

"Kym," Kat said in a strained voice. "Any minute now would be great!"

Kym redoubled her efforts, focusing all her energy on the water. She just needed to make enough for her to get started. Lights popped in her eyes as her head began to throb. Behind her came the unmistakable sounds of whipping water. Lance must be trying to beat something back. She was out of time. The pool was less than half full, but it would have to do.

Kym made two water bolts and ran to join the others. Kat and Lennax, both red-faced and sweaty, lowered their hands. The remaining sections of wall crumbled, and the giant constructs smashed their way through. Kat jerked her arms apart and a massive fissure opened in the ground in front of her. Three constructs fell in, but the others simply stepped out of the way. Lance whipped his arms up, and his tentacles pierced the glowing eyes of the closest giant. But they didn't stop. A barrage of green, pebble sized bolts flew from Lennax's hands, but they were no more effective than Lance's tentacles.

Kym threw a water swipe at the closest construct. It hit the giant's shins, which stumbled as the giant teetered. Her blast hit the giant in its middle, and it fell back even more. It landed on several constructs behind it, pinning them down. But Kym had no time to celebrate. More constructs stepped over, and on, the fallen as they pressed closer to Kym and the others.

Kym stepped back to the edge of the pool, which was nearly empty. If she started increasing it now, she wouldn't be able to fight. But how could she fight if they ran out of water? Kym pointed her hands at the water. It soared out of the pool and right over her head. Her heart racing, Kym spun around. The water split into four bolts, which formed a line in front of Lance.

"No!" she cried, but it was too late.

Lance's alignment blast ripped through five constructs, which disappeared in flashes of yellow, red, and silver. But it didn't matter. More constructs stepped forward, taking the place of the destroyed.

"Hang on!"

Kat wrenched her arms up, and Kym felt the ground below her shudder. The earth containing Kym, Lance, Lennax, Kat, and the pool of water rose into the air. Kym looked up at Kat. Her face was set, her arms extended, and she was breathing like she'd run a marathon.

"Kym," Kat said, her voice strained. "Do the more water thing. Lennax, keep the constructs away. I'm barely holding us up. Lance, don't be an idiot and use all the water!" Kat finished through gritted teeth.

Smiling, Kym did as Kat instructed. She increased the water while Lennax sent attacks down at the giant constructs. Once there was enough water in the pool, Lance joined Lennax on the attack. The earth platform shook violently, and some of the water splashed over the side. Kym reached after it, her heart racing. It stopped before it reached the edge of the platform and drifted back into the pool.

"What did I say?" Kat shrieked. "One more hit like that, and we're gonna fall out of the sky!"

With the pool reasonably full, Kym joined Lennax and Lance. Lance's tentacles pierced constructs as they reached up for them, while Lennax rained mini bolts down on them. Kym's heart sank. Lennax, no longer on the ground, was breaking chunks off their floating platform for his attacks. At this rate, they'd run out of earth to stand on before she and Lance used all of their water.

Their large earth platform, which started out ten feet wide, grew smaller, forcing the four of them to stand back to back. Lance and Kym's water supply dwindled as they drew closer together. There was only enough left to make a few bolts each. Lennax stopped using their platform as an earth source. He joined a red-faced Kat to help hold together what little ground they had left.

Kym reached out for more water, determined to keep going, but stopped before any flew to her hand. The crashes below and around her faded as she deflated like a balloon. They were out of time, and there was no point trying to put off what needed to be done. Kym's head drooped as her hand fell to her side.

"We can't keep this up," Kym panted, sweat pouring down her face as the constructs continued to try and pull them from the air.

"Yes, we can," Lance yelled. He, too, was covered in sweat, and he looked like he was having trouble keeping his eyes open.

"No. We can't," Kym yelled defiantly, the ground beneath her trembling. "We're nearly out of water, and Kat and Lennax can't keep us up much longer. It's over. We've done all we can."

"We aren't quitting!" Lance stared at the bolt in his hand. It exploded, and droplet-sized bolts rained down on the constructs.

Kym shook her head. Did Lance think she wanted this? Of course she didn't. Their job in this Trial was to last as long as they could. She needed to win this Trial. But they were backed into a corner. If they didn't back out now, they'd either fall, or get pulled, out of the sky. There was nothing more they could do.

"The girl's right," Lennax spat at Lance. "We're beat. Time to pull out before it's too late."

"I can do this!" Lance snarled, forming a glowing ring with his remaining water bolt.

Kym would've thrown her last bolt at Lance if she could have. What was wrong with him? If she could accept that they'd lost, why couldn't he? She had so much more on the line than he did.

Kym looked at Lennax, who nodded silently back. Kym lifted her bolt above her while Lennax took one last piece of earth from their crumbling platform. They shot their blasts into the air, filling the night sky with blue and green light.

Kat fell to her knees while Lance screamed in anger. The ground beneath Kym gave way. She closed her eyes, bracing for the impact. Through her eyelids, she saw a flash of yellow light. The sound of the giant constructs vanished as Kym's body became oddly weightless.

Kym's feet slammed into solid ground. Her knees buckled, and she collapsed to the floor. Her heart pounded so loudly she couldn't hear anything. She didn't care. Every part of her body was on fire. Using all the energy she could muster, Kym forced her eyes open.

She was lying on the ground in a dark, torch-lit tunnel full of people. The other pair of Earth Prized, a pair of Fire Prized, and all of Light Prized lay sprawled on the floor, their bodies covered in dust and sweat. Kat lay on the ground beside Kym. She was flat on her back, the heels of her palms pressed into her eye sockets.

Xander and Jazin arrived a few minutes later. A smile spread across Kym's exhausted face. She hadn't beat Jazin, but at least he hadn't lasted much longer than she did. He looked exhausted and had a large cut running down his thin arm. Strangely, this made Kym feel a little better. About ten minutes later, Tomark and his partner appeared. That meant Amber and her partner were the only ones left. Kym sat up, expecting them to arrive at any moment. They'd outlasted all the other groups, after all. It took nearly twenty minutes before they appeared in the tunnel.

Some of the Prized tried to stand when the Rulers arrived, but crumpled to the ground moments later. Kym didn't even bother. She doubted she could stand even if she tried. The Rulers didn't seem to mind. They walked in the middle of the collapsed Favored, their faces expressionless.

"Well done in the Second Trial," Zara began. "You were each given the opportunity to choose your clothes for the trial, which resulted in the trial affecting each group differently. We plagued you with wind, heat, cold, and rain until six pairs remained. Constructs were released, compelled to overwhelm you and force you to withdraw.

"Two teams will be eliminated based on their performance in this Trial. These Prized were the first to withdraw and therefore faced no constructs in the trial. Earth Favored, Brynar and Olerra, and Fire Favored, Farren and Railyn, you failed to answer the gods' call. You are unworthy of their glory."

CHAPTER SEVENTEEN

T H E
C H A R M

Protectorate dressed in green descended on the eliminated Prized. They helped them to their feet and left the tunnel with their heads bowed. Kym even saw tears falling down Brynar's cheeks. Kai and James, to their credit, kept their faces blank as they watched their Prized leave. But Kym could still see the rage flash behind their eyes.

"Now," Zara continued, "for the winner of the Second Trial. Your sole objective was to survive, which meant outlasting all the other Prized. Therefore, the Prized of Heirraph, Amber and Kensrix, are the clear winners of the Second Trial."

Kym looked at Amber and her partner, the only Prized who didn't look completely exhausted. Of course, Amber looked cool and intimidating—there were other people around, after all. She didn't even smile at being declared the winner, but Kym did see her narrow eyes widen a fraction. Kensrix, on the other hand, trembled from head to foot as his eyes darted to Amber every few seconds. What had Amber done in the trial to make him look so terrified?

"You," Zara said, inclining her head to Amber and Kensrix, "answered the gods' call and have taken a step closer to proving yourselves worthy of their glory."

Zara turned and started making her way back through the tunnel. The other Rulers and Prized followed, although the Prized fell further and further behind. Kym could barely pick up her feet. What she really wanted was to lie down and sleep for at least a week. However, the waiting room was full of servants, and Kym's dreams of sleep vanished.

"Have the Favored ready for dinner in two hours," Stailin barked at the servants, who bowed their heads in response.

Dinner? There hadn't been any dinners since the Calling started. Kym and Lance trained so often they usually only had time to eat in the evenings. Why were they having a formal dinner now? It couldn't be to celebrate the winners of the trial. If that were the case, why didn't they celebrate Xander and Jazin when they won the first one? There had to be something special about this dinner, but Kym couldn't think what it could be.

Veronica and Isabel grabbed Kym and marched her into the water practice room. They took Kym's clothes off the moment they were safely in her little bedroom. It was a slow process. Even the smallest move sent pain radiating through her body. But, after some time and many breaks, her maids led her to the small bathtub in the connecting bathroom.

"We've added medicine and oils to the water," Isabel said, helping Kym into the tub. "They should help with the pain."

Kym lay back in the sweet-smelling water, trying to relax. After a few minutes, her aching muscles did start to feel a little better. At least now she didn't feel like a million tiny needles stabbed her every time she moved. The medicine even quieted her mind, which felt oddly blank as Veronica and Isabel gently washed the dirt and grime from her body.

"How are you feeling?" Veronica asked, running a comb through Kym's floating hair.

"Really good," Kym said groggily. "Why didn't you use this stuff when I first started training? This is great. What is it?"

"It's only to be used in special cases. Lady Zara makes it. I believe she said it's an infusion of life energy and healing oils. It's not enough life energy to heal you, but it should help you recover faster. All of the Prized are using it. The Rulers want you ready for the Third Trial."

Isabel helped Kym out of the tub. She dried herself, slipped on a robe, and sat on the small stool in front of the mirror. Kym's body started to ache again by the time Isabel finished shaping Kym's hair into a single sheet down her back. Zara's healing oil didn't last long. At least the pain was less intense than it had been.

Veronica waited for Kym in the bedroom. She stood beside two blue trunks, their contents draped over every available surface. In her arms was a shimmering blue dress, with jewels in varying shades of blue and white arranged along the bottom hem. It reminded Kym of a wave. The long, billowing cuffs looked like they easily reached the floor.

"Why am I wearing that?" Kym asked, staring at the dress in Veronica's arms. She knew her maids wanted Kym to look her best, but this was over the top, even for them. "It's just dinner."

"My dear," Veronica said, stepping forward, "tonight isn't just a dinner. Tonight we celebrate all of the Prized who remain in the Calling. You will march into the room together, and everyone will cheer—"

"Do I have to?" Kym groaned. She was in the Calling to save her mom, not so other people could cheer and stare at her.

"Of course you must," Isabel smiled excitedly. "You've made it through the first stage of the Calling. The Team Trials are over. From now on, you answer the gods' call on your own."

It was like a weight lifted off Kym's chest. She'd forgot that she and Lance were partners for only the first two trials. Now, that was done. She didn't have to worry about Lance's lack of planning ruining things for her. From now on, Lance wasn't her problem anymore.

Kym smiled and didn't complain as Veronica and Isabel helped her into her dress. They circled her, checking for any last-minute imperfections. When they placed the final touch, a thin golden chain, around Kym's neck, there was nearly an hour until dinner. Kym walked over to the small sofa in the corner. Veronica and Isabel followed a few steps behind her as Kym plopped down on the stiff cushions.

"So." Kym turned to face them. "How was watching the trial?"

"Oh, it was wonderful," Isabel replied. "You did well, my dear."

"We weren't sure in the beginning," Veronica admitted. "You

had such a hard time finding water, not to mention Lan... But, you overcame those obstacles. You were very clever to share that shelter with the Earth Prized."

"Why did you stay?" Isabel asked. "You could've easily left when the fighting started. You may have lasted longer."

"I couldn't leave Kat," Kym said. "They'd helped us. And besides, there was no pulling Lance away from that fight."

"But—"

"Isabel, don't be foolish. Miss...Kat...?" Veronica looked to Kym for confirmation. She nodded, smiling. "Miss Kat is a dear friend of Miss Kym's. They've battled together many times. I knew Kym wouldn't leave the moment they found each other."

"Exactly. I wasn't around some stranger. Kat and I know each other. We know how to work together. I knew Lance, and I, had a better chance of surviving with her and Lennax by our side."

"I could not have said it better myself."

Kym turned around so fast she cracked her neck. Nila stood in the doorway, her hands behind her back, her face impassive. Veronica and Isabel sank into deep bows, murmuring greetings to their shoes as Nila glided into the room.

"Leave."

Veronica and Isabel backed out of the room, their eyes still trained on the shimmering green floor. Kym stood, panic rushing through her veins like ice. What was Nila doing here? She hadn't lost the trial. She was still in the Calling, trying her best, just like Nila wanted her to. Was Nila going to take the doctors from her mom anyway? She couldn't. Kym held her breath, her body trembling, and waited for Nila to speak.

"You have done well, Kymbralyn."

Kym couldn't stop the sigh from escaping her lips. Nila said she'd done well. Her mom must be alright.

"Very well, in fact," Nila continued. "When you first found your friend, Katarein, I did not know what to think. I worried your resolve would waver in her presence. But it did not. You would have failed much sooner if you had not joined forces with her and her partner. Once again, you made the right choice."

"Thank you," Kym breathed. The ice in Kym's veins turned to fire at Nila's words. If Kym really had a choice, she wouldn't even be there in the first place.

"I knew, when given the proper motivation, you would succeed in the Calling. Thus far, you have not disappointed me. Continue to battle the power of death in the trials, and your mother's care will continue. And when you win the Calling and prove water's dominance over death and the other elements, you can end her suffering yourself. Are you determined, Kymbralyn?"

"I'm determined," Kym said through gritted teeth. It took all of her willpower not to send every drop of water in the room flying at Nila.

"Good," Nila said. "It is because of that determination I have decided to give you this."

Nila held out her hand, revealing a small, wooden box. Kym took it, her eyes darting between Nila and the box. What was Nila doing? First, she reminds Kym of the threat she made against her mom, and now she's giving her a gift? Nila had never given any of her Favored a present as far as Kym knew. Why would she give Kym a gift now? Tentatively, she opened the box.

A necklace lay draped across a white, miniature pillow, but it was unlike any necklace Kym had ever seen. It wasn't made of metal or any other material she could think of. It was a simple, pure blue chain, much thinner than the gold one Kym wore around her neck. It looked so delicate Kym thought it would crumble to dust if she touched it. She tilted the box, and the chain glistened like wet stone in the candlelight.

"I don't know what to say," she said slowly.

"Come. I will assist you," Nila beckoned Kym toward her.

Nila lifted the box from Kym's hands. Gingerly, Kym followed Nila to the full-length mirror. She quickly pulled the golden necklace from around Kym's neck, carelessly tossing it to the floor. Then more carefully than Kym had ever seen her handle anything, Nila draped the blue necklace around her neck.

Kym's body felt lighter the moment the necklace touched her skin. It was so thin it felt almost weightless. The stiffness from the first two trials vanished instantly from her muscles. She felt like she could run for hours, and even then, she doubted she'd be tired. It was a wonderful feeling.

"What is it?" Kym asked, forgetting her anger as she placed her fingertips on the delicate blue chain.

"It is one of the four physical charms," Nila said, nodding knowingly at Kym.

"Um…" Kym had no idea what Nila was talking about.

"Of course," Nila said, sounding almost annoyed. "I forget how little you know, Kymbralyn. There are three elemental tiers: the pure elements—life and death, the planal elements—light and darkness, and the physical elements—fire, air, water, and earth. Magical users are most powerful when they are in their natural element. This leaves physical Favored at a disadvantage to planal Favored, who always have access to their element.

"So, the Rulers decided to even the playing field. One charm was constructed for each of the physical elements, spun from the crystal of the Conduit itself. They grant the wearer their highest magical potential at all times."

Kym stared at Nila. She hadn't understood a word Nila said. Sure, she knew that light and darkness were the planal elements— Ashlyn had told her ages ago. But everything else…Kym didn't even know where to begin.

"That's…um…I don't…" was all Kym could say.

"Kymbralyn," Nila snapped. "Where is your magic at its peak?"

"In the water," Kym said immediately.

"Correct. By wearing this charm, your magic will be just as powerful as it is underwater, even when you are not. The charm was made from the Conduit, and therefore links you to the pure source of magic. You will be able to summon water out of nothing, swim through the air like you do water, and because of the extra energy the charm provides, your magic will always be at its peak."

Kym's fingers traced the blue crystal thread around her neck. She wouldn't need to seek out water when she ran out, or even worry about the amount. With this charm, every problem she'd faced in the last two trials wouldn't exist. She'd be at her most powerful. With the charm, saving her mom wasn't an impossible task. But as she looked at the charm around her neck, a thought occurred to her that made her pause.

"Nila, is giving me this…it feels like cheating."

She knew how badly Nila wanted her to win the Calling. She'd already threatened her, so cheating didn't seem too far out of reach.

"Do not be ridiculous," Nila snapped. "The charms were made for the Calling. During the very first, we, the Rulers, saw the great disadvantage placed on the physical elements in the later trials. The charms even the odds. It is tradition for Lords Kai, James, and Stailin, and myself to present our chosen Prized with the charms after the Second Trial."

"Oh. Okay."

"Kymbralyn," Nila said, and her tone was suddenly serious. "Do not use the charm yet. Its power is great, and you should not test its limits without me there to assist you. Enjoy your accomplishments this evening. You have earned it."

Nila turned toward the door, leaving Kym by the mirror, still fiddling with the fine crystal thread that matched her eyes. Why would Nila give her the charm after Kym had caused her so much trouble? She wasn't Nila's favorite. It didn't make sense. Nila was nearly out of the room when Kym snapped out of her stupor. She spun around and took a few hurried steps toward the door.

"Nila—Lady Nila," she called.

"What, Kymbralyn?" Nila demanded impatiently.

"Are you giving a charm to Lance?" Kym knew Lance would lose his mind if he didn't get one.

"No," Nila said flatly.

"What?" Why would Nila give Kym a power boost and not Lance?

"Only one charm exists for each physical element, Kymbralyn. You and Lance are no longer a team, and I must choose which of you is water's best chance. As I said before, I know you will succeed."

Before Kym could say another word, Nila closed the door behind her. Veronica and Isabel crept out of the bathroom. Veronica picked the golden chain from where Nila threw it while Isabel fussed over Kym's hair and dress, her hands shaking any time they got too close to the charm. It seemed Veronica and Isabel were too stunned to speak, and Kym's brain was too overloaded with information to say anything.

Nila hadn't chosen Lance, her Master of Masters, to receive the charm. She'd given it to Kym. Why would she do that? Did she think Kym was better than Lance? No. He was far more powerful than she was, and knew things about magic Kym never dreamed of. So why would Nila choose Kym over him? Kym's heart sank as Nila's words swirled around her mind.

I knew, when given the proper motivation, you would succeed in the Calling.

That was it. As powerful as Lance was, he had nothing to fight for. That wasn't the case for Kym. If she didn't win, she'd lose everything.

Much to Kym's horror, the entrance hall was packed when she arrived. Favored, both eliminated Prized and others, filed in from every direction while visiting priests and other prominent city members talked excitedly amongst themselves. She watched Jax, Roetta, Peira, Larus, and Ryland hurry into the dining hall, all looking anywhere but at Kym and the other Prized. Kym didn't mind in the slightest. She wasn't there for them to stare at her.

She joined the other Prized standing a little off to the side, pressed against the wall by an army of servants and Protectorate. Lance stood on the other side of the group, his arms folded across his sapphire-studded shirt. He looked upset about something, but

Kym neither wanted, nor cared, to know. Dealing with him was no longer her responsibility.

"Isn't this great?" Xander asked, sliding up between Lennax and one of the Light Prized.

"What?" Kym asked.

"This," Xander smiled, gesturing around the entrance hall.

"Really? You're enjoying this?" Being thanked and bowed to by random people was bad enough the first time. Kym didn't want to relive it again.

"Kinda. This is my shot, and I'm not gonna waste a second of it."

"Your shot?"

"Yeah. Winning this, it's my chance to change things," Xander said, and Kym could see the eagerness in his eyes. "Melana's been trying to get rid of me since the festival, but if I win, there's no way she'd throw me out. It would prove I'm the best, and not even she could contradict that. I'd be a Pupil at The Great Fortress forever."

Kym stared at Xander, his dark blue eyes alight with excitement. She could see where he was coming from. The Calling was the ultimate test of magical power, which was all Xander wanted after growing up with little to nothing. If he won, Melana wouldn't be able to dangle his place at her palace in front of him anymore. It's what he'd always wanted. Kym considered never getting to leave Wadita. She shuddered at the thought.

"Would you please assemble in elemental order, Masters, Misters, and Misses," a green-dressed servant wheezed.

They did as instructed, their servants twittering around them like birds, making sure they all looked just right. Luckily, Veronica and Isabel did such an excellent job in Kym's room they only adjusted her hair. Lance, however, was a whole different matter. He barked orders at his servants, who changed everything from his undershirt to his shoes. Kym just smiled, and for what felt like the first time in months, it wasn't forced.

The doors to the dining hall opened, and Jazin led the Prized inside. Applause and cheers filled the air as they walked between the round tables. At the front of the room, a long table sat below the Rulers' raised one. The Rulers' guests sat at the tables nearest the front, while the rest of the Favored occupied the remaining ones. Kym looked around. Water Favored took up at least three tables, and they all looked like they'd rather be anywhere else. The eliminated Prized all sat at the back near the door. They looked miserable, like they were trying to appear as small as possible. Servants and Protectorate stood around the edge of the room, standing so still they looked like statues.

Kym stood behind her seat between Lance and the tall Air Favored who'd been Tomark's partner. Everyone else in the hall stood as well, staring past Kym and up to the Rulers. Kym turned, craning her neck to see Zara up at the high table. Zara gazed up at the ceiling, her arms spread wide, and silence fell over the cheering hall.

"We give thanks to the gods for all they provide. Great Mother, almighty Pheil, bestow your blessing on the Prized before us. They have seen your signs. May the worthy among them answer your call."

Zara sat in her throne-like chair, and everyone else followed suit. The servants rushed forward, balancing golden trays piled high with food. Veronica and Isabel appeared at Kym's side, their trays laden with thick steaks, roasted chickens, magnificent fish, steaming vegetables, potatoes in every form imaginable, and bowls of salad. Saliva flooded Kym's mouth as her stomach gave an approving roar. She hadn't realized how hungry she was. She couldn't even remember the last time she ate more than a few bites between training sessions. She dug into her plate, happily grabbing whatever her hands could reach.

Kym had barely taken two bites of her delicious meal when several priests from the front tables stood up. They made their way along Kym's table, bowing before each Prized and staring longingly at them before moving on to the next. Grudgingly, Kym stopped eating, trying not to look too disappointed.

"You prove Reta's might with your actions, Blessed One."

"Reta's will is known by your deeds."

"Because of you, Reta's waters will purify Princirum."

The other guests made their way to the Prized's table, their clothes adorned with colorful sashes and ribbons to match the element they supported. Kym noticed a few of them had black accents. She stared at them as they approached Jazin at the other end of the table.

"You lead the way," Kym heard one woman say to Jazin.

"A new era is here," another smiled.

Kym looked back at her plate. Did these people really believe following Thed and death was a better way? She couldn't believe it.

"Once again," Zara said when everyone returned to their seats, "the Rulers offer their congratulations to the final fourteen Prized, who will compete in the Third Trial of the Calling in three days at the Palace of Water. Lady Nila has graciously opened Wadita's doors to all those wishing to watch the trial. Good luck, and may the worthy answer the gods' call."

Kym stood with the rest of the crowd, staring longingly at her half-eaten food as Veronica carried it away. She yawned, and her brain was like a rock inside her head. She felt like her skin was vibrating. All she wanted was to lie down and sleep. But, since the trial was at Wadita, Nila probably wanted Kym and Lance there as soon as possible. Hopefully, she'd let Kym sleep until the sun came up for once.

"Nice bling," a voice said from behind Kym.

Kat was walking right behind her, her arms folded across her chest. She kept messing with something wrapped around her upper arm. It was a green armband, and it was so thin Kym would've missed it if the color wasn't so vibrant. Kat kept tapping the armband with her finger, and Kym smiled. Kat didn't have a subtle setting.

"Thanks. Your bling's cool too. Is it a—"

"Charm?" Kat interrupted. "Yup. Kai gave it to me while my maids forced me into this monstrosity," Kat indicated her flowing green dress covered in gold leaves. "It would've been cool if I'd known the charms were even a thing before an hour ago."

"Yeah," Kym nodded. "Who do you think got the others? Nila said there's one for water, earth, air, and fire."

"Let's find out."

Kat stuck out her arm and scooped Tomark out of thin air. He spun around, his dark, wavy hair flying around his face. Kym smiled, grabbing Tomark's shoulders to steady him. She felt like she hadn't seen him for weeks.

"You nearly yanked my arm off," he said, rubbing his shoulder.

"You'll live. Did Stailin give you the air charm?" Kat said, getting right to the point.

Tomark raised his hand and shook away the cuff of his puffy white sleeve. A silver band, just as fragile-looking as Kym's and Kat's charms, sat around his wrist.

"Knew it!" Kat said triumphantly. "There was no way Stailin would give the charm to that giant girl."

"Her name's Baeka," Tomark said gently. "And I was surprised he gave it to me, to be honest."

"Why?" Kym asked.

"Well, after everything that's happened the past few months, I thought he'd be more interested in backing Baeka over me."

"You deserve it," Kym smiled. "I wonder who got the fire charm."

"If Amber didn't get it, the whole palace will be on fire by midnight," Kat said.

They found Amber walking out of the dining hall with Jazin. She stopped while Jazin kept going, glancing over his shoulder every few steps. Amber's face was impassive. She furrowed her brows as Kym smiled at her, and her golden-brown eyes darted all around the hall. Kym suppressed a sigh. The hall was still full of people. Amber wouldn't be able to break from full Fire Princess mode. Kym just hoped she didn't scream at them.

"So, Princess," Kat said bluntly. "Did James give you anything tonight before the banquet?"

Kym braced herself for the explosion. Why would Kat do that? They all knew Amber was extra sensitive about being called Princess lately. But, much to her surprise, Amber didn't go off on Kat. Instead, she smiled, and her whole body relaxed. Amber held out her right hand, showing them the delicate, pure red ring on her middle finger.

"As a matter of fact," Amber said coolly, "he did. Lord James presented me with the fire charm. It is truly the greatest honor. I see Lords Kai and Stailin, and Lady Nila honored you as well."

"They did," Kym said, fighting the urge to tell Amber how ridiculous she sounded. "They chose us, just like last time."

"And they never regretted that choice once," Kat said, and all four of them burst into laughter.

The water training room was empty when Kym walked in a few minutes later. She went straight to her room, where Veronica and Isabel waited for her. They helped Kym undress, but left the water charm around Kym's neck as they handed her a slippery blue night-dress. Kym climbed into bed, grateful to finally be off her feet. She lay back on the plush pillows, and fell asleep instantly.

CHAPTER EIGHTEEN

A REAL CHANCE

Kym's room was dark when Veronica shook her awake. Flames flickered in the little fireplace, filling the space with eerie green light. It was like being inside a giant plant. Her travel clothes, a light blue tank top, matching pants, and a thin coat, sat waiting for her at the foot of her bed. Kym smiled, eagerly pulling the comfortable clothes on. At least she didn't have to wear another dress while riding in a carriage for hours.

Veronica and Isabel flew around the room, nothing more than blue-colored blurs, their arms full of Kym's possessions. Kym watched them pile more and more of her things into the line of trunks by the door. How had so much stuff gotten around? They'd been at Terradon for less than a week. Apparently, thanks to their constant grumbling, Kym's maids felt the same.

"I wish we'd known the Third Trial was at Wadita," Veronica groaned, sitting on the lid of one of Kym's trunks to force it shut.

"Agreed," Isabel huffed, red-faced and sweaty with her arms full of what looked like every shoe Kym owned. "We needn't have bothered with half of this."

Kym stepped back, staying well out of her maids' way. She knew leaving them to pack on their own was best for all of them—both for their sanity and Kym's safety. So for the next hour, Kym tried to not to get run over by her maids, which worked out reasonably well. Veronica, her arms piled high with so many things they covered her face, only bumped into Kym twice.

When Kym's belongings were safely back in their trunks, she followed Veronica and Isabel into the still-dark entrance hall. The front doors were open, filling the room with frosty air and revealing a pale grey sky tinged with red along the horizon. Kym's bright blue carriage sat ready at the bottom of the front steps. The water-construct horses stood like statues between the reins, while Protectorate stood beside the door. She climbed through the open door and found Lance already inside. His arms were folded tightly across his chest, and he had a surly look on his face.

Kym tried to not roll her eyes. Did she have to ride back with him? They weren't partners anymore. There was no need for them to appear as a team.

"You took long enough," he muttered, though still clearly audible.

"Can we not?" Kym sighed. She didn't want to spend the whole ride to Wadita arguing with him. "I'm sorry you had to wait. It took my maids a while to get all my stuff ready."

"Why didn't they work through the night?" he demanded.

"Because I let my servants sleep," Kym said flatly.

Kym turned away from Lance and stared out the window, even though it was too dark to see anything. She'd thought she was free of Lance. The partner trials were over, after all. Clearly, they were done being cordial with each other. Why hadn't Nila given them separate carriages? It wasn't like she didn't have enough.

"What's with the necklace?" Lance asked a short while later as morning light filled the carriage.

"What?"

"Your necklace," Lance stressed each syllable, like he thought Kym was hard of hearing. "Why are you wearing it? You never wear jewelry, except at dinners."

Disregarding Lance's knowledge of her jewelry habits, Kym looked down. Sure enough, a fine, bright blue crystal thread rested against her chest. She'd completely forgotten about the water charm. It was so light she couldn't feel it against her skin. Kym looked up at Lance. He furrowed his brow and stared at the charm like he couldn't quite see it.

"I forgot about it," Kym said genuinely.

"It's not like the ones you usually wear," Lance said, still staring at the charm. "No way your maids picked that out."

"Rude," Kym said, her blood turning hot. "I'm the one with the bad taste, not my maids. And it wasn't even from them. Nila gave it to me."

"Why'd Lady Nila give you a necklace?"

"Ask her."

"Let me see it," Lance demanded.

He reached across the carriage. Kym slid across her seat, her mouth open in disgust. Did he really just try and take it from her? Lance lunged forward again, and this time Kym wasn't quick enough. The tips of his fingers brushed across the charm. Lance jerked his hand back, his eyes wide, as he stared at his fingers. It was like the charm shocked him.

"No," he muttered, shaking his head. "It can't be."

"Lance," Kym said, but he didn't seem to hear her. He continued to shake his head while he twisted his fingers in his hands.

"It can't be. I'm the Master of Masters. It should be me."

"Lance," she repeated, recoiling into her seat a little. He was starting to scare her.

"Why'd she give you the charm?" Lance deflated as he looked at Kym.

"She—she said she could only pick one of us," Kym stammered. Why did they still need to ride together? Didn't Nila know this would happen?

"Why'd she pick you?"

Lance lapsed into silence, apparently too stunned to speak. He'd look at Kym every now and again, his mouth open, but no words ever passed his lips. Kym didn't mind. She was happy for the silence. She knew Lance would react badly when he found out she'd gotten the charm. But the knowledge seemed to have shaken him to his core. Gone was the confident Master of Masters, replaced by a stammering man who couldn't string two words together. Strangely, Kym felt sorry for him.

The sun was high when their carriage pulled into Wadita's front drive. Kym opened the door the moment it stopped. She wasn't sure where she'd go, but anywhere was better than being around Lance in his current condition. She stepped out onto the graveled drive. A tall figure, his blue robes billowing in the spring breeze, appeared in front of her, barring her path.

"Let me pass," Kym demanded. She stepped to the side, but Pro Hayden did the same.

"I have a message for you," Pro Hayden said. His eyes darted around, and Kym knew he was looking for Veronica and Isabel.

"You do?" she asked, not bothering to conceal her smile.

"You're to meet Lady Nila in the water dome at once to begin your instruction with the water charm."

Kym heard Lance groan somewhere behind her, but she ignored him. She stepped around Pro Hayden, who didn't move this time, and sprinted up the front steps before either of them could say anything. The entrance hall was deserted, and the stairs to the training rooms were open. She ran straight down, not bothering to go change. For the first time, the clothes her maids put her in were actually appropriate for what she was going to do.

She reached the bottom of the spiral staircase in a matter of minutes. Panting, clutching a stitch in her side, she pulled on the door between the two torches on the wall. It didn't open. Kym pulled again, harder this time, but still it didn't budge. Why would the door be locked? That only happened when someone was using the room. But all the Water Favored who used the room had been at Terradon for the Second Trial. So who was in there?

Kym looked on either side of the door, and something else caught her eye. The basins of water for the constructs weren't there. Why would Nila remove the constructs? It wasn't like Nila was lightening her security. All the other doors she passed on her way down still had their basins.

She pulled on the door for a third time, putting all her weight behind it. The door swung open with ease. She staggered back, tripped over her own feet, and fell to the ground. She stared up at the open door, pain blooming in her hands and tailbone. Why did opening a door have to be so complicated around here? Shaking her head, she pushed herself up and ran inside.

"What kept you?" Nila demanded, standing in the middle of the room.

"What...didn't you—"

"Two days remain until the Third Trial," Nila plowed over Kym. "You must master the power the water charm grants you in that time."

"I can do it," Kym said, her hand drifting to the crystal thread around her neck. How hard could it be, anyway?

"Good."

Nila waved her hand, her Marks glowing. Rumbling filled the room as the lowest sections of the curved wall rose. Water sloshed across the floor, covering Kym's shoes in seconds.

"You will start in the water," Nila said, the water level at Kym's knees. "Once you master the charm here, you will begin using it above the surface."

Kym invoked her Marks, the water as high as her chest. Her body shuddered, and pure blue light shone from Kym's neck. It was like every nerve in her body was vibrating at once. She looked down. The water charm glowed as bright as her Marks and felt slightly warm against her skin. It was like nothing she'd ever felt. With all this energy surging through her, no magical feat seemed out of reach.

Kym focused the incredible energy coursing through her on herself. She shot upward, the world a blur around her, and reached the domed ceiling in seconds. She turned sideways, but her momentum was too much. She collided with the ceiling, lights popping in her eyes.

Kym shook her head, trying to clear the ringing from her ears. Usually, she'd feel her energy decrease after swimming that fast. But as she drifted through the water, all she felt was the rush of energy from the charm. She propelled herself to the ground, this time restraining her energy, and glided gracefully to the bottom of the room.

Floating a few feet off the ground, Kym formed a water bolt in her hand. It appeared instantly, and she barely felt any of her energy pass into it. She threw the bolt at the opposite wall, not paying much attention to where it went. The bolt shot through the water, hitting the curved wall in an explosion of blue light. Kym stared at her hands. She didn't even need to push the bolt with her energy anymore.

Kym practiced blasts, swipes, shields, and compact bolts, which all acted just like the water bolt. Everything she tried required so little energy. But why? Curious, Kym unleashed a stream of attacks for five minutes. Normally, this level of exertion would have left Kym dizzy, but she felt just as energetic as ever. It was the best feeling she'd ever experienced. She could do anything.

Kym stretched out her hands, focusing on an image of a fish in her mind. The water in front of her glowed, twisting itself into the shape of a fish. Pride spread through Kym like fire. She'd never created a construct that fast before. Sure, this one was still as a statue, but it was better than any of her past attempts. Those never even formed a distinguished shape before her energy started to wane.

"Good," Nila said coolly. Kym had forgotten Nila was even there. Nila lifted her hand over her head, and the water level fell around them. "You see the power the charm grants you. Translate your skills to a waterless environment. Act as if there is water around. The charm will do the rest."

Kym stepped forward as several targets rose out of the blue ground. She held out her hand, imagining an orb of water floating above it, just like she did whenever she was underwater. Energy rushed through her like electricity from the charm, and a ball of water appeared above her hand. She smiled, and let her energy continue to flow. The water orb glowed and hissed, turning into a bolt. Kym threw the bolt at the nearest target, where it exploded against the surface.

Kym spent the rest of the day practicing on the targets Nila provided for her. Everything acted just like Nila said it would.

Water appeared at the slightest thought. Her attacks moved just as quickly as they did underwater, her shields lasted longer, and even repaired themselves when Kym let the charm's energy flow into them. To Kym, doing magic without any water around felt perfectly normal. With the charm around her neck, nothing could hold her back.

"That is enough for today," Nila said, raising her hand for the third time as the targets sank into the ground. "We must prepare for dinner. Your fellow Water Favored will have returned from Terradon, as have many of the priests and guests."

Much to Kym's surprise, she found Kenna standing in the entrance hall when she and Nila emerged from the stairs. Kenna's face was blank. Her usual arrogant smile was gone, and she stared at the floor as people walked past. She looked like a balloon that had been left out too long, drooping and weak-looking.

"Are the ground-level rooms prepared for the Prized?" Nila snapped.

"Yes, my Lady," Kenna said flatly, bowing her head.

"Why are you standing here? Go oversee the preparation of the guest quarters on the fourth floor."

Kenna backed away without another word. Kym watched her leave, and she couldn't help but feel sorry for her. Ever since Kym's arrival at Wadita, Kenna had been one of Nila's favorites. She'd done whatever Nila asked without question, and in return, Nila brought Kenna into her confidence. But now, it was like Nila wanted nothing to do with her. Kym felt a lurch somewhere in her stomach. Nila treated her the same way when she lost favor.

Dinner was very subdued. None of the Prized or the other Rulers had arrived. Nila sat by herself at the raised table, leaving Kym alone with Lance at the one below it. They didn't speak, but Kym caught him glancing at her several times. She ate as fast as she could, eager to avoid another argument. She ran from the room as soon as Nila released them.

The following morning, Kym found Nila waiting for her in the entrance hall. She hurried to join her but stopped when she was halfway there. The entrance to the training rooms was sealed. But why? Nila said Kym was supposed to practice with the charm again.

"Aren't I training with the charm today?" Kym asked.

"Yes," Nila said coolly. "Your training today requires a change of venue."

Nila turned and glided across the entrance hall, leaving Kym's mind swirling. Where was she going? Kym hurried after her, catching up with Nila as she opened one of the many doors around the entrance hall. Kym didn't understand. That was the door to the back garden. Why were they going outside? It wasn't like the water dome wasn't big enough. Twenty people could train in there and not bother one another.

Warm air hit Kym's face as she stepped out onto the grassy back garden. The greying clouds above had thinned, allowing glimpses of the pale blue sky beyond. Tiny flowers covered the once-bare trees and bushes as insects flitted between them. Even the grass, which had been yellow and brittle for so long, had the faintest tinge of green.

"You will complete your training with the charm with a combat review."

Nila waved her hand lazily toward the beach. Glowing human-shaped constructs rose from the foaming water. Kym ran forward, not waiting for Nila's signal to begin. She leaped over the little wall dividing the beach and the garden, landing silently on the sand. She invoked her Marks, and the charm's energy shuddered through her. Kym raised her hands, and water bolts appeared above them instantly.

Her attacks exploded against the first two constructs before they reached the shore, fading away like blue mist. Her confidence soaring, Kym made a new, larger bolt in front of her. She clapped her hands together, then quickly jerked them apart, and the bolt split into three. She stared at the closest construct, which stepped onto the damp sand, and flicked her wrists upward. Her tracking bolts arched high into the air, then, one after another slammed into the same construct.

Kym shot a blast through the next construct, leaving a hole in the middle of its chest. She smiled, her body shaking with untapped energy. This wasn't even a challenge. She swung her arm through the air, and her swipe cut the next construct cleanly in two. Kym raised her hand, another bolt at the ready, but stopped. There were no constructs left.

"Excellent," Nila said beside Kym, making her jump. "You have mastered the charm for combat. Now, swim through the air."

"Wait, what?" Swim through the air? What was Nila talking about?

"I told you," Nila said impatiently. "The charm grants you the power to use your magic at its peak. Underwater, you have complete control over your movements. With the charm, you will do the same in the air."

Kym didn't move. This was just like when she first came to Wadita. Nila would tell Kym what she wanted her to do but never explain how to do it. How was she supposed to swim through the air like it was water? It was air!

Kym closed her eyes, invoked her Marks, and imagined she was in the water dome. Her body was weightless, drifting slightly through the cool water. She felt the water pass through her mouth, turning into ice-cold air before it reached her lungs. This was where she felt most at home—at peace.

"Well done, Kymbralyn."

Kym's eyes snapped open. Nila stood directly in front of her, and their faces were level with each other. But how? Nila was at least two feet taller than Kym. She looked down. She was floating at least a foot off the ground, her body bobbing up and down with each breath she took.

"Fly to the top of the palace," Nila instructed, her face still as impassive as ever. "Then return."

Slowly, Kym turned to face the Wadita, trying not to wobble around too much. She didn't care what Nila said—this was nothing like swimming in the water. Underwater, drifting around while her hair floated around her made sense. But here, out in the air, it just felt all wrong. The air felt thick, pushing her body this way and that. It was the opposite of how she'd felt when she learned to use magic underwater for the first time.

Kym focused her energy on herself, staring up at Wadita's many towers. She soared upward, her hair whipping behind her. The sound of waves crashing on the beach lessened, replaced by rushing wind. She wasn't a fan of the sound. She preferred the dull, peaceful quiet of being underwater.

Kym tried to stop when she reached the tallest tower, but her momentum carried her forward. She drifted several feet past the tower before eventually stopping. Kym had never been this high before, having never visited Wadita's tallest towers. From here, the sea stretched on for an eternity, shimmering in the light from the now clearing sky. It was just perfect.

Kym drifted around. Wadita's front drive stretched for miles, disappearing into the horizon. Squinting her eyes against the morning light, she watched several tiny specks grow larger as they sped down the wide lane. Kym glided forward, watching the brightly colored objects grow bigger by the second. Carriages.

Kym spun around and flew headfirst to the ground. She flipped around a second too late, and her feet slammed into the soft beach. Sand sprayed in every direction, even onto Nila's shimmering blue dress.

"Kymbralyn! Explain this."

"Carriages," Kym said, righting herself. "I saw carriages coming."

"Training is over," Nila said flatly. She walked around Kym and started making her way back up to the palace.

"What?" Kym called after her. She'd only practiced with the charm a couple of times. How could training be over?

"I must attend our guests and my fellow Rulers. I will not see you until the Third Trial. I want you to have dinner in your room this evening. Rest well, and prepare yourself. I put my faith in you, Kymbralyn. Remember the consequences if you fail me."

Kym stopped dead in her tracks as Nila continued inside. The warm excitement she'd felt the past twenty-four hours vanished, replaced by icy dread. She'd completely forgotten about her mom. Learning to use the charm had driven everything else from her mind. How could she be so thoughtless? She wasn't practicing with the charm because it was fun. She needed to know how to use it. It may be the only thing keeping her mom safe.

Kym found the entrance hall packed with people. Servants dressed in grey carried trunks into one of the rooms on the ground floor, directed by the Wadita servants. Kym stayed where she was, not daring to step into the madness in front of her. If she could just go up to her room before anyone saw her. But there was a problem with that plan. The door to the bedchambers was on the other side of the hall, through the mass of running servants.

"Hey! Kym!"

Kym, so focused on the servants, hadn't noticed the other people standing off to the side. Tomark, his long, wavy hair tied in a bun on the top of his head, and Baeka, the other extremely tall Air Favored, stood awkwardly beside the front doors. Tomark's hand was in the air, and even though he was on the other side of the room, Kym could see the soft smile on his lips. She waved back, stepping toward him while he did the same. She couldn't stop the smile spreading across her lips.

"Hey," Kym said when they met in the middle of the hall.

"So," Tomark said, his head slowly turning in every direction, "this is Wadita? Doesn't look like a prison to me."

"Give it time," Kym smiled, warmth spreading through her limbs. "You'll see."

"Can I?"

"Can you what?" Kym asked.

"See it. Can you show me around?"

Kym stared at him. Why did he want her to show him around Wadita? It was just like all the other palaces. There wasn't anything special or exciting about it. She could show him her bedchamber, but how would that look? For one thing, Veronica and Isabel would literally kick him out if they found him in there. But Nila also said she wanted Kym in her room, most likely to stop this very thing from happening.

"What's there to see?" Kym finally asked. "Wadita is just like Alfonburg, and all the other palaces."

"Those palaces aren't right by the beach," Tomark countered.

Kym hadn't expected that. Did he really want to see the beach? It wasn't that exciting. Rocks, sand, and the occasional pod of dolphins. There wasn't that much to be excited about. Kym couldn't remember the last time she went down to the beach to relax. She only went there now for training, which happened on rare occasions.

"C'mon, Kym," Tomark said, his green eyes wide with excitement. "Let's go before the servants stop us."

"Fine," Kym shrugged.

She turned and led Tomark back out to the garden. It looked just the same as it had when she left it five minutes before. Kym stopped at the garden wall, leaning against it and letting the warmth seep into her arms. Tomark stood beside her, his eyes wide as he leaned over the wall.

"It's incredible," he breathed.

"I guess," Kym sighed.

"You guess? This is the most beautiful thing I've ever seen."

"Really?" Kym turned to look at him. "Alfonburg is in the middle of a forest. That's way better than this."

"Sure, the forest is nice. But here… you can practically see the edge of the world. There's nothing blocking you in here."

Kym had never thought of that. She'd gotten so used to Wadita since she arrived. Now, everything seemed normal to her. But hadn't she felt the same way Tomark did when she first came here? She'd never seen the ocean before, and seeing it for the first time, how endless it was, took her breath away. How could she have forgotten that? How had her life at Wadita become so normal?

"You okay?" Tomark asked as Kym remained silent.

"Hum? Oh, yeah. I'm fine," she said quickly, shaking her head.

"You sure?" Tomark looked at Kym. His green eyes narrowed,

and there were several lines across his forehead. "You seem a little off…"

"I'm fine," Kym assured him. "I'm just tired. Nila's been putting me through the wringer getting me used to the water charm."

"Stailin's been the same," Tomark said. "He had me up two hours before sunrise today to train before we came here."

"Miss Kym!"

Veronica's voice cut through the air like a whip. Kym jumped and turned around to see her hurrying across the garden. Her face was the sternest Kym had ever seen it. Her muscles tensed as Veronica closed the space between them with a few strides. What could she have possibly done this time?

"Yes, Veronica?"

"Lady Nila requests you remain in your chambers for the rest of the day. You need rest before the Third Trial. You really must come with…"

Veronica trailed off, her eyes raking over Tomark. Kym bit her lip. What was Veronica going to do? Tell her off? Attack Tomark? Both were equally possible.

"Well," Veronica said, her tone suddenly much softer. "Hello, Mister Tomark. Miss Kym, I'll see you inside in a moment."

Veronica backed away, and Kym wanted to hide her face in her hands. What did she think was going on out here? It wasn't like Kym and Tomark were up to anything. They were just talking. And why didn't Veronica tell her off? She'd scolded Kym for far less than ignoring Nila's instructions.

"So…" Kym sighed heavily, "I'd better go."

"Really?" Tomark smiled. "Just like that?"

"Just like that," Kym laughed. "Getting on my maids' bad side is the very last thing I want to do."

"Can I come?"

"Tomark!"

"Kym, c'mon. What'll happen?"

"My maids would kick you out in three seconds flat," Kym said confidently.

"I bet I can take them," Tomark smiled. "And since when did you follow the rules anyway?"

Kym wanted to say 'since Nila threatened my mother,' but she bit her tongue. The warmth inside her fading, she decided it was best to ignore Tomark's question. "I doubt it. They're former Protectorate. They'd kick both our butts, and we'd never be able to stop them."

Kym hurried inside, leaving Tomark by the garden wall before he could say another word. Her smile fell with every step she took. What would be so wrong with him coming to her room? It wasn't like other people never visited after all. She'd rather him be there than Lance any day.

Veronica stood waiting for her in the entrance hall, which was now full of more servants carrying trunks and shouting at one another. Kym expected Veronica to say something, but luckily, she remained silent as they walked up to Kym's bedchamber.

"Oh, good. You found her at last," Isabel said happily when Kym finally walked into her room. "Where were you, Blessed One?"

Blessed One? Kym couldn't remember the last time her maids called her that. They knew how much she didn't like it. That's when she saw the two Protectorate standing on the other side of the room. Kym stopped dead in her tracks. Her hands balled into fists, shaking at her sides as her face grew hot. Why were they even in her room? They never went into her bedroom at the other palaces.

"Where were you, Blessed One?" Pro Hayden repeated Isabel's question, stepping forward.

"She was taking some air in the garden," Veronica snapped, sounding very unlike herself.

Pro Hayden opened his mouth to speak, but Isabel was quicker, "We must bathe Miss Kym. Pro Hayden, you and your fellow are no longer needed here tonight. Leave. Now."

Pro Hayden looked like he wanted to object. No doubt his

orders were to stay with Kym no matter what. But was it worth getting his butt kicked by Kym's maids again? Apparently not, because he and his partner backed silently out of the room. Kym looked at Veronica and Isabel, trying to catch their gazes, but they were already making themselves busy getting Kym's room ready for the evening. What was going on with them? Why were Veronica and Isabel clearly defying Nila's instructions to the Protectorate?

"There," Veronica said, closing the door behind the Pros. "Now you can relax in peace."

CHAPTER NINETEEN

THE
THIRD TRIAL

"MISS KYM, YOU NEED TO GET UP!"

Kym's eyes snapped open, and she sat up so quickly the world spun around her. Veronica and Isabel loomed out of the darkness, their heads wobbling branches in the wind. Panic ran through Kym like electricity, rooting her to the spot. What was going on? Why was Veronica's voice trembling like that? Immediately, she assumed the worst. Was her mother alright?

"Quickly, Miss Kym!" Isabel said urgently.

Isabel grabbed one of Kym's hands and pulled so forcefully Kym was sure her arm would pop out of its socket. She steered Kym to the door, Veronica beside them, a lit candle in her hand. Something was seriously wrong. Veronica and Isabel would never let Kym leave her bedchamber in only her nightdress.

Kym followed her maids down so many passages, stairwells, and doorways she couldn't tell where they were. Neither Veronica nor Isabel said a word, half running, half walking through the dark that Veronica's candle barely made a dent in. Sweat beaded up on Kym's forehead as her pulse quickened. Where were they taking her?

Isabel opened what must have been the seventh door, and light spilled into the dark hall. Hushed voices floated into the corridor, echoing off the vast walls. Kym looked from Veronica to Isabel and saw her confusion looking back at her. Her sense of dread mounting, Kym stepped inside on trembling legs. Favored dressed in their nightclothes stood around the room. Most had their arms folded awkwardly across their bodies, while others looked half asleep.

What were they all doing here in the middle of the night? Kym, her mind racing, gazed at the scene before her. Ashlyn was on the other side of the room. Kat, her arms behind her head, stood only a few feet away. And they weren't the only people Kym recognized. Amber, Lennax, Tomark, Baeka, Xander, Lance, and Jazin were there. Kym's panic melted away. This must have something to do with the trial.

A door at the other end of the room opened, and Nila, Zara, and Melana glided inside. A white-togaed servant hurried in behind them, a small wooden chest in his arms. He looked oddly small standing behind the unnaturally tall Rulers, his eyes wide as he stared around the room. Clearly, he had no idea why he was there, and Kym shared in his confusion. Why would the Rulers bring a servant here?

"The Third Trial of the Calling will begin in a few moments," Nila said, smiling blankly. "You are to compete as individuals, and combat between the Prized is now permitted. For this Trial, each Prized will receive a sash."

Nila waved her hand. The servant stepped forward, opening his wooden chest. He walked around the edge of the room, handing long, shimmering pieces of cloth to the other servants. Veronica stepped forward, tying Kym's around her waist, while the other servants did the same. Kym looked at Nila, whose pale eyes were wide with excitement. Kym's muscles turned to stone as her throat closed up. They were starting the trial now? Before the first two, they'd had time to prepare, were given clothes, and waited hours for them to begin. Why was this one happening so quickly?

"Your objective is to collect sashes from the other Prized. The Prized with the most sashes in their possession at the end of the trial will be the winner. Losing your sash will result in your removal from the trial."

Zara stepped forward, invoked her white Marks, and swept her hand in front of her. The sash around Kym's waist shone pure white, then faded back to its regular orange.

"The sashes," Nila continued, "are bound to your person. They cannot fall off or be ripped away by anyone but you. Use magic to subdue your opponent, but remove the sash with your hands. Lady Zara."

Zara raised her hands again and flicked her wrists more aggressively than she'd done moments before. Kym gasped, bending over in pain, as did many of the other Prized around her. Her blood burned through her veins in an instant. Then, the pain faded. Panting, Kym examined her forearms. They looked perfectly normal. What did Zara do to them?

"Your magic," Nila continued as if the Prized hadn't just doubled over in pain, "will be available to you for five minutes each hour. The five-minute period will fall during different times every hour. May the worthy among you prove yourselves to the gods. Lady Melana."

Melana stepped forward and lazily waved her hand. Darkness filled Kym's eyes, and the floor beneath her feet trembled. Kym reached down and grabbed a fistful of her sash with trembling fingers. She exhaled, and continued until there was no air left in her lungs.

How was she supposed to get through this Trial when she only had her magic for five minutes every hour? There was no way she could take any of the others without her magic. But that was it. She wasn't the only one who'd be magicless. The others would be too.

The unmistakable sound of crashing water filled Kym's ears. Light bloomed in her eyes, the ground stopped rumbling, and warm air, much warmer than it should have been in early spring, swirled around her. Kym lifted her hand to her eyes, shielding her face from the sudden, intense light. Why was it so bright? Wasn't it the middle of the night?

A bright yellow bolt streaked so close to Kym's face she felt the heat radiating from it. She dove to the side, flattening her body against the soft sand, her arms covering her head. Multicolored flashes filled the air, accompanied by cries of pain as attacks reached their targets. Every thought fled Kym's mind as bodies thudded to the ground around her. She needed to get out of there.

Kym invoked her Marks, and energy surged through her from the water charm. She rose into the air, darting from side to side as attacks exploded around her. A bright red bolt streaked through the air in front of Kym. She held her hands out in front of her, and the bolt collided with her hastily made shield. It stopped the bolt, but disintegrated in a flash of blue light.

Kym didn't wait to see who attacked her. She zigzagged through the chaos, narrowly avoiding the oncoming attacks as the battle raged on. She moved around so much she didn't even know how many attackers there were. This wasn't going to work. She needed to get out of the range of the attacks.

Kym turned to the bright blue sky and glided up as fast as she could. The sounds of battle faded, and the world stopped spinning around her. When she'd reached a reasonable height, Kym slowed herself down. At least this high up, she was safe from attacks.

Something moving very fast slammed into Kym. She rolled through the air, her arms and legs flailing around, trying to right herself. Pain radiated from the middle of her back, and somewhere around her, she heard a rush of wind. Kym swung her arm in the direction of the sound, her water swipe soaring through the air. Maybe she'd get lucky and hit whatever it was.

"Hey!" a familiar voice called. "Watch it!"

Kym looked around, her arms outstretched, trying to steady herself. Tomark hovered a few feet in front of her, his wavy hair flying wildly around his head. He had one arm held up while the other massaged his shoulder. Every time his hand moved, he grimaced with pain.

"You didn't have to slam into me!" Kym sighed, relief spreading through her as she rubbed the sore spot on her back.

"Then don't fly like an idiot," Tomark smiled back. "Since when can Water Favored fly, anyway?"

Kym tapped the glowing water charm around her neck.

"Oh," Tomark said, nodding his head. "That explains your lack of skill."

A massive crash below them sent a shock wave through Kym's

body. She drifted around, looking for the source of the noise. A tiny speck dressed in green was fighting one of the Light Prized directly below them. Several car-sized boulders littered the ground, blocking most of the Light Favored's yellow blasts and bolts. One of the light bolts found its way between the boulders, and Kat sank right into the sandy earth.

Kym looked behind the Light Favored, who didn't know Kat's style like Kym did. Kat rose silently out of the earth right behind him, bright green bolts in her hands. There was a flash of green, and he fell before he could turn around. Kat stepped forward to retrieve the sash from around his waist, unaware of the massive girl running toward her.

Kym dove downward, reaching the ocean in seconds. She flipped around and landed with a splash in the knee-high surf. She directed her hand at the waves and whipped her arm at the running Baeka. A jet of water as thick as a tree trunk shot forward, hitting Baeka in the back. She flew forward ten feet and slammed into a tree at the edge of the sandy beach.

Kym ran over to her, rushing right past a stunned-looking Kat, who was still on her knees next to the Light Favored. Kym knelt beside the feebly stirring Baeka. Her hands shaking slightly, Kym fumbled with the sash for several seconds before pulling it free.

She'd never attacked anyone like that before. It felt, wrong somehow. Was Baeka alight? Kym shook her head. What was she doing? She wasn't going to win if she wasn't willing to get her hands a little dirty.

"I could've handled that," Kat's voice said from a few feet away.

"Sure you could've," Kym said, tying her new sash around her waist.

The temperature around them skyrocketed. Kym spun around, blood pounding in her ears. Amber was standing in the middle of a ring of fire. Three other Favored stood outside the circle, trying to throw attacks at Amber, but every time their attacks reached the ring of fire, the flames grew and glowed, stopping the attacks dead in their tracks.

Inside the circle, Amber held her hands next to her chest, then pushed them out. The ring of fire exploded like a bomb. Flames flew out in every direction, knocking back the three Favored attacking her. But the flames didn't stop there. They turned in the air, flying toward the closest targets, which included Kym.

Kym rose into the air and flew into the trees, her heart pounding in her ears. She heard the flicker of flame behind her and knew Amber's fire was gaining on her. She needed to go faster. But the mixture of palm, and vine-draped trees grew too close together. Kym slowed down, trying to maneuver between them. Desperate, she looked up. Could she get out of the trees and fly above them? No. The branches were just as close together as everything else, and Amber's fire was inches from her.

Fiery hot pain coursed through Kym's body. She clutched her arms, curling into a ball as she crashed to the ground. Luckily, she'd only been about four feet in the air, and the ground was oddly soft, so the fall didn't hurt nearly as much as the pain inside her. It was like her insides were being burned away. Then, the pain subsided, leaving Kym feeling dull and empty inside.

Tentatively, she stood up. She held her hand out in front of her. Her Marks were gone. She imagined a ball of water floating above her fingers, but nothing happened. Kym sighed. She figured it wouldn't work, but it was worth checking all the same. Their first five minutes with magic were over.

Kym turned around, expecting to see the forest ablaze with Amber's fire. The green vines, mossy ground, and smooth trunks were all completely untouched. There was nothing there. Not even the faintest trace of ash or smoke. But why? Where had it all gone? Then it hit her. Amber's fire was magical, and with her magic blocked like everyone else's, there was nothing to keep the fire going.

Kym doubled over, her hands on her knees, panting. Sweat poured down her face, but she didn't feel tired or drained. Was it

Amber's fire or the Rulers making it so hot? It didn't help that the air felt as thick as soup, either.

A branch snapped somewhere close by. Kym spun around, looking for the source of the sound. She couldn't stay here. If she could find a place to lay low until she got her magic back, she'd stand a chance.

Kym started jogging in the same direction she'd been flying. She'd be moving away from the beach, and since that was where most of the Prized were, she didn't mind. Something small and green appeared in front of her. Kym collided with it, knocked her feet out from under herself and fell back. She slammed to the ground, and the air vanished from her lungs. Why did she keep running into things?

"What the Nothingness," a harsh voice demanded. "Watch where you're goin' why don'tcha?"

"I could barely see you," Kym wheezed, pushing herself up onto her elbows. "You're a tiny person, dressed in green, running through a bright green jungle."

"Hey, I'm vertically challenged," Kat groaned.

Kym sat up, rubbing the spot on her shoulder where she'd collided with Kat. "What'd you hit me with?"

"My head," Kat said bluntly, her palms pressed against her forehead. "Not my best move."

Kym stood, immediately ready to sit beside Kat. But her eyes locked on the two sashes around Kat's waist. How could she sit beside Kat without her taking her sashes? Kat liked to win, and she wouldn't hesitate to take Kym's sashes if it meant winning. But would she, if she knew why Kym was really there? Kym looked up. Kat was eyeing her own sashes. Maybe they should stay a little ways apart.

"Do you know how many got eliminated?" Kym asked, trying her best to slide back from Kat without her noticing.

"Five," Kat shrugged. "You and I took one each, and Amber got at least three with that explosion of hers."

"At least three?"

"Yup. Everyone booked it to the forest when she let loose."

"Could we expect anything less from our Fire Princess?"

Kat snorted. "No. Setting the whole world on fire is her thing."

"She can't win this thing," Kym sighed, more to herself than to Kat.

"Hey, there are still two trials after this," Kat said defiantly. "Anything can happen between now and then."

"I wasn't even thinking about the whole Calling," Kym admitted. "It's this Trial. It's perfect for her."

For all of her talk about not liking to be the 'Fire Princess,' Amber really was putting on a show. She didn't break a sweat defeating three Favored at once. And like Kat said, setting things on fire was her go-to. No one could get close to her even if they wanted to. And now, she had the fire charm boosting her already-powerful magic.

Tomark burst out of the trees, his dark, wavy hair flying in every direction. Sweat poured down his face, and Kym noticed the edges of his silver shorts were singed and blackened. Kym relaxed, lowering her hands as she sat back on the ground. Kat, on the other hand, was on her feet, her hands balled into fists. Kym stared at Kat. She hadn't even noticed her stand up.

"What are you two doing?" Tomark asked tentatively.

"Well," Kat said, her hands relaxing, "Kym was just saying how none of us stand a chance against Amber."

"I was not," Kym said defensively.

"You so were."

"All I said was this kind of trial is right up Amber's skill set."

"What? Making people feel bad?" Tomark asked, smiling slightly.

"Haha," Kym said mockingly. "Overwhelming people. That's always been how she operates."

"I've gotta admit it, Kat, Kym's right," Tomark panted. "She's just too good at this kind of stuff."

Kat opened her mouth to retort, and her legs flew out from under her. Kym jumped back, watching as Kat crashed to the ground. What was happening? She looked at Tomark and saw her shock mirrored on his face.

"Get off me!"

Kat swung her leg around, and a deep voice cried out in pain. Someone must've grabbed Kat by the ankles. Kym tried to see who it was, but Kat flailed around too much. There was a scuffling sound, and Kym saw Kat's fist jab forward.

"What the Thed is your problem?" a deep, familiar voice demanded.

Kat stepped aside, panting, with a triumphant smile on her face. Kym looked at the ground, and her hands balled into fists. Lance had his hands cupped around his face, and streams of bright red blood trickled through the gaps in his fingers. He stared up at Kat, and Kym could see the fury in his eyes. But she didn't care. How'd he find them in the middle of a jungle? Why wouldn't he leave Kym alone?

"I fink you boke my bose," Lance said thickly.

"Good. That's what I was going for," Kat shrugged.

She bent down and started untying Lance's sash from his waist. He let go of his nose, reaching for Kat with blood-soaked hands. Kat elbowed him in the chest, and he fell back to the ground. Lance looked over at Kym, his eyes full of anger.

"Stop her!" he demanded as Kat pulled the sash from his waist.

"Why?" Kym asked. They barely tolerated each other. If the rolls were reversed…

Lance tried to sit up, but he slid into the earth, just like Kat had done countless times.

"What was that?" Tomark demanded, his mouth hanging open.

"What?" Kat asked, tying Lance's sash around her waist.

"You're brave as Kensrad. You just kicked the crap out of a guy who's two feet taller than you," Kym said.

"And…?"

"How?"

Kat rolled her eyes so intently Kym was surprised she didn't fall over.

"When little Miss Amber screamed at me when we were little, I learned how to take care of myself. And anyway, taking on the Masters is really easy. They all can't live without magic. They never expect you to punch them in the nose."

Of course, Kym knew what happened between Kat and Amber when they were little. Kat always said she'd forgiven Amber for what she did, but Amber's actions gave others permission to do the same to Kat. Too bad for them, Kym thought. She didn't want to be on the receiving end of one of Kat's fists.

"That's it!" Tomark said excitedly, his eyes wide.

"That's what?" Kym asked.

"That's how we eliminate Amber."

"You want to punch her in the nose?" Kat asked. "And you think *I'm* brave."

"No, not in the nose. It's like you said; the Masters have forgotten what it's like not to have magic. But Amber, she's never *not* had magic. If we were going to surprise her, it would be now."

Kym stared at Tomark. Of course, it was so obvious. Amber's magical knowledge was far deeper than even the Masters. Tomark was right; she'd never lived a day of her life without magic. If they could find her before they got their magic back, Kym had a chance of winning the trial.

"We should go. Now," Kym said.

"Like right now?" Kat asked.

"Yes. Tomark's right. This could be our only chance to beat her. I don't wanna wait 'til the next magic time has passed. She could wipe us all out at that time."

"It's been fifteen minutes, max, since we lost our magic," Tomark said. "If we could find her in the next thirty minutes."

"Kat?" Kym looked to Kat, who had her arms folded tightly across her chest. They couldn't do this without her.

"I'm in," she shrugged. "Let's go wrestle a Fire Princess."

They ran toward the beach, staying just out of each other's reach. Kym's whole body vibrated as she ran, her mind racing. She didn't even know if this plan of theirs would even work. And how would Amber take it? Would she be upset? Kym shook her head. She couldn't worry about hurting Amber's feelings. She had more important things to worry about.

It took them a while to find the beach. Kym hadn't realized how far she'd flown trying to outrun Amber's fire. Sweat poured down Kym's face when they reached the tree line, and her side felt like it was about to split open. Slowly, she peered around one of the smooth tree trunks. Amber sat propped on her elbows on the middle of the beach, her head tilted toward the sun. She wasn't even bothering to watch if anyone was approaching.

Kat stepped out from behind her tree but darted back a second later. Kym edged around the other side of her tree. Why wasn't Kat going after Amber? This was their chance. Jazin stood a few feet away from Amber, his eyes trained on the trees. Just like Tomark, Kym, and Kat, Jazin and Amber were working together.

"Well, now what do we do?" Tomark whispered.

"It's your plan, genius," Kat hissed.

"Could you just, I don't know," Kym said, thinking quickly, "knock him down on your way to Amber."

"You two could help," Kat said incredulously. "I can't do everything on my own."

"We'll help," Tomark nodded. "Get Jazin out of the way, and we'll take care of him."

Kat bounced on the balls of her feet. Kym closed her eyes, breathing deeply. Her body needed to stop shaking. They could do this. How hard could it be for the two of them to hold Jazin while Kat fought Amber? Maybe, if they got ahold of Jazin's sash, they could eliminate him too. This could be Kym's chance to finally beat him. She opened her eyes, her body trembling like a leaf in the wind.

Kat sprinted out onto the beach faster than Kym thought possible, barely making a sound. She slid to the ground, one leg stretched out in front of her. She kicked Jazin's legs out from under him, and he crumbled to the ground. Kat's slender leg whipped up in the air, then fell swiftly to where Jazin lay sprawled on the ground. Jazin's gasp of pain filled the air. Kat jumped up, and ran toward Amber.

"Hey, Amber! Can we talk?" Kat yelled conversationally. She leaped forward and tackled Amber around her middle.

"C'mon," Tomark said, darting out from behind his tree.

Kym hurried after him, running right for Jazin, who was staggering to his feet, clutching his stomach. She lunged forward, burying her face in the sand and wrapping her arms around Jazin's thin legs. He toppled over, falling face-first back into the soft sand. Jazin wriggled around, and his barefoot caught the underside of Kym's chin. She sprang back, pain radiating through her jaw as Tomark wrapped his arms around one of Jazin's. But that left Jazin with one free hand, which started clawing for Tomark's sash.

"No!"

Ignoring the pain in her face, Kym lunged forward. She grabbed Jazin's free hand and pulled, preventing him from using it. But Jazin was stronger than his slight frame led Kym to believe. Even with all her weight behind her, Jazin was slowly pulling his arm from Kym's grip.

"Get his sash," Tomark grunted.

"I'm kinda busy," Kym panted, fighting to keep hold of Jazin's arm. "You get it."

"What are you doing?" Jazin asked, his voice strained.

"Isn't it obvious?" Tomark asked.

"We're eliminating Amber," Kym panted. "Tomark," she added. Jazin's arm was nearly free.

Kym turned her head just in time to see Tomark let go of Jazin's other arm. He reached down, slipped his hand around Jazin's sash, and pulled. It slid weightlessly off him as Kym released his other arms. Jazin tried to snatch it back, but Kym shoved him hard in the chest. There was no way she was letting him get it back. He stumbled backward and fell into the sand, which gave way beneath him. He sank into the ground, eliminated from the trial.

"Good job," Kym panted, unable to stop herself from smiling. She'd finally done it. She'd beat Jazin.

"You too," Tomark said, wrapping Jazin's sash around his waist. "C'mon. Let's help Kat."

Kym turned to where she knew Kat and Amber must be and stopped dead in her tracks. Amber was lying flat on her back, one long leg stuck straight up in the air. Kat lay on Amber's airborne foot, her arms reaching down to try and snatch Amber's sash. Luckily for Amber, she was much taller than Kat. So, with Kat held high above Amber on her foot, Amber was able to swat Kat's hands away from her many sashes. Kym couldn't help but laugh.

"Just give me your sashes," Kat said irritably.

"No!" Amber said, swatting Kat's hands away.

"You're being stingy. You already won a trial. It's my turn."

"I want to win this one, too!"

"Um…" Kym didn't know what to do. She'd learned two critical lessons while fighting death demons with Amber and Kat: never let a death demon touch you, and never, ever, get between a fighting Amber and Kat.

"She…has that handled," Tomark said, clearly thinking along the same lines as Kym.

And Tomark was right. No matter how wildly Amber swung her arms, Kat inched closer to her sashes. Just another couple of seconds, and it would be over. Kym sighed, her body relaxing. They actually pulled it off. They'd finally beaten Amber at something.

A fiery arch burst from Amber's flailing hand, her red Marks twisting down her forearms. Kat's yell of pain rang out over the beach as she flew high into the air, landing with a thud in the sand. Amber staggered to her feet. She looked at Kym and Tomark, and the smile on Amber's face sent a shiver down Kym's spine.

"I win."

Amber snapped her fingers, and a bright red circle exploded from her fingertips. Kym didn't wait to see what Amber did next. She invoked her Marks and soared upward as fast as she could. A rushing sound behind her told Kym Tomark had done the same. She looked down. Flames covered the sand, and Amber was tying several sashes around her waist. Kym couldn't see Kat anywhere.

"C'mon," Kym hollered over the wind rushing around her. "We can take her."

"This isn't gonna end well."

Both she and Tomark flew back to the ground. Kym spun around, throwing bolt after bolt at Amber, but bright red flames rose to block every attack. Amber waved her arm, and the fire around her rose into the air. Terror coursed through Kym as she watched the swirling flames form into bolts, which lined up in front of Amber.

"Scatter!"

Kym didn't need Tomark to tell her twice. She darted off, focusing all of her energy on herself, zooming through the air as fast as she could. Kym looked over her shoulder. Amber's alignment blast ripped through the air, far larger than any Lance ever produced. But the blast wasn't alone. At least ten red bolts flew through the air, heading right for Kym and Tomark. She changed direction randomly, but the tracking bolts followed her every move.

Kym formed two bolts as the tracking bolts drew even closer to her. She spun around, throwing her attacks at the bolts pursuing her. The first missed, but the second hit the closest tracking bolt, which exploded in a magnificent display of red and blue light. Kym didn't have time to celebrate. The other four bolts were closing in on her.

Kym arched backward, soaring over the tracking bolts. She fired a blast, blowing through one more bolt as the other three drew even closer. She needed to stop attacking. If she didn't speed herself up, she'd be done for. But she needed to stop Amber's attacks as well.

Kym spun on the spot, her arms outstretched, and a glowing blue sphere formed around her. The first fire bolt exploded against the shield, and cracks spread through the sphere like spiderwebs. Kym fed more energy into the shield, and the cracks sealed themselves. The second bolt exploded against the dome, which shattered like blue glass around Kym. She turned, ready to fly away when the third bolt slammed into her chest.

Kym smashed into the crashing waves below with an almighty splash. Every part of her body ached, and she didn't know if she had the strength to move. Using all the energy she had left, Kym swung her arms forward. A gentle current swept her away, carrying her back to the beach.

Kym heard the sound of something splashing through the water. Hands, long and slender, slipped under her arms and pulled her from the water and onto the damp sand. Kym looked around, the world spinning around her. Three Ambers stood over Kym, wobbling slowly as they bent down over her.

"Kym? I'm sorry. I took it too far."

Anger bubbled up inside Kym. She took it too far? Kym couldn't think. She couldn't let Amber win. She needed to get her sashes. This was her chance. Kym awkwardly swung her hand around, and a feeble jet of water shot from her hand, hitting Amber in the chest. She staggered back, a look of shock on her face.

"What the Thed was that for?"

"You blasted me out of the sky," Kym groaned.

Amber reached down and started untying Kym's sashes, tears welling up in her narrow eyes. "I'm sorry."

She pulled the sashes from around Kym's waist. Kym reached up, her fingers brushing the soft fabric. She couldn't let them go. She had to hold on. But Amber was too fast. The ground beneath Kym gave way, and she fell into darkness.

CHAPTER TWENTY

NO LONGER ALONE

Kym's body felt strange, like it was slowly being stretched in every direction. But oddly, it didn't hurt. There was a dull throbbing in what used to be her back and left leg, but both were distant and detached. She tried looking around, but there was something wrong with her eyes. Everything appeared dark and dull. Where was she?

Kym's arms, chest, and back screamed in pain. Her left leg throbbed slightly and she couldn't even feel her right. Hurrying feet, hushed voices, and labored breathing assaulted her ears. Light flooded her eyes, obscuring her already-shaky vision.

She tried to sit up, but hands, gentle and small, pressed firmly on her shoulders, keeping her down. Her skin exploded at their touch, like every part of her body was being ripped apart. Voices, familiar voices, called out for assistance, but she couldn't place them. It didn't matter. All that mattered was Kym's body was being destroyed.

Someone new stepped into Kym's limited line of vision, their face shrouded in darkness. Intense, white light flooded Kym's blurry eyes, and tears slid down her cheeks. Calm warmth washed over her, easing some of the pain and leaving a dull thumping in her back and legs. Hands, not the gentle hands on her shoulders, pressed forcefully into the small of her back. Kym screamed as white hot fire bore into the spot. She tried to move, to escape the inferno, but she couldn't. The fiery pain faded, and her back and legs felt perfectly normal.

Slowly, Kym's vision and mind cleared. She was staring at a

vaulted blue ceiling. The gentle hands lifted her up and several pillows appeared behind her back. She was in the room she'd been in before the Third Trial started. Several beds had been added since then, and most were surrounded by servants. Zara walked away from Kym's to another bed across the room, flocked by several white-togaed servants. The green-clothed servants backed away as she approached. Kym tilted her head. Was that Kat? She couldn't tell.

"Oh, Miss," Isabel said, stepping into Kym's line of vision. "Thank Pheil you're alright."

"What happened?" Kym asked groggily.

"Don't you remember?" Veronica asked, stepping forward so Kym could see her.

"It's all fuzzy." Kym closed her eyes, trying to remember. "We were trying to get Amber's sash but…"

"Your plan didn't work," Veronica said sadly. "Your magic returned, and Amber overpowered you, Mister Tomark, and Miss Kat."

Slowly, it came back to her. Kat and Amber's ridiculous wrestling match. The exploding circle. Amber's tracking bolts blasting Kym out of the sky. Crashing to the ground. Anger bubbled up inside Kym like lava. What had Amber been thinking? Would Amber's inability to control herself get Kym eliminated?

"When you crashed on the beach, you broke your back and one of your legs," Isabel said.

"What?" Panic surged through Kym as she looked down at her leg. It looked perfectly fine.

"The break in your back prevented you from feeling the pain in your leg," Isabel continued. "Lady Zara finally got around to healing you."

Gingerly, Kym flexed her bare feet. They seemed to work fine. She ran her hand slowly over her lower back, down the spot where she'd felt Zara's fiery life energy heal her. But like her feet, it felt normal too. Kym swung her legs off the edge of the bed, standing as her maids tried to stop her. They needn't have bothered. Everything, from her legs to her back, felt fine.

"Is the trial over?" she asked. Aside from the few Prized she encountered, she had no idea what happened to the rest of them. She didn't even know how she did. Had she done well enough to keep her mother safe?

"It is," Veronica said. "Miss Amber and Miss Ashlyn were the only ones left after you, Mister Tomark, and Miss Kat were eliminated. Miss Amber beat Miss Ashlyn, but the battle took time."

It took Zara and her servants twenty minutes to treat everyone's injuries, all of which Kym would call severe. Most were covered in burns and cuts, and several had limbs sticking out at odd angles. Zara examined each Favored, whispering to her servants, who'd run off and return with several potted plants. Zara then pulled the life energy from the plants, reducing them to blackened dust, and forced the glowing white mist into their wounds while the Prized screamed.

Kym wandered around the room. She needed to find her friends. She saw Tomark first, sitting up in his bed on the other side of the room. He looked perfectly normal, although not much remained of his charred grey tank top. Kym's body relaxed as she ran to him. At least he was in one piece.

"Hey. You okay?"

"Yup," Tomark smiled, pulling on the new grey shirt his servant handed him. "Zara fixed me up. Amber's super blast thing blew me out of the sky. Apparently, I was burned pretty bad."

"Well," Kym smiled, "I can't tell the difference."

"Thanks," Tomark laughed, his wavy hair bouncing around his face. "How about you?"

"Amber messed me up, I guess," Kym said, unable to keep the anger from her voice. Why had she taken it so far?

"Well," Tomark said gently. "We did kinda ambush her. And you're fine now. Where's everyone else?"

They walked around, peering between servants, trying to find the others. They'd only made it halfway through the hall when the doors burst open. Silence fell over the room as the Rulers glided in, and the smile on James's usually emotionless face sent a shiver down Kym's spine. Of course he'd be ecstatic. Amber just won her second trial in a row.

"Before we reveal the results of the trial," Zara began, "I will give you an overview of what transpired. During the first five minutes, most of the Prized battled on the beach, while a few sought refuge in the surrounding jungle. Five Prized were eliminated; Light Favored Vespar, Air Favored Baeka, Light Favored Alva, Light Favored Jerark, and Fire Favored Kensrix. Water Favored Lance and Death Favored Jazin were eliminated while your magic was blocked.

"In the second magical span, two battles happened simultaneously; one on the beach, the other deep in the jungle. The beach battle resulted in the elimination of Earth Favored Katarein, Air Favored Tomark, and Water Favored Kymbralyn. In the jungle, Darkness Favored Xander and Earth Favored Lennax were also eliminated.

"The two remaining Prized battled once their magic was restored. The Light Favored, Ashlyn, fell at the hands of the Fire Favored, Amber, who emerged from the trial in possession of all the sashes. Thus, the clear winner of the Third Trial is the Prized of Heirraph, Amber."

The room erupted into polite applause. Kym saw Amber, her shimmering red nightdress torn in several places and missing a sizable piece down the left side, grin subtly as she inclined her head to the Rulers. Kym's hands balled into fists, and she turned rigid as stone. She knew she should be happy for Amber. But after what Amber did during the trial, Kym couldn't bring herself to do it. She needed to talk to her.

"Four Prized have been eliminated based on their performance in the Third Trial. They were the first Prized to have their sashes taken from them. Therefore, the Light Favored Vespar, Jerark, and Alva, and the Air Favored Baeka, all failed to answer the gods' call, and are unworthy of their glory."

The eliminated Prized left the hall with their servants, their clothes in tatters but otherwise unhurt. Kym looked around. There weren't that many Prized left. From the twenty four they'd started with, less than half of them remained. How long had it been since the First Trial? So much had happened since the Calling began. It seemed like a lifetime ago.

And as she looked around, something else occurred to Kym. Kat, Tomark, Amber, Xander, Ashlyn, and Jazin were all still in the Calling. She'd expected at least one of them to be eliminated at this point. With them making up the majority of the Prized, odds were some of them wouldn't make it through the Fourth Trial. Kym needed to make sure she did.

"The Fourth Trial," Zara said, calling Kym back to her surroundings, "will take place tomorrow afternoon at Solaris. You will depart first thing in the morning."

The Rulers left the hall, leaving Kym and the others alone with their servants. Kym's body, although healed, felt like lead. Why couldn't they wait a few days before the next trial? They'd gotten plenty of time to recover after the first two. Sure, the Third Trial started without warning, but Kym had thought that was part of the trial. She couldn't begin to imagine what the Fourth Trial would be.

Kym and Tomark found Kat and Xander standing together near the middle of the room. Kat's clothes were singed and burned, just like Kym's and Tomark's, but Xander's looked far worse. Little holes dotted his purple tank top and shorts, and there was a lot of dried blood running down his left leg.

"What happened?" Kym asked, nodding to his leg.

"That old Master with the earth arm," Xander huffed.

"Lennax?" Tomark asked, which Kym thought was unnecessary. Who else did they know who had an earth arm?

"Yup, he did this thing where he shot about a hundred tiny bolts at me all at once."

"Tiny?"

"They were like the size of marbles. They broke my shield and just kept on coming."

"He tried that on me too," Ashlyn said, joining them along with Amber and Jazin. "It seems to be his go-to move."

Ashlyn looked just as singed as Kym, Kat, and Tomark. Her red hair was coated with ash, and there was a great deal of it smudged across her face. But she didn't look nearly as bad as Amber. Her long dark hair, usually perfectly straight, was a tangled mess, and there was a lot of dried blood on her arms.

"What happened to you two?" Kat asked, apparently reading Kym's thoughts.

"We both got a little carried away," Amber said, uncharacteristically modest.

"Both?" Ashlyn blurted. She sounded upset. "I didn't trap you in a ball of fire!"

"You what?" Kym, Xander, and Tomark asked at the same time.

"She was moving so fast," Amber said defensively. "I couldn't get a clean shot."

"So the next logical thing was to wrap her in fire?" Kat asked dryly.

"I wanted to win. I apologized."

Amber's words brought Kym's anger exploding to the surface. It was just like what she did to Kym. Why did she have such a hard time seeing she was hurting her friends? She had to know what she was doing was wrong, didn't she?

"Sorry's not gonna cut it this time, Amber," Kym said harshly.

"She apologized," Jazin said, his eyes darting between Kym and Amber. "She knows she took things too far. We're all trying to show Princirum we deserve to be here. That our existence isn't a bad thing!"

"Jazin, you need to stop," Tomark said, and Kym was shocked to hear the sternness in his normally gentle voice. "This is bigger than you feeling the need to assert yourself."

"I'm not—"

"This isn't the first time Amber's pulled something like this. Once, she almost blew me and Kym off a cliff."

"That was one time," Amber said defensively.

"Fine, then explain everything that happened today. You took things way too far with me, Kym, Tomark, and Ashlyn. You blew me up, blasted Kym and Tomark out of the sky, and wrapped Ashlyn in fire!" Kat said hotly.

"It's a competition, Kat," Jazin said. He turned to face Kat, and Kym watched his pale face turn pink. "We're all fighting to win. You attacked me, remember?"

"I tripped you, and the others held you down until they got your sash. That's different."

"How?"

"Because we know where the line is!" Kym shouted angrily. "We weren't trying to hurt you. We know when we've taken things too far, Amber!"

"I…I said I was sorry!" Amber stammered, and Kym could see tears shining in her eyes. "We're all supposed to be trying to win this thing."

"You always say you're sorry, Amber! But we're friends. Doesn't that mean anything to you?"

"You know it does," Amber snapped, and Kym could see Amber's anger was starting to reach its tipping point. "You know what you all mean to me."

"Then act like it! I need to win this thing, Amber! I have to! But I'm not gonna walk over my friends to do it!"

Kym couldn't see straight. She had more at stake than any of them. If she didn't win the Calling, her mom could die. But she wasn't going to win by hurting her friends. There had to be a better way.

"You guys," Xander said, stepping between Kym and Amber. "Knock it off. This is crazy."

Kym stepped back, and her muscles tensed as she looked at Amber. She wiped away the tears clinging to her golden eyes, which stared unblinkingly at Kym. What was wrong with her—and all of them, for that matter? They'd never fought like this before.

"Everyone shut up," Kat said, her voice unnaturally stern. "This is dumb. We're not gonna shout at each other over nothing. She turned to look at Kym, who felt oddly empty inside. "Kym, go to your room. Relax. Take some space. Same goes for everybody."

"Kat's right," Tomark said. "We're all tired. What we need now is rest."

Happy for an excuse to leave, Kym walked out of the chamber, Veronica, Isabel, and two Protectorate guards joining her at the door. Her body shook with suppressed anger. All she wanted was to climb into bed and not think about Amber, or the Calling for the rest of her life.

The torch-lit entrance hall was packed with people; servants running this way and that, visiting priests, esteemed city officials, and Favored from every palace. Kym's anger turned to annoyance as her entourage half led, half dragged her through the mob. All bowed their heads to Kym as she passed, and some hurried up to her, the blue additions to their wardrobe clearly visible.

"You answer Reta's call!"

"Your waters will cleanse Princirum of death!"

"The Vanquisher of Water! Vanquish death!"

Kym's stomach churned as they pressed in on her, their arms outstretched, trying to touch some part of her. Luckily, Veronica and Isabel kept everyone at a reasonable distance as they hurried her across the room. The crowd burst into cheers of delight when she reached the bedchamber door. She glanced over her shoulder. Jazin stood in the hall, surrounded by a group of supporters, their black accessories twinkling.

"You show us a new path!"

"You answer Thed's call!"

Kym shook her head as she followed her maids up the stairs. There were more death supporters than after the Second Trial. They had to know death's growing power, which they were cheering for, was why people were getting sick. But they supported Jazin anyway. Did they really believe following death was the best thing for everyone? If Jazin won the Calling, what would it mean for Princirum? A shudder ran through Kym's spine. She didn't want to find out.

When Kym woke a few hours later, fiery afternoon light replaced the early morning glow that filled her room when she arrived. Several trays of food sat on the small table in the middle of Kym's sitting room. The smell of roses and lavender drifted in from the bathroom, where Kym heard her maids talking in hushed voices. Still slightly on edge, Kym climbed out of bed.

After a nice long soak, where she almost fell asleep three different times, Kym settled down to eat, happy to be confined to her bedchamber. The argument with Amber crept into her thoughts as she ate. In the light of a new day, she knew she'd handled it wrong. She shouldn't have let it turn into a screaming match, even if she'd been right. After all, Kym was fighting to save her mother's life, and she wasn't hurting her friends to do it. Maybe, after having it shouted at her, Amber would snap out of Fire Princess mode.

The sky outside slowly shifted from red to indigo. Kym yawned. Even after sleeping all day, she was ready to call it an early night. There was nothing like sleeping in her own bed. She hadn't realized how much she'd missed it. Veronica and Isabel bustled around the room, getting it ready for the evening, along with packing for the next four years.

"So far as we know, none of the other trials will be held here," Veronica said, running around the room with the oddest assortment of Kym's clothes.

"And when you make it to the Fifth Trial," Isabel assured Kym, her arms too full of Kym's clothes, "who knows when you'll return. It's always best to be prepared, my dear."

Kym walked over to the other side of the room, not daring to get in her maids' way. She pulled the heavy, blue drapes over the windows and balcony doors, rubbing the soft fabric between her fingers. On any other day, her maids would have been appalled to see her doing anything so ordinary. When was the last time she'd done something like this herself? She struggled to remember. How sad was that? She couldn't even remember the last time she shut the windows?

Something large swept past the balcony doors. Kym jumped

back, her heart pounding like a drum in her ears. What was it? It was too large to be any kind of bird. And besides, it was still too cold for birds to be out flying at this hour. Slowly, cautiously, Kym stepped toward the glass doors, her eyes raking the darkness, her body tense.

The dark shape zoomed by the door again, but this time, it did not fly off. It landed gracefully on the balcony, and Kym could just make out a lot of wavy brown hair in the combined light of the moon and the person's silvery Marks. Her mouth dropped open, her heart racing in her chest. What was Tomark doing on her balcony? How'd he even know which room was hers? How many other rooms did he peer into before finally finding hers? The thought brought a smile to Kym's lips.

"Miss Kym, that is not your job." Isabel's disapproving voice made Kym's heart race even faster.

She spun around, jerking the curtains closed, concealing Tomark. Had Isabel seen him? She couldn't have. Kym had stood in front of the doors the whole time. But if Isabel got any closer and readjusted the curtains, she'd definitely see something on the balcony that shouldn't be there.

"You know what?" Kym said, thinking fast. "I want to go to sleep. You two are free to go for the evening."

Veronica emerged from Kym's closet. "Are you sure, my dear?" she asked, joining Isabel and Kym by the balcony doors. "It's early, even for you."

"I'm sure," Kym nodded, trying her best to sound convincing. "I want to rest for the trial tomorrow. And you two have worked so hard," she added, and she actually meant it. "If we're not coming back until the Calling is over, you deserve a break too. Take the night to relax. I insist."

Veronica and Isabel glanced sideways at each other. Kym held her breath, waiting for them to say she needed their help to pack. They knew she didn't like having them there when it wasn't necessary, even though their definitions of necessary differed drastically.

But they smiled, bowed their heads, and backed out of the room without another word.

Kym sighed, turned around, flung the drapes carelessly aside, and opened the balcony doors. Tomark had his back pressed against the ornate railing, his arms folded loosely across his chest. He smiled at Kym, who couldn't help but smile back, warmth spreading through her like fire. He looked so cool and relaxed. But that didn't explain what he was doing on her balcony.

"What are you doing here?" she asked, laughing slightly.

"I wanted to talk," Tomark said seriously. His tone was so at odds with his body language it made Kym feel uneasy.

"Okay," she said slowly. What did he need to talk to her about so badly it couldn't wait until morning. "What's up?"

"Not here."

Tomark's silver Marks burst into life on his arms, and he shot upward. Kym stared after him. What was going on? First he sneaks onto her balcony, and then he wants her to run off with him? Aside from it coming completely out of nowhere, if they got caught, they'd both be in serious trouble. Nila had so many Protectorate at Wadita now. They were bound to spot two flying teenagers. But Tomark never did anything without thinking it through, so what was his plan? She invoked her Marks and the water charm, and drifted up after him.

Kym glided upward, and silently thanked Wadita's servants for their punctuality. All of the windows she passed were shut and curtained, shielding Kym and Tomark from prying eyes. She followed behind Tomark, who flew to the very top of Wadita. He hovered over the tallest tower, giving Kym time to catch up. She stopped beside him, bobbing slightly up and down while Tomark stayed right where he was. Slowly, without speaking, they landed on the top of the tower.

"What are we doing up here?" Kym whispered, though she doubted anyone could hear them. "If someone sees—"

"No one's gonna see us," Tomark said gently, sitting down on the tower's flat roof. "And weren't you the one convincing me to sneak out not too long ago?"

Kym sat down next to Tomark. It was true that she'd convinced him, and Amber, to sneak out on the weekends so they could escape the palaces. But that was before the Rulers had them watched day and night. That was when the Rulers actually liked Kym and the others. They'd sit around a fire Amber made, complaining loudly about the Rulers while they tried to figure out what they were up to. It seemed like a lifetime ago.

"A lot's changed since then."

"I know," Tomark nodded. "That's what I wanted to talk to you about."

"What?"

"Downstairs, after the trial, you didn't seem like yourself. The way you yelled at Amber—"

"I've yelled at Amber before," Kym cut across him, her insides turning icy. Were they really talking about this? "Back when we fought the squid demon. Remember? She nearly blew up the cliff we were standing on. And every other time she's taken things too far."

"I know," Tomark said calmly. "But today, you were on a whole other level, and you took it out on Amber."

"I didn't," Kym said feebly.

"Kym, we've all seen it. Ever since the Calling started you been acting like a different person. I know it's a lot of pressure. It's a big thing, what we're trying to do. The winner could do so much good for a lot of different people. It's just as important as what we did as Vanquishers. But you're letting that Lance guy put himself all over you when you clearly don't like him, and Kat said you shut her out the last time you two talked."

"When'd you talk to Kat?" Kym said defensively.

"She had Ashlyn bring them both into my room earlier. They're worried about you, but you won't talk to them. I said I'd try."

"So, you've been talking about me?"

"We're worried about you," Tomark repeated. He turned to face

Kym and put one of his hands on top of hers, making her skin tingle. "Something's going on, but you're not telling us. How can we help you if you shut us out? We're your friends, Kym. We want to help you, but you need to tell us what's going on."

Kym stared into Tomark's dark green eyes. She knew he wanted to help; he always did. He was even in the Calling so he could try and help people he didn't even know. But it wasn't his job to save her mother. It was hers. She had to win the Calling, something she never wanted to be a part of in the first place. There was nothing he could do to help her, so what was the point in telling him? Somewhere deep inside Kym's mind, a tiny voice answered back.

You can't do this alone.

"I just…do you ever feel like you don't know what we're doing anymore?"

"Kym, you know I have," Tomark said calmly. "We've all struggled with being Favored. But this, it's something different. What is it? You know you can tell me."

"I…" Kym stopped herself before she said any more. She couldn't tell him. She looked into Tomark's kind face, and the words poured from her mouth before she could stop them. "Nila threatened my mom."

"What?" Tomark snapped, anger flashing across his normally kind face. "Why would she do that?"

"To make me…" Kym gasped, tears welling up in her eyes. Each word was like a knife in her heart. To say these things out loud, to Tomark, made them real somehow.

"To make you what?"

"Be in the Calling. I didn't want to do it, and when she picked me as a Prized, I told her. She said she's been having doctors care for my mom all this time, and if I don't win, she'll send the doctors away. But…I'm not like Amber. I can't plow over my friends, even to save my mom. There has to be…"

Kym lapsed into silence, tears sliding down her face. Thankfully, Tomark didn't try and break it. He merely slid a few inches closer to Kym, and wrapped his arms gently around her shoulders.

All the tension and pressure building inside her over the past several months melted away, replaced by a warmth beating deep inside her chest. Here, in this moment, after weeks of fighting to save her mom, she wasn't alone.

Slowly, Tomark's arms fell from Kym's shoulders. She smiled up at him, and was happy to see him smiling back. He put his hand on her face, and gently brushed away the tears from her cheek. She pulled back, pressing the heels of her palms into her eyes. Tomark stood up, offering her his hand as he smiled down at her. She took it, and he pulled her to her feet.

"C'mon," Tomark said gently, jerking his head to the edge of the tower. "We'd better get back."

Kym's maids woke her early the next morning. With no clothes provided for the Fourth Trial, Veronica and Isabel decided Kym should be prepared for anything. They dressed her in some of her training clothes, along with a light cloak to keep her warm on the journey to Solaris. Kym left her maids in her room; they still had more packing to do since she dismissed them early the night before.

Black, purple, yellow, green, blue, red, and silver carriages all sat on the graveled drive, pairs of Protectorate waiting by their open doors. Kym climbed into the only blue one and found Lance already inside. She took the seat opposite him as the carriage lurched forward, ignoring his annoyed expression. She didn't see why he was so upset. Nila never told them when they were leaving. But, much to her surprise, Lance didn't say a word the whole ride to Solaris.

The sun was high when they reached the glittering yellow palace, nestled in rolling green fields. Kym climbed out of the carriage, sweat glistening on her brow as she threw her cloak over her arms. It was warmer than it had been in months. Kym closed her eyes, feeling the warmth spread through her face.

A servant dressed in yellow led Kym, Lance, and their Pros inside. Their room on the ground floor was identical to the one at Terradon and Alfonburg, down to the benches surrounding the shallow pool. Kym followed Lance onto the surface of the water, making several water orbs float around her one by one. The servant returned before she'd made five.

"Follow me please, Master and Miss."

Lance followed the servant out into the entrance hall, Kym a few feet behind him. The servant led them through another door, where most of the other Prized were already waiting. Like Kym, they were dressed in training clothes, and the usual chatter that preceded the first three trials was absent. It didn't take long for the other Prized to arrive, since only ten of them remained.

The doors to the room opened, and Zara, Philip, Evanna, and Melana drifted inside. Zara raised her hand, calling for silence, which Kym felt was unnecessary. Everyone stared at the Rulers, and tension coursed through the air like electricity. Kym took several breaths, trying to calm her shaking body.

"For the Fourth Trial," Philip said coolly, "combat between the Prized is permitted."

"For this Trial, you must retrieve what has been hidden and return it to the starting point undamaged," Evanna said cryptically.

"Your magic," Zara continued, not stopping as the Prized exchanged confused looks, "will be limited once again. Until you locate what has been hidden, you will only have access to basic elemental manipulation."

Zara waved her hand through the air. The insides of Kym's arms burned, but it wasn't the same feeling she'd experienced during the Third Trial; that had been like fire in her veins. This felt more like boiling water. At least she wasn't starting the trial with nothing.

"You will gain full access to your magic once you have found what is hidden," Zara continued. "Lady Melana."

Melana raised her hands, and darkness seeped into Kym's vision for what felt like the hundredth time. She'd become so used to it at this point that it didn't even unsettle her. She took a deep breath, trying to clear her mind, but it was too full of questions. She needed to find something, but the Rulers hadn't said what they were looking for. But how could Kym find it if she didn't know what *it* was? During the other trials, the rules had been so specific. For the first time, it really felt like she was going in blind.

The floor beneath Kym's feet gave way, and her stomach lurched as she hurtled downward and forward at the same time. She squeezed her mouth shut, breathing deeply through her nose, the wind whistling in her ears. The ground slammed to a stop, and she staggered forward several steps. Then, slowly, light crept in on the edges of Kym's vision.

C H A P T E R   T W E N T Y - O N E

T H E
F O U R T H   T R I A L

Sweat poured thick and fast down Kym's back. Her eyes darted from side to side. Walls of grey, brown, and black rock rose up every way she looked, and a bright yellow sun shone over her head. Where was she? No trees. No grass. No flowers. No bright colors of any kind. She was somewhere in the middle of the mountains.

Kym moved without thinking. She ran forward, not bothering to look at the others, her feet sliding slightly on the gravely ground. She waved her arms wildly, desperate to not fall over, and kept going. Sounds of battle rose behind her, but they differed from the one she'd grown accustomed to. Gone were the high-pitched whirs and flashes of energy; there were only crashes, booms, and screams.

Kym invoked her Marks and jumped into the air. She crashed to the ground, a cloud of dust billowing around her. She pushed herself back up, pain radiating from her hands and knees. Why hadn't it worked? Swimming was one of the earliest magical skills she'd learned. Wasn't she manipulating the water around her when she swam? Even with her magic limited, she should still be able to swim in the air, especially with the water charm. Apparently, the Rulers thought otherwise. Seething, she stood up and continued on foot.

Kym held her hand out as she ran and imagined a ball of water floating above it. She closed her eyes, and energy pulsed through her from the water charm. She opened her eyes a fraction. A small ball of water floated above her fingers. Kym sighed. At least she didn't have to waste time trying to find water somewhere in these mountains.

Kym walked on, the hot sun beating down on her. Sweat drenched her clothes after five minutes, and her breathing grew more labored as she wound her way through the rocky paths. She made grape-sized balls of water, which she sent into her mouth every few steps. She couldn't control the temperature, but the luke-warm water was better than nothing. At least she wouldn't dehydrate while she wandered around aimlessly, looking for Pheil knew what.

Kym's eyes moved constantly, searching for something, anything, that could be what she was looking for. All she could see was rocks and dirt, which all fit perfectly in her current environment. The Rulers hadn't told them what they were looking for, so whatever they were supposed to find must be obvious, at least to the Rulers. But nothing seemed out of place.

Kym's frustration mounted as she turned down another empty canyon path. Would it have killed the Rulers to tell the Prized what they were supposed to find? Unless having them wander around like idiots was part of the trial, they could have given them a little more to go on than "find what was hidden." It wouldn't have been difficult. But Kym knew the Rulers would never give them clear instructions. They liked knowing more than everyone.

Heat rose around Kym in waves. The air popped and cracked around her as bright orange flames encircled her. Kym spun around. Kensrix stood a few yards from her, his dark hair flying around his head. A burn covered his right arm, and his red Marks were glowing.

"Ahh!"

Kym dove to the side, her heart pounding in her ears. Kensrix's jet of flame soared through the air, scorching the place she'd stood moments before. She swung her arm, and a jet of water whipped through the air. It slammed into Kensrix's chest, pushing him back and leaving him drenched. Frantically, Kym threw another stream of water at his feet, hoping to trip him up.

Kym didn't wait to see if it worked. She shot a hose-like jet of water at the fire behind her, clearing a path in the wall of flame. She sprinted through the gap, not bothering to look behind her, her heart pounding like a drum in her chest. If Kensrix was still behind her, she'd know soon enough. Several minutes passed, and all Kym could hear was the sound of her own feet. She chanced a glance over her shoulder. The rocky path behind her was deserted.

She slowed down, her heart rate returning to normal as she looked around. She had no idea where she was or how to get back to the starting point once she found whatever she was supposed to find. The dark peaks around her slowly shifted to vast, tan arches. It was like two different mountain ranges collided, and she was walking through the resulting mess. The smooth, tan arches grew larger the farther Kym looked, with the biggest one sitting at least a fifteen-minute walk away.

Kym sighed. She still had no idea what she was doing, and going to the arch seemed as good a plan as any. She might as well check it out. At least now, she was doing something productive. It was better than wandering around and waiting for something to happen or for someone to attack her.

Her legs shook violently when she reached the arch. She hadn't realized how steep the incline was. Every breath she took sent a sharp pain running through her side, and no matter how much water she made for herself, she always had room for more. If there wasn't something up at the arch, she'd have wasted so much time and energy on nothing.

The large arch grew out of the top of a massive rock. Kym pushed herself onto the top of the boulder, and stopped dead in her tracks. Eight people sat on the summit, their hands bound in chains, their heads slumped forward. They wore dark, mud-colored clothes and ranged from an old man who was at least ninety to a little girl who couldn't be older than eight. Small, ornate boxes sat on their crossed legs, the same dull color as their clothes.

Kym stared at the people. Why had the Rulers put them here? What was she supposed to do? Free them? Take the chest and run?

Both? She thought back to before the trial, and Evanna's words came back to her. *Retrieve what is hidden, and bring it back undamaged.* Did that mean the chest? She hadn't seen it at first, and the people weren't exactly hiding.

Gingerly, Kym approached a young man with short brown hair. His head bobbed up and down, and his chained arms were wrapped around the wooden chest in his lap. Kym tried to pull the chest from him as gently as she could. It didn't move. It was like the chest was glued to his arms. Kym put all of her weight behind it, but still, the little wooden box wouldn't leave his grip.

Kym staggered back, panting. Yanking on the chest wasn't going to work. There had to be something she was missing, something she hadn't seen. She stepped back to the edge of the boulder and looked at the whole line of chained people. But it wasn't an entire line. There were two gaps in the group. Two Prized must've beaten her to the arch.

But how'd they free the people? For the first time, Kym tried to think like a regular Favored. How would they try and get these people out? She knew the answer instantly; with brute force. A shudder ran through Kym's spine. How could she attack a defenseless, unconscious person? She couldn't.

Whatever Kym did, she needed to do it soon. Kensrix or any of the others could arrive at any moment, and fighting here, around all these sleeping people, was the last thing she wanted. She wasn't going to let these people get hurt.

"Hey," she whispered, shaking the shoulders of a girl about her age. "Get up."

Nothing happened. No matter how forcefully she tried to rouse them, their heads remained drooped and unresponsive. What else could she do? Her only other option was to use magic, but what good would that do? All she could do right now was control water. She could splash some water on them, but would it do anything?

A loud crash echoed through the narrow canyon walls, bombarding Kym's ears. She needed to do something, and fast. She crouched down at the end of the line and shook the shoulders of a little girl. Nothing happened, and another booming crash filled the air. Kym invoked her Marks, spinning around on the boulder's rough surface. The open expanse of rock in front of her was empty. Desperate, Kym turned back around and grabbed the girl's wrists.

"Get up," she pleaded.

There was a flash of blue light, and the chains binding the little girl vanished as energy surged through Kym like electricity. The girl's head jerked up so quickly it made Kym jump. Her eyes fluttered open, darting wildly around as she gasped. Kym watched her little body tremble as her mouth fell open. This girl had no idea where she was.

"It's alright," Kym said gently, helping the girl to her feet, the dark brown chest still held tight in her arms. "You're safe now."

"Where am I?" The girl whispered in a high voice, almost like a songbird.

"Um…"

What was Kym supposed to say? She wasn't even sure where they were herself. A mountain range of this scale couldn't be anywhere near Solaris's rolling green hills. No doubt the Rulers built this whole thing just for the trial. But how was she supposed to tell this little girl she was there as a prop in the Calling? The idea made Kym's stomach lurch.

"It doesn't matter," Kym said quickly, trying to sound braver then the felt. "I'm gonna get you out of here."

"You are?" the girl asked, glancing down at the chest in her arms.

"Yes," Kym said confidently, making up her mind on the spot. "You and that chest. What's your name?"

"Revein."

"Nice to meet you, Revein," she smiled. "I'm Kym."

Kym offered Revein her hand, and after a few seconds, she took it. She shifted her dark brown chest under her arm as Kym led her down the boulder-topped arch. More crashes filled the air, these even louder than the others. Kym didn't know who was causing it, but they were getting closer. The sooner she got Revein out of there, the better. Hopefully, they'd be able to slip past without any of the other Prized seeing them.

Kym led Revein around the opposite side of the boulder and started down a narrow path she'd never been down. She'd rather avoid the way she'd come, given all the crashes and booms coming from that direction. Revein's grip on her hand was so tight her fingers went numb after a few minutes. But Kym didn't complain. How could she ask her to let go? How did Revein, who looked no older than nine, get here in the first place? Had the Rulers grabbed people at random and thrown them into the trial without telling them anything? Kym's heart fell. Sadly, that didn't sound too far out of character.

Kym had absolutely no idea where she was. She was either going the right way, and they'd be out of there soon, or they'd end up wandering around the mountains until someone found them. Should she turn them around and try to find another way? The dark mountains from the start of the trial were nowhere in sight. She looked down at Revein, who still looked just as terrified as ever. No. She couldn't do that. Revein had suffered enough in this trial. Kym wasn't going to make it any worse than she had to.

Slowly, the tan stone around them shifted back to the vast, dark mountains Kym arrived in. Her insides swelled at the sight of them. This must mean they were going the right way after all. She watched the heat rise off the surrounding stone in waves. Revein finally let go of Kym's hand, wiping the almost constant stream of sweat from her face. Kym made water for her to drink, which she swallowed loudly.

Footsteps bounced off the high stone walls of their narrow path. Kym stepped forward, placing herself between Revien and the unknown newcomer. Kym held up her hand, ready to attack at the first sign of trouble. Lance barreled around the corner. Scrapes covered his muscular arms and legs, and the bottom half of his blue tank top was burned away.

"What the?" His head turned wildly in every direction, his eyes wide. "Where'd you come from?"

"That way?" Kym said cautiously. She jerked her head over her shoulder. "Who got you?"

"Amber," Lance growled. "Your friend's crazy."

Kym couldn't help but smile. Sure, she and Amber weren't in the best place, but she was happy that she'd cut Lance down a few pegs. By the look of it, he'd barely gotten away from her.

"She wants to win," Kym said coolly. "And so do I. So, if you don't—"

"Where'd you get that?"

Lance's eyes narrowed, focusing on something behind Kym. As subtly as she could, she turned her head. Revein was looking around Kym's back, the dark brown chest visible under her arm. Kym looked back at Lance, who'd taken a few steps closer to Kym and Revein. She invoked her Marks, pointing her hand menacingly at Lance, her heart pounding in her ears.

"Go that way," Kym said pointedly. "You'll find what we're looking for over there."

"Why'd you bother bringing her?" Lance said, still inching toward Kym. "Clearly, the Rulers want us to get the chest."

"We're not partners anymore, Lance," Kym said firmly. A ball of water appeared above her hand. "You do the trial your way; I'll do it mine."

Lance's eyes darted between the water floating above Kym's hand and Revein. He licked his lips. Kym shifted her feet on the rocky path, strengthening her stance. She had two things Lance wanted; Revein and her chest, and water. She doubted he'd seen more than a drop since the trial started.

"Give it to me."

"Excuse me?" Kym squared herself up. Was he talking about the water, or Revein and her chest?

"You already know where to find the others," Lance said, his tone uncharacteristically dark. "And you have the charm. You can get another and still beat me back. You owe me this."

"I owe you?" Kym couldn't believe what she was hearing.

"Nila gave you the charm," Lance spat. "It should've been mine.

I deserved it. I'm her Master of Masters. But she gave it to you, a Favored who doesn't even want to be here. Hand it over!"

Lance pulled his hand backward, his Marks glowing. The ball of water floating above Kym's hand lunged toward him. She reached forward, focusing her energy on the ball, but Lance's grip on the water was too strong. It soared through the air and into his outstretched hand.

Four high-pressure jets of water burst from the ball. Kym dove backward, practically tackling Revein to the ground as she covered her little body with her own. Lance's attacks slammed into the rock wall behind them, boring several small holes in the dark stone. Loud cracks filled the air, and chunks of rock broke away from the wall.

Kym curled herself over Revein's head as pieces of rock fell around them. Several landed on her back, but Kym bit her tongue, holding in her cries of pain. What was Lance doing? Even if he wanted to take Revein and her chest, he was going to hurt both of them before he did that, which was against the Rulers' instructions. Kym wouldn't let him hurt this little girl, no matter what he wanted.

Kym got to her feet. The ball of water in Lance's hands had expanded to the size of a beach ball, providing him with plenty of water to do real damage. He sent a much larger jet of water at Kym, but she was ready this time. She swung her arm just as the water reached her. It bounced away from her and into the rocky wall.

Pain seared Kym's side as another jet of water shot past her. She glanced down, and saw a deep cut just above her right hip. Kym's body shook with rage. She threw two bolts at the ground near his feet. He staggered back, tripped over a rock, and fell with a thud. The ball of water floating in his hand exploded, drenching him and the earth around him.

Kym waved her hands. The water covering Lance and soaking into the earth rose into the air and flew into her outstretched hands. Energizing the water, Kym threw a swipe at Lance. He gasped in pain as he toppled back into the hard rock. Kym walked up to him, covered in dirt and dust, his eyes wide with anger. Kym waved her hand, the image of what she wanted clear in her mind. Shining blue bands appeared around Lance's legs and arms, binding him like Ashlyn bound Xander during the festival.

"What the Thed are you doing?" Lance spat. He writhed around on the ground, but nothing he did made a difference.

"You're staying here," Kym said quietly. She focused on the bands around Lance and flicked her wrist. They glowed momentarily brighter before returning to their usual glow. "The bands will disappear in thirty minutes."

"I'll send you to Nothingness for this!" Lance's voice trembled with rage.

"Maybe you will," Kym said quietly. "And I may deserve it. But you…you'll attack anyone to get what you want."

Kym turned around. Revein was still on the ground, covered in dust. She stared at Kym, who felt her anger at Lance melt away as she looked into those wide, brown eyes. Slowly, Kym turned back to face Lance. He bared his teeth, and his dark blue eyes were full of fiery rage. But Kym, after everything they'd been through together, felt nothing toward him.

"Good-bye, Lance."

Kym walked back to Revein, still crouched on the ground. The mixture of shock, terror, and possibly joy on her face made Kym feel uneasy. Revein, who hadn't taken her eyes off of Lance since he showed up, now only had eyes for Kym. She offered the little girl her hand, and she took it. She pulled her to her feet, trying her best to keep her face and voice calm.

"Are you alright?"

"Who was that?" Revein asked tremulously.

"He's…" Kym glanced over her shoulder at Lance lying bound on the ground, looking more pathetic than ever. "He's just someone I used to know."

"You…why'd you save me?" Revein stammered in her birdlike voice.

"What?" Kym asked. She hadn't expected that. "Of course I saved you. Why wouldn't I?"

Revein shrugged but didn't say any more as they walked past

Lance. Every few steps, Kym glanced down at Revein, who wouldn't look up from her bare feet. Kym hadn't even noticed she didn't have shoes. Why did she find it so shocking that Kym would save her? She would've done it in a heartbeat, regardless of the circumstances. She remembered, as though from another lifetime, the death girl they had locked away in Tenbatter. She, like Revein, hadn't chosen to be where she was. Kym couldn't do anything to save the death girl. She wouldn't fail Revein the same way.

Chunks of stone sat unnaturally upright in the middle of the path, and unmistakable signs of fire and wind scarred the rocky mountain walls. More than one person had fought here. Oddly, the thought made Kym relax. At least she was on the right path. Hopefully, they'd be out of there soon.

The path opened up, revealing a deep mountain valley. However, Kym wouldn't call it a valley. It was more like a large stone tube with several canyon paths leading out of it. She'd been so focused on getting out of there when the trial started she hadn't registered what the starting point looked like.

Somewhere to Kym's left, she heard the sound of hurrying feet. She pulled Revein back into the safety of their narrow path. Slowly, her palms filling with sweat, she peered around the stone wall. A small boy, a few years older than Revein by the look of him, swayed out into the narrow valley. Amber, her arms folded across her chest, drifted behind him. She had her nose in the air and looked almost bored.

"Good," Amber said flatly. "I thought we'd never make it here at the rate you were going."

"What now?" the boy panted.

"Now we leave," Amber said cooly. "This is where the trial started, and it is where it ends."

Amber turned slowly on the spot, taking in the smooth walls surrounding her. Kym followed her gaze. Amber knew the Rulers better than anyone, and as far as Kym could tell, there was no exit that she could see. Maybe, if Amber found the exit, Kym could get

Revein out of here before Amber got her boy through. Amber didn't seem to be in much of a hurry.

"There." Amber pointed lazily at the section of stone wall opposite the canyon entrances.

Kym stared at the wall, trying to see what Amber saw. That stretch of dark stone looked just like the rest of the walls surrounding them. The only thing that seemed different about it was the color. A seam of tan stone ran through the dark wall. It was so thin Kym hadn't noticed it.

"That lighter layer is the same color as the arch where I found you," Amber droned at the boy. "It doesn't match the rest of the rock here. It is the exit."

Kym's eyes darted between Amber and the faint line of lighter stone. Could she be right? It was a stretch, even for Amber. Just because the color was the same as the arches didn't mean it was the exit. There had to be something she wasn't saying, or she thought was obvious. The boy looked more tired than Revein. Kym doubted neither he nor Amber had drank anything since the trial started. This was her chance.

"Alright," Kym whispered to Revein, crouching down in front of her. "You see that arch in the wall over there? When I tell you, I want you to run as fast as you can to it. Can you do that?"

"What about you?" Revein breathed.

"Don't worry about me," Kym smiled, brushing Revein's hair from her face. "You just focus on getting to the wall. Nothing's gonna happen. I promise."

"Okay," Revein squeaked.

Slowly, Kym stood up, her muscles tense and rigid. Her heart pounded in her ears, and the world around her grew oddly quiet. She stared at Amber, gliding toward the colored arch on the wall. If Revein stood a chance of getting out in one piece, this was Kym's moment.

"Now!"

Not even bothering to look at Revein, Kym sprinted at Amber. Her water bolts flew from her hands, exploding on the ground in front of Amber. She jumped backward, her face impassive as her eyes locked on Kym. Her bright red fire bolt flew through the air so quickly Kym couldn't make a shield. She dove to the ground, dirt and dust flying around her as her arms and side seared with pain.

"Get to the wall!" Kym heard Amber order.

Kym shot a blast at Amber. She deflected it, then turned her attention to the boy and Revein sprinting to the wall. Kym saw the bright red sphere form in Amber's hand and fear spread through her like ice. Amber wouldn't attack Revein so her hostage would be first, would she? Kym's heart sank. Amber had done worse to her friends in the last trial.

Kym frantically waved her hand. A single, glowing blue band appeared around Amber's ankles. She toppled forward, her fire bolt vanishing in a flash of red as a cloud of dust bloomed around her. Kym looked to the wall. Revein and the boy were feet away from the exit. Kym turned back to Amber, who was pushing herself back to her feet. Kym raised her hand, ready to strike again, and the ground beneath her gave way.

Her body hurtled downward and forward before jerking upward. Bright lights appeared in Kym's eyes, obscuring her vision. The sounds of hurrying feet and several familiar voices filled Kym's ears. Gentle hands appeared out of nowhere, helping Kym into a sitting position. She blinked several times, trying to bring the world into focus.

She was in the same room where they started the trial. She and Amber sat in chairs on opposite sides of the otherwise empty room. Their hostages sat on stiff, wooden chairs along one of the walls, looking both overwhelmed and relieved. Servants ran around the room, their arms full of bandages, spare changes of clothes, pillows, and many potted plants.

"Revein." Kym tried to stand, but the hands that helped her sit up held her down.

"You did well, my dear."

"You and Miss Amber came in at almost the exact same time. It was too close for us to see."

Turning around, Kym saw Veronica and Isabel crouched behind her. They each held a damp cloth in their hand and were wiping the dirt from Kym's skin. Scrapes covered her knees, legs, and hands, her back throbbed uncomfortably, and blood oozed from the cut on her side. But she didn't care. Revein was safe.

"Where's everybody?" Kym looked around the room. She and Amber couldn't be the first ones back, could they?

But they were. It took nearly an hour for the others to arrive. Most looked worse than Kym, covered in large cuts, bruises, and burns. Somewhere, deep down inside her, Kym felt hopeful. Could she have actually won the trial and kept her mom safe? She and Amber basically tied, and looking at the hostages, Revein was definitely in better shape than Amber's. Kym's body relaxed. For the first time since the Calling started, she'd finally done something right.

"Congratulations on completing the Fourth Trial," Zara said after addressing everyone's injuries. "The goal of this trial was left purposefully vague, allowing your true priorities to shine through. Your task was to retrieve a hostage from the arena and return with them undamaged. The chests they carried were worthless."

Confused murmurs swept through the room. Kym glanced around. The other Prized, like Lance, must've thought the chests were the things to protect. Kym looked over at the hostages. Most of them bore signs of injury from the trial, but nearly all of the chests were in pristine condition.

"Therefore," Phillip said, bringing the murmurs of the Favored to a halt, "the winner of the Fourth Trial is not the Favored whose hostage left the arena first, which was the Fire Favored, Amber, but the one who got their hostage out of the arena with the least amount of damage."

"So," Zara said, taking a step forward, "the winner of the Fourth Trial is the Prized of Reta, Kymbralyn."

CHAPTER TWENTY-TWO

THE PARADE OF GLORY

RELIEF SPREAD THROUGH KYM'S VEINS LIKE COLD WATER, AND something warm stirred deep inside her. She hadn't won the trial because she'd gotten some box first or was the best at magic. She won because she'd kept Revein safe. The others had been wrong. And by saving Revein, she'd kept her mom out of danger. For the first time since the Calling started, Kym finally felt like she'd done something right.

"Kymbralyn's hostage sustained damage to her clothes and two superficial scrapes on her knees," Zara continued.

"This was the least amount of damage any hostage received. The Prized whose hostages received the most damage failed the trial. The Water Favored, Lance, Light Favored, Ashlyn, Death Favored, Jazin, and Earth Favored, Katarein, failed to answer the gods' call. You are unworthy of their glory and no longer have a place in the Calling."

Kym's happiness vanished in a flash. She stared at her friends' downcast faces. How'd all three of them get eliminated? Ashlyn couldn't have done worse than Amber. She cared deeply about others and would never put someone in harm's way if she could help it. Something must have happened that was out of her control. On the other hand, Kat's elimination came as a surprise to no one.

Kym watched Kat, Ashlyn, and Jazin leave the room in silence. Ashlyn waved feebly at Kym, Tomark, Amber, and Xander, who stood in the middle of the room with Lennax and Kensrix, while Kat looked like she wanted to punch something. Jazin left the room with his head hung low, his long arms hanging limply at his sides. Kym's insides swelled with pride as she watched him go. Not only had she won the trial, but she'd beaten Jazin. Finally, she'd done what Nila wanted her to do. She'd beaten, and eliminated, death from the Calling. This had to prove Thed's power wasn't as strong as it seemed. There was no way Nila could send her mom's doctors away now.

Zara and the other Rulers closed in around the remaining Prized. Kym noticed Evanna and Phillip standing a little behind the others, shaking with suppressed rage. Kym didn't have to imagine why. Neither of them had a Prized left. Of course, James looked like his birthday had come early. He was the only Ruler with two Prized remaining.

"Congratulations," Zara said, beaming down at them. "By advancing to the fifth and final Trial of the Calling, you join an elite and prestigious class of Prized. No Favored living has accomplished what the six of you have these past weeks. You have brought pride to your Rulers, and your service to the gods will not go unnoticed.

"The Fifth Trial will take place at Crystal Palace in five days. However, you will not depart for Crystal Palace tonight. First, you will attend the Parade of Glory."

Kym's body deflated at Zara's words. Once again, the Rulers showed their frustrating habit of giving everything unnecessary, over-important names. The Parade of Glory? What were they even going to do? It couldn't be a real parade, could it? Kym's discomfort quadrupled at the thought.

"The Trials of the Calling have been streamed to the cities, who have loyally and enthusiastically followed your progress. Those esteemed members of the cities who earned the privilege to watch the trials in person returned to the cities after each one to give their own thoughts on what they witnessed. Every citizen of Princirum eagerly awaits the Fifth Trial to see which element will reign supreme.

"But now, you are tired after your ordeals and deserve rest before the Parade of Glory tomorrow. Good night, and may the gods bless and guide you all."

The Rulers swept silently from the room. Kym stared after them and locked eyes with Nila. Her face was just as impassive as ever, but Kym thought she saw something flicker in Nila's dark eyes. Could Nila actually be proud of Kym? The thought made Kym's insides squirm even more.

"Good job," Tomark whispered, wrapping one arm around her. She shuddered slightly as his hand found her shoulder. "You're nearly there."

"Thanks," Kym sighed, her discomfort melting slightly at his touch. She glanced over at Amber, whose face was as blank as the Rulers'. "Amber doesn't look too happy."

"Amber hasn't been 'happy' since the Calling started," Tomark said, which Kym had to agree. Another thing to look forward to once the Calling was over; they'd get normal Amber back.

"I can't believe Ash got eliminated," Kym said as they walked over to the door. "What happened?"

"Kensrix," Tomark jerked his head in Kensrix's direction. "He's picked up a few of Amber's tricks. He set everything on fire whenever he saw anyone."

"He did that to me too," Kym said, thinking back to her own altercation with Kensrix in the trial.

Servants stood off to the side of the glittering yellow entrance hall, waiting for them. Veronica, Isabel, and Tomark's servants stepped forward as Kym and Tomark drew nearer.

"The next couple of days are gonna suck," Kym whispered, so only Tomark could hear.

"I know," he said. "But I guess it's a good thing since Zara said the people are all really excited."

"I guess," Kym said tentatively, unsure if she believed him or not.

The sounds of an explosion jolted Kym from a dreamless sleep. She sat bolt upright, her heart pounded as she invoked her Marks, ready to fight. Two blue blurs ran around her room, babbling on as pieces of fabric flew in every direction. Kym slumped back, her pounding heartbeat subsiding slightly. Of course, Veronica and Isabel were in a state. Kym would need her best clothes for the parade, which explained why her room looked like a closet exploded.

Kym sank beneath the sheets. Maybe, if she didn't move, her maids would leave her alone? They didn't. They yanked her out of bed so quickly Kym thought they might break her arm. Veronica dragged her into the little bathroom, where the tub was so full of healing oils and scents it made Kym's head ache.

"You need to soak for at least an hour," Veronica said matter-of-factly as she helped Kym into the tub. "To look your best."

"If only we had a week to prep this instead of half a day," Isabel lamented.

Kym did as she was told, not daring to speak. She'd never seen her maids this bad. Even her prep before the Festival of Creation was smoother. This parade was clearly important to them. They were bound to go a little overboard.

By the end of her soak, Kym was the one on the verge of snapping. Veronica and Isabel burst into the room every couple of minutes, something to show Kym held in their arms. They'd back out before she opened her mouth, promising something different and better. Half the time, she couldn't even see what they were showing her.

Her maids released her from the sweet-smelling tub, wrapped her in a robe and forced her into a chair to start her hair. However, they wouldn't let Kym see what they were doing. There wasn't even a mirror in the bathroom. All Kym could see of their work was sections of her blond hair falling in her face before being pulled back into place.

Veronica led Kym back into her little room when they'd finished with her hair. The clothing explosion was nowhere to be seen as Kym stepped onto a little podium. Kym tried hard to keep her frustration to herself. What was so special about this parade that was causing all of this craziness? In response to Kym's thoughts, Veronica slipped a thin strip of fabric over Kym's eyes.

"Really?" Kym groaned, unable to hide her annoyance. "Is this necessary?"

"We don't want to spoil the surprise," Kym heard Veronica's voice somewhere to her left.

So, blind and defenseless, Kym gave herself over to her maids' capable hands. They'd never let her down before, after all. Smooth fabrics fell over her body, and as the weight rested on her shoulders, Kym's legs began to shake. Whatever she was wearing, it weighed a ton. Tentatively, she leaned forward a fraction. It was like dragging a bag of rocks behind her. Could she even walk in something so heavy? For the first time since meeting them, Kym feared her maids had taken things too far.

They slipped her feet into very tall high heels. Veronica and Isabel each took one of Kym's hands and led her, still blindfolded, off the dressing platform. Kym started panting after the first few steps. What was the dress made of? Finally, after a lot of whispers and last-minute adjusting, her maids removed the blindfold. Kym looked in the full-length mirror in front of her, and something other-worldly stared back.

The dress was pure, shimmering gold, flowing weightlessly around her. However, the dress's gold color was almost unnotice-able thanks to the twinkling sapphires covering the fabric. The train was at least two yards long, and her skin was the same metallic gold as the dress. The only thing that Kym recognized from the outfit was the water charm. She didn't look like a sixteen-year-old girl, or even a young woman. She'd transformed into something else entirely.

"This…" Kym didn't know what to say.

"We know," Veronica said, and although there was pride in her voice, there was also understanding there. "This isn't your style."

"Lady Nila was specific with her requests for your parade wardrobe," Isabel said.

"I—I look like…"

"Like a Favored of Princirum," Veronica smiled, squeezing Kym's hands. "And a Prized of Reta."

"We're so proud of you, my dear," Isabel added, placing both of her hands on Kym's shoulders and giving them a little shake.

"Where are we going first?" Kym asked, still unable to take her eyes away from the mirror.

"The City of Luxmont. We are in Lady Evanna's realm, after all. It won't be long now."

Her bedchamber door burst open not ten minutes later. Her heart pounding, Kym looked over her shoulder, expecting to see Nila. But it wasn't the Ruler of Water walking toward her.

"Blessed One." Pro Ormana, the Protectorate who'd taken Kym to see her mom, bowed her head.

"We're here to—"

"Get the Thed out," Kym cut across Pro Hayden, her voice no more than a whisper. Her face grew hot and her hands shook at her sides. She already felt miles from herself in Nila's parade outfit. She barely tolerated the Protectorate on a good day. Today, she didn't want them anywhere near her.

"Blessed One, our orders come from—"

"Get out!" Kym shouted, her anger spilling out of her in waves. She pointed to the door, and her Marks burst into life on her arms.

"You heard her," Veronica barked, stepping between Kym and the Pros.

"We will escort Miss Kym to the carriages ourselves," Isabel said, closing the door swiftly behind Ormana and Hayden.

Kym turned away from the door. She knew she shouldn't have yelled at Ormana and Hayden. After all, they were just doing what Nila told them to do. But that was the problem. Kym was sick of doing what Nila wanted her to do. The sooner the Calling was over, the better. But before that, she had the parade to deal with.

Kym never thought she was uncoordinated, but walking in her parade dress was the hardest thing she'd ever done, and that included fighting death demons. Even though the fabric billowed around weightlessly, it still felt like she was dragging a dead body behind her. The heels didn't help, which were taller than the ones she usually wore. In the end, Veronica lifted Kym's train while Isabel held Kym's arm, steadying her.

Six different carriages sat on the curved front drive—two red, one blue, one silver, one purple, and one green. Kym climbed into the blue one with difficulty. She wanted to kick off her shoes the moment she sat, but the dress was so tight she wasn't sure she could bend over. She couldn't even lean against the cushioned backrest for fear of ruining the gold dusting on her skin.

It took another ten minutes before her carriage lurched forward. Kym sighed, trying to calm her nerves. This was precisely why she didn't want to do the Calling in the first place. Parading through the streets, dressed like something from another world, was not why she was here. Would she have to speak? The thought twisted her stomach into a knot.

Kym looked down at her shimmering dress and golden skin. What would the people from her old life think of her now? They'd probably think she was the most ridiculous thing they'd ever seen, and she'd agree with them. What would her dad think? He hadn't liked the way she acted when she visited him before. How would he react to this?

Kym's carriage stopped outside the City of Luxmont's massive walls. The door opened, and Pros Hayden and Ormana stood outside. She ignored them and exited the carriage, taking in the area before her, which buzzed with activity. Priests, servants, and Protectorate ran in every direction, yelling orders and guiding people to the correct places. Kym's Protectorate led her silently from her carriage to a bright blue chariot. Four pure white horses stood before it, their ears turning this way and that as people ran around them.

"Up you get, Blessed One," Pro Hayden said flatly.

Kym climbed into the chariot, which was in the middle of the line, as gracefully as she could. It was harder than it looked, and no matter where she stood, a section of her glittering train always hung off the back.

Amber, whose bright red chariot was right in front of Kym's, didn't have nearly as much trouble. She looked completely at home as she glided onto her chariot unaided. Tiny, glistening rubies covered Amber's fair skin. To Kym, it looked like Amber had been sprayed with blood.

"Ready to go, Miss?" asked a gentle, familiar voice.

Kym spun around so quickly she nearly lost her balance. She clung to the edge of the chariot and couldn't believe her eyes. Veronica and Isabel stood on either side of her chariot, but their clothes were unlike anything Kym had seen them wear. Gone were their simple blue dresses, replaced by tight, fitted robes accented with blue. Why were her maids dressed like Protectorate, and where were Pro Hayden and Pro Ormana?

"What are you doing here?"

"Isn't it obvious, my dear?" Isabel asked.

"We're here for you," Veronica smiled.

"What?" Kym shook her head. What were they talking about?

"All of the Prized are assigned Protectorate during the Parade of Glory," Isabel said. "Lady Nila thought it would be best if you were protected by people you were familiar with."

"Really?" After everything Nila had done, Kym had a hard time believing Nila cared at all about what Kym felt.

"Well, we did ask her to allow us to take up the spear again for you," Veronica admitted. "She didn't object to the idea."

"Thank you," was all Kym could bring herself to say.

It took another fifteen minutes for everyone to get ready. Each Prized's Protectorate would walk behind their chariot, just in case anything happened. Kym couldn't see why the Rulers were giving them Pros for a parade. The Prized were more capable of stopping anything that might happen than the Protectorate were.

Xander's chariot moved first. He held his hands in the air as his chariot rolled into the city, his shimmering violet clothes so sheer Kym could see every one of his muscles. Booming drums assaulted Kym's ears as his chariot vanished beyond the walls, accompanied by the unmistakable screams of the crowd. The sound made Kym's throat constrict, and her heartbeat grew louder in her ears.

Kensrix's chariot went next. Like Amber, he was covered in rubies and looked like he'd been dipped in glistening blood. When his chariot entered the city, the cheers grew even louder as the drums continued to beat. Amber's chariot followed Kensrix's, and she was in full Fire Princess form, barely moving a muscle as her chariot lurched forward. The crowd gave its loudest cheer yet, but Amber kept her slender hands firmly behind her back, not acknowledging their presence.

Kym's body trembled. Any second now, her chariot would start to move, and she'd be on display for the whole of Princirum to see. She gripped the side of the chariot so tightly her knuckles shone white through the golden dust on her skin. Kym thought back to before the Calling, before she was a Vanquisher, and even before she was a Favored.

Back then, everyone ignored her because her aunt and uncle spoke out against the Rulers and the gods, and Kym wanted nothing to do with magic. And now, a whole city cheered her on because of her magical accomplishments. How'd she even get here?

Kym shook her head. It didn't matter how she got here or what happened in this stupid parade. All that mattered was winning the Fifth Trial and saving her mom. If she had to stand like an idiot in a dress to do that, she would.

Kym's chariot lurched forward. She closed her eyes, taking one final moment for herself before every eye turned to her. Why did she need to do this? The explosive cheers jolted her eyes open. Crowds of people lined either side of the wide main avenue, while elemental banners hung from the tops of the tall glass buildings. Massive holo projectors, like the one her father used to read the news, sat along their path, projecting the whole parade up into the air for those too far back to see.

The crowd, which Kym noticed was kneeling, pressed their heads to the ground every time a chariot passed. Once they'd up righted themselves, they'd resume their clapping. Kym lifted her hands into the air, trying to smile as she waved at the crowd. They cheered and screamed her name, but as she passed, she noticed their faces. Every single one of them looked like they were in pain.

Many watchers wore blue, red, green, purple, and silver sashes, no doubt to show support to whichever Prized, god, and element they supported. Naturally, those wearing blue sashes cheered the loudest as Kym rode by, but they weren't the ones that caught her eye. Every once in a while, she'd spot a black sash mixed in among the others. But that made no sense. Who were they even supporting? It couldn't be Jazin. He wasn't in the Calling anymore. Why were people still determined to support death when its fight was over?

It took thirty minutes to reach the Temple at the city center. The horses walked at a very slow pace, allowing everyone a chance to see and cheer for Kym and the other Prized. The Temple, constructed from white stone, was identical to the one from Kym's memory, down to the worn steps and cracked columns. Xander and Kensrix stood at the top of the massive stairs, while Amber glided up the worn slabs of graying stone, flanked by her Protectorate.

When Kym's chariot reached the steps, she climbed out and made her way up the old steps, Veronica and Isabel right behind her. The high priest, dressed in billowing white robes, stood waiting for her. She bowed low as Kym approached and directed her to her place beside Amber. Tomark, who looked like he'd been dipped in molten silver, stood on Kym's other side, while Lennax stood next to Tomark.

"My children!" the high priest called over the cheering crowd, her hands held above her head. "For the first time in the lives of most of you, the glorious gods have made their plans for us known. I saw their signs, and summoned their chosen among us, their Favored, to answer their call!"

More cheers from the kneeling crowd. Kym stared down at them. Not one person looked happy. What was going on? Her eyes drifted to the edge of the crowd, to those closest to the buildings. A gust of wind disturbed the elemental banners hanging over the nearest buildings, revealing the damage hidden beneath. Kym's insides turned to ice. Blackened cracks ran up the sides, and some had sizable chunks missing—the unmistakable signs of a death demon.

Kym stared at the damage, unable to look away. What happened here? Why hadn't she, or any of the other Vanquishers, come to stop it? She looked down the line at Xander and Amber. Had the attack happened during the Calling? Why hadn't the Rulers told them about it? Kym's hands trembled at her sides, balling into fists as her face grew hot. Were the Rulers so determined to get more power that they'd let the cities get attacked? How could the stupid Calling be more important than keeping the people of Princirum safe?

"These Prized follow in the footsteps of the first Favored, bravely battling to answer the gods' call," the high priest continued over the now-silent crowd. "And now, they present themselves to you. Prized of Kensrad, and Favored of Darkness, Xander!"

Xander stepped forward, and the crowd resumed its cheering. At the foot of the steps, a massive projection of him burst into life, glowing fifty feet high. Kym's stomach churned at the sight of the hologram. She looked down at the base of the steps and saw five more massive projection disks. Kensrix stepped forward next, and his hologram burst into life as the crowd, mostly those dressed in red, cheered his name. The cheers grew even louder as Amber stepped up, but died away quickly as the projected Fire Princess glared down at them.

"Prized of Reta, and Favored of Water, Kymbralyn!"

Kym stepped forward, her hands still shaking at her sides. She braced herself, knowing what would happen when she reached the edge of the stairs. The hologram of her burst into the air, and she looked more otherworldly than when she'd first seen herself in the mirror. She waved at the crowd, smiling as their screams filled her ears. They cheered and shouted Kym's name, but she saw no joy or excitement on their faces. It was like cheering for Favored, who'd never set foot in their city, was causing them pain, and Kym couldn't blame them. Standing there, covered in gold and jewels, she'd rather be anywhere else.

But there was something else that made Kym feel uneasy. While everyone's faces were turned in her direction, as required, no one actually looked at her. That's exactly what she used to do whenever the Rulers came to her school. She wanted nothing to do with magic after it caused her whole town to shun her for something she hadn't even done. And now, these people wanted nothing to do with Kym because of the magic she never wanted. How could this be part of the gods' plan for her?

The crowd gave Tomark and Lennax the same reception they'd given Kym, Amber, Kensrix, and Xander. They clapped and yelled the Prized's names, but only seemed genuinely happy when Lennax stepped back to join the others. Kym shared their enthusiasm. This was the most uncomfortable she'd ever felt in her life, and all she wanted was to get into some regular clothes and leave the city unseen. Hopefully, the high priest would wrap things up quickly.

"Four days from now," the high priest called down to the crowd. "These six Prized will compete one last time to prove which element will reign supreme and determine which god will bestow their good fortune upon us all."

A ripple moved through the crowd as the mass of faces in front of her shook their heads. Kym had to focus hard to stop her mouth from falling open. No one ever disagreed with the priests, especially not the high priest. The only people Kym ever knew to do that were her aunt and uncle, and they'd been killed for their disobedience.

Several stones flew out of the crowd, barely reaching the temple steps. Spears appeared out of nowhere around Kym as the Protectorate descended down the temple steps. But the appearance of the Protectorate didn't stop the crowd. They pressed on, passing through the towering holograms of the Prized as they approached the stairs. Kym watched, transfixed, as their black sashes glittered in the holo-light.

"High Pro Varen," the high priest hissed at the Protectorate standing beside her. Her voice wasn't just worried. She sounded terrified. "Contain this. Before they see."

High Pro Varen stepped forward, his spear held tight in his hand. "Protectorate, *d'naity drah*!"

The word stirred something in Kym's memory. She'd heard it before, but she couldn't think where. At High Pro Varen's command, the Protectorate lining the steps charged forward, their spears directed at the advancing crowd. Kym froze. Why were the Protectorate attacking the crowd, and why were the people not backing down?

"Get out!" A voice shouted from the depths of the crowd.

"Your gods won't help us!" another yelled.

"Thed will lead the way!"

Kym held her breath and glanced sideways at High Pro Varen. He watched the scene unfolding before him, and several lines formed between his stern eyes. Kym looked back down into the crowd, which, even with spears pointing right at them, continued to press forward.

"Agni!"

High Pro Varen's command sent a shiver down Kym's spine. She knew that strange word. It was the same command the Pro Ormana used when the man hadn't left her alone when she'd visited her father. Kym turned and watched the line of Protectorate draw back their spears and lunge into the angry mob.

CHAPTER TWENTY-THREE

WHATEVER IT TAKES

"No!"

Kym's scream of terror mingled with the shrieks of the crowd. People ran in every direction. The Protectorate forced their way into the mob with their spears raised, but some managed to push their way onto the Temple steps. Kym needed to do something. She needed to help. She invoked her Marks and ran forward, but two sets of hands grabbed her firmly by the upper arm.

"Get inside!" Kym had never heard Isabel's light and gentle voice so forceful.

"Make way!" Veronica barked.

The priests standing behind them parted, and Veronica and Isabel dragged Kym through the massive Temple doors. The sound of scuffling feet followed her as the others hurried in behind her. Several priests swarmed forward, pushing the heavy Temple doors closed the moment Xander and Lennax crossed the threshold. The sounds of the chaos outside faded inside the deserted Temple until only silence remained.

Kym's body trembled, and no matter how much she breathed, no air entered her lungs. That didn't just happen. She didn't see priests attack a crowd of defenseless people. She didn't care how angry the crowd was or what they said. They could've stormed the steps and ripped the clothes from her body for all she cared. Nothing warranted attacking them.

And why were they so angry? For so long, Kym thought her distain for magic and the Favored was something only she felt. But those people, they were saying things that no one ever said. Would the Rulers have them arrested? They'd done far worse to Kym's aunt and uncle when they spoke out.

"Let go." Kym's voice shook so badly, it was a miracle Veronica and Isabel understood her. They released Kym's arm without hesitation.

"Come, my dear," Veronica whispered, her voice once again soft. "You're alright. You're safe."

Safe? Kym hadn't considered her own safety once. She was more worried about what was happening to the people outside. She stared at the doors, but no sound passed through the ancient slabs of stone. But that didn't stop the words ringing through her head like a gong.

Get out! *Thed will lead the way*!

"Kym," a very familiar voice said behind her.

No. It couldn't be. Kym spun around. Her father, dressed in his best Temple clothes, stood between Veronica and Isabel. Kym's anger melted at the sight of him. Tears welled up in her eyes as she stepped into her father's arms.

"What...how..."

"The families of the Prized were invited to show their support during the Parade of Glory," Isabel smiled.

"And of course, they're welcome at Crystal Palace to watch the Fifth Trial," Veronica added.

Kym barely heard Veronica and Isabel. All that mattered was her dad. In his arms, her worries faded away, like they had so many times in her past. She buried her face in his chest, not wanting to pull away. But, as she felt his arms around her, she couldn't ignore what was missing.

"How's Mom?"

Slowly, Kym felt his arms loosen around her. They slid down her sides until they vanished altogether. Kym kept her face hidden in her father's worn shirt. She didn't want him to see her face. Nila hadn't said a word about her mom's condition since the Calling started. Kym assumed the doctors were still there. She was still in the Calling, after all. Did her dad know those doctors were there because of her? She doubted it, and wanted to keep it that way.

"She's…at home," Kym's father croaked.

"Has there been any improvement, Mr. Collins?" Kym heard Veronica ask. "Miss Kym has been so worried about Mrs. Collins."

"Elena's fine," Kym's dad said, and there was a note of coldness in his voice that Kym rarely heard.

She pulled away from her father. He was staring at Veronica and Isabel, dressed in their new Protectorate robes. Kym could see the anger in his eyes at the sight of the outfits. How could she forget? The Protectorate hunted down her aunt and uncle. Of course her dad wouldn't be happy to see them.

"Dad, this is Veronica and Isabel," Kym said quickly, stepping between her father and her maids. "They're my servants back at Wadita."

"They don't look like servants," Marek said, his voice dark.

"They are," Kym assured him.

"We're pulling double duty during the Parade of Glory," Isabel said gently. "We wanted to ensure your daughter's safety. It's our duty to care for her."

"I appreciate that." Marek Collins relaxed at Isabel's words, and so did Kym. "And Elena…she's hanging on."

Kym breathed a silent sigh of relief. Her mother was still alive. Her eyes grew hot as tears threatened to spill down her face. Kym turned away, looking around the hall as she willed her tears not to fall.

They were standing in the Temple's large antechamber. The Prized stood a little ways apart from each other, surrounded by their guards and at least one other person. Tomark stood closest to Kym with two people in their late seventies. His grandparents. Of course, his parents weren't there. They'd died during a death demon attack when he was little.

Amber stood between two people who looked so different Kym couldn't help but stare. The man on her left, tall and proud-looking, dressed in glittering red clothes, had to be her father. A short, thin woman with the same narrow eyes as Amber's stood on her other side, fiddling with the faded hem of her orange dress. Xander's mother, a slender woman with dark, curly hair, stood beside her son, looking simultaneously proud and terrified. Her shabby dress looked like at least four other people had worn it before her.

"We must hurry," the high priest said, her voice shaking slightly. "We need to get the Prized out of the city before this gets any worse."

The other priests nodded and directed the Prized, guards, and families deeper into the Temple. Where were they going? The main doors were the only way in and out. Kym had never been inside the massive, round room when it was empty. It seemed odd, seeing all those benches with no people to fill them. The silence didn't help. Every step echoed off the vast, stone walls.

"Here," the high priest said.

She stepped aside as two others moved forward, each holding a thin, metal rod. They drove their rods into the ground and pushed, lifting a slab out of the stone floor. Three other priests hoisted it to the side and dropped it with a crash. Kym stepped forward, craning her neck to see down into the darkness.

A set of stone steps descended into the earth, leading to who knew where. The high priest stepped forward, a much shorter, clear rod in her hand. She hit a button on the bottom, and pure white light shone from it, illuminating the way.

"The passage leads beyond the city walls," the high priest explained as she descended the steps. "The journey won't take long."

Everyone followed the high priest down into the passage. Once they were safely inside, the priest who stayed behind slid the stone tile back into place, sealing them in. No one spoke as they walked through the dim tunnel, which reminded Kym of the tunnels she'd explored beneath Crystal Palace during the Festival of Creation. That night seemed like a whole lifetime away.

They walked until they reached another set of steps. These stairs, unlike the stone ones beneath the Temple, were carved into the earthy passage itself. The high priest and two others pushed away another stone tile, flooding the tunnel with warm, evening light.

Kym emerged from the stairs, blinking rapidly as her eyes adjusted to the intense afternoon light. They were just outside the tall city walls. Their carriages stood waiting for them, the doors already held open by the drivers. But they weren't the only things there.

All of the priests, Protectorate, Prized, and family members bowed as the Rulers raced toward them. Zara and Phillip led the charge, and Zara had a look on her face that Kym had only seen on very rare occasions, like when Thed, the god of death, revealed himself at the festival or when Phillip and Jazin first arrived. What were the Rulers even doing there? Weren't they supposed to be at Crystal Palace preparing for the Fifth Trial?

Zara swept past everyone until she towered over the high priest. She flattened herself to the ground, like she was trying to make herself as small as possible.

"Rise," Zara said, and there was a venom in her voice Kym thought only Melana was capable of mustering.

The high priest sprung to her feet, trying her best to straighten her shimmering white robes. She was at least three feet shorter than Zara, who loomed larger than usual as she stared down at the woman with dark eyes.

"My Lady," the high priest stammered. "I…I don't know—"

Zara held up her hand, and the shaking woman fell silent at once.

"You failed me," she hissed, her voice ringing through the silence. "Under your charge, this celebration of the Prized and the gods was an utter disaster. Your people show no respect for the gods. I expected more from the priest who first saw the signs of the Calling."

"You will send word to the Cities of Silvaura, Termubra, and Contellus," Phillip said. His voice was just as cold as Zara's, but Kym thought she saw a triumphant glimmer in his pale eyes. "You will confess your failures to the other high priests and urge them to do better. You would not want to anger the creators of Princirum, would you?"

"Of course not, my Lord," the high priest flung herself at Phillip's feet. "I will send word at once, my Lord."

The priests practically ran from the Rulers, leaving them with the Prized, their families, and guards. Kym couldn't help but feel sorry for them as they scurried back inside the city walls. Sure, she didn't like the priests, but even Kym could see what happened during the parade wasn't their fault. How could they know the people would riot at the sight of the Prized? Sending in the Protectorate didn't help. All it did was make the whole situation worse.

"You must be proud of your daughter, Mr. Collins," a cold voice said behind Kym.

She turned around. Nila drifted toward Kym and her father, towering over them. Marek fell to his knees, resting his forehead at the hem of Nila's glittering blue dress. Isabel and Veronica gave their usual bows of respect, bending so their backs were level with the ground. Kym, on the other hand, didn't move a muscle.

"Rise," Nila drawled. Slowly, Veronica and Isabel righted themselves, but Marek stayed where he was.

"My Lady Nila," Marek said to Nila's feet. "I am ever grateful to you. I can never repay the compassion you've shown my family."

"You are too kind, sir," Nila said, the corners of her mouth twitching.

Kym bit her tongue to stop herself from screaming. How could her father say that, after everything magic had done to their family? The deaths of her aunt and uncle. Kym being forced to leave home. Her mother's sickness. What had Nila done to make him grateful?

"You are the kind one, my Lady," Marek said, still on the floor. "Because of you, my wife has received exceptional care these past months. If it hadn't been for you, I don't know…" Marek tailed off, and Kym heard the pain in his voice.

"It is my pleasure," Nila said coolly, her eyes drifting to Kym. "I reward my Favored for their loyalty."

Kym's internal scream was so loud she was surprised no one heard it. So, Nila was rewarding her for her loyalty, was she? The thought dug inside her, boring its way into the deepest parts of her being. She balled her hands into fists at her side, fighting her every impulse to throw a water bolt at Nila. But she knew she couldn't. So, Kym smiled and inclined her head to Nila, trying to keep the anger from her face.

Veronica and Isabel led Kym to her blue carriage, her dad hurrying behind them. They helped Kym inside, carefully lifting the train of her gown and placing it on the floor. Isabel removed Kym's shoes while Veronica stood to the side. Her head moved constantly, her spear held tight in her hand.

"There's no time for you to change here," Isabel said, placing Kym's shoes on the floor of the carriage. "We'll make adjustments when you arrive at the City of Silvaura."

"Really?" After everything that happened, all Kym wanted was to put on something that was actually comfortable.

"I'm sorry, my dear," Isabel said. "The carriages need to leave right away."

"I'll see you there." Marek reached inside and grabbed her hand. "I'm so proud of you."

Kym opened her mouth to respond but the carriage lurched forward, and her father's fingers slipped from her hand. She stared out of the window, watching Veronica, Isabel, and her father shrink away into the distance.

Kym's carriage skidded to a halt outside the City of Silvaura, stars twinkling in the dark sky. A miniature city of multicolored tents sat outside the city's walls. It reminded Kym of the ones outside Crystal Palace during the Festival of Creation. She wanted to find Tomark, or Xander, or even Amber. She hadn't spoken to any of them since the Fourth Trial, and she need to talk to someone about what happened. But they were nowhere to be seen. Neither was her father. She'd expected to see him as soon as she arrived, but the only faces she recognized were her maids. They were back in their usual, light blue dresses and pulled Kym into a tent the second her carriage door opened.

After standing in the hot sun, running into the Temple, walking through a tunnel, and sitting in a carriage, there was barely any golden paint left on Kym's skin. Veronica and Isabel wiped off what little remained with sponges before handing Kym a floor-length, sheer blue nightgown. They didn't say a word as they helped her into the small bed in the middle of the tent. Thankful to finally be off her feet, Kym lay back on the soft pillow and almost instantly fell asleep.

The next morning, Kym stood on a small pedestal while her maids dressed her, re-coating her skin with golden paint from a large bucket. She expected them to finish after they fussed over her gown and hair. She was wrong.

Isabel sat Kym on a stool and applied powdery blue makeup around her eyes. Veronica, a pair of tiny tweezers in hand, placed little sapphires all over Kym's bare shoulders and upper torso. They were just like the ones on her gown. But this didn't make sense. Veronica and Isabel said they were happy with Kym's outfit. Why were they changing it?

"Lady Nila's request," Isabel said, her voice uncharacteristically flat. "We're to up our standards for this leg of the parade."

"After what happened yesterday," Veronica added, placing a gem on Kym's collarbone.

Kym and the other Prized gathered outside the city walls. Kym stepped onto her blue chariot and saw her outfit wasn't the only one that changed. Strings of silver thread shimmered in Tomark's dark, wavy hair, Xander's clothes were even more revealing, exposing more of his muscular physique, and Amber wore a bright red tiara, which Kym had only seen her wear once. The chariots made their way into the city, and the Protectorate followed behind the Prized. However, it didn't escape Kym that their spears were already drawn.

The crowds cheered and bowed, just like the day before. Kym waved, her skin twinkling like a golden blue star. She spotted more death supporters in the crowd, and their looks of discontent were more prevalent than the ones from the last city. They looked like they'd rather be anywhere else. Members of the city patrol stood among the kneeling crowd, batons held ready at their sides. Did the High Priest of Silvaura anticipate another riot? Did he order the city patrol to keep the people under control?

Kym mounted the Temple steps, and she was surprised to find her dad waiting for her at the top. He offered her his hand, which she took after hesitating a moment. What was he doing there? He hadn't been part of the parade yesterday. Why was he there now?

Kym's dad led her to her spot in the lineup. Tomark walked up next, who was welcomed by his grandmother, followed by Lennax, joined by an older woman who looked just like him. Once they all stood in front of the Temple, the high priest started presenting the Prized. Unlike the previous city, this high priest didn't take as much time during his presentation. He'd announce one Prized, and before the crowd stopped its required cheering, announce the next.

Kym preferred this approach. It made things move along much faster. The sooner the Parade was over and done, the happier she'd be. Before Kym knew it, her presentation had come and gone. As Lennax stepped back into the line, members of the crowd stood, waving black banners over their heads.

"Thed guides us!"

"Serve the people, not yourselves!"

The Protectorate descended the Temple steps in silence, pushing their way through the crowd. They forced the Thed supporters back to their knees, their spears held menacingly at their sides. But the damage was done. More black-clad supporters took up the call while the first fell silent.

Kym stepped forward. Why were they Protectorate attacking these people? They weren't throwing stones or rushing forward like the people the day before. They were just speaking their minds. Why was that so wrong?

Long, gentle fingers wrapped around Kym's upper arm. Kym turned around, expecting Veronica and Isabel to drag her to safety.

But all they did was pull Kym back to her place in line. The high priest didn't acknowledge the disturbance. He continued with his speech, calling on the gods to bless the Prized in the Fifth Trial.

The parade in the City of Termubra didn't go much better. Veronica and Isabel added flakes of gold to her now slicked-back hair. More Protectorate patrolled the crowds, standing every ten yards or so, their spears held at the ready. More Thed supporters filled the crowd, glaring at the Prized as they rode by.

Kym couldn't stop herself from staring. How were there more of them than the previous day? Why were they declaring themselves to Thed, who was still the enemy of the other gods? He wasn't saving them. He was making them sick. And supporting him was why the crowd was full of Pros. Why couldn't they see that?

Kym tried to smile and wave as her chariot rolled through the streets, but that was harder than she thought. The chant of '*serve the people, not yourselves*' rose like a wave from the Thed supporters, and by the time she reached the Temple, she could barely hear the high priest speak as the crowd swelled in anger. It took every ounce of control Kym possessed not to throw attacks into the line of Protectorate standing at the edge of the Temple stairs.

Kym dreaded returning to the City of Contellus. There, the people shunned her for more than half her life. How would they react now, seeing Kym being paraded into the city like she was better than they were? Would they still ignore her, or would their apparent dislike of anything magical outweigh their memories of her? If the first three cities were any indication, no one was going to be happy when the Prized arrived.

Kym's maids added sapphires to her face and golden hair, applied more blue makeup to her eyes and cheeks, and topped it off with a shimmering blue band around her forehead. And her wardrobe wasn't the only thing that changed. Three young Water Favored arrived by carriage that morning, dressed in simple blue clothes. They were to walk behind Kym's chariot, water dancing around her under their supervision.

The priests upped their game as well. Protectorate moved

through the crowds, and more of them lined the street, their spears angled toward the kneeling people. More holo projectors had been set up along their route as well, projecting the parade's progress high into the air for all to see.

Kym heard the roar of the crowd before Xander's chariot entered the city. Unlike the first three cities, the displeasure in their cries was evident. Kym's golden skin shuddered as she took a few breaths to calm herself. Here, she'd always been invisible. What she wouldn't give for that to be the case today.

Kym's chariot rolled into the city, now pulled by a pair of massive, water construct manta rays. Streams and sheets of water swirled around her waving arms, looking like ghostly extensions of her dress. She watched from the wrong end of a telescope, faces she recognized jumped out at her from the crowd, oddly magnified as she locked eyes with them; an old neighbor leaning on his cane, a classmate who'd never acknowledged her existence, a teacher who always forgot her name. Her stomach lurched at the sight of these links to her past, who all wore the same hateful expression, black banners held in their hands. She looked ahead, but more faces from her past were there as well.

Kym was grateful when her chariot reached the Temple steps she knew so well. Her father waited at the bottom, this time escorting Kym up in a fitted blue suit. The crowd swelled as he led her up the steps to the high priest. He was just as Kym remembered him. He was younger than the other high priests and looked absolutely thrilled as he bowed to Kym. The sight made her skin crawl more than the displeasure of the crowd.

"We, my children, are twice blessed by the gods this day," he shouted over the roars of the crowd, which the massive Protectorate presence barely contained. "The great purifier, Reta, and the bringer of judgment, Rai, honor the City of Contellus today. Kymbralyn, Favored of Water, and Tomark, Favored of Air, called our great city home before joining the gods' chosen few, their Favored amongst us."

Kym stomach lurched. Why did the priest need to single out her and Tomark? It was bad enough being recognized by the people who knew her. Now, everyone would remember.

Kym's father and Tomark's grandmother led them forward, and Kym forced on a smile. They stood a little ways apart at the top of the steps, their massive holo projections shining into the air. Under the command of the Water Favored, a wave crested behind her as streams of water swirled around her arms.

There were so many Protectorate in and around the crowd, they could only stare at Kym and Tomark with displeasure. But that was enough to knock the wind from Kym's lungs. She stared into the crowd, at the people she used to pass in the street every day, their hatred of her contained by a small army. Kym glanced down at her glittering body, covered in more wealth than most people saw in their lifetime. What happened to helping those who couldn't help themselves?

Nila happened. She put Kym's mother's life on the line. The people of Princirum could hate her as much as they wanted. All that mattered was saving her mom. If she didn't, all of this would be for nothing.

Relief washed over Kym as she climbed into her blue carriage. The horror show of a parade was over. She'd arrive at Crystal Palace in a few hours, where she'd try to wash off the ridiculousness of the past four days. She didn't have time to dwell on angry crowds or her discomfort and shame. Those things were mere distractions. All that mattered now was winning the Fifth Trial.

Kym was alone, nothing but open sea in every direction. Behind her, the sky was black and empty, while the last rays of sunset danced on the horizon before her. She struck out, trying to reach those last golden beams. The water was so warm, so peaceful. If she just kept going, she'd leave the cold blackness behind forever.

"You're not done," a dark, cold voice rumbled from the icy water behind her.

Cold waves crashed around Kym, sweeping her beneath the surface. She tried to swim out, her heart pounding in her ears, but the icy current was too strong. She opened her mouth, desperate for air, but the water stayed wet and unbreathable as it entered her lungs. Kym reached out, longing to reach the warmth above her. But all she could see was darkness.

Kym sat bolt upright, her body drenched in sweat. Her massive bedchamber at Crystal Palace seemed oddly dark, given that everything was white. She lay on her back, staring up at the high, vaulted ceiling as her heartbeat slowed. Today, she had one task, and it was a simple one—save her mom.

Veronica and Isabel arrived as the sun rose, once again back in their blue dresses. They let Kym stay in bed while they zoomed around the room, claiming they were "tidying" the already-spotless space. Clearly, Kym wasn't the only one who was nervous.

Kym couldn't stand being still. She needed to do something. Practicing magic wasn't an option; she needed to conserve her energy for the Fifth Trial, whatever it ended up being. Luckily, the day was full of pre-Trial preparations. Veronica and Isabel washed and dressed Kym in a glittering blue dress with a weightless train. After the outfits from the Parade, this outfit felt oddly subdued.

Kym followed her maids to Crystal Palace's Temple. She, Tomark, Xander, Lennax, Kensrix, and Amber stood silently outside the massive doors, waiting for their cue to enter. Xander led them inside when the doors opened. The massive, round room was filled with benches, all facing the large altar at the center. Six smaller altars sat in niches around the curved outer walls. Shafts of light filled the room, crisscrossing through the air from skylights in the ceiling.

Favored filled the back rows, while Masters, prominent city officials, and friends of the Rulers sat near the middle of the room, facing the altar of Pheil. Kym glanced sideways at she walked down the aisle, and something strange caught her eye. The high priests, who'd been present throughout the Calling, weren't there. Clearly, after the disastrous Parade of Glory, they were no longer welcome at the palace.

"Great Pheil," Zara said, standing in the middle of the Rulers, who all stood before the altar of Pheil and Thed in the middle of the room, "Queen of the gods and bringer of life, we beseech you. Your chosen, your Favored, have answered your call and kneel before you, humble and willing. May only the worthiest among them answer your call."

Zara moved down the line of Prized, placing her hand on each of their shoulders. Kym's insides squirmed as Zara's slender fingers rested on her skin.

"Those of you," Zara continued, "who wish to extend your gratitude to the gods' Prized may step forward."

Everyone rose from the glittering white benches, forming tight lines in the Temple's many aisles. Kym tried not to look uncomfortable as people sank to their knees in front of her, bowing at her feet as they wished her luck. Some even placed small gifts at her feet. She wasn't sure what was worse—the genuine way the city members wished her luck or how the Water Favored clearly did it out of obligation. Kym let the world around her drift away, focusing instead on a single thought. At the end of the day, this would all be over.

"May Reta reign supreme," an elderly woman said, tears welling up in her eyes as she placed a small statue of Reta before Kym.

"May Reta reign supreme," Kenna said, barely making eye contact with Kym.

"May Reta reign supreme," a young couple whispered, gently stroking the hem of Kym's dress.

"May Reta reign supreme," Lance snarled through gritted teeth, staring right into Kym's eyes.

When the line of people dispersed, Veronica and Isabel led Kym from the Temple. However, they didn't take her back to the bedchamber. They led Kym to a chamber she'd never been to on the second floor. It was empty except for a few chairs, a long table along one wall, and a stone pedestal in the middle of the room. Kym was about to sit when the door opened. Nila glided into the room, a servant cowering behind her, a large, blue box in his outstretched arms.

"Your clothes for the trial," Nila said as the servant placed the box on the long table. "Dress Miss Kymbralyn, then leave her here."

Veronica and Isabel nodded, not looking up from the floor.

"You are very near the end, Kymbralyn," Nila continued, turning back to Kym. "Because of your service, death will not reign supreme. I knew you would prove water's might, and the gods' good fortune will guide us all in our endeavors. All you needed was the right...motivation."

"Nila," Kym said, fighting to keep her voice calm. Why was Nila acting like the last five days weren't a complete disaster? "This...it can't be worth...didn't you see what happened in the cities?"

"That was... unfortunate," Nila said slowly. "The rise of Phillip has given the people a false sense of change. But, you will show them how things are meant to be. You will restore balance in Princirum."

"It doesn't bother you that—"

"You wear the Water Charm," Nila cut across Kym, her voice as stern as steel. "You are the Vanquisher of Water. Do not hold back. Do this, and all you have fought for will be yours."

Kym's hands balled into fists as Nila glided from the room. She didn't want to hold back. She wanted to let her anger fall on the one who caused her so much pain. But attacking Nila was pointless. All that mattered was the trial.

Kym breathed through her nose, trying to forget Nila, the people's anger, and her mother's life hanging over her head. Somewhere, Veronica and Isabel opened the blue box. It contained a simple, sleeveless blue dress and matching sandals. It took them longer to get Kym out of her first dress than it took them to put on the new one.

"You're nearly there, my girl," Veronica said, squeezing Kym's hand.

"We are so proud of you," Isabel smiled, running her fingers through Kym's hair. "So proud."

"Thank you," Kym croaked, although she felt she'd done nothing worthy of praise lately.

She wrapped her arms around them. Kym thought back to the first time she'd met her maids. She couldn't understand why she needed them. Now, she couldn't imagine getting through this without them.

Veronica and Isabel backed out of the room, their eyes full of tears, leaving Kym alone. She paced around the room, her heartbeat increasing with every step. There was a tray of food on the back table, but Kym didn't touch a bit of it. Her body shook as she glanced out of the vast window. How much longer did she have to wait? She wanted to get this over with.

A flash of blinding white light filled the room. Kym stumbled back, covering her eyes as the light burned her retinas. Slowly, she lowered her hand. The pure white form of Zara floated in the middle of the room, her face impassive. This was no hologram projection. This was Zara's magic.

"My children, tonight you witness something that only occurs once in a generation. In a few moments, the final, Fifth Trial of the Calling will begin. Until now, the Prized have been unaware of what this Trial entails.

"The Fifth Trial is a fight to the last Prized standing. However, some Prized will not have access to their magic at the start of the trial. Those who have performed the best in the Calling will begin with magic. The remaining Prized will regain their magic in one-minute intervals, with the last receiving their magic five minutes into the trial. Amber, Prized of Heirraph and Favored of Fire, will begin the trial with her magic, followed by Kymbralyn, Lennax, Xander, Tomark, and finally Kensrix."

Kym gasped, the insides of her arms alight with pain. She doubled over, clutching her forearms as the pain receded.

"The rules of the Fifth Trial," Zara continues, "are the same as the previous two; do whatever it takes to accomplish your goal. A Prized will be eliminated when they are knocked unconscious. Prized, step onto your pedestals. The Fifth Trial will begin at the sound of the gong. May the gods bless your endeavors, and may the worthiest among you answer their call."

Zara's glowing white form faded away as silence filled the room. Kym stepped up onto the pedestal, her entire body shaking. She closed her eyes and took a deep breath, hoping to calm her frantic mind. This was it. All she needed to do was beat five other Favored in a fight, and she'd save her mom.

Kym opened her eyes, but all she could see was darkness. The sound of rushing water filled her ears. Something pulled Kym forward, and her feet left solid ground. She spun on the spot, her body exploding into the void as she hurtled through space. Her feet slammed into solid ground, and her body collided back together. Then specks of light bloomed in her eyes.

CHAPTER TWENTY-FOUR

THE
FIFTH TRIAL

KYM STOOD IN THE MIDDLE OF A SMALL STONE ARENA. A GIANT wall of black earth, at least one hundred feet high, ringed the edge of the enclosure. Piles of stone, pools of water, and pits of fire littered the ground. Kym's eye's darted around, trying to take it all in. Unlike the other trials, this place was designed for a show. Bright lights shone from beyond the wall, and muffled cheers from the massive crowd reached her ears.

The Prized stood on pedestals, forming a ring in the center of the arena. Kym turned her head as little as she could to either side, not daring to move. Tomark and Lennax stood on her left, while Amber and Kensrix were on her right. Xander was directly across from her, and she could see the nerves on his face. None of them spoke, and aside from the slight turn of the head, they were as still as statues. Blood pounded in Kym's ears, drowning out the distant noises of the watching crowd. Her body trembled with each breath, which barely filled her lungs.

The silence stretched for an eternity. How long were they going to wait? Zara said the trial would start at the sound of a gong, but there was only silence. Kym's stomach gave an uncomfortable lurch. She wanted to get started. Anything was better than standing, waiting for something to happen.

A low hum rumbled through the enclosure. It grew louder and louder, and seemed to emanate from the arena itself. Kym covered her ears with her hands, trying to drive off the ringing in her head as her body vibrated. The humming faded, and the arena fell back into silence. The trial had begun.

Kym didn't move a muscle, even though she knew she needed to run. The information from her brain couldn't reach the rest of her body. To her right, Amber raised her arms, her red Marks glowing. Kym's heart stopped. Amber was going to eliminate her before she even had magic to defend herself. The bright red fire bolt illuminated her blank face, and Kym, still unable to move, braced herself.

Amber spun around, throwing the bolt in the opposite direction. It streaked through the air and struck Kensrix right in the chest. Kym's mouth fell open as Kensrix flew through the air and slammed into a pile of rocks. What just happened? Kym was sure Amber would go for her first. She'd beaten her in the last Trial, after all. Why'd she attack Kensrix?

"One down," Amber said flatly. Her fire blast left her fingers before Kensrix moved an inch.

Kym's body jolted into action. She was defenseless, at least for the next thirty seconds, which was plenty of time for Amber to take them all out. So, she ran. She dove behind a large boulder as the air around her filled with bright red light. Amber's attack made the boulder tremble as pieces of rock fell around her.

Kym peered cautiously around the side. Flames covered the open space between the pedestals, and the rest of the Prized were nowhere to be seen. Amber stood in the very center of the chaos, tongues of flame flying through the air like ghosts. She was using her time as the only one with magic to overwhelm the rest. Kym had to admit it was a smart move.

She tucked back behind her boulder and focused her energy, but her forearms remained bare. She couldn't have much longer to wait. More crashes filled the air, and debris rained down on Kym. She couldn't wait any longer. She needed to win the trial, and she wasn't going to do that crouching behind a boulder.

Kym peeked around her crumbling shelter. Amber's back was to her, several bright red bolts floating around her, shooting blasts in every direction. There was a large pile of rocks next to a shallow pool fifteen feet away. This was her chance. Kym closed her eyes and took a deep breath. This had to work.

She rolled out from behind her boulder, and sprinted toward the large pile of rocks. The unmistakable hissing of bolts filled her ears, but she ignored it. She quickened her pace, the pile of rocks was just feet away. She leaped into the air, her arms outstretched. She'd made it.

"Ah!" Pain radiated through Kym's body as she skidded across the ground.

The fire bolt hit Kym's side, knocking her away from the rock pile and pool. Instead, she landed beside a pit of fire. She tried to push herself up, but her arms buckled, and she fell back to the ground. The hem of a red dress drew nearer, and Kym rolled onto her back. Amber raised her hands, and the fire from the pit soared into the air. Kym instinctively raised her arms, covering her face, and braced herself for the impact.

There was a flash of blue light, and energy surged through Kym like electricity. A dome of glowing blue water appeared around her as Amber's fire descended. The flames skidded off the dome, flying in every direction, but left Kym untouched. Amber's blank stare faltered as she waved her hand, directing her own fire away from herself.

Kym didn't wait for Amber to recover. She dissolved her dome and threw a bolt at Amber. It ripped through Amber's half-formed shield, and she flew back, landing with a thud on the hard ground. Kym scrambled up as Amber did the same.

Kym glided into the air, the full power of the water charm surging through her. Streaks of red zoomed past her, and Kym veered around. Several fire pits glowed red, and countless bolts launched from their depths at Amber's command. Kym moved as fast as she could, but Amber's aim was good. The attacks streaked past her, and Kym felt the heat radiating from them. Below her, Kym saw someone dressed in silver crouched behind another large boulder. Tomark. Kym swooped down without hesitation, Amber's attacks raining down around her.

"How's it going?" he asked almost conversationally, the world crashing around them.

"Oh, you know," Kym panted, throwing two bolts in Amber's general direction.

"Thanks for making me a target," Tomark said as three spiraling red blasts zoomed over his head. "I don't think we're supposed to team up," he added.

"You think Xander and Amber won't fight together to narrow the playing field?" Kym asked.

She waved her hand above her head, and a glowing blue disk appeared over her and Tomark.

"Besides," she pressed on. She looked into Tomark's dark green eyes, and the crashes around them faded away. "I'm not attacking defenseless people. I won't."

"I appreciate that."

Warmth spread through Kym at Tomark's words. At least there was one person who wouldn't attack her on sight. The shield above their heads shattered in a flash of red and blue. Kym jumped up and fired a blast, but Amber was faster.

Kym's attack bounced off Amber's shield, flying off course and exploding against the massive stone wall, leaving a sizable crack behind. Amber directed her hand at the fire pit closest to her; the flames turned red as they twisted into a massive sphere.

"Run!" Kym shouted as Amber flicked her wrists toward Kym and Tomark.

The massive red comet exploded out of the ground, twice as tall as Kym. It soared through the air, filling the dim arena with bright red light. Out of the corner of her eye, Kym saw Lennax, the cracks of his stone arm glowing green, racing not away from the comet but right at Amber. A bright green blast shot from his hands and collided with Amber's comet. The explosion sent dirt and rocks flying in all directions. Kym turned away, shielding her face with her hands. Lennax jumped into the air and slammed his stone fist on the ground. The earth beneath Amber's feet split open and cracks spread like a spider's web across the earth.

Kym swung her arm. A jet of water flew through the air and struck Lennax in the side, knocking him off balance. However, he was more agile than Kym expected. He righted himself after staggering back a few steps and turned to face Kym. Chunks of earth flew up from the ground to his hands, where they glowed bright green. Kym braced herself, ready to deflect his attacks.

Three bright red bolts hit Lennax in the chest, one right after the other. He spun through the air like a top, his feet pointed to the sky, his cries filling the air. He crashed to the ground, a massive cloud of dust billowing around him. Kym, her heart racing, turned to face Amber, who was already readying another round of attacks.

Kym's swipe hit the ground right in front of Amber's feet, forcing her to jump back. Kym took off in the opposite direction, blood pounding in her ears. Luckily, there was a giant fissure between them, which should buy her a few seconds. That didn't stop Lennax. He was back on his feet on Kym's side of the gash, and running straight for Tomark.

"No!"

Kym frantically waved her hands, and the water from three pools rose into the air. It swirled around Lennax on all sides, looking like a tower of warped glass. Kym, still focusing on the water, let the energy around herself flow, and she rose into the air. She flew over the trapped Lennax, there was a flash of bright green, and pain radiated from Kym's middle. She drifted through the air, but Lennax's attack wasn't strong enough to blast her from the sky.

The water swirling around Lennax fell. It knocked his feet out from under him and carried him several yards away on a muddy wave. Ignoring the pain in her stomach, Kym flicked her wrists. A jet of muddy water launched Lennax into the air. This was her chance. She waved her hand, and three small bolts appeared in front of her.

She focused on Lennax, momentarily frozen in midair as his body fell, and flicked her wrists. The tracking bolts zoomed after Lennax as he crashed back to the earth. The first knocked him to the ground, while the others hit him right after, filling the air with dust. Kym soared down, landing as the unconscious Lennax sank into the earth.

Panting, her head pounding, Kym leaned down onto her knees. Sweat poured thick and fast down her face. She'd done it. Lennax was out, and so was Kensrix. That was two Prized gone out of six, but the thought didn't make Kym feel better. Eliminating Lennax had been easy enough. She barely knew him. But now, it was down to Tomark, Amber, Xander, and Kym. Now, to save her mother's life, she needed to fight her friends.

Several loud crashes brought Kym back to her surroundings. Xander had his magic, and just like Kym expected, he stood side by side with Amber. They were throwing everything they had at Tomark, who rolled and jumped all over the ground, narrowly avoiding the attacks flying at him from all sides. The bottom fell out of Kym's stomach. Tomark didn't have his magic yet.

Kym ran as fast as she could. Pain surged up her legs, which felt like a million needles were stabbing them at once. But, Kym didn't miss a beat as she sprinted to the closest pool. She fell to her knees, skidding the last several feet across the rough ground. She shoved her hands into the water, an image clear in her mind. Energy flowed from Kym's arms, and the water in the pool began to glow.

The shark construct rose soundlessly out of the glowing water. It floated above the surface, rising and falling slightly as it remained completely still, like a blue statue. More crashes filled the air, and Kym focused harder than she ever had before. The single thought filled her mind until there was nothing else: Get Xander.

The shark burst to life, snapping its jaws and twitching its fins as it wheeled around. Luckily for Kym, Xander was focused on Tomark, who was still barely avoiding the combined assault from him and Amber. The shark's massive jaws snapped around Xander's leg, and his screams filled the air. The construct pulled Xander away by his bleeding leg, while Tomark and Amber froze, staring as Xander struggled against the construct's jaws.

Tomark dove behind a boulder, taking advantage of Amber's momentary freeze. Kym's blast hit the ground at Amber's feet, who jumped back as the air filled with dust. Kym waved her hand, and the water from the pools nearest Amber surged toward her, forming one massive wave. A bright red strand of flame cracked through the air like a whip. It cut cleanly through the wall of water, and struck Kym in the chest.

Pain coursed through Kym as she staggered backward. Tentatively, she looked down. The top several inches of her dress were gone, and the skin of her upper chest shone bright red. Gingerly, Kym prodded the burn with her fingers and gasped in pain. Sweat poured down her face and onto her chest, which felt like acid against the bright red welt.

Amber's fire whip cracked through the air once again, but Kym was ready for it this time. Her shield exploded in a flash of blue when the whip made contact, but luckily, it stopped the fiery attack from striking her again. Frantically, Kym threw two swipes in Amber's general direction. A massive wall of flame, at least twenty feet long and just as high, exploded into being, waves of heat radiating off it. Kym's swipes exploded on contact, not even making a dent in Amber's defenses.

Sweat poured into Kym's eyes, and her body throbbed like a drum. Even with the power from the charm coursing through her, she wasn't sure how long she could keep this up. Amber was determined to win, apparently no matter the cost. In a distant part of her mind, she could sense her construct was still intact. But how long would that last? Xander knew more about constructs than anyone she knew. Would he return to Amber's side after he destroyed the construct?

The wall of fire surged away from Kym, condensing into Amber's outstretched hands. Kym's heart rate quickened even further. Amber's compact bolt quivered as she lifted her hand above her head. Kym racked her brain for something to do, but Amber's hand was already coming down. It was too late.

A silvery blast streaked past Kym's right ear, hitting the red compact bolt before it left Amber's hand. The flash of red energy blew Kym back. She skidded across the ground, pain radiating through her shoulder. Kym gritted her teeth, pushing the pain from her mind as she staggered up. Tomark stood on the side of a boulder, his silvery Marks shining on his forearms. Kym couldn't stop the smile from spreading on her lips. Tomark had his magic at last.

"Thanks," Kym winced.

"Don't mention it," Tomark said. Both he and Kym ran behind his boulder. "She's not holding back, is she?"

"She's on a whole other level," Kym said. "She's gone way past Fire Princess. I can't beat her on my own."

"You don't have to," Tomark said, giving Kym's hand a quick squeeze. "I'll help you."

"What?" Kym stared into Tomark's green eyes. Watching each other's backs was one thing, but actually helping each other? "Why?"

"Because," Tomark smiled, pulling Kym to her feet. "You need to win more than I do."

Warmth swelled inside Kym that had nothing to do with her injuries. Together, they stepped out from behind their boulder. Amber was staggering out of a pool, a large cut across her forehead, her red dress singed and soaking. She raised her hand, and flames burst around her. Kym instinctively covered her face, but the fire vanished as soon as it came. Amber stood where she was, just as disheveled but completely dry. She stared at Kym and Tomark, and even from that far away, Kym could make out the blank, cold look on her face.

Tomark took to the sky, and Kym ran toward Amber, just like they'd done countless times fighting death demons. The fire in the pits closest to Amber rose into the air but flickered away as Tomark rained bolts down on Amber. She staggered back, looking wildly in the air for Tomark, and that was all Kym needed. Her bolt hit Amber's staggering feet, and she toppled backward. Kym shoved her hands forward, and her blast hit Amber right in the chest. She flew through the air like a doll, landing with a loud thud on the hard ground.

Kym sprinted toward Amber, while Tomark landed gracefully a few yards away. Even after all that, Amber was already pushing herself up. Tomark waved his arms. A massive gust of air lifted

Amber into the air like a leaf. Kym stopped running. She stared up at her friend, her arms and legs waving wildly as she flew toward the sky. Amber, the fiercest person Kym knew, was utterly helpless.

"Kym!" Tomark yelled, recalling Kym to her surroundings. "Hurry! I can't hold her for long!"

Kym's head whipped around. Flames from the nearest fire pits flew through the air to the struggling Amber, spinning like a top high above them. It was only a matter of seconds before Amber found a way out. Tomark was right. To save her mom, she needed to take Amber out.

Kym raised her arms. Four tracking bolts appeared in the air before her. She looked up at Amber, focused her energy on her airborne friend, and flicked her hands upward. There was a flash of bright purple, and pain surged through Kym's right arm. Something large latched painfully onto her shoulder and hoisted her into the air.

Blood poured down Kym's chest from deep, empty puncture wounds. Panicking, she looked down. Xander was limping toward Tomark and Amber, his leg a bloody mess and his clothes in tatters. Kym threw a bolt wildly over her head, and whatever construct Xander made released its grip. Kym plummeted to the earth, wind roaring in her ears. She focused all of her energy on herself and stopped, suspended in midair, a few inches above the ground.

Kym relaxed and flopped on her stomach. The pain in her shoulder coursed through the rest of her body. She didn't want to look at it, but how could it be worse than what she imagined. Slowly, she glanced down. There were four large holes in her left shoulder. Blood ran from each one, seeping into her blue dress. She was wrong. This was much worse than she imagined.

The edges of her vision fuzzy, Kym struggled to roll onto her back. Tomark zoomed over her, but he didn't stop. Where was he going? Kym tried to sit up but stopped as her insides turned to ice. Somehow, Amber had freed herself from Tomark's tornado and was sprinting right toward Kym. Every other thought vanished from Kym's mind. She needed to move, and she needed to do it now.

Kym focused all her energy on herself and rose into the air. She threw a steady stream of bolts, blasts, and swipes down at Amber, who jumped from side to side, easily avoiding them. Amber waved her hand at one of the fire pits, and a giant fireball launched into the air. Kym stopped attacking, focused her energy on herself, and shot off to the opposite side of the arena.

But the giant ball of fire must have been more than just flame. It pursued Kym, following her erratic flight path like a massive tracking bolt. The dark, black boundary wall loomed in front of her, and Kym veered upward at the last possible moment. She shot high into the air as the large fireball crashed into the wall.

A giant plume of smoke and dirt exploded into the air on the other side of the arena. Kym froze in midair, unable to think as she stared at the spot. Fear coursed through her body like ice, eclipsing the pain of her many injuries. What happened? She'd completely forgotten about Tomark flying off before. Who caused the explosion? Was Tomark still in the trial? An explosion of that size could have taken out both Tomark and Xander. And if one of them managed to survive, would they be in any condition to fight?

"Ah!"

Pain and heat burned around Kym's middle. Something fiery red and hot was wrapped around her waist. Kym struggled, trying to turn herself and see what was forcing her back to the ground. But its grip around her was too strong. Kym threw attacks wildly over her shoulders, but nothing she did caused the fire construct to release her. As the ground drew closer, Kym waved her arms in a last-ditch attempt. Water from the five nearest pools sloshed onto the ground, forming a gigantic bubble.

The force of the crash sent hot, steaming water and dust flying in every direction. Kym bounced off the ground like a rag doll, skidding across the rough ground until she slammed into a large pile of light grey stones. Every part of her body ached, and stars flashed continuously across her vision. She stayed where she was, not bothering to move. She didn't have enough strength to blink, let alone sit up or perform magic. All she knew was intense, pulsating pain.

Amber emerged from the clouds of steam and smoke. She

stopped a couple of feet away from Kym, her face blank as she looked at the small red sphere floating above her hand. Kym stared at the fire bolt. She couldn't let it end this way. She couldn't give up. If she gave up, Nila would send her mom's doctors away. She had to keep fighting.

But as she stared at Amber's bolt, it began to change. The smooth, round shape broke down, swirling like a glowing red cloud above her slender fingers. Fear overtook Kym's pain. What was Amber doing? She'd never seen a bolt do anything like that before.

Amber raised her hand, the swirling, red energy floating above it. Kym's eyes darted in every direction. Where could she hide? Amber's arm fell, and the fiery red energy flew toward her. Kym tried to move, but her body was in too much pain. She was stuck.

A scream of pain ripped through the air. Kym watched, seconds stretching into an eternity, as Tomark flew in front of her, his clothes torn and bloody. Amber's attack struck him in the chest, filling the world with bright, red light. Tomark fell to the ground, his body limp and lifeless, a bright red burn spreading across his chest. Kym reached out to him, but the ground swallowed his body.

Kym's insides turned to ice. Tomark had just sacrificed himself so she could stay in the trial. Why would he do that? There was no logical reason. But of course, Kym knew why he did it. His soft, gentle voice pushed its way to the front of her mind.

You need to win more than I do.

Emotions swirled inside Kym like a storm, most of them moving too fast for her to even register. But as she looked at Amber's momentarily stunned face, one emotion kept resurfacing— anger. She wouldn't let Tomark's sacrifice go unanswered. She needed to win.

The water blast left Kym's hands before she knew what she was doing. Amber flew backward, caught off guard by the speed of Kym's attack. Kym rose back into the air, energy pouring from the charm around her neck. Long streams of water grew from her arms, forming two long tendrils. Kym stared down at Amber, crouched on her hands and knees, and there was only one clear thought rushing through her mind: Amber needed to go.

She swung her arms down, and the tentacles of water slammed into the ground, leaving deep craters in their wake. Fire from four different pits flew to Amber, and she threw her compact bolt up at Kym with incredible speed. Kym's tentacles whipped through the air, striking the compact bolt before it could even get close to her. The force of the explosion sent her flying backward, but she righted herself and sent four tracking bolts down at Amber. Amber spun on the spot and vanished in a flash of bright red flames. Kym veered around, but she wasn't fast enough. A bright red arch hit Kym right in her stomach.

She fell, slowing herself just before she smashed into the ground. Kym staggered to her feet, her ears ringing, her vision growing darker as her arm seared with pain. But she didn't care. Amber couldn't win. Somehow, that would make everything right. Behind her, Kym heard the unmistakable crackle of flame.

Using what felt like all the energy she had left, Kym turned around. Amber stood right next to her, four bright red bolts arranged in a line in front of her. Amber's alignment blast collided with Kym's temple before she raised her hands. Her head exploded as she teetered backward. Pain overtook Kym's senses, and the world around her faded away.

CHAPTER TWENTY-FIVE

THE
UPSET

The inside of Kym's head was on fire. The throbbing she associated with overusing her energy was there, but that was a mere discomfort. She tried moving, rolling over, something. She only managed a slight twitch. Panic coursed through Kym like fire. What was wrong with her? Why had her body turned to stone?

Kym couldn't breathe. Her panic rose, and so did the throbbing inside her skull. She wanted to open her eyes, but they were just as motionless as the rest of her body. How'd she even get here? She tried to remember, but the fiery pain in her head quadrupled.

Something brushed against her fingers, gentle as billowing steam against her frozen skin. She felt it, but it was so faint she barely registered it on top of all the throbbing. But she had felt it. Kym's breathing slowed slightly. At the very least, she could feel. Something was near her, and if she could just open her eyes, she'd see it.

It was like drilling a hole in stone with a feather. Kym felt like she was pushing a boulder up a steep hill, her eyelids always fighting to close again. But, little by little, the slits of her eyes crept open. The room she was in was so bright, her first impulse was to close her eyes again. But she couldn't. It took too much to open them to stop now. Besides, she needed to see who was beside her.

Sounds wound their way into Kym's ears as the pounding in her head increased. Voices. Not distant, unknown voices, but voices she knew, and knew well. The light, singsong voices seemed to be on her left, while the much rougher and more welcome one was to her right. She knew the singsong voices at once. How many times had they pulled her from sleep in complete darkness? She didn't need eyes to know Veronica and Isabel were there, watching over her.

Kym forced her eyes open even wider, and more bright light flooded her exhausted pupils. Slowly, more slowly than she wanted, Kym looked to the right. A smile grew inside her, even if it couldn't appear on her frozen, motionless face.

Kat stared down at her, her short brown hair curtaining her worried face. The concern in Kat's eyes was even more frightening than Kym's inability to move. Kat never worried about anything. If she was worried, something must be seriously wrong.

"Hey," Kat breathed. She extended her arm, and the faint, ghost-like sensation reappeared on Kym's hand. "You did good."

Kym tried to open her mouth, but she couldn't make her lips move. She needed to speak. Kat knew what happened and why she was here. The pounding in her head increased, and her breathing became quick and shallow. The ghost of Kat's grip grew stronger. No doubt she saw the panic in Kym's eyes.

"Hey. Hey," she said quickly. "Don't do that. Don't worry. You're gonna be fine."

"Miss Kat," Kym heard Veronica's voice say from somewhere behind her back. "Please don't give Miss Kym false—"

"She'll be fine," Kat cut across her. "She's not wandering Nothingness yet."

Kym's panic rose from horrible to extreme. What was so bad that her maids didn't want Kat to give her false hope? And why couldn't she remember what happened to her in the first place?

"Zara's gonna be here any second," Kat said, quickly glancing over her shoulder. "She's patching up Xander, and then she'll undo whatever damage Amber did to you. If Jazin wasn't over there, I'd…"

But Kym didn't hear what Kat would do. Her sluggish brain burst into overdrive at the sound of Amber's name, flooding her pounding head with images. Attack raining around her. Tomark diving in front of Kym to save her. Amber's alignment blast hitting Kym in the temple.

Even her closed lips couldn't stop Kym's moan of pain. Tomark. He'd taken Amber's attack, eliminating himself so Kym could stay in. An image of Amber standing over her, a shapeless bolt floating above her hand, entered Kym's mind. She'd never seen a bolt change its shape before. What had Amber done to it? And what had the attack done to Tomark?

Kym needed to sit up, to find Tomark and make sure he was alright. But her body still wouldn't move. What had Amber's alignment blast done to her? It hit her in the side of the head, so why was her body stiff as stone? How much damage had Amber done? Could it even be fixed?

"Remember when Ashlyn hit her head about twenty times at the festival?" Kat said, correctly reading Kym's thoughts. "She passed out, remember? None of us could get her to respond, but Zara fixed her. She'll do the same for you, or else," Kat added, smiling broadly.

The little joke loosened the tension in Kym's chest, but only slightly. Kat was right. Kym had been sure Ashlyn wasn't going to make it after she passed out at the festival. But Zara had reversed all of the damage, and Ashlyn was fine. But were Kym's injuries comparable to Ashlyn's? She didn't remember Ashlyn ever being awake but unable to move.

Pure white light bloomed in the air behind Kat. Kym's insides relaxed even more. She knew exactly what it was, even if she couldn't see it. Life magic was pretty distinct, after all.

"What's taking so long?" Kat hissed, more to herself than to Kym. "Xander's injuries weren't even bad. He was fighting Tomark, after all. She should've come to you first."

Kat turned back to face Kym, and she was happy to see her face had relaxed slightly. If Kat was starting to calm herself down, Zara couldn't be too far away. She stared up into those light brown eyes, which looked softer than they usually did. For the first time in a long time, Kat wasn't glaring at her. Kym stared back, willing her gratitude to pass between them. Surely, Kat knew what Kym was trying to say. She always knew what was on Kym's mind.

A rustling to Kym's left made Kat look away. The ghostly pressure on her fingertips vanished, and Kat disappeared from Kym's limited line of vision. And, even though she couldn't see them, she heard her maids back away as well. This little change in her surroundings sent Kym's heart racing. Throbbing filled her ears and head, causing her already considerable pain to skyrocket.

A tall figure loomed over Kym, their face cast in shadow from the pure white light above. Kym didn't need to see Zara's face to know who stood above her. Kat and her maids wouldn't leave her side for anyone else. Zara's long, slender fingers descended on Kym, who braced herself for the pain she knew would come. Zara may be a healer, but she wasn't gentle.

Pain radiated from every spot Zara's fingers made contact with, and Kym felt them all. While Kat's touch had felt distant and other-worldly, Kym knew exactly where Zara's hands were as they worked their way up and down her screaming body. It was fortunate Kym couldn't open her mouth. If she could, she'd have screamed when Zara's fingers found her temples.

"Her broken bones and tissue damage are superficial," Zara snapped, turning slightly to her right and looking down. "They will heal as we address the rest of the damage. Do not bother tending to them."

Other wounds? As far as Kym was concerned, the only thing wrong with her was her splitting head. What other injuries did she have? They couldn't be too bad since Zara didn't even want her helper tending to them. Feeling even more confused than she'd been when she woke up, Kym focused on Zara, still speaking to the unseen person.

"The damage she sustained to her brain is severe," she said flatly. "I can feel the life fading from that area. Gather all of the materials you can and bring them here. The older, the better. Why did he insist on coming here?" she added, more speaking to herself than to anyone else. "Because of him, I lost valuable time."

Kym had no idea what Zara was talking about. Who wasted her time? Zara wasn't the type of person to waste time if she was needed elsewhere. Who made her late? Kym couldn't think of a single person. For a moment, she considered one of the Rulers, but that didn't make sense. Zara ignored them, and even kicked them out of rooms when they annoyed her.

"What kept you?" Zara demanded, bringing Kym back to her surroundings.

"Sorry, my Lady," said a soft, timid voice. It was familiar to Kym, but she couldn't place it.

She tried to concentrate, but the pounding in her head reached a tipping point. Even the simple act of trying to identify a voice sent the room spinning. A moan of pain forced its way through Kym's closed mouth. Zara's head twitched in her direction like she'd forgotten Kym was there.

"Quickly," Zara said, and there was a note of urgency in her voice that hadn't been there before. "Time is short."

The sound of heavy things scraping across the floor filled the air. Kym didn't need to imagine what was happening around her. Zara needed to pull the life energy from living things to heal others, and given her assessment of Kym's injuries, she required a lot of it to put Kym back together. Once again, Kym remembered Ashlyn's injuries after the Festival of Creation. She'd hit her head several times and required the most life energy to heal, even though she looked perfectly fine. Kym had a feeling she was in a similar situation.

The air around her filled with shimmering, white mist. Kym braced herself as best she could in her frozen state. In the past, healing her minor injuries had been excruciating, and her current injuries weren't minor at all. Feeling crept into her ghostly limbs as the glittering white cloud drifted around her. Kym watched the mist surge toward her head, and knew Zara was pulling it toward her. It was time.

Kym felt Zara place her hands on her throbbing temples. Her mouth opened, and her screams filled the air. The pain was terrible, but it was nothing compared to the life energy. Zara forced the white-hot life into Kym through her temples, and the burning pain surged through her head. Kym's body shook as the life consumed her. She wanted to run, to escape this horrible agony. Surely it didn't need to be this painful.

"Hold her," Zara said, her voice strained as Kym continued to struggle.

Hands, more hands than she expected, grabbed Kym's flailing limbs. Kym's insides jolted. She could feel the hands holding her. Who was there, and why did they need to keep her still? She looked around, but all she could see was the swirling cloud of life dancing around her head. She continued to struggle, straining against the arms pressing into her.

"C'mon, you moron. Lay still," Kat's rough voice said very close to her ear.

"It's almost over," a softer, lighter voice whispered on Kym's other side.

Kym's whole body relaxed at the sound of the new voice. Ashlyn. She was there too. The hands holding Kym relaxed, and some made their way down Kym's arm, squeezing her fingers tightly. The pressure of their touch was enough to make Kym stop fighting. She clenched her jaw, fighting her every impulse to cry out as Zara continued to set her brain on fire.

Slowly, like the dying embers of a fire, the pain in Kym's head subsided, along with the aches and pains all over her body. Tentatively, Kym opened her eyes. Zara was gone, but Kat and Ashlyn, and Veronica and Isabel, were there, smiling down at her. Kym felt the corners of her mouth curve upward and was happy to know she could smile. She sat up, flexing her hands and feet, which moved as she intended. She felt perfectly normal.

"See, that wasn't so bad, was it?"

Kym would've smacked Kat if she hadn't burst out laughing. It felt good, the laughter and joy surging through her. Sometimes, she knew just what to say to make Kym feel better.

"Then you try it next time," Kym gasped.

"Didn't look so bad," Kat shrugged.

"Well then," Ashlyn said, "Next time, we'll have Amber blast your brain. See how much you like it."

"No thanks," Kat said quickly, shooting Ashlyn a look. "I'm good."

"Miss Kat and Miss Ashlyn," Veronica said, nodding curtly to each of them. "Thank you for being here. I know it meant a lot to Miss Kym having you by her bedside."

"Lady Zara is tending to Mister Tomark," Isabel smiled. "You should offer him your company."

"I'll go too."

Kym stood up, looking every direction for some sign of Tomark. She saw his bed on the other side of the room, and heard his screams of pain as Zara treated him. Her heart froze in her chest at the sound. His injuries must be bad to elicit such a sound.

"No," Isabel said, grabbing Kym by the wrist. "We need to get you ready for the results."

Veronica and Isabel pulled Kym away as Kat and Ashlyn joined Tomark. Several sets of screens were set up around the room, and they led Kym to the closest one. Kym barely noticed as they removed the tattered remains of her clothes from her healed body. Once Isabel said "results," the ramifications of Kym's actions fell on her like a ton of bricks. She remembered why Amber blasted her. She'd lost the trial. She'd lost the Calling.

The pain inside her was more severe than any injury she'd received. Her body trembled uncontrollably, and her heart ached so bad she wanted to rip it from her chest. After everything she'd done and endured, none of it mattered. She'd lost, and now, Nila was going to order the doctors to leave. Kym's mom was going to die, and it was all her fault.

She sank to her knees, tears streaming down her face, no more than a crumpled shell. Veronica and Isabel fell beside her, and Kym knew they needed her to stand. She only had on her underclothes. But how could she stand when every part of her was destroyed?

"It's alright, my love," Isabel said, pulling Kym into a tight embrace. "You fought well."

"But—but I—"

"It's not over yet," Veronica said, also wrapping her arms around Kym. "Once Mister Tomark is healed, Lady Zara will reveal the results."

"Reveal the results?" Kym blubbered. "But Amber won."

"The trial, yes," Isabel said. "But not the Calling. Not yet."

"You mustn't give up, my love," Veronica said, wiping the tears from Kym's face. "Hope isn't lost yet. You can still save her."

Once again, Kym underestimated her maids. How long had they known why Kym was in the Calling? Surely, not the whole time. They must have found out after Nila talked to her, either when she gave her the charm or before the Fifth Trial. Her maids were right. Amber may have won the trial, but Kym had done well in the Calling overall. There was still a chance.

"It is time," a young boy dressed in a white toga said in a timid voice once Tomark was healed and redressed.

Kym recognized the boy's voice. It was the same one she'd heard at her bedside. He was the same servant Xander attacked when he tried to steal the Conduit during the festival. Kym would never forget his screams as the darkness constructs bit his dark skin.

Kym wrapped her arms around Veronica and Isabel before the Prized and their companions left the room. Jazin stood at Amber's side, her face blank as they followed right behind the young boy. Another Fire Favored walked beside Kensrix, while an older woman led Lennax along, and their faces were so similar Kym was sure they were related. That left Kat and Ashlyn, who placed themselves between Kym, Xander, and Tomark.

They walked in silence behind the white-togaed boy through Crystal Palace's vast halls. It only took a few turns before Kym knew where they were going. She'd walked the corridors to the throne room enough times to know the path. When they reached the deserted hall outside the throne room, they found the doors shut.

"When the Rulers finish deliberating," the young boy said. "they will announce the results of the Calling."

He backed out of the hall, leaving them to wait in silence.

Kym's stomach twisted uncomfortably. She didn't know which was worse, knowing that the next few minutes would determine her mother's life, or that she genuinely didn't know what the results would be. There'd been a twist in each trial. Why wouldn't there be one for the Calling as a whole?

"This is ridiculous," Jazin whispered to Amber. "You won. It shouldn't take them long to decide that."

It took another fifteen minutes before the throne room doors opened. The Rulers walked out, their cheeks flushed as they lined up in front of the gathered Favored and Prized. They all looked forward, barely moving their heads as they glared at Kym and the others.

Kym stared at them. What happened in the throne room to make them so mad? Zara stepped forward, and the impatient tone she'd used when healing Kym was even more prominent.

"We would like to congratulate the winner of the Fifth Trial of the Calling—the Prized of Heirraph, Amber." Zara clapped politely, as did the other Rulers and Favored. "She was the last one standing. Therefore, as per the instructions for the trial, she is the clear victor. Now, we must anoint the winner of the Calling. I am pleased to announce that the winner of the Calling is none other than Tomark, Prized of Rai and Favored of Air."

Silence filled the hall as Zara's words echoed around them. Tears welled up in Kym's eyes, and she felt like she'd been punched in the stomach. She'd lost the Calling. Because of her, her mother was now going to die. And Tomark won. But how? It made no sense. He didn't win the Fifth Trial; he'd sacrificed himself so Kym could save her mom. Looking around, Kym saw her confusion, along with anger, on several of the others' faces.

"Me?" Tomark stammered, his voice quiet. "How could I win? I didn't win the trial, or any of the trials. It should be Amber."

"You, Tomark, are the true winner," Zara said pointedly, and Kym saw her eyes dart quickly to either side, taking in the other Rulers. "You won because you are the only Prized who truly accomplished everything set before you during the trials. The Calling not only tests a Favored's magical prowess. It tests their innate qualities.

"The First Trial tested your ability to work with others. You listened to your partner and, together, you made a plan to retrieve your chest. The Second Trial tested your instincts. You survived second-longest because you made choices in the moment. You didn't worry about what might come next. The Third Trial was a chance to utilize your resourcefulness. You allied yourself with other Prized and joined forces to eliminate a more powerful enemy. The Fourth Trial tested your compassion. You cared for your hostage, and consoled him after he was injured by another Prized, putting his needs above your own. Finally, the Fifth Trial was the test of self-sacrifice. You sacrificed yourself so another Prized could continue. That is the greatest sacrifice anyone can make. Tomark, you are the true winner of the Calling."

"If Tomark did all of that," Kat asked, unable to hide her scrutinizing tone, "why'd it take you so long to announce the winner?"

"There was…confusion among the Rulers about the legitimacy of Tomark's victory," Zara said slowly. "You see, Tomark is the first Favored to display all of the qualities we look for. Before now, no Prized have shown these qualities. So, we determined the winner based on the magical might they displayed in the trials. But now, after centuries, we have our first true winner of the Calling.

"Tomark." Zara gestured for him to join her. Silently, he stepped out from between Kym and Kat. "By winning the Calling, the gods will grant you one request. They will appear to you in the throne room. Consider your request. You earned it."

The Rulers stepped aside, all looking murderous. Through tear-filled eyes, Kym watched Tomark walk past them and into the empty throne room. He glanced over his shoulder as the doors closed behind him, and Kym, even in her despair, smiled at him. She'd lost, but there was nothing she could do about that. He deserved his victory.

"This is a disgrace!" James snapped, not even bothering to contain his anger. "Amber should be the one speaking with the gods! She proved herself in the trials. She was born for this! Zara, if you had only listened—"

"Tomark was victorious," Stailin gloated, smiling so broadly Kym thought it looked painful. "He was the only Prized who displayed the necessary qualities. You must know this, James. Why else would you try to speak with Zara on your own?"

"We have never picked a winner based on the qualities, Stailin," Nila snapped. "Kymbralyn deserves the honor more than your Favored. She fought to stay in the trial. Your Favored sacrificed himself rather than fight."

"You have made your feelings on this point clear, Nila," Phillip droned.

Kym stared at the Rulers, who weren't bothering to hide their argument from the Favored. This was why it took them so long to announce the winner? They couldn't decide whether to follow the rules of the Calling, or do what was best for them? Kym knew better than most how much winning the Calling meant to the Rulers. But if she could accept Tomark as the rightful winner, they should too.

"C'mon," Ashlyn whispered, jerking her head toward the opposite side of the room. "I'd rather listen to anything but that."

Kym and Kat followed Ashlyn to the farthest point from the Rulers they could manage while staying in the hall. Lennax, Kensrix and their companions walked past them, leaving the hall in silence. Bright, multicolored light emanated from the gap around the throne room doors, and the Rulers fell momentarily silent.

Kym stared at the ancient-looking doors, the multicolored glow burned into her retinas. The gods must have appeared to grant Tomark's request. She wondered what he would ask for? Of course, he knew what Kym would ask. But she'd been so obsessed with saving her mom she never bothered asking what he'd request. The thought made her writhing insides feel strangely hollow.

"They could argue about dirt," Kat muttered.

"What?" Kym asked, not really listening.

"The Rulers," Kat said impatiently. "They're arguing over

something that doesn't matter anymore. Tomark's with the gods. They can't do anything to change that."

"It's ridiculous," Ashlyn said, shaking her head.

"Is it?" Amber asked flatly, Jazin and Xander right behind her. "For a Ruler to fight for their Favored?"

"Amber," Kym said, her temper eclipsing her grief, "you're more than capable of fighting your own battles."

"Poor Kym," Jazin said in mock concern. "You got in a little fight with Amber, and she hurt you. Big deal. She did what she needed to do to win."

"For Nothingness sake! She gave Kym brain damage, you idiot!" Kat snapped.

"And she didn't even win!" Ashlyn said.

"We knew what we were signing up for," Xander said, stepping between Kat and Jazin. "We knew the Calling could get messy."

"I didn't sign up for hurting my friends," Kym said, glaring at Xander. After everything he'd done during the Festival of Creation, he should understand where Kym was coming from.

"I never tried to hurt any of you," Amber said slowly.

"Oh, Pheil, Amber. You tried to blow us up during the third Trial!" Kat shouted.

"And you nearly burned Kym alive in the fourth," Ashlyn added.

"It was a contest," Jazin said. "Didn't you want to win?"

"Of course I did," Kym said, tears welling up in her eyes. "I wanted it more than anything. The only reason I did this stupid thing was to save my mom."

"What?" Kat and Ashlyn asked at the same time.

"I never wanted to do the Calling," Kym pressed on. This was the time. She needed to tell them. Besides, telling them couldn't make things worse. "I told Nila that, and she said if I didn't compete, she'd order the doctors to stop caring for my mom. I did all of this to keep her alive. But I'm not willing to hurt my friends to win. Not even to save my mom."

Kym was back in the Fifth Trial, lying on the ground while

Amber held a bolt in her hand, a bolt that lost its defined shape right before Tomark jumped in front of it. That act sealed Tomark's win. But what had Amber done to the bolt to make it do that?

"Amber," Kym said, but no one could hear her over all the arguing. "Amber!"

The group fell silent, and turned to look at Kym. Her palms filled with sweat as she looked at them, but she didn't care. She needed to ask Amber something, and being angry wasn't going to help. She took a deep breath, hoping to calm herself down a little. It didn't really work.

"Spit it out," Amber demanded coldly. "Don't be shy."

"What did you do to the bolt that hit Tomark?"

"What are you talking about?" Jazin demanded.

"The bolt that eliminated Tomark from the trial," Kym said, still addressing Amber. "How'd you make it lose its form? Energized elements maintain their shape."

"I did not change the shape," Amber said curtly. "You are confused, Kym."

"Like Nothingness she is," Kat snapped. "We saw you do it, Amber. The whole of Princirum saw what happened."

"Oh, right." Amber shrugged. Kym fought every impulse not to throw a water bolt at her. Why was she acting like this? "It just happened."

"You could've really hurt Tomark, or Kym," Ashlyn said.

"But she didn't," Xander said.

"Are we seriously talking about this?" Amber asked. She sounded almost bored, which sent Kym's blood boiling.

"Yes, Fire Princess. We're talking about this!" Kat spat, sounding just as mad as Kym.

Kym didn't understand. What was going on with Amber? Sure, they were all trying to win the Calling. Kym certainly was. But no matter how badly she wanted to win, she'd never act the way Amber did. It was like she didn't care if she hurt anyone, so long as she won.

But that was the problem. Amber didn't win. Kym expected

Amber to set Princirum on fire when she found out she'd lost. But she didn't. She didn't even speak up for herself. And now, when accused of attacking her friends, she sounded almost bored.

"Amber," Ashlyn said, bringing Kym back to the conversation. "Don't you feel bad for taking things too far? We're friends! We're the ones who know you, the real you."

"I thought you wanted to be more than the Fire Princess," Kat said, her tone cold. "Guess when push comes to shove, that's who you are. I guess you don't feel…"

Kat trailed off. Kym glanced sideways, taken aback by Kat's falling off of the offensive. She'd never passed on an opportunity to tell Amber off. Nearly all of the color had drained from Kat's face. She stared at Amber, her mouth open, like she'd had the wind knocked out of her.

"Amber," Kat said, her voice no higher than a whisper. Kym heard something in Kat's voice that she'd hardly ever heard there before. "You don't feel anything."

It was a statement, not a question. Kat's usual joking manner was nowhere to be seen. Kym looked from Kat's shocked face to Amber's blank one. Realization bloomed from the depths of Kym's mind. Amber hadn't hesitated when attacking her friends in the Calling. She hadn't reacted when she'd lost the competition she was born to win. Kat was right. Somehow, Amber wasn't feeling anything.

"As usual, Kat, you are wrong," Amber said, speaking like she was reading from a prepared speech. "I am perfectly capable of feeling. I do not, however, experience emotions."

O N E   F I N A L
C H O I C E

"How do you not feel things?"

Of all her friends, Kym was surprised to hear Xander ask the question. He looked just as confused as Kat and Kym, while Ashlyn looked like she was about to be sick. Jazin was the only one who didn't seem floored by Amber's announcement.

Kym's brain felt like someone had just pummeled it to mush. With knowing she'd lost her chance to save her mom and Tomark's surprise victory, this was too much. How could Amber not have emotions? People couldn't turn their emotions off whenever they wanted. It made no sense.

"She just said she feels," Jazin said defensively, as though Xander had asked something rude. "She doesn't experience happiness or anger or all the other emotions anymore."

"What are you talking about?" Kat sounded disgusted.

"I thought it was obvious?" Amber asked, looking at each of them. "Emotions held me back. Without them, I see everything clearly. Those little things like love and happiness do not matter in the grand scheme of things."

"When did this happen?" Kym demanded.

"After the Third Trial. Jazin showed me my friendships would ruin my chances of success. I couldn't let anything stand in my way. Winning the Calling is expected of the Fire Princess."

Kym's hands balled into fists. Every fiber of her being wanted her to run forward and punch Jazin in the jaw. How could he let Amber do this to herself? Didn't he know being the Fire Princess, and caring for no one, was the opposite of what Amber wanted?

Because of him, Amber had finally become the thing she'd resisted for so long.

"You're all avoiding the obvious question," Ashlyn said slowly. "Amber, how'd you do this?"

"I assume you know about the Cladium?" Amber asked. The word stirred in Kym's memory, but Amber pressed on without hesitation. "There is one for each of the six lower elements. Each one utilizes an element to control an aspect of human existence. The Fire Cladium controls the natural fire inside a person—their emotions. But simply controlling my emotions wasn't enough. I snuffed them out."

"Oh, Pheil," Ashlyn breathed.

"I think I'm gonna be sick," Kat muttered.

"Please tell me you're joking?" Kym breathed, her stomach twisting uncomfortably.

"Why would I joke?" Amber asked flatly, "I no longer find things humorous."

"You can reverse it, right?" Xander asked.

"Of course, but why would I? For the first time, everything is clear."

"This is crazy," Kat burst. "You can't live without your emotions, Amber."

"They're part of being human," Ashlyn said. "You just can't get rid of them and expect things to be fine."

"What's done is done," Jazin said. His shoulders fell as Kym and the others glared at him. "Guys, I've tried—"

"How could you let her do this!"

Kym hadn't realized she'd stepped forward. She stood mere inches away from Jazin's pale face. Up close, she saw he was trembling. He was afraid, and he should be. He'd sent Amber down the path Kym, Tomark, Kat, Ashlyn, and Xander had spent months pulling her away from. Thanks to Jazin, Amber was lost.

"I…I thought…" was all Jazin could stammer.

"You thought? You didn't think, Jazin. If you'd bothered to

think about Amber, then you'd know being the Fire Princess is the last thing she wanted."

"But…"

"But what?" Ashlyn demanded. "What could've been worth this?" she waved her hand at Amber's impassive face.

"She wanted to win, but after the Third Trial, all of you were still in the Calling. She was devastated after she took things too far because she cares for all of you."

"Well, that's not a problem now!" Kat spat.

A shudder ran down Kym's spine. She felt Lance's twisted grip on every fiber of her body. At the time, she couldn't understand why someone would want to do that, and now that she was staring it in the face, she still didn't. She had more reason than any of them to want to win the Calling. But, even to save her mom, she'd never destroy herself to do it. This wasn't what magic was for. The Favored were supposed to battle death, not mutilate themselves.

She looked into Amber's blank face, seemingly bored by the arguments raging around her. Anger once again boiled up inside Kym. She looked into the blank eyes of the girl she once considered one of her closest friends, and pity and disgust overwhelmed her rage. That girl was gone, replaced by a cold, unfeeling stranger.

Pandemonium erupted around the hall. The Rulers' arguing reached its peak as they shouted and screamed at each other. Kat, Xander, and the others weren't much better, as their arguments about Amber were nowhere near finished. So much noise bounced off the walls, Kym barely understood what Kat said to Jazin, and she stood right next to her.

Kym wanted to leave, just walk out of the hall and forget all of this. There was no one standing at the entrance to the hallway. There was so much happening around her, no one would notice if she slipped away. Maybe, if she was fast enough, she could see her mom before it was too late.

Kym stepped forward, glancing over her shoulder one last time. The doors to the throne room opened, and Tomark stood on the threshold, a look of utter shock on his face. Kym immediately walked toward him, and Tomark did the same. They met in the middle of the room, surrounded by the incoherent screams and ramblings of too many arguments.

Silently, Tomark grabbed Kym's hand. Warmth spread inside Kym as she followed him, but he didn't lead her out into the hall. Instead, he dragged Kym back to their circle of friends, still in the midst of their argument.

"Hey!" Tomark bellowed, bringing Ashlyn and Jazin to a stop mid-sentence. "What the Nothingness is going on here?"

No one spoke. Ashlyn's head drooped, and Xander looked like all of the air had been knocked out of him. Jazin stepped back to stand beside Amber, who barely acknowledged his presence. The only one of them who looked like she wasn't ready to stop arguing was Kat.

"Oh, good. Who'd like to tell the person who literally just won a goodness contest what Amber's done?"

Tomark let go of Kym's hand and stepped into the middle of the circle. No one said a word. Kym felt even worse about the whole thing. Kat was right, after all. The true trials of the Calling determined whether the Favored would do the right thing during the competition. Amber certainly hadn't done that.

"Someone say something?" Tomark said, turning slowly on the spot.

"Um…well, Amber…she…" Ashlyn said before trailing off.

"Amber used the Fire Cladium on herself," Xander said.

"I don't know what that means," Tomark said, but Kym could tell by the look on his face that he knew it wasn't good.

"Apparently, Fire Favored can control emotions. So Jazin thought it was a good idea to tell the Fire Princess to put hers out about halfway through the Calling," Kat said.

"Oh, Pheil. Amber," Tomark breathed. Unlike the others, he wasn't angry. He looked sad. "Please tell me this isn't true."

"I didn't say that," Jazin said feebly, glaring at Kat.

"You might as well have," Kym snapped.

"It is true," Amber said flatly. "Jazin showed me my connection to the five of you would hold me back in the Calling. He was right. For the last two trials, my emotions didn't drive me, and I did well in each one."

"At the expense of your friends," Ashlyn whispered. "You did this to win a stupid competition."

"Of course, I did. If the Fire Princess didn't win the Calling, what's the point of being the Fire Princess?"

"You didn't win!" Kat threw her hands in the air.

"But that's not who you are," Tomark said.

"This isn't who we are," Ashlyn said. "I thought we were friends."

"I don't know about you, Ash, but those two haven't acted like our friends for a long time," Kat huffed, staring at Amber and Jazin.

"It was a competition," Xander repeated. "Things were bound to get messy—"

"And now you're defending them?"

Kym couldn't listen to another word. How could this be happening? The friends she'd come to rely on since becoming a Favored were at each others' throats. Why did the Calling even have to happen? If the stupid priest hadn't seen the signs, Amber would have her emotions, and they'd all still be friends. What was the point? Of any of it?

Why couldn't things go back to the way they were before? Back when things were simple. When all she worried about was whether or not she'd make it through a day of training. She didn't know about fighting Rulers, invading gods, secret prisons, or any of the other things she'd learned during her time at Wadita. She wanted the life she had before her magic revealed itself that night in the river.

But that could never happen. As much as she didn't want to admit it, her time at Wadita had changed her. She trained all the time, did what Nila wanted her to do just to stay on her good side, and completely forgot about helping those who didn't have help. She'd competed in the Calling, not to make Princirum a better place or even stop the spread of death. She did it because Nila gave her no other choice. This wasn't what she'd signed up for.

"I quit." Kym's voice was so soft none of the others heard her. They were all too absorbed in their own argument. "I'm leaving."

"Kym's right," Ashlyn nodded, clearly not understanding what Kym said. "We should go to bed. This fighting is getting us nowhere."

"No, Ash," Kym said, and she was surprised that her voice was calm. "I can't do this anymore. I quit."

"What do you mean, you 'quit'?" Xander asked. "You can't just leave."

"Watch me."

Kym turned on her heel and walked toward the exit. Behind her, she heard the sounds of hurried feet. Kym didn't stop. Who would reach her first? She wasn't surprised when she felt Tomark's hand slip into her own.

"What are you doing?"

"Kym, stop," Kat said, and she looked even more stunned than when she'd learned about Amber's smothered emotions. "Think this through."

"I have. I don't want any part of this." She gestured around the room. "I never did. Fighting my friends to prove which element and god is best isn't what I want to do with my life."

Kym glanced over at the Rulers, who no longer looked angry or upset. They all stared at the chaos in front of them like it was some kind of unexpected treat. If Kym didn't know better, she'd have said they looked happy. But why? The answer fell immediately into Kym's hands. It was, really, the simplest explanation.

"You wanted this," Kym said to the Rulers.

"Excuse me, Kymbralyn," Nila said. "I am afraid I do not—"

"You wanted this to happen," Kym cut across Nila, and the anger that flashed in Nila's eyes was apparent to everyone in the room. "You wanted us to turn on each other."

"Nila," Melana said silkily, "you let your Favored show you such disloyalty?"

"Remember the day before they announced the Calling?" Kym

turned to her friends. They all looked like they thought Kym had lost her mind. On the contrary, Kym's mind hadn't been clearer.

"Not really," Kat said slowly.

"Should we?" Ashlyn asked.

"We all tried to get them"—Kym waved her hand over her shoulder at the Rulers—"to tell us what was going to happen, but they wouldn't. They just said they didn't mind us being together."

"Kym, that was a good thing," Xander said. "We hadn't been allowed to see each other for months."

"But we never bothered asking why. Don't you see? They knew this would happen. Once we were all in the Calling and forced to fight each other, they knew we would turn on each other. And I was so focused on saving my mother, I didn't see what was happening around me."

Kym faced the Rulers, who looked down at her like she was something rotten. They didn't even bother trying to hide the anger in their eyes. It was like she'd spat in their faces. But Kym didn't care. If they were upset, Kym knew she had to be right.

"The bond you share," James said, "is unnatural."

"What's unnatural about friendship?" Ashlyn demanded.

"Favored from different elements are not meant to be together," Evanna snapped at Ashlyn, and Kym was surprised to see Ashlyn stand her ground. "It upsets the balance of nature."

"The Thed it does," Kat said. "These people are the only ones I can be myself around."

"That is because you refuse to accept the role that has been assigned to you," Kai hissed.

As each of her friends stepped forward, Kym's chest grew lighter. The gratitude she felt for each of them was undeniable. They weren't going to let her do this alone. They'd stand with her, and what was more, they sounded like they agreed with her.

"We've been idiots for thinking you would change," Tomark said, glaring at the Rulers. "You're still the same scared children you were when Thed showed himself at the festival. I agree with Kym. I'm out."

"Count me in," Kat said. "I thought you'd changed when you let us fight death demons. But we've only fought one in the past six months."

"I'm leaving too," Ashlyn breathed. "I thought being a Favored made me special, but after all of this, I don't want any part of it."

"Well, the choice is easy to make when there are no emotions to cloud your judgment," Amber said. "If there is even a choice to be made. I am staying, my lords and ladies."

Amber glided forward, taking her place at James's side. Nila, Evanna, Kai, and Stailin looked like they were on the verge of ripping Kym, Tomark, Ashlyn, and Kat apart. But strangely, Kym didn't care. She'd lost the Calling; Nila was already going to take her mother away from her. There was nothing she could do to Kym to make things any worse.

"A line has been drawn," Zara said, stepping forward. "Those of you who haven't declared your allegiance, do so now."

Kym looked at Xander, and she could see the fear in his eyes. He'd lost the Calling too, so his power was still tied to Melana. She knew he wouldn't leave, not after how hard he'd fought to become one of Melana's pupils. Kym and the others wanted to leave, but that didn't mean Xander or Amber should too. If they wanted to stay with the Rulers after everything they'd been through, that was their choice.

"I…" Xander stammered.

"I know," Kym smiled. "It's okay."

Xander's shoulders fell as he crossed the room to stand with Melana. Jazin walked over to Phillip's side, his eyes darting between Kym, Kat, Ashlyn, and Tomark, and his own pale fingers. Personally, Kym didn't care. His staying meant nothing to her. And after he didn't stop Amber, Kym was happy Jazin was no longer going to be part of her life.

There they stood; Amber, Xander, and Jazin with the Rulers, Kym, Tomark, Kat, and Ashlyn on their own. And even as she felt their eyes on her, a huge weight lifted from her shoulders. She didn't need to watch what she said or did anymore. No longer did she need to follow the Rulers' crazy rules. As of that moment, she, Kat, Ashlyn, and Tomark were free.

"Is this your final choice?" Zara asked, her icy voice ringing through the hall.

Kym's eyes flashed to either side, and she saw all of her friends standing their ground.

"It is."

"Very well."

Slowly, Kym and the others turned to leave. She held her breath, unable to believe the Rulers were letting them walk away. If she hurried, maybe she'd be able to see her mother—

A wall of dark stone shot out of the glittering white floor, sealing the doorway. Kym invoked her Marks, the power from the water charm surging through her as she spun around. On either side of her, Tomark, Ashlyn, and Kat stood ready to fight, their Marks shining brightly. But it wasn't her friends' readiness to fight that sent a chill running through her body. It was a feeling she hadn't felt for months, a cold nothingness emitting from somewhere deep inside her.

On the other side of the room, the Rulers stood shoulder to shoulder. Kai's hands were outstretched, and in the glowing light from his green Marks, Kym saw something she'd thought she'd never see again. The Rulers' faces were pale and sunken, with dark veins running across their skin like cracks. All the color had vanished from their eyes, which turned velvety black.

"You have something that belongs to us," they all said in unison, and Kym heard a deep, dark voice mixed in with the voices of the Rulers.

"Oh, Pheil," Tomark said, and Kym heard his voice shaking. "It's Thed. They're all possessed by Thed."

"No. Thed would need them all to agree, and they never would," Kym said, trying to convince herself more than anything else.

For a god to possess someone, both the god and the host needed to agree to the possession. Even with how much she hated the

Rulers, Kym couldn't imagine they'd agree to let Thed in. He was their enemy, after all.

"The Rulers are weak," Phillip said, stepping forward. And even though Kym heard Thed's voice, Phillip's own voice rang out clearer than before. "The bringer of death has grown stronger since the festival. He waited, ever the patient planner. He knew it was better to take small steps, rather than mount an attack."

"As Zara told you at the Festival," Zara said, although there was little trace of her voice left, "the power of death is parasitic. Dear Melana granted me a small foothold in Princirum, but my strength is bound to Nothingness. To remain here, I needed anchors to the world of the living. The people were easy, submitting to my influence with ease. But they were too weak, and my power quickly overwhelmed them. When I was strong enough, I granted my power to two who would further my cause; a Ruler and Favored of Death.

"The people renounced the other gods, turning to one who could show them a new way. But, my hold on Princirum was not final. To anchor myself completely, I needed the children of the gods. But I was too weak. I could only whisper in the Rulers' ears, turning their attention to other, frivolous matters. The Calling sealed their fates. They fought amongst themselves, and my power and support grew unchecked. And now, while the gods granted an insignificant request, I pulled the Rulers into the arms of death."

"The sick people in the cities," Ashlyn said. Kym glanced sideways. Ashlyn wasn't looking at the Rulers, but at Kym.

"The girl," Kat said, also looking at Kym, and that's when it dawned on her.

"My mom." Bolts appeared in Kym's hands without her even thinking. "Let us leave."

"You said you no longer want to be Favored," Nila said, and Kym could hear Nila's voice clearly over Thed's. "Only the Favored may possess the magic of the gods."

Kym and Kat moved at the same time. Their blue and green bolts flew through the air, hitting the ground in front of the Rulers' feet. Yellow and silver blasts followed, and the Rulers scattered.

They launched themselves in different directions, caught off guard by the speed and synchronization of the attack. But for Kym and the others, it was second nature. Fighting as one was what they did.

"We need to get out of here!" Ashlyn shouted, bolts flying from her hands.

"Kat! Door!" Kym yelled, throwing two more bolts at the Rulers, who were all starting to stand.

Kat ran toward the blocked exit, while Kym, Ashlyn, and Tomark faced the Rulers. Ashlyn vanished in a flash of yellow light, appearing instantly on the other side of the room. Kym followed Tomark into the air. She glided around the domed ceiling, throwing attacks randomly down at the Rulers. If she, Ashlyn, and Tomark could keep the Rulers' attention focused on them, it should buy Kat enough time to make them a way out.

The Rulers jumped this way and that, their bright, elaborate clothes swirling around them, but they didn't attack. But why? Kym doubted Thed would have them hold back. The loud crashes and flashes of green below her told Kym that Kat was hard at work. She didn't have time to worry about the Rulers. They were nearly there.

"End this."

Multicolored blasts filled the air at Zara's command. Kym spun around, narrowly avoiding two green blasts which exploded against the ceiling. She swerved around, avoiding chunks of glittering stone, and threw a bolt down into the attacking Rulers. A bright red blast slammed her in the stomach. She fell out of the air, crashing into the ground. Pain pulsed through Kym as she pushed herself to her knees. She and the others needed to get out of there as fast as possible.

Something wrapped tightly around her throat. She looked around for the source of the attack, unable to breathe. There was nothing around her. She clawed at her neck, her heart pounding in her ears. She felt long, slender fingers beneath her own. Opening and closing her mouth, Kym looked to the floor. She saw her shadow, along with the shadow of an elegant woman, her hand wrapped around Kym's throat.

"I have waited for this for quite some time."

Melana threw Kym against the wall, knocking what little air she had out of her. Kym gasped, clawing at her neck as she watched the chaos before her. Tomark knelt on the ground, his entire body engulfed in flames. Kat stood trapped in a column of light, her skin bright red. Ashlyn's lower body was completely encased in earth like some unfinished statue.

"Enough," Kym heard the mixture of Zara and Thed's voices say.

Melana's hand withdrew from Kym's throat, and she crumpled to the floor, gasping for air, her ears ringing. Someone grabbed her by the arms and dragged her across the cool ground. She tried to wrest her wrist from their grasp, but it was useless. They dropped Kym in the middle of the floor, and she stayed where she was, not daring to move. She watched as Kat, Tomark, and Ashlyn fell in a heap beside her.

"We will do them one by one." A hand grabbed Kym's face, forcing her to look upward. Zara stared down at Kym, her black eyes shining in her colorless, dark-veined face. "You could have had your heart's desire, but you chose wrong. Your choices caused this, so you will watch the fate of those who emulate your choices. Amber, hold Kymbralyn up. We will start with Katarein."

Zara let go of Kym's face, and she fell back to the floor. Her choices? It hadn't been Nila threatening her mother. It had been Thed, whispering in Nila's ear all of this time. How could she have missed it? But what was Kym supposed to watch, and why were they starting with Kat? She tried to force herself into a sitting position, but every part of her body screamed in protest.

Someone grabbed Kym's upper arms and pulled her to her feet. They dragged her from the middle of the room, where only Kat remained, held in a kneeling position by a frightened-looking Xander and Jazin. Kym turned her head around. Where were Tomark and Ashlyn? All she saw was Amber's impassive face staring back at her.

"Amber, please," Kym begged, tears streaming down her face. "We're your friends."

Amber punched Kym in the windpipe. She gasped, unable to say another word. Amber turned Kym to face Kat, who struggled against Xander and Jazin, but they were a lot bigger than she was, and uninjured. What were the Rulers going to do to her? To them? And why did Kym need to watch?

The Rulers held out their arms, and Jazin and Xander ran from the center of the room. A glittering cloud of green mist appeared around Kat, matching her Marks, which glowed on her arms. Kat stopped trying to stand, apparently caught off guard by the appearance of the mist. The Rulers pulled their hands into their chests, and the green mist around Kat flew toward them. Kat's chest jerked forward, and a combination of white and green mist burst out of her body.

Kat screamed; a high-pitched wail of pain Kym had never heard her make. She was in agony. Kym tried to run forward, but Amber's grip on her was too tight. She watched the last wisps of mist exit Kat's body, leaving the air around her strangely dark. The Rulers relaxed their arms, and Kat's little body crumpled to the floor, convulsing and twitching.

Deep in the recesses of Kym's mind, a memory worked its way to the surface. Nila had just saved Kym after she'd yelled at Melana, who'd wanted to rip the magic out of Kym for disrespecting her. The idea had scared her, ripping something out of her that she thought was unremovable. She looked at little Kat, now lying off to the side, her body still twitching. Her Marks no longer glowed green, but looked blackened and burned as blood oozed from the thin lines onto the floor. For wanting to leave, the Rulers were going to rip the magic from their bodies.

Another scream forced Kym to tear her eyes away from Kat. Ashlyn knelt in the middle of the room as the Rulers ripped the mixture of white and yellow mist from her chest. Ashlyn's head hung backward, her eyes rolling into the back of her head as her body shuddered. She collapsed to the floor once the mist left her body. Jazin, his face stony, stepped forward, and dragged Ashlyn's body to join Kat while Xander forced a struggling Tomark into her place.

The sight of Tomark, his hair in tangles, his skin raw and burned, drove every thought from Kym's mind. She lunged forward, breaking free of Amber's grip. She needed to get to him. She had to save him.

Kym screamed as pain radiated from her upper arms. Unable to breathe, she looked down. Flames glowed beneath Amber's slender fingers, which were wrapped around Kym's arms. She was burning Kym to stop her from moving.

"You were told to watch," Amber said flatly, not even reacting to Kym's screams. "Your time will come."

Xander forced Tomark to his knees, and a silvery grey cloud appeared around him. The Rulers pulled it from him as they'd done with Kat and Ashlyn. Kym turned away, tears streaming down her face. She couldn't watch this. Not Tomark.

Pain exploded on Kym's neck as one of Amber's fiery hands turned her head. Kym had no choice but to watch. Tomark's screams filled her ears, and Kym's eye's flooded with tears as she watched the last of her friends fall to the floor.

Jazin and Xander dragged Tomark off to the side with Kat and Ashlyn while Amber forced Kym forward. But she needn't have bothered. All of her fight vanished as she stared at her friends bleeding on the floor, Tomark's fingers twitching beside Kat's. She didn't resist as Amber placed her before the Rulers, their black eyes alight with victory.

Blue mist appeared around Kym, and she couldn't stop her heart from racing. She knew what was coming, and there was nothing she could do to stop it. She watched her magic fly into the Rulers' outstretched arms, and for a brief moment, she found herself feeling sad. How odd it was, watching something she never wanted slip through her fingers. Kym felt her chest jerk forward as something inside her struggled to break free. She took one final breath and closed her eyes.

It felt like knives cutting through every piece of Kym's soul. Her blood boiled as the Rulers ripped her apart from the inside. Her body, no longer under her control, shook violently. Her heart beat erratically, the strain too much for it to bear.

The world around her slipped into blackness. There was no sound. All she knew was the certainty of pain. She felt the slow, dulling release as her body began to fall. There was nothing left for her here. Soon, when the pain faded, she'd see her mother again. Her father was wrong. The gods didn't have a plan. Not for her. With no more fight to give, Kym descended into Nothingness, finally free.

Glossary

AIDAN (AY-dihn) – Water Favored

ALFONBURG (AAL-fon-berg) – the Palace of Air; home to Lord Stailin and the Air Favored

ALVA (AAL-vuh) – Light Favored

AMBER – Fire Favored

ASHLYN (AASH-lihn) – Light Favored

BAEKA (BAYK-uh) – Air Master

BRYNAR (BREYE-nehr) – Earth Favored

THE CALLING – a magical contest among the Favored; used to determine the will of the gods

CHARMS – one for each of the physical elements; elevates wielders magic to its peak

CHLOE (KLOH-ee) – Water Favored

THE CITY OF CONTELLUS – one of Princirum's four cities; located at the border of Contellus

THE CITY OF LUXMONT – one of Princirum's four cities; located at the border of Luxmont

THE CITY OF SILVAURA – one of Princirum's four cities; located at the border of Silvaura

THE CITY OF TERMUBRA – one of Princirum's four cities; located at the border of Termubra

CLADIUM (CLAAD-ee-uhm) – magic used to control an aspect of human existence; utilized by planal and physical elements

THE CONDUIT – Princirum's source of magic

CONTELLUS (Con-TEHL-uhs) – the realm of earth

CRYSTAL PALACE – the Palace of Life; home to Lady Zara

DEATH DEMON – a creature infused with and radiating death

ELENA COLLINS (EH-layn-uh) – Kym's mother

FARREN (FAIR-ehn) – Fire Master

FAVORED – those in Princirum who can magically control one of the elements

FESTIVAL OF CREATION – Princirum's eight day religious festival; celebrates the gods' creation of the known world

THE GREAT FORTRESS – the Palace of Darkness; home to Lady Melana and the Darkness Pupils

HAYDEN (HAY-dihn) – Wadita Protectorate

HEIRO (AIR-oh) – Air Favored

HEIRRAPH (AIR-aaf) – god of fire and love

HIGH PRIEST – highest rank of the priesthood

HIGH PRO – highest rank of Protectorate in a city

IGMONTIS (Ihg-MOHNT-ihs) – the realm of fire

INFERON (Ihn-FAIR-on) – the Palace of Fire; home to Lord James and the Fire Favored

ISABEL (IHS-uh-behl) – Kym's ladies maid

JAX (Jaax) – Water Favored

JAZIN (JAY-zihn) – Death Favored

JEAN (Jeen) – Water Favored

JERARK (JEHR-ark) – Light Favored

KATAREIN (KAAT-uh-rain) – Earth Favored; goes by Kat

KENNA (KEHNN-uh) – Water Favored

KENSRAD (KEHNS-raad) – goddess of darkness and bravery

KENSRIX (KEhns-rics) – Fire Favored

KYMBRALYN (KIHM-brah-lihn) – Water Favored; goes by Kym

LADY EVANNA (EE-vaan-uh) – Ruler of Light and daughter of Thilg

LADY MELANA (Meh-LAHN-uh) – Ruler of Darkness and daughter of Kensrad

LADY NILA (NEYE-lah) – Ruler of Water and daughter of Reta

LADY ZARA (ZAR-ah) – Ruler of Life and daughter of Pheil

LANCE (Laans) – Water Master; Nila's most trusted master

LARUS (LAHR-uhs) – Water Master

LENNAX (LEHNN-aax) – Earth Master

LORD JAMES – Ruler of Fire and son of Heirraph

LORD KAI (KEYE)– Ruler of Earth and son of Thray

LORD PHILLIP – Ruler of Death; chosen by Thed as his Ruler

LORD STAILIN (STAY-lihn) – Ruler of Air and son of Rai

LUXMONT (LUHX-mont) – the realm of light

MAREK COLLINS (MAIR-ehk) – Kym's father

MASTER – title given to a Favored when their training is complete

MATT (Maatt) – Water Favored

NOTHINGNESS – the realm of the dead

OBSIDIAN (Ahb-SIHD-eeuhn) – the Palace of Death; home to Lord Phillip and the Death Favored

OLERRA (OH-lehrruh) – Earth Master

ORMANA (OHR-maanuh) – City of Contellus (later Wadita) Protectoate

PEIRA (PAIR-uh) – Water Master

PHEIL (FEEL) – goddess of life and family; the Great Mother; Queen of the gods

PHYSICAL ELEMENT – fire, water, air, and earth

PLANAL ELEMENT – light and darkness

PRIESTHOOD – a branch of the Princirum faith; sworn to guide the people through the gods' plan

PRINCIRUM (PRIHNC-ee-ruhm) – a land of magic created by the gods

PRIZED – title give to Favored competing in the Calling

PROTECTORATE – a branch of the Princirum faith; sworn to protect the temples and those loyal to the gods; given the title 'Pro'

PUPIL – name taken by all Darkness Favored

PURE ELEMENT – life and death; the original elements

*R*AI (RAY) – god of air and judgement

*R*AILYN (RAY-lihn) – Fire Master

*R*ETA (REHT-ah) – goddess of water and purification

*R*EVEIN (REH-vayn) – hostage in the Fourth Trial

*R*OETTA (ROH-ehtt-uh) – Water Master

*R*ULER – title given to the children of the gods

*R*YLAND (REYE-lihnd) –Water Favored

*S*ERVITUDE- a branch of the Princirum faith; sworn to serve those blessed by the gods

*S*ILVAURA (SIHLV-ohr-uh) – the realm of air

*S*OLARIS (Sohl-ARE-ihs) – the Palace of Light; home to Lady Evanna and the Light Favored

*S*TEKAR (STEHK-are) – Air Favored

*T*ENBATTER (TEHN-baat-ter) – the Rulers' prison

*T*ERADON (TEHR-ah-don) – the Palace of Earth; home to Lord Kai and the Earth Favored

*T*ERMUBRA (TEHR-muh-bruh) – the realm of darkness

*T*HED (THEHD) – god of death; King of Nothingness

*T*HILG (THIHLG) – goddess of light and wisdom

*T*HRAY (THRAY) – god of earth and the harvest

*T*OMARK (TAH-mark) – Air Favored

*U*NDARUNCI (Uhn-duh-RUN-see) – the realm of water

*V*ANQUISHER – Favored charged with destroying death demons; one for each element (light, darkness, fire, water, air, earth)

*V*ARREN (VAIR-rehn) – High Pro of the Ciry of Silvaura

*V*EILIX (VAY-lihx) – Wadita Protectorate

*V*ERONICA (Ver-ohn-ih-cuh) – Kym's lady's maid

*V*ESPAR (Vehs-pahr) – Light Master

*W*ADITA (Wah-DEE-tah) – the Palace of Water; home to Lady Nila and the Water Favored

*T*HE *W*ARDEN – Earth Favored; in charge of Tenbatter

*X*ANDER (ZAAN-der) – Darkess Favored

ACKNOWLEDGMENTS

Writing this novel was difficult in more ways than I can count. I experienced so many things during the process of writing this book, and it will forever be a time capsule for my 2020. 2020 was a hard year, and that had an affect on my writing. Inspiration was hard. Some days—and even months—I didn't have the energy or brain power to open my computer. I felt stuck, and that was really hard for me to work through. This was the first book I've ever written with actual deadlines and release dates in place.

Timelines were made. And for the first time, I really had to sit down at my desk and push through my slumps. This was by far the hardest part. Pushing through when I knew my writing was not my "best" was really hard for me. I don't like doing something if it isn't "good", and this year I had to embrace the fact that for the most part, my first, second, and even third draft wasn't going to be the "perfect" thing I'd envisioned in my head. And that was hard. After releasing a book that was polished and that I loved, it was hard to go back the beginning and write things that I didn't like. But I knew I could do it. I'd done it before. I just had to get it done.

For the first time in my writing life, I experienced "burn out" while trying to write the first draft of this book. I was so tired, and so out of creativity I had to step away for nearly two months. Thankfully, my family is amazing. They helped me in whatever way they could think of—whether that was letting me refinish a dresser on a whim, or giving me a safe space to be frustrated. They are also the worlds best sounding boards. They tell what I need to hear, even if I don't want to hear it sometimes. I am so thankful to my family for all the help they gave me!

I would like to thank all of my friends for their support as well!

They are constantly asking me how things in "author land" (what I call my strange mind) are going. Their support helped to keep me accountable, since I never wanted to say, "Things aren't going well. I haven't done anything."

Next, I need to give the world's biggest shout out to my amazing critique partner! Dani, your insight is unparalleled! This book truly wouldn't be what it is toady without her comments and thoughts! Whenever I didn't know what to do, you were an amazing mind to bounce ideas off of! I am forever grateful to you!

I also need to shout out my amazing BETA readers! They all rose to the challenge of reading this book in a very unpolished form, and they were all excellent!

Kayla, your enthusiasm was and is limitless! You literally jumped at the chance to when I asked you to BETA read, and your comments made me even more excited to share this story.

Kristen, I have no words. I called you very last minute (the night I was sending out the book) because I really needed a different perspective, and you didn't disappoint! Your keen eye caught things others overlooked, and it was so much fun hearing your thoughts.

Schuyler, my brother. I know you will tell me when something is not right, and I really need to hear that sometimes. Thank you for always reading things when I asked, even when I'd randomly show up with four new pages that I needed fresh eyes on.

This book would not be what it is today without the talents and skills of my amazing editor, Suzanne Johnson, and wonderful cover designer, Wesley Goulart.

Suzanne, I had such a good time working with you on my first book, and I was so excited to get to work with you on the second. You saw all of the little mistakes I failed to see, even the ones that were blatantly obvious. Your fresh eyes and encouraging words helped get me through the final stretch with this book, so thank you!

Wesley, I knew exactly what I wanted on this cover. I had such a clear image of it in my mind, and you were able to make that image a reality. From the first mockup you sent me using a random picture for the background and undrawn placeholders for the characters, I knew I made the right choice in having you design this cover. It is everything I could have wanted and then some! I thank you for all of your hard work.

And finally, I want to thank you—my amazing readers. Your love and support for these books makes me excited to keep writing them. I love that you love Princirum and hope that, like me, you get lost there as well! So, all have to say to you is thank you.

ABOUT THE AUTHOR

Logan Young is a Colorado-based young adult author. As a child, his overactive mind never shut off, constantly filling his head with all kinds of stories and new worlds to explore. It didn't take long before those stories found their way onto the page. Deciding he wanted to pursue writing as an adult, he attended the University of Colorado, Boulder and graduated in 2017 with a Bachelor of Arts in English, Creative Writing. When not writing, Logan enjoys an active lifestyle, but is always on the lookout for his next idea.

Hear about Logan Young's new releases, cover reveals, publishing news, and much more before anyone else!

WWW.IMLOGANYOUNG.COM

instagram.com/imloganyoung

goodreads.com/imloganyoung

bookbub.com/authors/logan-young

facebook.com/imloganyoung

twitter.com/imloganyoung

WWW.IMLOGANYOUNG.COM/THEPOWEROFPRINCIRUM